HE WAS THE ONLY
MAN WHO DARED
TO CALL HER
BLUFF AND
CHALLENGE
HER TO
LOVE....

"IS THIS WHAT YOU WANT?"
HE ASKED HUSKILY,

moving upon her, easing his hard body higher, pressing against her intimately, separated by the silk.

"No," she managed in an uneven whisper, her heart racing, her body softening, dampening. "Not ever with you."

Solomon eased open the white silk, his face dark and flushed as he studied her, his fingers trembling, warm against her skin. Cairo closed her eyes, her body wrapped in the pleasure she had only just discovered. She opened her eyes to Solomon's harsh face, the intense fires beating against them both.

Then his mouth was brushing hers, tantalizing, nibbling on her bottom lip, circling, nudging her upper lip. Solomon's beard chafed her skin as he opened his lips, breathing hotly against her cheek, his body tense above hers.

"I haven't wanted a woman for a long time. If you meant to stir me, you're doing a daisy of a job. . . ."

The Wedding Gamble

by
Cait Logan

A Dell Book

Published by
Dell Publishing
a division of
Bantam Doubleday Dell Publishing Group, Inc.
1540 Broadway
New York, New York 10036

The trademark Dell® is registered in the U.S. Patent and Trademark Office.

ISBN: 0-440-22241-9

Printed in the United States of America

Published simultaneously in Canada

August 1996

10 9 8 7 6 5 4 3 2 1

OPM

Dedication

To those western men of courtly style who, while sitting around their lonely campfires, wrote romantic letters to their "daisies." To the same men who respected, cherished, and adored their lady loves. I've always loved these romantic cowboys.

To Fort Benton, Montana. Located on the upper Missouri River, Fort Benton was originally a fur trading post and is a historical blend of Native Americans, fur traders, keelboat and steamboat men, vigilantes, ranchers, cowpunchers, and tradespeople. Fort Benton exists today, its 1870s and '80s buildings magnificent and intact as they overlook Front Street and the Missouri River. Thank you, Joel Overholser, Fort Benton's River and Plains Society, and Sharalee Smith, for preserving Fort Benton's riveting history.

To Mike Shamos, curator of The Billiard Archive and author of excellent billiards books, for his help and patience. The history of billiards (including women, who weren't always welcome) is fascinating. Marie Antoinette and Napoleon's Josephine were devoted players, as is our fictional heroine, Cairo.

To those who have encouraged and supported me and to my new editor, Mary Ellen O'Neill, for her enthusiasm and vision.

Prologue

The Barbary Coast, San Francisco, 1880

"Y ou leave my mother alone, you miserable excuse for God's humanity," a child's voice raged from the doorway. "You can't have my ma now," the girl ordered as she swept into the small, dirty room.

A woman had just died in the cold, gloomy prostitute's crib, shrouded with the scent of sex.

The child's fierce black eyes glared at Solomon Wolfe, who was kneeling by his sister, Fancy. She lay dead on her pallet, and he was gripped by the past, by what she had just told him. He held her fragile hand, death cooling the blue veins. The six-year-old girl pushed back the rags covering her matted hair and drew an evil-looking, sharp knife from her tattered cloak.

"Leave my mother alone, you spawn of a she-goat, or I'll cut you. I've got friends waiting for my whistle. We'll cut you and feed your manhood to the harbor sharks, or sell it to the voodoo lady. . . . Don't worry, Ma, I'll protect you," she said, a lisp sliding through her missing front teeth.

"Garnet?" Solomon asked softly. This was the child he had just promised to raise.

He thought of Fancy at the same age, happily excited about Christmas. Fancy had given her daughter those black eyes. . . .

Garnet would spend Christmas morning burying her mother.

She hitched up her sagging pants and ran her sleeve beneath her runny nose. "That's me—Garnet. One an' the same. That's my ma sleeping there, fishbait, and you leave her alone. She ain't been up to working lately. I've been taking care of her and I don't care how much money you got, you ain't having her now. Get out."

The girl's dirty hand poked the knife at Solomon's face. "Let go of her hand. Don't try to sweet-talk her or me. It won't work."

From the busy street below, prostitutes hawked their wares from cribs, drunken seamen yelled back, brawls drew wagers, and music spilled from the gambling pits where a man could be shanghaied easily. At seven o'clock in the evening, the famed Barbary Coast began stirring to life.

Solomon carefully placed Fancy's thin, lifeless hand on her sunken stomach. He rose to his feet, age and years of a hard life weighing him as he towered over the girl. This was Fancy's daughter, the one he had promised to take to a good "growing place" with sunlight and wild-flowers.

Just moments before Fancy's rattling whisper had told him how she came to work on the Barbary, how she had been seduced and sold into slavery. Lying on her dirty pallet, sick, used, and dying, she still bore traces of the beautiful sister Solomon remembered and had searched for years to find. *"They told me you were dead,"* she had whispered, her eyes shimmering with tears and death. *"Duncan sold me to one house after another."*

For years, Solomon had thought his sister was dead—because she didn't want him to know what she had become.

Fancy had a child now, a fierce dirty urchin threatening him with a knife and looking up at him uncertainly. He ached, remembering Fancy as a girl; she had looked just like Garnet. "Garnet, I'm your mother's brother. I'm your uncle."

Garnet squinted up at him, then glanced down at Solomon's gun belt, the holster lashed low on his thigh. "My ma had a brother once, but he's dead. I've got plenty of uncles. High-falootin' ones, too, not used old gunmen like you. Look at you, holes in your boots and you're not even sporting a gold tooth. What kind of a gent doesn't sport a gold tooth on the Barbary? Go away, let my ma rest. Do it, or I'll make you sorry. Go on up to Ella's crib. Tell her that Garnet sent you, fishbait. I get a cut for sending her customers."

"I'm not dead. Your mother wanted me to take care of you, just like I took care of her," Solomon said slowly. But he hadn't taken care of Fancy, had he? He'd been too involved with showing off for a married woman, for showing how tough he was on the Montana frontier. Then Fancy was gone and he'd spent years looking for her, believing she was dead, and then, finding her.

They'd had just two hours before she died.

"Ma knows that I can take care of myself and her. I been doing it since I was a kid. Look." Garnet dumped a sack of gold pokes and wallets onto the rickety table that held Fancy's laudanum bottles. She threw one of the pokes at the rat scurrying into a hole; the curses she hurled at it came from the salty seamen on the infamous Barbary Coast.

Garnet brushed the small mountain of gold watches, pokes, and wallets with her knife. "See? I can pay for Ma's medicine just fine."

She stopped and sniffed loudly. "What's that smell? *What is that?* Soap? Goddamn soap?" she asked, outraged. She tramped to the basin that Solomon had used to clean Fancy. Then because she had asked it of him—because his dying sister had wanted to see his face without his beard—he had quickly shaved in the same water. Garnet peered into the cold, cloudy water and bent to sniff it.

Then she pivoted to him and lifted the knife higher. "You brought soap in my ma's place and smeared it on her? Now she'll really get sick, you backside of a pachyderm. Don't you know that soap can kill people?" she demanded.

"Your mother won't need more medicine," Solomon stated softly, and swallowed the wad of emotion clogging his throat. "Let me take you to someone you know, while I take care of your mother."

The child's eyes widened as she looked at her mother. "Ma?"

The uneven, high, fearful sound tore at Solomon. Long ago Fancy had cried for their parents, slain by Blackfoot arrows, in just the same heartrending way. He'd remember the sound forever. He wondered when he had last thought about religion, or anything but surviving. Now Fancy's child needed him, and he struggled to comfort her. Because he had had little softness in his own life, Solomon recalled what an old man had said to Fancy. The words fell stiffly from his lips. "She's gone to heaven, Garnet."

Garnet hurled herself, a small flying body covered with rags, down to the pallet. She shook the dead woman. "Ma? Ma, wake up!"

Fancy's pale, lifeless hands slid to the dirty floor. "Ma!" Garnet wailed, alarmed now and shaking her mother harder.

Solomon remembered Fancy's hands cupping baby chicks, her expression luminous and innocent. His heart twisted painfully; the brittle scars protecting it shattered for a heartbeat. He wished he had Montana's wildflowers for Fancy now. He rested his hand on Garnet's thin shoulder. "Let's go, Garnet. I'll take you to someone while I make the arrangements for your mother. Who do you know?"

She shook off his hand. "Mister, I know men like you wanting little girls. I ain't goin' nowhere with you. Ma?"

Solomon inhaled sharply. He'd seen women and children cry, grown men sob for loved ones, but he'd never given comfort. He didn't know how. An aging gunfighter knew one thing—how to survive. What did he know about raising Fancy's daughter?

He'd promised his sister on her deathbed. He'd take care of Garnet, whether she liked it or not.

Footsteps pounded up the stairs and men cursed before the thin door crashed open. "That's her. That's the whore's little bastard who took our money!" A man with a big belly led two other, thinner men into the room.

Solomon turned slowly, braced his legs wide in a gunfighter's stance, and hoped that his speed would hold just one more time. The men behind Big Belly were professionals, their eyes flat and dull. Solomon knew that look; he shared it. He rested his palm on the butt of his Colt and inhaled slowly. The men were younger, probably faster, but just maybe they didn't have his seasoning. A shootout wasn't always won by the fastest gun, but by "edge."

The gunfighters, dressed in fancy clothes, and Big Belly paused in the doorway. Solomon stood in front of his sister and her crying child. "My sister just passed on. The girl is my niece. You'll have to go through me to get her."

Garnet's heart-wrenching cries continued and Solomon focused on the men's eyes. He waited for them to make the first move.

"You can have what's on the table. Take it and go . . . or call it," Solomon ordered, trying not to be distracted by his niece's sobs. She needed him at his best now, protecting her. He focused on the three men in front of him.

"The kid is a pickpocket, a little thief," Big Belly stated, his jowls settling down into his starched collar. "She just worked my place and some customers can't pay me now. Scoots in and out so fast no one can see her. Crawled right between the legs of my barkeep and scooted down a hole in the floor."

"She's coming with me," Solomon said softly.

"Look at that iron and the way he's packing it. He's a shootist," one of the gunfighter dandies muttered. "Boss?"

"Looks like an old Kipp Knutson," another man stated warily. "Rangy . . . has the same stance and come-get-me look. But Kipp is maybe eighteen or twenty."

Solomon didn't flinch, but the mention of Knutson took him back twenty years and into the frontier cattle ranches of Montana Territory.

"You know Kipp Knutson?" one of the men pushed. "You two sure look alike. Saw him on a St. Louis riverboat. They paid him for a shooting exhibition. Course, he dresses fine."

Solomon refused to talk. A distraction now could cost, and he was the only protection his niece had at the moment. "Call it," he repeated. "Or leave. The girl is coming with me."

Big Belly glared at the crying child and walked to the table. He scooped the gold pokes, coins, and wallets into the cloth sack. "Take her. You're welcome to her. You got until tomorrow night and then this crib better be empty. I've got a new working girl coming in. I find that kid on the Barbary and I'll snap her stringy neck."

Solomon nodded and watched the men leave, and wondered how a worn gunfighter could deal with a six-year-old girl. He'd taken care of children before for brief times, dealing with the kidnappers and transporting them to eager parents. He'd tended women torn from their rapists. But his commitment was short-term, leaving behind a deadly trail. Cold, deadly memories hurled themselves at him—dead men lying in the street, in saloons, out on the prairie. He'd hunted for Fancy and led a life looking over his shoulder to see who wanted to build a reputation by killing him.

He was thirty-six just two days before, riding his horse and eating cold tinned beans for his birthday supper. He'd been regretting never having planted a garden or flowers for his love; he'd been mulling the sweetheart letters he'd always wanted to write . . . but a man had to have someone to write to, didn't he? Then he'd heard that Fancy was alive on the Barbary and that hope drove him.

Fancy was gone, but she'd left Garnet. Solomon found his sister's features in the little girl. He mourned for Fancy, silently cursing himself for not finding her soon enough. Then a vision slid by him—a young, carefree Fancy smiled through a bouquet of Montana's wildflower sat him. He swallowed hard and promised Fancy that he'd do his best with Garnet. She'd have the best life he could give her.

Garnet glared at him through her tears as Solomon paid the minister at the cemetery. "You killed my ma with that goddamn soap," she accused in the first words she'd spoken since discovering him in her mother's room. The little girl, grieving and furious that her mother was gone, raged at him. "You think that preacher-man would have missed his watch? Why did you make me give it back?"

"Garnet, there will be no thieving at your mother's grave," Solomon said quietly as he ran his hand through his hair and ached for Fancy.

The dawn touched Fancy's new stone, and the working girls sobbed as they wound away from the cemetery, clustered like shivering blackbirds. They expected to end as Fancy had, used and tired, lying in rags in a cold, dirty room—if they were lucky.

"You killed my ma with soap," Garnet said louder as she began to edge from Solomon. "I'll be on my way now. I've got my rackets to run . . . percentages . . . cuts of the take. I'll do just fine on my own," she stated unevenly, and slashed her thin, dirty arm across the tears streaming down her cheeks.

Solomon knew he should touch her somehow . . . to let her know that he cared.

How? How did he comfort a little girl who had just lost her mother? For a man who kept to himself, whose protection was his silence and isolation, reaching out to this small image of Fancy was like reaching through a rock wall. Solomon tried to remember what he'd seen others do in the same situation. But he was brittle, too empty, and couldn't find the warmth this little girl needed.

The flowers laden with morning mist quivered in a slight breeze, and he listened to the sound of water dripping from the petals. Garnet was Fancy's daughter and she needed whatever he could find inside him to give. He hesitated, then placed his open hand on her head and shook her gently.

Garnet accepted the gesture and glanced at her mother's new grave. "You did okay with the stone and the preacher, mister. I know that it cost a heap of coins to give Ma that big, fancy stone and the flowers. You sent her out high, wide, and handsome. I'll pay you back when I can. So now I guess I can go with the girls, huh?" she asked hopefully. "And don't get any ideas that because . . . because you held me on your lap when I blubbered last night that you can just take me away from my pickings. You weren't that comfortable and you don't say things that a body needs to hear. Seems like Ma's brother would know how to make a heart feel better—that's what my ma said—a body should always try to make hearts feel better, she said."

Solomon inhaled the damp mist and crouched beside his sister's grave. The small, fragile blue and yellow flowers quivered beneath his stroking hand. Fancy liked Montana yellowbells that bloomed in March; she knew how to make hearts ease. He saw her running over the hills surrounding Fort Benton, picking wildflowers, and pelting him and Ole with juicy sarviceberries. Her hair was black and thick then, gleaming in the sun like a raven's wing; her eyes sparkling with mischief and life. The old man had beamed, cherishing Fancy, and had loved his "sweet, little, precious orphans."

On his deathbed, Ole had willed his ranch to the children he loved, Fancy and Solomon.

Solomon was just sixteen then and ready to jump into life, when Buck Knutson asked him to work for him.

Knutson. The name slammed into Solomon, hitting him with the cold past. Twenty years earlier, Solomon been a hot, wild youth, out to build a fast gun reputation. Buck Knutson had promised young Solomon anything, everything to sire a child on his child bride, Blanche.

Full of pride and just a dose of mother's righteousness, with Ole's deathbed condemnation ringing in his ears, young Solomon had resisted for two years. Then Blanche Knutson's high manners and sweet, soft body had drawn him to her bed. Buck had lied about his child bride's age; Blanche was just thirteen when he married her and fifteen when Solomon made love to her.

On her deathbed, Fancy had filled in the missing pieces: Buck's top man, Duncan, had seduced Fancy at fifteen, "On the boss's orders." Knutson didn't want Fancy mixing with his high class young bride so Duncan had sent her to work in one bordello after another, far from Choteau County, Montana.

"Duncan told me you were dead," Fancy had whispered. Solomon's chest tightened and he rubbed an old bullet wound that ached in damp weather. Jealous of Solomon, Duncan had made certain that the young gunfighter came after him, searching for Fancy. The scars on Solomon's wrists and the bullrope stripes marking his back were Duncan's signature work.

Solomon knelt to smooth the dirt on his sister's grave. Duncan had laughed about his seduction of Fancy when Solomon faced him in the street that day. That was Duncan's fatal mistake.

Solomon took the small, grubby hand that rested tim-

idly on his shoulder. Now he had Garnet, a mouthy urchin whose dirty face was stained with tears for her
mother.

Garnet's slight weight leaned against him and Solomon braced himself.

What did he know about the tenderness a little girl
would need? Or making a home and settling down?

He'd made a promise and he would keep it as best he
could.

Solomon considered the only home he'd known. Just
maybe Ole's ranch was still his. "We're going to where
your mother and I grew up, Garnet. She wanted you to
have fresh air and lots of sunshine. An old man left us
his ranch, and I thought we'd see about settling in there.
You can pick wildflowers, just like she did."

Would Ole's ranch be waiting?

He studied Garnet's tangled hair, her dirty face. She
badly needed a bath. She needed a woman's touch, the
gentling of a feminine hand—

The unfamiliar ice of fear snaked through him, fear
that he couldn't do the job.

He'd just spent most of his money on Fancy's funeral.
Leaving Garnet in the care of a good woman—until he
could send for her—would cost.

She needs you, Solomon. Fancy had whispered. *My little
girl needs you and don't let anyone take her from you. She's
the best part of me.*

If he couldn't find the right words to say to his dying
sister, how could he raise her tiny image?

But he would. So help him, God. He would raise Fancy's daughter the best way that he knew how.

"I like the Barbary. I like the smell of whiskey and fish
guts and good strong perfume," Garnet muttered. "Don't
want no wildflower ranch in Montana. Not me. When I

grow up, I'm going to be a faro girl, maybe a blackjack dealer with scarlet skirts. There's lots of opportunities here on the Barbary for smart kids like me. No ranch in Montana. No stinking, bawling cows."

Garnet fingered the tiny locket Solomon had given her; it held the pictures of his parents. She looked up uncertainly at him. "Ma's hair was black as yours. It turned white quick," she said. "I guess I could take care of you like I took care of her. You sure as hell don't know anything about keeping pickings."

Solomon watched the small hand curl around his scarred, calloused fingers. She eyed him and pushed back a matted length of hair. "You got kids, Solomon?" she asked in a lisp between her missing front teeth.

"Maybe," he answered truthfully, examining the notion that he had a son—Blanche's son.

A son. The boy couldn't be Buck Knutson's. Blanche's young body had been so hot, squeezing him, desperate for his seed. Buck had promised to send her back to her destitute, abusive parents if she proved barren.

Garnet nodded, her black eyes like Fancy's, too wise for her years. "Ma said some men don't know about their kids. Some men don't care," she said.

"I do," Solomon returned grimly, meaning it.

"You ever kiss a kid's cheek, mister?" Garnet asked hesitantly, tears shimmering from her eyes. They dropped slowly onto the tiny flowers of her mother's grave. "'Cause Ma said kisses make hearts feel better and right now, mine is hurting bad."

one

"Show us some fancy shooting, Cairo," Dud Harply called from the crowd of men surrounding her.

"Love to, boys," she murmured as the men parted, making a path for her. Her old friend, her fortune, the massive mahogany billiard table waited in the center of her ornate gambling parlor—Cairo's Palace. She glanced at Harvey Murtle and smiled lazily. "Got your money ready, Harvey?"

"Maybe I'll beat you tonight," he returned with a leer.

Cairo touched his beefy shoulder with her fan. "Could be."

She'd take everything in his pocket and give it to his wife. The next time Pris Murtle came to Cairo's back door, a beaten housewife needing care, Cairo would give her Harvey's money and send her down the river.

Cairo eased the hem of her elegant blue evening gown away from a man's dirty boot and flicked him a frown. "The tonsorial shop is across the street. You can have that bath and a shave and come back," she murmured pleasantly.

She lifted her head, letting the overhead lamps light her blond hair and turned her glittering smile to the men who came to see—Cairo Brown, Queen of the Billiards, trick shooter, and high-class lady. Cairo touched the soft fringe of hair running across her forehead with a fingertip of her long blue evening glove and surveyed her empire, a profitable kingdom created by trick shots, charm, endurance, and grit. She'd fought her way through the male-only Butte billiardists and cut her reputation in tournaments and in private play. They left her alone now, except for an occasional game to test her. Most of the professional billiardists didn't like playing women, feeling it was beneath them. And now this was her empire. From crystal bottles and fancy glasses to polished brass spittoons and elegantly served meals, her establishment reeked of money waiting for her taking. Men weren't allowed to place side bets on her; they paid to come into her business, to eat in her restaurant, to drink at her bar, and play at her billiard tables. They paid to see her play her challengers.

The Missouri River's ice had just thawed, allowing transport of buffalo robes and gold, and the men needed her brand of relaxation. It was theirs . . . for a price.

Cairo's Palace was packed, men drinking at the bar, raising their glasses to her, men playing cards at the table, and men waiting for her to start the evening with her famed trick shots. The heavy hand-carved cherry bar glittered with liquor bottles lit by overhead chandeliers. The smoky air was filled with the scent of expensive cigars, the best whiskey, beer, and ale, and the scent of men, freshly bathed and splashed with bay rum.

She glided through the crowd, acknowledging the compliments with a practiced light smile. These men came to see her and she gave them their money's worth—high-society silks and bustles, a polished smile, and a glimpse of elegance on the frontier—every night but Sunday.

Quigly moved at her side—massive, black, and immaculate in his butler's suit. He scanned the men, looking for any sign of trouble. Murtle was a known troublemaker outside Cairo's Palace. She allowed him admittance because she took his money regularly, and used it to help women and children who came to her for aid. While the steamboats rested against the river levee, danger roamed the streets, and the town's taverns were rowdy, Cairo demanded elegance, good manners, and filled pockets.

She smoothed the old billiard table, which dominated her ornate gambling parlor. The porous Italian slate was slightly rough, the green Belgian cloth covering the slate smooth and fast. They were old friends, she and this massive polished table that was her fortune. The dark mahogany frame was smooth beneath her brilliant blue evening glove; her skill would take her out of this rip-roaring frontier town on the Missouri River and put her in New York society and in the best of the tournaments. A triangle of red balls waited on the green cloth, numbers scrimshawed into each one. Cairo touched the smooth vulcanized rubber cushion framing the tabletop. She loved those small celluloid balls and the sound they made when they collided or sank into the table's leather pockets. She loved the clicking of the score beads over the table; the sound always meant a win for her and money in her bankroll.

She breathed in the scent of money, wallowed in it sumptuously. She recognized the player in her, the excitement and anticipation of a good game beating through her. She loved billiards, the sport and the challenge.

Cairo fluttered her fan and studied the men. A practical woman, Cairo knew how to play her average looks to her advantage, how to accentuate her honey-brown eyes, how to lengthen her face with a daring décolletage. Men came to see her, to glimpse a creature from another, enchanting world, and while they were visually consuming her from headfeathers to ballroom slippers, she was fattening her purse.

She'd paid dearly for her skills, for Cairo's Palace, and nothing was stopping her now. It was already late May. By May next year, or when the ice first broke on the Missouri River, she'd pack herself into a luxury steamer and travel to St. Louis. One more year of stuffing her purse lay ahead and she'd have the investment she needed for New York. She sent a glittering smile into the room and noted the men preening for her attention.

She inhaled the scent of fine Sultana and Nabob "house" cigars. She was the best. She thought it; she acted it. Because if she didn't believe, neither would they.

"Evening, ma'am." A wolf hunter showed his darkened teeth in an admirer's smile. He arched his neck against the clean starched dress clothes he was forced to wear in her parlor. The cattlemen needed these rough men to keep their stock safe, but they didn't socialize with them. Wolfers usually kept to their own kind, much like the animals they hunted and poisoned. A word from her and Quigly would evict him quietly.

"Good evening, Jake," she returned in her smooth, cool, practiced tone. "I'm glad you could come tonight."

The wolfer blushed, his eyes bright with hunger as he glanced down at the silk roses on her bosom. Then

Quigly loomed close—almost seven feet tall, black and muscular—and Jake cleared his throat and backed away.

Cairo slowly removed her long evening gloves, inhaled their luxurious Oriental fragrance, then folded them and handed them to Quigly. She slid a glittering diamond from her finger and placed it on the gloves. Quigly haughtily eyed the blue feather boa running from her shoulder down to her waist; he'd just given her instructions not to ruin the line of his design by pressing too close to the table. The blue French silk roses along her bustle whispered against the dark wood.

Quigly grimly pushed his lips together, disdaining the "mutilation of beautiful silk." Cairo winked up at him and he loftily refused to rise to her bait, his bald head gleaming in the light.

She gently rolled her shoulder, letting the men catch the long white arch of her throat and testing the tightness of her puffed sleeves; Quigly had fitted her perfectly, allowing her easy movement.

She slid a glance at the tall gunfighter leaning against the paneled wall, his thumbs hooked into his gun belt. He looked down on his luck and fitted into the shadows, watching her. She'd seen hundreds of such men, that flat-eyed killer look settling on them like a shroud.

Cario inhaled slowly, taking her cue case from Quigly and placing it into the waiting hands of an old man who adored her. The ancient fur trader, dressed in a too-large evening coat and short pants, swept the Palace and kept it clean. "May I have the pleasure of proclaiming your beauty tonight, Cairo . . . ma'am. . . . You're awful pretty tonight, Cairo," Skinner said in the gravelly tone of a man whose vocal cords had once been partially cut.

"You're looking pretty yourself," she said, enjoying his blush as she lifted the two pieces of her custom cue from the case. Skinner was honored, beaming his pride at the rest of the men. She traced the roses engraved on the butt of her cue, then lifted the shaft to tighten it into place.

Money. Gold. The pockets of the men moving through this frontier town were stuffed. Fort Benton's miners, fur traders, and farmers offered an inventive woman a world of opportunities. Across the Canadian border, the North-West Mounted Police at Fort Macleod used the old outlaw Whoop-Up Trail for the transport of their wives, food, and necessities. Drovers—cowboys—and miners kept to the taverns and the fleshpots, shooting their guns in the air while an attorney talked on his home telephone—if buffalo didn't rub against the poles and push them over.

Cairo tested the balance of her cue stick, smoothing the ornate, inlaid pearl and rosewood shaft with a lover's touch. This is what she knew—how to play billiards, how to entrance men into wagering and losing. She ran the cue chalk lightly across the tip of her cue, careful not to let the dust fall onto her table. Quigly grumbled when he had to clean the cloth, and the dust could change the spin of her ball. She glanced at the lamps overhead, noting that they were properly trimmed, keeping the shadows and heat from the fifteen red celluloid balls on the table. Quigly ran a cloth over the white cue ball, cleansing it of the men's fingertips, and glared a warning at the crowd.

Cairo moved through her rituals with dedication, concentrating on what she must do, focusing on her cue meeting the balls. She ran her fingertips over the hard cone of chalk Quigly held, careful to keep the application light. *"Not too much, old girl. Keep the dust away from the table,''* Bernard Marchnard had instructed her so many years ago.

Bernard. Sweet Bernard with his cravat, silk brocade vest, and monocle. The destitute English nobleman who had fallen upon hard times. Fascinated with royalty, the cowboys gave Bernard an edge, and he used it. *"Woo the crowd, old girl. Then take their gold."* He'd taught her and called her a "natural," rising to the challenges and to the romance of the game.

She sent a soft smile to the crowd and wondered how much she would earn tonight. The freighter with his hair oiled and neatly parted in the center looked as if he would play her, his buffalo-hide shipping payroll in his pocket. A son of a wealthy family preened when she glanced at him, and she knew that "Daddy" would mourn his financial loss in the morning. Several merchant businessmen bet cautiously and an English second son, spending his family's fortune on the high plains, would likely play. It would be a good night.

While the town ladies worried about taking care of the bachelors, knitting their socks and cooking for them, Cairo made them happy simply by removing her evening gloves.

Cairo moved to the end of the table and leaned over it, aligning her shot. She placed one hand on the table, resting the cue beneath the bridge of her finger. She played like a man, taught by the best English billiards man on the frontier. Bernard had taught her how to dazzle the crowd, how to make them wait.

Her instincts to win moved in her now, rising to envelop her, dismissing the crowd of men allowing her shooting room. The cue was smooth in her hands, balanced perfectly, aimed at the exact spot on the cue ball.

She breathed deeply, concentrating on the imaginary line running from the cue ball to the fifteen balls forming a triangle on the green cloth.

The cloth was smooth, fast, and perfect for her style and strength. She closed her eyes, focusing on the spin of the cue ball, seeing it smash into the other balls. She opened her eyes, refocused, and shot. The cue ball smashed into the triangle of red balls, hitting the exact spot she had visualized. All fifteen balls went flying against the cushions and into the leather pockets.

There was nothing but her and the table and the balls. The cue was a part of her, doing her bidding, her pleasure. She nodded briefly to the men who were cheering, then nodded to Quigly to add ten more balls. The shot was difficult, calling for a drop of spit on the right ball. Cairo licked her thumb and slid it over the surface of the ball. She breathed slowly, feeling the small drops of perspiration on her upper lip.

Quigly moved gracefully, patting her face with a lace handkerchief scented with lemon balm, her favorite. Cairo inhaled again, slowly lined up for the shot, and held her breath, just as Bernard had instructed her. The twenty-five red balls crashed against each other, flying into the pockets and the men roared jubilantly for their queen, Cairo Brown.

Ethel Brown, dirty little child starving on a poor Missouri dirt farm.

Bernard had changed her life. *"Ethel, we'll give you a name that makes you special. A name no one else has . . . something so magnificent that people will remember it, and you. That's part of the game, my dear. Being special and knowing it,"* Bernard had said, looking down at Ethel as she jammed food into her mouth. *"I always loved the city of Cairo. That's it. You are now Cairo,"* he had said, and dubbed her with his elegant walking cane.

Cairo inhaled sharply. Nothing was taking her back to poor times. She would be in New York in just one more year. . . .

She smelled money in the room. She thrived on the scent of it and the knowledge that it would take her to New York. She'd go to operas, move in high society. . . . She'd experience everything that Bernard had told her about. She'd take every high-class name from her newspaper clippings and search them out.

Then they would be hers and she would travel to Europe—to the Italian villas, to Vienna, to Paris. . . .

Cairo smiled at the men, their faces lit by pleasure. They weren't allowed to use this table, this friend who had traveled miles with her across the border into the land of the whiskey traders. Nor were the men allowed to use her English carom table or to touch the balls that were for her use alone. They used the house cues, the house tables of lesser quality, and when they wanted to challenge her, she was waiting.

She knew about waiting. Waiting for her father to trade horses that he had "doctored." Waiting for crumbs to fill her aching stomach.

Quigly removed all the balls and replaced them with three ivory balls, the cue ball and two others, near each other at the opposite end of the table. Cairo sipped the ice water and lemon he served her from his small tray and studied the two balls at the far end of the table. After carefully drying her hands on Quigly's precisely folded cloth, she chalked her fingertips and bent over the table. She hit the cue ball, directing its spinning path slowly toward the opposite side, then it curved and hit the two balls precisely, sending them into opposite pockets.

The tiny blue satin sleeves tightened slightly over the muscles in her upper arms, and Cairo knew that few women could match her strength or concentration. She refused to use the heavier cue stick that men had decided the weaker sex needed for power; she refused to take the feminine stance they had determined would "balance her anatomical imbalance."

She inhaled, held the air in her lungs, closed her eyes, and when she opened them, she met the cold black ones of the gunfighter. He glanced impatiently down at her bodice, where her breasts had raised slightly over the blue silk and lace.

The man was one of those, she knew instantly, nettled by his glance at her bosom. He was one of the imperial all-male club, wearing his masculinity like a flag— "Women aren't built anatomically correct to play billiards" . . . "Women are too weak to play properly" . . . "Their feeble minds can't comprehend the complexity of the physics involved in billiards."

Cairo stared at the stranger and knew that more than anything, she wanted to prove him wrong. "The massé," she said, and the men cheered.

Quigly placed three ivory balls close together against the table's side; he handed her another, shorter, heavier cue with a special leather tip. Cairo inhaled and stood close to the table, lifting the butt of the cue high—almost straight. The difficult shot required skill and follow-through, the ball hit by the vertical massé stroke would jump over one ball to "kiss" another.

In an uncustomary distraction, Cairo narrowed her eyes at the stranger, letting him know that she was the champion of the house and that she had earned her reputation by skill, not in the bedroom.

She dedicated the shot to her mentor, Bernard, then

concentrated on the mechanics of the shot. Holding the butt of the cue vertically and aligning the tip with a bridge of her fingers, she plunged the cue downward, striking the ivory ball. It spun into the air and came down to nudge the outside ball into a pocket. The men's cheers drowned the sound of the evening's usual gunfire in the street.

She answered a compliment automatically and noted that the tall, tough-looking gunslinger had moved closer. The lines on his face were deep, his shaggy hair slightly gray at the temples. Beneath heavy black brows, his eyes were veiled, a man who revealed little of his emotions. His cheekbones were high, his jaw covered by a neatly trimmed beard.

Cairo recognized the grim set of his mouth. The man could have been thirty or fifty, lean and tough, and had lips that had never tasted a smile. The man reminded her of someone . . . the jut of his cheekbones, the dark color of his skin, and those black slashing eyebrows above a nose that had been broken more than once.

Black suited him; the stranger's collarless shirt and pants had seen better days, his gun belt was worn. In a short time, the scuffed toes of his boots would become holes.

She pushed her uneasiness away. She'd faced predators all of her life. Emotion never paid, and she turned to the men with her famed cool smile and asked the question that she asked every evening except Sundays. "Would anyone like to play?"

She softened the invitation with a smile and added, "For money, of course."

The big gunfighter was irritated now, his eyes flashing as he observed the ripple moving through the men. The men, enjoying themselves with drink, cheer, and Cairo's performance, didn't notice the small child at the stranger's side.

Cairo thanked Matthew Jones for his praise and sipped the julep that Quigly had just handed her. She didn't allow children in her establishment, which was solely for the pleasure of men. But there was something about the child, about the way she latched her small hand on to the gunfighter's belt and how she had ruffled the man's flat, still expression.

The stranger stood almost four inches over six feet, and in the bright light glittering off the liquor glasses and glancing off the huge mirror, it was clear that he was irritated. Cairo's lips pushed away a small smile and she decided to let the child stay. The girl stood in braids and rags with her hand hooked on the gunfighter's belt as if she would not let him escape.

The man looked doomed. His impatient, harried expression endeared the child to Cairo even more.

The girl reminded Cairo of herself as a child. She'd had to be persistent to survive. As a child, she'd tried to drag her father away from his pleasures, betting and trading away horses that she'd grown to love. . . . Maybe this child could succeed, getting her way, where Ethel hadn't.

There was a quick exchange between the tall gunman and the child, then the girl screwed up her face as if she might cry. The lines on the stranger's face slowly shifted into wary, reluctant submission. He nodded impatiently, the light glinting off his black hair. Thick and waving, the rough cut ended low on the back of his collar. He inhaled slowly, too patiently, then grimly locked his legs in a fighter's stance and turned back to watch Cairo.

He was focused on her, watching her with his predator's eyes, his challenger's eyes. She'd seen the look many times and savored teaching those men how to lose. Excitement trickled up her spine; her pulse leaped and all her senses told her that this was the man who would play her tonight.

While she enjoyed the child and the man's byplay, Cairo turned her mind to making money. "I'd love to play one of you gentleman."

"I would be honored to oblige, Miss Cairo," Benjamin Dove said, sweat glistening on his forehead. She made quick work of Benjamin, a boy trying to be a man. She almost felt sorry for him as Quigly took his gold coins. Benjamin's father wouldn't be happy tomorrow. Of course, he wouldn't face Cairo with his anger, because she knew that he was keeping company with another man's wife. Cairo swept her hand up to her hair and smoothed the huge sausage curls and the delicate spirals around her face.

Cairo glanced at the slight disturbance in the crowd— the man and the child outlined clearly in the lamplight. The girl had just picked a cowboy's pocket and the stranger had taken it, handing it back to the man as if it had fallen. The stranger said something to the girl, who glared up at him. Cairo liked the girl and the way she nettled the man.

Cairo played Rufus Baylor, an English nobleman out for good times on the American West frontier, and spending his family's fortune along the way. Rufus lacked Bernard's class, losing poorly.

"Gentleman, surely there is one of you who wants to play me?" Cairo yawned delicately and smoothed the feather headdress Quigly had lovingly created for her.

The stranger moved through the men surrounding Cairo and looked down at her steadily. "Yes?" she asked, nettled when he didn't speak. "Did you want something?"

She allowed her eyes to drift slowly down his worn clothing and boots. "The stakes are high at my table," she murmured, then glanced at the little girl squinting up at her.

The girl tugged at the gunfighter's belt. He frowned, bending to listen to the child. He said something in a deep, dark, rich voice, and the girl stuck out her bottom lip. "Well, she *does* look like a real fancy whore," she muttered.

Cairo lazily arched an eyebrow, amused as the man turned to her. To a child, she would look like an expensive working woman. The man's black, shadowed eyes locked on her face and she shifted uncomfortably. Few men would dare to pin her with that bold, assessing stare.

"Would you like to play?" she asked lightly, sweeping her hand to the table, in an invitation.

The man held her eyes as he slowly eased his gun belt away, wrapping it expertly around the well-used gun. He placed the deadly weapon on the green cloth of the table.

Cairo noted the deep scars on his wrists before the man tugged his cuffs down. "That's your bet?" she asked with practiced disdain.

He nodded stiffly, pride and arrogance flashing in his eyes for a heartbeat. Then he tugged a small chain from his neck and tossed a worn wedding ring onto the table.

"It's all he's got, lady," the girl said, and the stranger's dark face jerked down to stare at her. Clearly unafraid of this tough, seasoned gunfighter, the girl returned the stare belligerently. "Well, it is. We just got off that damn riverboat an hour ago. Do you know this town only has one street? The gents here don't have gold teeth," she noted indignantly.

Cairo swept her evening fan up to her face, spreading it open to hide her smile. Over the expensive painted roses, she looked up at the man. Clearly he wasn't happy about the girl's revelations. "Hard times?" she asked smoothly, not bothering to shield her amusement.

"Are you all mouth?" he drawled in deep, too-soft voice that swirled around her, snaring her into a private duel.

Men who challenged her often were taught to mind their manners, Cairo thought coolly, forcing away the slight wave of anger that he had created. This man didn't know how to talk to a lady; tonight was his night for learning. She concealed her rising temper with a small curve of her lips. "Very well. I'll match you with this."

She nodded to Quigly who tossed a small bag filled with gold dust onto the table. "You *do* know how to play?" she asked the man in a bored tone.

"I'll try," he murmured.

"Fine. I ask that you do not use chalk dust over my table. It dirties the cloth. And try not to tear the cloth. It is very expensive, from Belgium. If you prefer, we can ask for a referee." She wanted to let him know that she always called the shots, that she intended to win.

He shook his head, declining the offered referee.

Cairo glanced at the little girl and the past tore at her. "Quigly, there should just be time to bring this sweet little girl a glass of milk and something to eat." Cairo glanced up at the stranger and smiled. "This won't take long, Quigly. Hurry, please."

Quigly's aloof stare was locked with the little girl's hard one. "Would the young lady like to retire to the kitchen?" he asked in his proper English accent, and the girl's mouth gaped.

"Hell, no," she stated baldly, gripping the stranger's hand. "I want beer. With foam."

"She'll have milk. I'll pay for it," the man said tightly,

his head lifting slightly with pride. He placed his hand on the top of the little girl's head, shook her gently, and nodded to a table. She inhaled, slumped her shoulders dramatically, and marched to the table as if it were a guillotine. She plopped herself into a chair, propped her chin on her small fists, and glared back at him.

"Bring her a tray, please, Quigly," Cairo asked. "She can eat at a table. This will just take a minute." Cairo then turned to the man. "Since you don't have your own cue stick, perhaps you'd like to select one from the wall rack. The house cues are better than most."

She allowed him a small, taunting smile. She resented his height, towering over her, when the top of her head barely reached his chin. She met the steady gaze of those dark eyes sheltered by thick lashes. "They were collateral on bets . . . from challengers. The rules are ball numbers equal points, sixty-one out of a hundred and twenty wins the frame. Twenty-one frames in the game. Winner starts the next frame. Shall we begin?" she invited, tasting the sharp edge of her need to compete, to pit herself against a challenger and test her skills.

The man's arrogant look, his expressionless eyes staring at her, dug at things she didn't want uncovered. She was just the perfect one to teach him manners. He'd shoot too hard on the fast cloth and she'd have him easily.

Solomon smoothed the expensive cue stick, tested the hard tip, and roughened it slightly with sandpaper. The table was fast, an advantage to the woman, and he'd have to shoot slower, restraining his greater strength. Cairo Brown swept her hand across the table, inviting him to shoot first. "Why don't you warm up? Try not to damage the cloth, please," she repeated distinctly.

He nodded briefly—her hand had never known hard work, the skin soft and smooth, the fingernails tapered and short.

He glanced at Garnet, who was mashing food into her mouth and stuffing it into her pockets. Beside her, Cairo's huge black bodyguard sat at the table with elegant disdain. His white gloved hands were placed exactly on his knees.

Garnet needed food and shelter, and Solomon had just wagered the only valuable possession he had, his nickel-plated Colt model Lightning with a hair trigger and special rosewood butt. Only a seasoned hand could handle the light double-action revolver. He'd had other guns—they had been his livelihood.

His mother's wedding ring was all he had to remember of her, retrieved from the burned wagon by Ole. He'd hoped to give it to his sister.

The fancy woman's blond hair shone beneath the lamplight as she continued moving around the men, talking with them. The light caught on the satin dress, the tightly fitted lace bodice with a blue feather boa running from her shoulder across her bosom and down to the blue and purple underskirt.

She moved languidly, gracefully, circling the crowd, like a beautiful swan circling her domain. Solomon leaned over the table, formed a bridge with his fingers on the shaft of the cue, and braced the edge of his palm on the expensive cloth. He tested the cue's butt with his other hand, running the tip through the bridge of his finger, and knew that whatever Cairo was doing now, she was watching him with stealthy little glances. Like a cat stalking her prey, searching out the weaknesses.

Solomon inhaled very slowly, focusing on the shot, lining the cue ball's path to the other balls.

He inhaled again, steadying his nerves—just as he had when he prepared to meet another gun.

The sight of Cairo's pale breasts gripped him. They weren't lush, but high and proud, shimmering in their tight, lacy confinement. He pushed away the rush of unexpected heat, not willing to be distracted when his only protection lay on her billiard table.

He glanced at Garnet, distrusting the child who could work a crowd without being seen, and found her nodding drowsily. Quigly's massive white gloved hand slid behind her head and caught it gently as she fell asleep on her chair.

Cairo's expensive perfume curled around Solomon, and he looked down into her whiskey-brown eyes. They were hard eyes, predator eyes, though skillfully shadowed by her dark lashes. She licked her lips, moistening them, and he wondered how many men had been distracted by the full soft contours. Or by the pale mounds swelling over her tight bodice.

Solomon disliked the heavy sensual punch low in his body. He was too old, too worn to feel that kick, the sudden urge to bury himself in a woman's soft body.

Cairo Brown sent him a quick look under her lashes, not a flirtatious look, rather a sizing up of an opponent. Then she smiled at him, slowly, confidently. "I'll help you feed the child. Maybe there are a few odd jobs you can do around town to pay for buying your gun back . . . though it's well used and you might want to save up for a new one."

She smoothed the lace on the front of her skirt. "What's your name? I like to know who I'm playing."

"Solomon. Solomon Wolfe," he added, remembering his father's pride in the name. He wanted the same for

Garnet—to know she had a bloodline with pride. He hoped to teach her that before fate separated them.

Cairo reached to touch him, just as she had the other men, a light, claiming touch to disarm him, to ensnare him, and he caught her wrist. "No."

The lift of her eyebrows was eloquent. A frown skipped across them when he held her wrist too long, testing her strength before allowing her to draw away.

"You'll pay for that, Mr. Wolfe," she said when she finally spoke, her eyes flashing up at him and the color in her cheeks rising swiftly.

Solomon did not dismiss her threat. He never took opponents lightly, of either sex. He watched the tiny vein pulse low in her throat, just below the expensive cameo held by a black velvet ribbon, then he allowed his gaze to lower, touching her breasts.

Cairo inhaled sharply and Solomon lifted his gaze to her indignant one, holding it. He'd gotten to her, playing his edge before the match. He allowed a tight, insolent smile to touch a corner of his mouth, a slight mockery.

"Let's play," she said suddenly, a touch of anger biting into the soft, husky, languid tone of her voice. She took a towel and dried her hands. She tossed it to Solomon and took her cue from the table. "I said let's play," she repeated briskly to Solomon.

He nodded and noted the slightly impatient tone to her voice. Solomon knew that he had caused that slight edge, the need to prove that she could best him. He would remember that about the woman—a natural gambler, she took challenges like a hungry cat.

two

"Fifteen-Ball Pool, unless you prefer something else," Cairo said, stating the game she played with other challengers. The gunslinger nodded curtly, studying the balls placed into the triangular shape called the pyramid. The man had wagered his last possession. Because she worried about the child in his care, she decided to offer him a way out of her challenge. "We'll stop right now, Mr. Wolfe, and you'll have your gun and your ring. All you have to do is unscrew the cue and place the two pieces on the table. That means you admit you are beaten. There's always another day. I'll be here waiting."

He stood there, big, seasoned, and ominous, legs braced, watching her. She sensed that he'd face what would come his way and take the consequences, a proud man, asking for nothing. Cairo shifted restlessly, smoothing her bodice. She was used to being the object of men's stares, but desire or admiration was not stamped on the stranger's face. He disliked being touched—his hand had locked to her wrist when she had tried the ploy that often gave her the advantage.

Waiting for her to continue, he smoothed the cue stick with his fingers. They were long, slightly scarred at the knuckles, lean and strong. His fingers had curled slowly around the cue stick during his warm-up shots, finding the balance and testing the tip. A player who gave that much attention to inspecting and roughening the cue's tip had experience.

His hands ran over the wood, testing it, warming it, loving it and making it his, making the stick become a part of him, an extension of his will, his power. *"Never trust a player with a lover's touch, because he plays with his soul and heart and brain . . . that man will be a good player and a bad bet,"* Bernard had said.

Cairo lifted her chin. She'd been riding boredom, needing a challenge. From the look of the man, he'd met a struggle of his own. His expression gave little away, the shadows stalking his face as he ignored her offer. His bones thrust at the sun-darkened skin covering his cheeks, and she wondered when he had last had a meal; the child had crammed food into her mouth and had instantly fallen asleep. The man and the child were riding hard times like so many others; if he was addicted to gambling, Cairo pitied the child. He met her impatient glance and held it, wearing his I've-made-my-decision attitude like a dark, swirling, ominous male cloak.

Cairo had little patience with men who could not provide for their families; she had less patience for men who were not prudent when facing bad times. "Very well. We lag—shoot our balls as close to the cushion as possible—to see who shoots first and bursts the pyramid," she said, referring to breaking apart of the triangular arrangement of balls. "I'll call my shots, but if you're not up to it—"

He nodded, watching her with that steady, assessing look. The silent taunt brought her fighting spirit leaping out of her, and she wanted to vanquish him.

Whoever he was, he knew how to nettle. She had fought too long to remain free of male restraints and ownership. Men gossiped that Bernard was her keeper, and she saw no reason to disillusion them.

The stranger studied her face, tracing the angles, looking beneath the smooth mask she presented to her challengers. Some men didn't like women players and she began her routine warning. "I don't play with the usual stance of a woman. If that bothers you—"

"It doesn't," he said curtly, his beard gleaming in the lamplight. The smoothly tapered cue sliding through his fingers had been wagered and lost to her from a St. Louis hustler. The cue's balance and feel was excellent.

Cairo smiled coolly, placing herself at the long end of the table, and shot her ball toward the opposite cushion. It rolled, slowed, and stopped two inches from the cushion.

Solomon angled his tall body down, sighted carefully, and Cairo held her breath as his ball slowly rolled past hers, stopping one inch from the cushion. Cairo nodded, forcing her brilliant smile. "Well done. You may begin the match with bursting the pyramid."

"Delighted," Solomon murmured in a rich, deep voice that caused her to look at him sharply. The word slid oddly over the lips of a tough westerner. Dukes and barons murmured words like "delighted"; gunfighters didn't. The hair on the nape of her neck lifted in warning, and she fought the wave of anger surging through her. This man, down on his luck, dared to taunt her!

"This crowd can turn nasty when they find a hustler," she noted lightly, stepping back to allow him room. He braced his hand on the green fabric. He rested the cue stick precisely on his thumb, bridging it with his forefinger. The scars on the backs of his knuckles gleamed and his shirt cuff slid higher to reveal bracelets of more scars.

Solomon nodded, concentrating on the shot that would scatter the balls into the pockets. The cue ball hit perfectly, the balls smacked into each other, and several of the balls pounded into the pockets. The shot was strong, arrogant, and done by a man who knew how to temper his strength. Cairo used her cue to slide the scoring beads above the table. "You've played before, Mr. Wolfe."

He rounded the table, sending the cue ball against the other balls, one after another, and the frame ended without Cairo playing. Cairo shrugged lightly, disliking his dismissal of her. Men did not ignore her as a woman or as "The Champ." Quigly's bass voice boomed over the stunned crowd as the last ball shot into the pocket. "Frame one to the challenger. All one hundred and twenty points."

Cairo glanced at Quigly, who still held the sleeping child's head in one white glove on the table. His other gloved hand was braced on his striped trousers, and Cairo frowned when he smiled placidly at her. Quigly had often noted that Bernard was her last true competitor, and clearly he recognized the challenger as a potential winner.

Solomon broke the next pyramid, played expertly, then missed a shot. Cairo decided to finish him off quickly and grind his arrogance into dust. She shot expertly, the red balls whizzing into their pockets.

"It's still your turn," Solomon said, standing back and bracing the butt of his cue on the floor.

"You're good, Mr. Wolfe," Cairo returned, forcing her voice to a pleasant tone. "But I am better."

His impassive gaze dropped slowly to her lips, then down to her bosom. "Nice dress," he said while she fought the hammering of her heart.

She wanted to launch herself at him. "Thank you. It's very expensive. Please make certain that you stay your distance from me," she murmured, and took her position at the end of the table to burst the pyramid for the second frame. Her fingers locked to the cue too tightly and she forced the shot, the balls breaking, but without her usual finesse. "Deuce," she said, calling the ball she would pocket next.

She focused, locked her mind and body into the game before her, calling the balls before sending them into the pockets. She cleared the table and focused on beginning the next frame when Quigly's booming announcement startled her. "Frame two . . . to the champion. Best of twenty-one frames, by agreement of the champion and the challenger."

"Frame three to the challenger," Quigly announced after she had missed a shot and Solomon finished the frame.

On the fourth frame, he broke the arrangement of balls in the same hard, fast way. Five balls were left on the table, which he quickly sent into the pockets, calling them as she had done. The fifth frame he missed a shot and she won.

Cairo dusted chalk on her hands and roughed her cue, recognizing Solomon as a genuine competitor. His skills had grown from his first practice shots; a powerful shooter, he acted instantly, smoothly, rather than using her slower, thoughtful style. She inhaled slightly, focusing on the balls, and was startled to find Solomon's gaze locked to her chest. Few men dared to look at her so boldly, tracing her breasts and slender, agile body. She'd dealt with outlaws, stuffy noblemen, and bawdy men from the frontier. None of them nettled her like this tough gunslinger down on his luck. *"Delighted,"* he had dared to say. The taunt echoed in her mind, angering her.

"Is that all you?" he asked lightly, glancing down at her bosom again, and she realized she had been holding her breath with anger.

She slowly pushed the air from her lungs just as she pushed down her rising temper. She knew how to distract, how to balance a tough game in her favor; the stranger was playing the same game, and she would cram his loss down his throat. She shot too fast, her fingers too tight and trembling on the cue and missed a shot, leaving Solomon to finish the match, which he did neatly, calling the balls that would be hit. Solomon lifted his cue stick to move the scoring beads, while Quigly announced, "Frame six goes to the challenger. The current champion is behind."

Cairo glanced at Quigly, irritated by his "current champion." Still holding the child's head in his glove and sitting very straight, he smiled back at her blandly. She noted that he had lit one of the house's best cigars and was puffing with delight, as if he was really enjoying himself.

Bending his tall body slightly, angling his hands and the cue, Solomon began the seventh frame, calling the balls as he shot them, and including the location of the pocket. His deep voice ground on Cairo's nerves. "Deuce into left side pocket . . . three ball, right corner."

When he leaned down, the worn cuffs of his shirt lifted, exposing the light rough scars running across his wrists. Concentating on a shot, Solomon glanced at her and frowned when he saw her noting his scars. His lips tightened, and he played coolly, systematically pitting himself against the balls.

When he won, he glanced at Cairo. Her face was pale, furious. She didn't seem to notice the youth standing just behind her, his hand resting possessively on her shoulder. Dressed in a frilled shirt and string tie, a black frock coat and trousers, the young man wore his tooled gun belt low, his weapon expensive with etching and pearl handles. He matched Solomon's height and his coloring was just as dark. Solomon held his breath, noting the jutting cheekbones that he and Fancy both possessed. Without his beard, Solomon's jaw lay just as square as Kipp's, a dimple in the exact place in his chin.

The youth looked over Cairo's head to Solomon, taking in his worn clothes, his missing gun belt, and the gun on betting shelf. He nodded curtly. "I'm Kipp Knutson," the boy said.

The name, his age, and the boy's features said he was Solomon's son. Solomon's chest tightened. He'd never thought about having a child, and now he was looking at his son.

He'd missed a young lifetime.

Cairo moved restlessly and he glanced sharply down at her. The boy adored the older woman; it was written in the softening of his eyes, in the tenderness of his voice when he murmured, "Cairo, you are a perfect daisy tonight."

The words were soft and husky, meant to appease her wounded pride.

Then Kipp took Cairo's hand and kissed the back of it gallantly. "Dine with me tonight, my beauty?"

"How you do talk," she murmured absently. She'd hated losing the match; her smile was brittle and forced.

Solomon continued to study Kipp, a younger image of himself. He pushed down the excitement racing through him, the startling pride that Blanche and he had created a life between them.

"Wait for me, will you, Kipp?" Cairo murmured, patting the youth's smoothly shaven cheek. "I'll have our dinner served in my apartment. I won't be long."

Quigly carefully lifted the dress over Cairo's head. "You're in a froth, madame," he announced in his distinct rumbling tone.

"What do you expect?" she asked impatiently, loosening and stepping out of her petticoats.

"Please be careful with the lace, Miss Cairo. You know how hard it is to replace. May I recommend that you soak in the chamomile bath that I have prepared? Perhaps that will soothe you."

" 'I'm not a trick shooter, ma'am,' " she mimed Solomon Wolfe's deep voice. " 'A little rusty. I'll be back.' "

Quigly carefully arranged the dress in the giant carved walnut closet. "You appear to be irritated. Perhaps—"

Cairo rounded on him. "Quigly, you will not insinuate that I am 'indisposed.' The man peered down my bosom. Do you know how difficult it is to shoot with an exposed bosom? The man made certain he was at the opposite side of the table each time I shot."

"Being an admirer of a woman's fine figure does not

condemn a man. Perhaps he was admiring my handiwork and the lovely drape of this gown."

She stared at him, this huge elegant man who was her friend and her protector through hard times in the past. "Yes, I allowed myself to be rankled," she admitted tightly.

"Yes, madame. Quite true. But one could suppose that out of the goodness of your warm heart, your generosity . . . you were worried about the welfare of the ragamuffin."

She lifted an eyebrow and began plucking the long tortoise-tone pins from her hair and tossing them into a crystal bowl with claw feet. "I've been matched to the toughest billiardists in the territory. *I did not give him that game.*"

"Another day then. Perhaps you'll regain your losses."

Cairo leveled a dark look at him. Solomon Wolfe had stepped into her world and challenged her. While the other men in the parlor remained gentlemen within her prescribed boundaries, she doubted that Solomon realized the leash she kept on her establishment. "I had an off night, Quigly."

"An unusual night, indeed, Miss Cairo," Quigly agreed with just the right amount of amusement to cause her to throw her corset cover at him. "In fact, I do hope that Mr. Kipp will not suffer from your wrath."

"Kipp understands," Cairo returned, rolling her garters and silk stockings down her legs. "Solomon Wolfe is a man who badly needs lessons concerning gallantry."

Quigly caught the small bundles thrown at him; he skillfully unrolled and draped them over his arm. "Shall I prepare lamb chops for two, perhaps adding—" Quigly grimaced and continued—"an amount of those horrible fried potatoes for the gentleman?"

Cairo wrapped her black robe around her, jerking the sash closed. "Dinner for two, of course. But steak for him, and green beans. Kipp waited for me to have dinner."

"The epitome of a gentleman. A *young* gentleman," Quigly said soothingly, then muttered, "A steak-and-potato man through and through. You were right to note that he needs his vegetables, as growing boys do."

Cairo ran her fingers through her hair, then began brushing it rapidly. "This is beef country. And yes, he is younger than I am, Quigly, but only by a few years. I enjoy his company. He enjoys mine."

"Barely eighteen years to your . . . ah . . . twenty-eight? A well-preserved twenty-eight, may I say. A true friendship," Quigly murmured, catching the brush she had thrown at him. "And what of the challenger tonight, madame? What brought the roses to your cheeks, I wonder?"

"I was angry," she stated flatly, jerking her sash tighter. "That poor child looked ill-kempt and starving."

"The man looked no less. In fact, he reminded me of a lone wolf, protecting his only cub. A cub who is a skillful pickpocket, may I add."

Cairo plopped down into her day lounge and stared out into the starlit night. When the game was finished, she refused to run for her room, but had continued to talk with her customers.

When the stranger had passed her, his gun on his hip, her gold dust in his pocket, and carrying the sleeping child, he glanced at her sitting on the edge of the table, shooting the cue behind her back. "I'll be back," he had said, meeting her eyes.

She had nodded and smiled, but when his gaze fell to her breasts, raised by the trick shot she was performing, she dropped her smile.

The man's grim expression hadn't changed, but Cairo disliked the light in his eyes—amused, arrogant, male—taunting her. She shifted impatiently on the day lounge, disliking the way she rose to Solomon Wolfe's challenges. She had her first royal headache in years—since Bernard's death—and Solomon Wolfe was the reason.

The knock at her apartment door was Kipp's, and sensitive to her emotions, Quigly asked, "Shall I tell the young gentleman that you have a headache?"

His tone implied that she was brooding about her loss and wanted to hide. Cairo lifted her head. She would deal with Solomon Wolfe when he came again. "Ask Kipp to wait, will you?" she asked with her best, glittering smile. "I'll change into a lounging gown."

"May I suggest the adorable purple lace with the fichu?" Quigly asked, moving his three-hundred-pound, well-dressed body toward the front door of her apartment. "It's already laid out on madame's bed. I'll tell the chef that it's lamb and steak—"

"I'm certain Kipp will enjoy whatever we serve," Cairo interrupted, impatient with Quigly because she sensed that he was pleased by her loss.

"The young gentleman is always adoring and complimentary, unlike your challenger."

"Stop reminding me that Kipp is younger, Quigly. And Mr. Wolfe is not my challenger."

"Mmm. Is he not?" Quigly asked, unruffled by the blue silk shoe hitting the massive palm of his outstretched hand. He lifted his other hand to catch her second shoe. "Well done."

Kipp lifted his champagne glass to her. "You've been brooding, Cairo. You've barely eaten. Have a glass of champagne and relax."

Cairo yawned delicately and wondered when he would leave. She needed meditation, exercise, and a long, soothing bath before she could sleep. "Kipp, you're such good company, but I'm afraid that today has been tiring."

"How about a ride tomorrow? We'll take a picnic and ride toward the Highwood Mountains. I'd like to be alone with you," Kipp said, his voice inviting her to respond. He took her hand and brought her palm up to his lips. "You're beautiful, Cairo. Never more beautiful than tonight."

He kissed her wrist while she thought of Solomon's scarred ones, and when Kipp's lips touched her inner elbow, she eased her arm away, smiling at him. She did enjoy Kipp, his charm and his manners, but—

"Your mind is on the stranger, isn't it? Do you want me to take care of him?" Kipp asked, his black eyes flashing at her, his head lifted in pride. He stood up and began to pace the floor, his hand resting on his fancy gun butt. "I won't have you upset. Tomorrow I'll find him and his brat and pay their passage downriver."

Cairo rose to her feet. Kipp was too ready to protect her, too possessive. "Kipp, you will do no such thing. A gambler expects losses."

Kipp's fingers circled her wrist, drawing it to his mouth. "Marry me, Cairo. Let me take you away from this . . . from these men looking at you. You could dress for my eyes alone."

"Kipp—" She didn't want to hurt him, nor would she bend to his demands.

"You think I can't give you what you want, don't you?" he asked softly, his finger caressing her cheek. "But I can, Cairo. In a few months—"

"Kipp, you're riding with a dangerous bunch. James

Taloose was in a knife fight and Tom Jordan in a drunken brawl. Rats Davis is addicted and dangerous."

She leveled a look at him. Kipp's intelligence deserved more than running with a bad bunch. "You've pled their case with the sheriff and found reasons they shouldn't be charged with their crimes. Why don't you go to the East, to college? With your intelligence, you could easily become a lawyer."

His face tightened, scowling down at her. "Don't lecture me, Cairo. My school days are behind me. If you let me marry you, you won't need to work, to spend time with the riffraff."

"I like my customers, Kipp. I like talking with them."

"And I like having my woman to myself," he stated too sharply.

"That's enough," Cairo said coolly, after a pause. "We're both tired."

The youth reminded her of someone else, his hair gleaming and the sharp angles of his face shadowed by light. There was a flash of arrogance in him that she'd seen recently. Who did Kipp remind her of? "Good night, Kipp," she said, moving toward her front door.

"*Chérie*," he murmured huskily, coming to stand beside her. "Let me stay the night. Let me kiss you just once. . . ."

"Kipp, until tomorrow," she returned smoothly, though she disliked his insistence.

"Tomorrow," he said curtly, then bent to kiss her cheek. "You're not angry with me, are you, *chérie*?"

When she looked up into his boyish grin, Cairo couldn't resist smiling. Kipp could be beguiling, learning how to please her, and teasing her with French endearments. "Out."

* * *

Solomon lay fully dressed on the quilt beside his sleeping niece. The hotel room was cheap but clean, the halls filled with women plying their trade, with drunken Texas drovers, and with businessmen's quiet knocks and hushed demands. Garnet's sleep was restless, punctuated by mumbling and movements of her hands and body each time a drover shot his gun or shouts echoed wildly in the night.

Still unused to dealing with Garnet's quick emotions after five months, inexperienced in sharing his life, Solomon reached to place his open hand over Garnet's head. The gesture settled her and she sighed one last shuddering time before turning to curl against him. Solomon let the child find her spot, her face pushed against his upper arm, like a puppy, safe for the moment. The movements of her bony body stilled, and her small hands gripped his arm.

She smelled. Garnet despised baths and having her hair washed, and she refused to let the kind-hearted women along their travels bathe her. When Solomon promised to stay in the room, to sit by her bath, Garnet would swish a rag over herself. She had accused him of killing her mother with soap and refused to let him lather her hair. Solomon had used yucca and soapwort and had managed to keep her clean—until the last bit of their trip when she had stepped into a coal bin to hide from the man chasing her. He had dragged her from the bin and had her by the nape of her neck, shaking her when Solomon found them.

Garnet had smiled hopefully up at him through her mask of coal dust. "Hi, Daddy," she'd said cheerfully to him; then to her captor, she'd said fiercely, "My daddy has killed a thousand men. Maybe a million. I'm his little darling."

Fancy's daughter wasn't an easy child and Solomon wasn't meant for fatherhood.

Through the shadows of the night, lit by the streetlamps, Cairo's flashing, thunderous eyes struck at him. Solomon had heard whispers of how an English gentleman had kept her, and every slow, graceful movement of her hand declared that she had never worked. Solomon had actually enjoyed testing her temper.

He had intended to nettle her, to give himself the advantage, but the sight of her lips tightening beneath their gloss and the color rising in her cheeks had tantalized him.

He forced his mind to the next morning and the land he prayed would be waiting for them.

Solomon closed his eyes. Praying. How long ago had the minister prayed over Ole's grave?

Garnet stirred beside him, her knees jabbing into his thigh. She flopped to her back, her small hand resting on his chest.

What did he know about keeping her safe, helping her grow up into a woman? Children needed decent food, a home, and—

Solomon inhaled sharply as fear skipped through him.

Garnet's hand sought his beard, stroking it once before she curled against him again. Solomon closed his eyes, remembering the billiard tables that he had played, the hustlers that he had taken and the quick brawls in smoky beer halls.

The woman was a trick shooter, a strong one, but she could be distracted. She had a habit of closing her eyes to concentrate before a difficult shot, and if that focus was broken, she shot too soon.

She had focused when Kipp's hand had brushed her shoulder and she hadn't liked the intrusion.

Kipp. Solomon opened his eyes, watching the moon's reflection on the Missouri River wash across the room's ceiling. His stomach tightened painfully. He had a son. His features were stamped from the same mold.

"Are you Solomon Wolfe?" an old drover had asked as Solomon had carried Garnet out of the parlor. When he nodded, he knew that the old man recognized the name, and Blanche, if she were still here, would come calling.

Blanche. Soft, white, round Blanche who wanted the heat of a young, promising man to keep her happy. She'd begged him to stay, not to search for Fancy.

Kipp's youthful face was too hard and he was likely very fast. If his luck held, Solomon could keep the boy from the trail his own life had taken. Just maybe.

At ten o'clock in the morning, Solomon adjusted Garnet's sleeping body in front of him on the saddle. She had refused to stay in the hotel room and he wanted to keep her close; he couldn't afford her antics now.

Because Solomon had beaten "The Champ," he was able to rent the horse and purchase food. In the livery and the emporium, people wanted to know if he would be playing Cairo again. Though he disliked asking for credit at the store, for food and staples for Garnet and himself, the excited storekeeper had asked, "Are you the man who beat Cairo Brown? Are you having another match? The missus won't let me out nights. If I was to say that I'd extended you credit and was keeping an eye on my investment—"

The old ranch spread out before Solomon, a stream wandering along the meadow, lined with cottonwood trees. The first day of June sunlight caught the old adobe bricks, the unpainted boards, the gaping hole in the tin roof, and the broken corral and long sheds for wintering the animals. Weeds grew up and into the house, the old pipe chimney slanting at an angle. Birds flew in and out of the windows.

A sense of homecoming filled Solomon as his eyes wandered over the ranch. Sagebrush and sarviceberry bushes grew everywhere, enclosing the ranch yard. Wild roses would bloom later, adding pink to the prairie. Solomon thought of the old Nez Percé woman who collected sprigs for her grandchild's cradleboard: "Keep away ghost from child. Flathead believe plant in grave keep dead from howling. . . ."

Ole had made them drink rosehip tea to ward off fevers. . . .

Cattails swayed in the pond, and Ole had allowed the Indian women to gather the down. They packed it in their babies' cradleboards to prevent chafing.

Disturbed by their passing, a hawk cried and flew from the wild plum grove near the stream.

Garnet's seaman's curse hit the sweeping wind and she sat up straight. She leaned forward, studying the time-battered house. "No. Ma's room was better. Where are all the people?"

Solomon traced an old dog-travois trail that marked the wild grass. Not far from Ole's ranch was a small mound with stones arranged carefully, where for years the Blackfeet had run buffalo over the top of a cliff, killing them. Time had rounded the cliff, but the land remained, wide and free. "This is our land, Garnet. Five hundred acres of nothing but coulees—ravines—dry land, buffalo wallows, and sagebrush. We're home."

"Home? The Barbary wasn't as bad as this. Sell it. Just because some goddamn old man gave you and Ma this godforsaken rat hole doesn't mean we have to stay here." She huddled back against Solomon. "First you get up at the crack of dawn—people don't even have their eyes open that time of morning. Then you want to desert me . . . then you haul me from livery to store—you bought a mountain of goddamn soap—and you plop me on this . . . this bag of bones that pees and poops while it walks, and—Solomon, where are all the people?" she asked again fearfully.

"You'll have only my pockets to pick, Garnet. And I think there is a bag of candy in my shirt right now," Solomon returned, wondering if the small stream would hold water in a dry summer. According to the land office, the property was still in his name and Fancy's. Someone—and Solomon would discover who—had paid taxes throughout the years, and Knutson "boys" were keeping an eye on the spread, keeping squatters and Indians out. Fancy's death certificate had satisfied the clerk, and now Solomon was the only owner. When he could afford a lawyer, he'd have Garnet listed as his heir.

"Ghosts," Garnet muttered, scanning the old adobe and log house, the rusted tin roof. "What's that?" she asked, pointing to antelope grazing on the fields.

"Dinner," Solomon said, sliding his rented rifle from its holster. He noted the sight was off; he'd shoot to the left.

Garnet turned to him, horrified, her fingers paused in his shirt pocket. She forgot the candy bag. "You want to kill them? They're so pretty." She placed her small hand on his beard and blinked up at him. "Don't kill them, Solomon. They might have babies. Then they'd be orphans just like me."

Solomon held the antelope in his rifle sights for a moment, then quickly shoved the rifle back into the holster. He nudged the horse with his knees, guiding it down the slope to the old ranch. Garnet, a city child, would soon learn about the western frontier menu.

He held Garnet close to him, giving her the security she needed. She gripped the scars on his wrists, scars that no one touched—because the girl needed to lock on to something—someone whom she believed was safe. He knew the feeling; after burying his own parents, he had needed Fancy's small hand in his.

Who had kept the land for him? Why were Knutson's men keeping an eye on the old spread?

"Listen to the wind blow through the cottonwood leaves," he said to Garnet, whose fingers were digging into his arm. "Listen to the music."

He saw Fancy running to the creek to get water, a long-legged sprite with wild black hair.

Garnet needed the sun and the strength the land could give her. If he could keep her safe . . .

"You're daft, Solomon. Crazy as a drunken sailor," she answered as a jackrabbit ran from the bushes. The horse sidestepped and nickered uneasily when Solomon quieted him.

"How about that jackrabbit for dinner?" he asked as Garnet's head jerked around at each new sight, each new sound. "Think of it as pickings."

"He's so furry and cute. I knew a South Seas cannibal once, big as a mountain. He lived in a cage and he wanted to eat everything, just like you."

Garnet kept close at Solomon's side until they came to the door. She was afraid one of the house's many snakes would kill him and clung to his leg, begging that he wouldn't go in. When he entered the house, she ran to a post and latched on to it. When he stepped outside to reload the first time, she yelled, "You're all I got, you worthless old man. Don't you go being some slimy snake's dinner!"

Later he placed the bucket filled with snakes on the ground outside and asked, "Dinner?"

Garnet wrapped her arms around his legs and gaped at the bucket. Solomon wondered when he would get used to wearing a gun on one leg and a frightened child on the other. He shouldn't have teased her, but she reminded him so much of Fancy. . . . He placed his hand on her head and Garnet nestled against him.   "You're not funny," she said grudgingly. "Let's go."

"Let's sleep here and I'll tell you about the stars."

"I know about the stars. Ma's sailors told me. Let's go back to town and you can play that woman again. She's got fine eats and a real fine propped-up bosom. I'm going to get me one when I grow up. Or I could run socks under my tits like a whore I once knew—"

"Garnet, do you remember about the words you weren't going to use anymore?" Solomon asked softly, though the memory of Cairo's breasts tantalized him. He wondered how she would feel, soft in his hand. He glanced at the bucket of snakes. If there was a woman he didn't want in his bed, it was a worthless, male-provoking betting lady.

When tears came to Garnet's eyes, Solomon reached down to lift the frightened girl up on his hip. Though he wished he could afford a hotel room for her comfort, he couldn't. "You're right. I'm an old man, Garnet. My bones ache from riding that nag. Do you think we could sleep here for tonight?"

Garnet's arms curled around his neck and she shivered, holding him tightly. "There's snakes here. Lots of them. Did my ma ever lay outside and look up at the stars?"

"Sure did." Fancy dreamed of riches, of a man giving her pretty things, talking sweet to her, of all the things she would have when she became a woman—then Duncan swept it all away.

As her brother, Solomon should have seen what was happening . . . should have protected Fancy's loving heart. . . . But instead he'd had his head filled with pride and his gunhand building a reputation; his body had followed Blanche's invitation despite his will.

Kipp. Solomon had a son.

A giant horned owl soared against the horizon and Solomon knew that one day Kipp would come looking for him, wanting to take him. Solomon closed his eyes; he felt two centuries old, weighted by the men he had faced, by the old wounds, by his guilt.

He always did the job. . . . He ran his fingers through his hair. What was he doing with Fancy's child? What did he know about settling down? About keeping a child warm and safe and happy?

Solomon gritted his teeth. Fear wouldn't help him think straight; if fear for Fancy hadn't been running him, he might have found her sooner.

"You're gritting your teeth again, Solomon. You're doing that more all the time." Garnet scanned the rolling land, the old house, and the stream. "We need a pee pot, Solomon. I don't like the thoughts of snakes waiting to chomp on my backside. Good God's britches! What in the hell is that?" she asked, gripping him with all her strength when the first wolf howled. "Dinner?" she asked hesitantly, locking both arms around him, her thin body trembling.

"That's a wolf. They look like big dogs and you stay away from them," Solomon whispered, comforting her.

Garnet quieted and Solomon's thoughts shifted back

to Cairo. He wondered when was the last time he'd felt the dark, rich tug of desire knot his belly that he had experienced looking at the billiards woman.

She had a high-class, look-down-her-nose attitude that just begged to be challenged. Wrapped in silk, satin, and feathers and gleaming under the house lights, Cairo Brown knew how to attract and distract men.

A female without a woman's tender softness could make men jump to her tune, and Kipp's attraction to her was evident. A woman who took off her gloves as if she were peeling off her clothes for a man could cost Kipp his life.

For the first time, Solomon was glad for the days he'd spent in smoky halls learning the game. Because Cairo Brown's silk purse was going to help him get started as a cattleman and as a father.

Garnet held him tight. "If you hold me tonight, Solomon—you know, not just put your hand on my head, but maybe put your arm around me, I'd try real hard not to pee on you when I sleep."

"I purely thank you for that, Miss Garnet," Solomon murmured wryly. In the last months, he had washed more clothing than he had in years. Washing the little girl's drawers every morning was a routine he was glad to stop. Hanging them over a stove to dry was a nightly chore. He'd worn damp but clean clothing several times.

"I like that fancy lady. She didn't try to slobber all over me," Garnet said, eyeing an old buffalo walking slowly down toward the stream. "Lordy! A living, walking mountain," she exclaimed, holding Solomon fiercely.

"A buffalo. An old bull who had to leave the herd. Probably driven out by a younger one." Kipp, a younger gun, would be coming after him, Solomon thought.

"Ooh," Garnet murmured in a sympathetic tone. "Poor old buffalo-thing. Can we keep him?"

The old bull walked wearily down to the water, drank, then settled heavily upon the ground to stare off into the evening.

Solomon knew the lonely feeling. "You stay away from him, Garnet. But he's got a home here . . . for as long as he stays."

Home. What did he know about ranching or making a living from the land?

But he would learn. With nothing but hell at his backside and nothing to offer either Garnet or Kipp, Solomon promised to do his best.

three

From the balcony overlooking her billiard table, Cairo surveyed her domain. She inhaled and moved into the scents of expensive house cigars, finely aged mash whiskey, beer, and money.

She shifted slightly, smoothing the jade silk of her gown and tugging up the matching gloves. They reached her upper arms, tight over the slight muscles. She flexed them gently. She had exercised with Quigly, pitting her agility and speed against his strength and bulk. She relished beating Quigly at the Chinese wrestling game that kept her fit, easing her tension. Dressed in silk pajamas, bound by a sash, she had felt free and in control.

She ran her glove over the carved cherrywood banister hauled upriver from St. Louis. Quigly's concession had been reluctant. She'd sat on his back, locked his thumb in a painful grip, and made him say the words "Yes, O magnificent one. You have won."

Then later, during Quigly's daily luxurious massage, she noted him humming gleefully. "I'll beat him next time, Quigly," she had muttered as he rubbed jasmine oil into the backs of her thighs.

"Yes, madame, of course you will," he had returned easily.

She looked over her bare shoulder at him. "I dislike the feeling that you view me as that man's pickings."

"Of course, madame. I apologize profusely. He is only a minor talent compared to your championship ability. He is not worthy of you. You were just having an off night. Perhaps you were still upset by the poor woman who had been beaten by her drunken husband."

Cairo inhaled slightly, allowing the new scent mixed with ambergris to soothe her. Quigly, a master at creating scents, had chosen an exotic jasmine to match her jade gown with tiny seed pearls on the bodice. The pearls matched some of those in her elaborate, twisted coiffure.

Cairo waved to a longtime customer and began to descend the staircase slowly. She continued smiling at the men but noted their expressions: They'd seen her lose.

Edge. She had to grab her winning edge over the customers, and quickly. Winning and losing were partly done in the mind, and she didn't want to lose anything— not now, not when New York was waiting.

Kipp lounged at the bar, an expensive, well-polished boot braced on the brass footrest. His eyes lit when he saw her and she returned his smile, spreading it over the crowd. Though she enjoyed Kipp, she didn't want her customers to think his attraction to her was returned. Part of the men's fascination with her was that she was alone, her heart unattached, the lady who had given her love once to a man who had adored her—Bernard.

"Act like a princess in an ivory tower. The gentlemen will

all want to rescue you and when they can't, they'll do the next best thing—lose their money to you."

Kipp came to her side at once, smoothly taking her hand and placing it on his arm. She turned slightly, avoiding the kiss he would have placed on her cheek. "*Chérie, ma chérie,*" Kipp murmured. "The jade color becomes you."

"Why, sir," she murmured, miming a deep southern accent. "How you do talk." She slowly noted his frilled shirt with tie and stickpin, evening frock coat, and pressed trousers. "You are looking beautiful yourself." Then she slid her hand from Kipp's to touch a customer's brocade vest and then to move through the crowd.

The table awaited, her table, the elegant mahogany friend bequeathed to her by Bernard. The scrimshaw numbers on the red balls would roll in her favor tonight. She talked to the men, thanked them for coming, and began her trick-shot routine.

Solomon Wolfe had taken something from her, and she wanted it back. He'd taken a portion of the absolute confidence that she had earned with years on the frontier, that she had scraped and dedicated her life to earning the reputation of "The Champ." The men were waiting now, waiting for the return of Solomon Wolfe to answer her challenge.

She drew off her gloves and gave them to Quigly. She'd make Solomon pay, Cairo decided as she placed two cue sticks together and allowed the ball to roll down them, successfully hitting another ball and sending it into the pocket. She allowed Kipp to place his hands on her waist and lift her to the table, where she sat, the cue stick behind her back, braced to shoot.

The men's rumbling conversation stopped, and Cairo

concentrated on her last shot. Her ball went into the pocket, then she took another one, rolling it beneath her palm to create an arcing path across the table.

She could sense Solomon Wolfe and smell his clean scent of fresh air, soap, leather, and woodsmoke. So he'd come to win again, had he? Before acknowledging him, she'd continue—

Two big hands circled her waist and lifted her from the edge of the table. Solomon Wolfe plopped her down to her feet. A small pearl, dislodged from her coiffure, bounced to the floor and lay by the scuffed toe of his boot. Garnet, looking rested, her hair neatly braided, bent to retrieve the pearl and bit it gently. "Real," she noted with authority, and popped it into the small bag tied to her waist.

"Give it back, Garnet," Solomon's deep voice ordered softly, though he didn't take his eyes from Cairo's furious ones.

"No. She lost it. I found it. It's mine," Garnet stated, glaring up at him. She squinted up at Cairo's hair. "Do you think you'll lose any more?"

"I'm not in the habit of losing anything," Cairo answered smoothly. "Quigly?"

He loomed beside Solomon, his expression disdainful as he glanced down at the small girl. "If the young lady would like to follow me, the cook has outdone herself with tonight's fare of ragout of pork with chestnuts, served with potatoes and apple rings. Then perhaps a torte—"

"No rags for this child and you can't talk right, mister. I don't want no tarts. I am a female myself and the thought turns my guts. It makes me puke," Garnet said as Solomon's big hand lay on her head. He shook her

gently and she glared up at him as if reluctant to be reminded of something. The meaningful bond that passed
through the two sets of black eyes was easily seen. He
shook her gently again and nodded significantly toward
Cairo. With a scowl, Garnet fished through her bag and
grudgingly handed the pearl to him.

Slumping her shoulders dramatically, Garnet marched
off to the side table. She glared at Solomon and he nodded approvingly to her. Quigly took the pearl from Solomon and slid it into his pocket. He closed his lids,
inhaled slowly, and lifted his eyes to the crystal lamps
before following the girl.

Solomon placed his rolled gun belt onto the table, the
wedding ring rolling across the green cloth.

His lingering gaze trailed across the seed pearls on Cairo's bodice, and the sharp edge of anger rose instantly in
her. "Very well," she murmured. "Let's play. I'll match
your wager with a better one, just to make the game more
interesting. The cue stick of your choice, and—"

"I'd like a good bed and cooking pots. Not your fancy
ones, but ones that will do for beans."

He'd asked for too little; the thought goaded Cairo as
she lifted her hem away from his boots. He had intruded
enough upon her life. "That's little to ask. Since you are
evidently in destitute circumstances, I'll raise that with
a sizable gold dust poke, say . . . oh, ten ounces."

He nodded briefly, the lamplight skimming across the
shadows of his face and glistening on his beard. Cairo
noted that it had been trimmed and washed. So she had
provided him with soap, had she? Sympathy for the child
would not be in his favor tonight. "Your cue stick?" she
asked; a graceful movement of her hand indicated the
wall rack.

Just watching him walk toward the rack, selecting a stick without hesitation, and sauntering back to the table infuriated Cairo.

His eyes drifted over the seed pearls on her bodice again and Cairo fought not to suck in air. She smiled tightly. "I'm ever so interested to see if your luck holds."

His gaze traced her throat lazily and finally lifted to meet the heat of her eyes. "I can only try."

Cairo lifted her skirts away from him as she swished to the end of the table. "Yes. Do," she shot back curtly.

He took his time bursting the triangle, and Cairo held her breath with each shot, praying for a miss. At the end of the second frame, she got her chance and finished the balls.

On the third frame, she leaned over the table and noted the drift of his gaze to her backside. He slowly followed the line of her skirts to her ankle. Cairo shot too fast and Solomon stepped up to the table.

She found herself standing, arms crossed in a blatantly defensive position. She never allowed her body to show her moods, but the gunfighter had raised her hackles. She forced her arms down to her side, holding her cue loosely.

He moved by her to angle a shot, coming too close. She was forced to move against the table and resented giving an inch to him. He lifted his eyebrows in her direction, his expression bland. Oh, he knew what he was doing, she thought. Knew it and wallowed in it.

She also knew how to prod a competitor. She touched him lightly in passing, moved her silk- and satin-clad body against his taut arm. He tensed and she reveled in her ploy, gaining confidence from the tightening of his broad shoulders as if taking a blow. Another time, she touched his wrist briefly with her fingers and smiled slowly. "All you have to do is to place the two pieces of the cue stick on the table," she murmured.

Solomon's lids shuttered his eyes, but she sensed she'd gotten to him, scored a hit. Cairo lifted her lips and smiled her slow, sensual, almost drowsy inviting smile, allowing her fingers to drift across his chest.

He caught her wrist, his eyes flashing beneath his lashes, his jaw taut. "I really want those pots and that bed. So I'm not likely to place my cue stick on the table, am I?"

She undertood what he meant. He would get what he came after, or go down trying.

From the crowd, Kipp stepped close, looming at Cairo's side. "Cairo?" he asked sharply, his hand resting on the butt of his gun.

Slowly Solomon raised his face to the younger man, as tall as himself. He held her wrist and she sensed storms flying over her head.

"Back off, son," Solomon murmured before slowly releasing her.

Kipp stared coldly at Solomon and Cairo nudged him with her shoulder. "Shall we play?" she asked easily, though her fingers were shaking.

Solomon nodded, then leaned to make a shot. Cairo swallowed, her body taut. She watched the expert shot and was forced to smile for appearances. A champion never shows bad temper, Bernard had said.

Bernard hadn't been ogled by a black-eyed gunman.

Solomon lightly ran a finger over the balls, his eyes locked with hers. The hair at the nape of her neck lifted and Cairo fought shivering.

Minutes later, she forced another tight, cold smile and made her concession to the winner of the match. "You have your choice of cookware in the kitchen. Quigly will show you the beds."

She caught the narrowing of his lids and remembered that he too was a predator. "Except mine," she added carefully, her nails digging into her palms. She couldn't bear him sleeping in the bed she adored. "You have your choice of any bed in the house—except mine. It wouldn't suit you."

He stood in her path, legs wide spread, cue stick held loosely in his big hands. He nodded once and she didn't trust the humor lurking in his black eyes.

Forced to ease around him, Cairo carefully tucked her skirts away from his worn boots. She placed the necessary smile on her lips and shot him a furious look as she left the parlor.

Her head held high, Cairo promised herself that Solomon Wolfe would rue the day he ever taunted her.

Cairo eased aside her lace curtain to look down on Fort Benton's notorious Front Street. In the fresh morning air, black-clad Chinese people carrying fresh vegetables moved among drovers wearing chaps, prostitutes, and housewives. A farmer herded sheep—"woolies"—from the sternwheelers down the busy street. It was filled with Red River carts, oxen teams loaded and ready to travel the Whoop-Up Trail to the Mounted Policemen's Fort Macleod. Children pulled a wagon of river fish to the butcher's, and hunters' horses were laden with fresh fowl and antelope. A wood cutter, known as a wood hawk, bargained with a farmwife while her husband waited.

Cairo's gaze brushed a drover herding cattle through the street and she inhaled sharply. Solomon's black hat, his straight, broad shoulders, and the way he commanded the horse beneath him could be easily recognized. While he was dressed in the same worn black outfit as when they met, Garnet was dressed in a new floppy hat with ribbons and wildflowers and wore a new blue shift. She proudly rode a paint pony beside him. The brown and white pony pulled a small cart loaded with supplies, and Garnet touched the prancing animal frequently, proudly showing off her new pet.

"Twelve cattle. Not prime, but mostly cows, and an old longhorn bull from Texas," Cairo muttered. "He's riding a good horse, an Appaloosa. I'm glad that Mr. Wolfe is investing my money wisely. According to local gossip, Mr. Wolfe once resided in this community. He began his career here as a young gun hand with a hot temper."

Cairo studied Solomon's shoulders and the expert way he held the reins. Quigly looked past her. "That's the new racing horse he's purchased from the Nez Percé, an Appaloosa mare. He appears to have a talent for gathering females of any species."

Quigly stepped back and lowered a tray onto her elegant claw-foot table. "Morning tea, Miss Cairo? I'll be going to Chinatown later and must be certain to purchase oolong tea. I understand a new shipment of silk is in at Mr. Fong's. I thought we would try silk knickers next, using the remnants of the silk I've been saving."

Cairo drank her tea quickly, much to Quigly's horror. She didn't like the restless feeling in her, the waiting to play Solomon again. Eagerness and pride hurt a champion's concentration; she knew how to pace herself and for the moment, she needed a distraction from her defeat. "I'll want a riding outfit. I want to practice with my dueling pistols. I'm riding a short way out of town. If Kipp comes here, please invite him to visit me."

If you don't want to continue, just place the two pieces of your cue stick on the table. Solomon had taken her offer and repeated it in a challenge she could not refuse, and she had raised her wager against him. "It isn't that he's a better player, Quigly, it's that—"

"Purple silk . . . ten yards of muslin . . . mmm? Yes, of course, Mr. Wolfe isn't a better player. But he has the ability to distract you with ungodly ease. One look down your bosom and you are in a froth, ready to fling yourself at him."

Cairo narrowed her gaze, focusing her attention on the man who would surely return to answer her challenge tonight. "I've lost far too much to him. It can't go on."

"You could eliminate him from the challengers. Refuse to play him," Quigly answered, sitting and placing a napkin on his lap.

"I've come too far to allow Solomon Wolfe to stop me now," Cairo said very quietly. "New York is just one year of work away from me, and then I'll be in the social circles. I don't want them to think that I had to work on the western frontier. I want enough money to make them think that I inherited from my English father and that billiards is my sport, not a means to make money," she said.

"I know your plans. I've heard them often enough. From dear Bernard and from you. A never-ending litany," Quigly murmured in a bored tone. "World-class tournaments in New York City. Society balls, etcetera, etcetera. . . ."

Solomon glanced up to her window, staring at her through the lace. His look promised that he would answer her challenge tonight. He touched the broad brim of his black hat with his fingers and nodded.

Cairo inhaled sharply and slowly eased the lace curtain down. "That man . . . that man does not know when he is well off. I am not afraid of Mr. Solomon Wolfe."

"Yes, madame. Perhaps tonight? I really wish he wouldn't bring that urchin with him. She has the manners of a farm animal. She is actually proud of how loud she can belch and break wind." Quigly's slightly bored tone lifted with interest, his eyes gleaming with excitement. "I need you to try on the petticoat before you go. I've decided to try for a detachable train, and the proper length is a necessity. My new sewing machine is a delight."

Cairo watched Solomon's broad back, the arrogant tilt of his head as he rode out of town. "Please see that any leftovers from the kitchen are delivered to Sarah's boardinghouse. She's been taking good care of the women and children we send her. And buy extra muslin, Quigly, and sweets. Those poor McDonald children need new clothes and . . . place money in their account at the shoemaker's, will you? Their father is not allowed to have access to that money. Make certain you inform the shoemaker that I will not trade there again if he allows Peter McDonald, that bully, that wife- and child-beater, to touch money given to those children. Also see if Sarah needs anything for the woman she has just taken in—"

"The gambler's woman thrown into the river without her clothes?"

"Yes. And see that the church's quilting circle and the new school receive one thousand dollars each in their accounts. I know the ladies don't want to acknowledge me, but they do appreciate my money. Some of which is rendered from their dear spouses. If you would like to do the river woman's hair, or help her dress, arrange to bring her here in the morning. With the shortage of women here, wives are always needed, and she may like the idea.

If not, we can pay her passage from here. Right now, she needs to feel an amount of pride."

"Quite so," Quigly agreed grimly. "Yes, I will help her."

Cairo returned to the setting room. She smoothed her pantalettes and eased a small waxed packet between her breasts. She adjusted her corset cover to conceal the slight bulge; while Quigly was concerned about the ruined line of her clothing, she was dedicated to surviving. She had long ago learned the uses of sleeping doses in a threatening man's drink and was never without them. Or the small knife in her garter. "I'll want a good wrestling match early in the afternoon, Quigly. Be forewarned. I will be at my best—"

"Ah, yes. Since you have been playing with Mr. Wolfe, my poor weak body has paid dearly."

"Mr. Wolfe has scars on his wrists. Do you suppose he's been in jail?" She'd seen marks like that—on her father.

Missouri, torn by war, had little use for crooked horse traders. Her father had sold a rogue stallion to the Union army. Old Tex couldn't be ridden, but he knew how to herd the other horses back to her father. Buford Brown been tied to a tree and whipped in front of his weeping wife and six children. But he'd lived, because a skinny little girl, just nine years old, had stepped in front of the lash. "Ain't you got no kin? No mams and kids and grannies? Think how they'd feel if they knew you killed my pa and we starved. Can't you please let him live? Please?" little Ethel had begged.

Quigly frowned. "I've seen slaves with marks like those on Solomon's wrists. Men who had hung by their wrists for days, weeks. Or men who fought with every drop of life in them to get free. Desperate men."

She poured another cup of tea and closed her eyes, savoring the blend. Solomon had his weaknesses and she would seek them out. "A light dinner tonight, fresh fruit and a green salad, broiled fish. I'll want to nap and meditate before I play tonight . . . the scent of chamomile oil would be relaxing—"

"Perhaps sautéed chicken bosoms with a sprinkle of parsley and later a wedge of scented geranium cake. Madame, we are almost out of chamomile due to your need for soothing since Mr. Wolfe made his appearance. Lemon balm is also soothing—"

Cairo leveled a stare at him. "I do not want to hear more about Mr. Wolfe, Quigly. You are always brewing oils, lavender, ylang ylang, chamomile, and whatever to burn as scent therapy or to use in my baths and massages. My use of chamomile has nothing to do with Mr. Wolfe. By the way, please see that we have adequate lemons to use for my hair rinse, will you? That awful shade of light brown is coming back."

Cairo went to the window, easing back the curtain to trace Solomon's path out onto the prairie. He'd been tormenting her, quietly, efficiently, feeling out and testing her weak spots. He had stalked her, sensitized her, and ruined her focus.

Two could play at that game.

Solomon listened to the day begin on the prairie, to the sound of a cow calling her new calf. The old longhorn bull bawled, sensing a cow's sexual heat, and the rooster that a farmer's wife had given him began to crow.

Garnet slept beside him, a child afraid in a new place. As soon as he could make a cot for Garnet, the little girl would have to sleep alone.

Solomon lifted his arms behind his head, his strained muscles protesting, the old scars aching.

The billiards woman excited him in ways he had forgotten.

He'd seen too much, been in too many battles not to know that she had pitted herself against him.

His son wanted Cairo Brown as a lover, but she held him off, moving away from his possession easily. The lady didn't like tethers. He rubbed his scarred wrists briefly and realized he shared that dislike.

When Solomon had found out about Duncan's seduction of Fancy and her note, he'd been too eager for revenge. Solomon had approached and accused Duncan; a blow from behind had sent Solomon into unconsciousness. He awoke in a cave, hanging by his wrists, chained to the rock wall. Wielding a bullrope, Duncan had almost killed Solomon, leaving him hanging in that cave for days.

Garnet snored lightly and reached to pet his beard in her sleep. Then she turned to her side and snuggled the kitten that Cairo's butler had given her. Quigly's skillful ploy kept Garnet busy during last night's match.

Mourning doves began to coo and a mockingbird trilled. In the corral, the Appaloosa mare, Hiyu Wind— a Chinook word for "storm"—returned a nicker to another horse up on the knoll overlooking the ranch.

Solomon eased from the iron-rail bed and slid into his boots. He jerked on his shirt and gun belt, lashing the holster to his thigh as he eased open the house's door. Out on the ridge, outlined against the pink dawn, a rider dressed in skirts slid from her horse.

Minutes later, Solomon slid down from Hiyu Wind's bare back to walk toward Blanche Knutson.

In the dawn, she was more beautiful than he remembered, her skin milk-white against the rich black curls drawn back from her smooth brow. Her blue eyes widened in pleasure as he walked toward her, her generous mouth welcoming him with a wide smile. "Solomon. My dear sweet Solomon. You have returned, just as I knew you would."

She took his hands, gazing up at him fondly. "Still the same . . . rugged, tight-lipped, and saying things with your eyes that no righteous woman could refuse. How I've prayed, how I've waited for you to return."

He eased his hands away, bracing himself against the lash of time, the memories filling him. He'd loved her desperately, fighting the command of his hot, youthful body and losing to her invitations. Invitations that her much older husband encouraged. Looking through the years, Solomon knew that Buck had skillfully arranged for his young wife and her lover to be alone. "Tell me about our son, Blanche," Solomon said, removing her open hand from his chest.

She inhaled, her hand rising to cover the lace at her throat. The velvet riding costume fit her torso tightly, her full breasts thrusting at the cloth, her waist nipped into a small drape that circled her hips to the back. The velvet material revealed a lace petticoat and kid leather buttoned boots, so small that Solomon remembered fitting her bare sole into his hand.

"So you know and you've come back for us. Your son and myself." She turned to him, her eyes lighting, catching the dawn, as she wrapped her arms around his neck.

Her lips were warm, soft, tantalizing. Her teeth nibbled on his bottom lip, an invitation that had driven him into white heat as a youth.

Solomon stepped back. "Buck got his wish for a son after all."

Blanche's expression lit with pride. "Yes. Kipp was such a beautiful child, Solomon. He reminds me so of you. Black hair, black temper, ramrod-straight pride. He told me about the man at that Brown woman's billiard parlor, and oh, how I prayed it was you. Now that you've come, say you'll stay at the ranch with us, let us be the family that we always should have been. I've never stopped loving you, Solomon. Not for a moment."

"Even when you refused to come with me to find Fancy?" The bitter memories slashed through him, and he saw Fancy's childish handwriting again. *"I'm going with my own dear true love. I'll write. F."*

Blanche's lovely smile died slowly. "Surely you know now that I couldn't have left Buck. You didn't know where Fancy was, how long it would take to find her—and he needed me. Then there was the baby I suspected you'd given me. How could you ask that I endanger myself and your child, by riding off to God knows where?"

"But I didn't know there was a child, did I? Was it ever intended that I should know? Did Buck know I fathered his baby?" Solomon asked grimly. "Who acted as stud for your other children? Does Kipp have brothers and sisters? How much did Buck pay them?"

The words were harsh, demanding, ripping from him like bullets and winding him. He disliked revealing his emotions and knew the danger of exposing them. He realized his fists were curled tightly and slowly forced his fingers to open. "A man should know when he's a father, Blanche."

"You're shocked. Discovering that you are a father after all these years has temporarily upset you. You'll realize that I acted wisely. Buck died five years after you left. He would have killed you if you . . . if you had tried to acknowledge Kipp as yours. He wanted more children, of course, so I had Edward. Buck didn't want Kipp to remain an only child. As his wife, how could I refuse a dying man? And you were off in search of Fancy—"

"Let's talk about Kipp. I hear he's riding with a wild bunch now. Is Buck's money going to buy him out of the hangman's noose?"

Blanche turned away. "Kipp is just a boy living life. I'm certain he's doing nothing illegal. He's his father's son. He's trying to impress that harlot Brown woman, though I do not know why. . . . Solomon, she used to run a traveling billiards game with some old English fool who doted on her. When he died, she set up shop here. She's probably making extra money upstairs with her customers. I have no idea why men drool over her."

She turned, shaking her hair loose with one hand and unbuttoning the velvet bodice with her other. "Oh, Solomon, I'm so hungry for you. No one has ever satisfied me like you did . . . ever. . . ."

She tugged away the laces of her camisole, freeing her lush breasts to the dawn. "I ache for you, Solomon, honey. Ache for your mouth, your body locked with mine. I can give you everything now. You can take your rightful place at my side. All this land—she swept her hand across the ranch and beyond—"I've kept this for you. Take me . . . take me now, here."

She pulled open his shirt, locked her arms around his neck, and stroked his hair. "I love you, Solomon. Only you. I've waited for this moment. Waited for you to come back to me."

He eased her wrists from him. "No, Blanche."

"I ache for you, honey," she protested, arching up to kiss him. "Please make this ache go away."

"No," he said quietly. The time for loving Blanche had passed. He wondered distantly if she had ruined him for trusting other women. He'd never trusted a woman after Blanche and her refusal to come with him. Those years were long ago and he didn't need a woman's softness to keep him warm now.

"You're tired. Tired from traveling, from working on this ranch. Come to my home . . . I'll have my cook serve us breakfast in bed. We can stay there for days."

"What do you mean, you 'kept this' for me?"

"Why, my boys and the ranch hands kept the Indians and the squatters off, and I paid taxes when they were due, honey. I know how attached you are to old man Johnson's land. Not that you'd want to live in that shack when you can stay in my home . . . when you can run my gorgeous ranch. Think of the parties we'll have. Think of the social position you'll have at my side. I am a matriarch of Fort Benton now, dear one. You'll have power—"

"I'll pay you back, Blanche," Solomon said slowly, aware of her bare breasts nestling, rubbing against his chest. When he was a boy, Blanche's body set him on fire, but now he saw her as a shallow, grasping woman.

"Pay me back now, honey," she whispered huskily with an inviting smile, placing his hand on her breast, moving it slowly until she groaned, arching into him, her hand searching his trousers—

"Tell me what you know about Fancy, Blanche. About why she left," Solomon asked so softly that Blanche paused and glanced up at him.

. He removed his hand and she licked her lips, breathing heavily. "Do we have to relive the past, honey?"

"Yes, we do." He was cruel now, losing the dispatch that had kept him alive, the cool reasoning, so much a part of him. He wanted to hurt Blanche, to make her pay for his lost years with Kipp.

Solomon glanced at a noise in the shadows and found Garnet picking her way through the sagebrush up to him. She glared up at him and placed her hands on her waist. "I wet myself because you weren't there to wake me up to use the pee pot. You promised me you wouldn't leave me. I got scared." She glanced at Blanche who was quickly buttoning her velvet bodice. "Lady, I'd be mighty proud of those melons myself."

Solomon placed his hand on Garnet's head and rocked her gently. She pouted up at him. "Well, I'm a kid. I get scared sleeping alone, and here you are wanting to poke some female who hasn't got the sense to play in her own bed . . . 'cause yours is filled, with me. See?"

She held her wet drawers away from her legs and continued studying Blanche's bosom. "Did you get 'em back in?" she asked curiously.

Solomon shook her head gently and Garnet nudged her head against him, returning the odd caress. This small girl held the only softness in his life. He didn't want her involved in the cruelties of the past. "This is an old friend. Garnet, say hello to Blanche."

"Should I leave and let you two have at it or what?" Garnet grumbled.

"Hello, Garnet." Blanche looked at Solomon and smiled warmly. "Yours?"

"Now she is. Garnet is Fancy's daughter."

Blanche's blue eyes darted to Garnet, reading the same fierce features as Solomon's and his sister's. For a moment she frowned, and Solomon wondered about her thoughts. What did she know about Fancy? About Duncan's use of her? Had Blanche played a part in Fancy's descent?

A deep chill swept through Solomon, stilling him. A

vain woman, Blanche had hated the beauty of other women and Fancy had been so vibrant. . . .

Then Blanche smiled warmly. "She's welcome, too. I've always wanted a daughter," she said.

"You wouldn't want me. I pee in beds."

Blanche, visibly shaken, took a few steps back. She forced a tight smile. "You'll grow out of that, my dear."

"Well, at least I don't have lice anymore," Garnet stated proudly.

Blanche's hand rose to her throat. She glanced at Solomon, then down to the child. "Yes . . . well . . . that's good. Solomon, I'll be expecting you. . . . Help me mount, please?"

When Blanche rode away with one last lingering, inviting look, Garnet took Solomon's hand. "She's helpless, not worth spit. She wouldn't last one day on the Barbary."

Solomon watched Blanche ride into the morning sun. He disliked the dark anger swirling through him, the need for revenge. For a moment, he'd wanted to take her cruelly, to hurt her as he knew Fancy had been hurt. But he'd never had a woman like that and he never would.

He lifted Garnet up to the mare's back and the girl shook her head. "I suppose you're all set to poke her now, though the thought is disgusting. Two old people . . ." She shuddered. "Just disgusting."

"You went to see that bastard, didn't you?" Duncan demanded as Blanche swung down to the ground. She tossed the reins of her horse to him, reminding him that he was her employee, then stalked past him toward the massive, elegant house she wanted to share with Solomon.

Duncan grabbed her shoulder, spinning her around. Her hand raised and caught him on the cheek. She'd come from her dreams and found herself in a reality as ugly and deformed as Duncan's shattered hand and leg. "Don't manhandle me, Duncan. I don't like it."

He sneered down at her, ignoring the burning imprint of her hand on his cheek. He smoothed his blond hair, so like Edward's, the same crisp textures and waves. "I've touched you plenty and you'd raise the dead with the noise you make under me."

She hated him for reminding her of her needs that only Solomon could fill. Blanche breathed heavily, facing Duncan. His eyes skipped down to her bodice, narrowing on an opened button. "You've been whoring with Wolfe, haven't you?" Duncan asked.

"No." Blanche turned and walked toward the two-story mansion. She'd borne Buck the sons he wanted and she had paid dearly for the carved white gables, painted columns, and the two thousand acres of prime land, grain, and stock.

Blanche tossed her hair, freeing the black soft strands to the High Plains wind; Solomon would come back to her. Men did not refuse Blanche Knutson. She'd give Solomon time to come to his senses and she'd bribe the girl, then Solomon would be hers again. Magnificent, strong, arrogant Solomon.

In the house, Blanche ripped the velvet ribbon from her throat and tossed it onto a carved English parlor table. "Mary, heat my bath and be quick about it," she ordered the Mexican woman hovering in the parlor doorway.

Blanche raced up the elegant stairway to the master bedroom, which had been hers before Buck had died. She flung herself onto the lace-draped bed and stared at the ruffled canopy. She gripped the pillow, pushing it beneath her aching breasts. She frowned, thinking of the past. Solomon had run off, chasing his tramp sister, a fifteen-year-old girl that Duncan and the others had boasted about having. Duncan had said she'd taken up with a traveling tinman, a tinker, running away from Solomon's protective eye.

Buck had wanted another child the instant he'd held Kipp—a squalling, big baby boy with a heavy thatch of black, waving hair. Buck was insistent, plaguing and taunting her and offering her magnificient jewelry to find another lover, to "breed" again. Then in his dark rages, he hurt her badly. She had no one to turn to for help, and she had to protect Kipp. Before Kipp was barely three months old, Blanche found another dark-skinned man, one who reminded her of Solomon with his hot glittering eyes and a hard thrusting body. William had pleasured her and Buck had known about her affair, pleased and waiting his second child. But the baby was too dark, with a coppery tint to his skin. Grief squeezed inside Blanche, fleeting and dulled by time. After beating Blanche for mating with an Indian, Buck had killed William and ordered her to kill "her redskinned bastard."

But Blanche had loved her baby, the little life she'd carried. An Indian woman had promised to raise him away from the ranch, to go to Canada and to keep him safe from Buck's men.

Blanche cupped her breasts. *Solomon*. She needed him, needed his strength at her side. Needed him in her bed.

The bedroom door opened and clicked shut, the lock turned. "Duncan, get out," she ordered without turning toward the man who had been her lover, her tethered beast, for years.

The preying beast knew her weak moments, when she had to have a man lodged deep inside her—Duncan knew her sometimes better than she knew herself and she hated him for that.

Duncan flipped her to her back, his face harsh with desire. He jerked up her skirts and tore away her drawers, entering her roughly, despite her pummeling fists.

The fever caught her and Blanche cried out, giving herself to her needs as the man suckled, bit her breasts, and roughly thrust himself into her. When Duncan collapsed on her, she pushed him away, rolling off the bed and cleansing her body immediately. She faced him, smoothing her clothing shakily and trembling with anger and passion for Solomon . . . only Solomon.

Duncan lay back on her pillows, watching her.

"You're pathetic," she said, her body shaking with fury. "How dare you!"

"You looked like you needed the ride," he returned easily, rising to cleanse himself. "You got a son from me, didn't you? Edward is a fine specimen, so I guess my bad hand and lame leg didn't matter at the time, did they?"

"Stay away from me from now on."

"Because you've got plans for that worn-out bastard, Wolfe?"

"I've always loved Solomon."

"Hell, Blanche. You've loved the whole lot of us, haven't you?" Duncan asked with a leer.

"If Solomon suspects that you had his sister all those years ago, that you started her whoring with the traveling tinkers and the drovers, he'll come after you," Blanche returned with a small, tight smile.

"I'll be waiting. Solomon and I go way back. You just remember how back then you couldn't stand his sister. How she caught men's eyes, even old Buck's. You had to talk long and sweet to get him turned against her, didn't you?"

Fear skipped through Blanche. Duncan was capable of hurting anyone, and she ruled him by her power and holdings. He had no heart, only a cold hollow abyss. "You hurt Solomon and you'll pay."

"Now, wouldn't that be a shame for you to lose Kipp's daddy so soon," Duncan sneered.

"You say anything to Kipp and I'll—" Rage ripped through her, shaking her violently.

"He's too taken with that billiards woman to notice just how much he looks like his pa." Duncan strapped on his gun belt, his movements still awkward after years. His fingers were permanently curled, his gun hand shattered by a bullet; his left hand served him now slowly, clumsily. Another bullet had shattered his kneecap. Blanche had never discovered who shot him, nor did she want to know. One day Duncan's intrigues and his enemies would kill him. "What will people say when they know you've had three sons by three different men? That you spawned an Indian's brat? Where will your fine upstanding reputation be then? I'll tell you where—in a cowpile. By the way, Edward got a bit too frisky with a tart in town and he needs money to shut her up. Either that, or I'll see that she takes a long swim in the river. She'd just fit into a sack."

Blanche went to the high carved-cherry bureau. She scooped out a handful of gold coins and flung them at him. She enjoyed Duncan's awkward movements to retrieve the gold glittering on the Oriental carpet. "Don't hurt her and don't touch me again, Duncan," she repeated softly. "Or I'll see that Edward is removed from my will."

Duncan's hard, narrow face tightened as he slapped his dusty hat against his hand. "You wouldn't disown your own son, Blanche," he stated with a sneer. "You're too fine and loving a mother."

"Edward is the only reason you're still here," she reminded him.

"You're a hot woman, Blanche." He placed his hat on his head and nodded. "Until the next time you're feeling lonesome."

"Not ever for you, Duncan. I can't bear your touch."

Fifteen minutes later, Blanche soaked in her scented bath and planned how to entice Solomon to her home. He'd have the little girl—clearly he was attached to the child with her matted hair and wet drawers. Blanche forced herself not to frown; wrinkles would mar her perfect complexion. "Mary, come massage buttermilk into my face," she ordered to the woman bringing in another bucket of hot water.

Solomon. Kipp needed his father, a strong man. Edward needed Solomon to temper his anger, to settle him. Edward barely recognized her wishes, starting brawls constantly, costing a fortune in keeping prostitutes and the townspeople quiet.

Solomon would look beautiful in a frilled shirt and a black frock coat. He'd be perfect at her side on the ranch, in Fort Benton society, or trips to St. Louis and the East. He was a man who drew respect, and she would have him.

Blanche closed her eyes, remembering his harsh face lit by the pink dawn. The man she wanted was still there—hot, passionate, waiting. She'd seen the fire dance into Solomon's black eyes, his expression tighten fiercely with the emotions running deeply through him, just as he once looked when he caught her scent. She'd wait for him to come to his senses.

four

"All you have to do is to place the two pieces of the cue stick on the table," Solomon repeated quietly to Cairo that night.

Her quick flush of anger dismayed and shocked her. Solomon could rake out an emotion she had concealed for years, like taking a smoldering coal from an old fire and blowing upon it, nudging it into life.

"You are insolent," she stated between her teeth, stepping back when he would brush a pink boa feather from her cheek. She felt the fancy confection of ribbons and feathers trembling in her perfectly arranged blond curls. "Don't touch me, Mr. Wolfe. I always finish a game and *I* am not the bet."

Solomon's black eyes flickered over her warm face, touching her lips before moving down her throat to her bosom. She placed her fingers over her rapidly beating pulse, distracted by his hunter's stare, seeking out her weaknesses. His gaze held hers, amusement tempered with desire, heating her worn nerves.

Solomon Wolfe had that effect on her, tearing at her nerves, prowling around her walls, her experience, and lifting the hair at the nape of her neck. She touched the frothy pink headpiece Quigly had created to match her evening dress and resented Solomon down to his dusty, worn boots. He was toying with her, becoming a better shot the more they played. She knew he had let her win, toying with her, drawing her on.

He had her reputation and a good portion of her savings in his dark, scarred fist. Cairo smiled at the men who came to see her every night, to admire her as a winner. She detested the sympathy in Elmer Makin's rheumy eyes, the cocky vulture grin of young Evans, who was certain that she would lose to him one day. She was losing her pride every time she played Solomon, a worn, hard-eyed gunfighter, who probably wasn't that fast anymore.

Cairo slanted a glance at Solomon's lean, broad-shouldered body and down to the gun he constantly wore on his thigh. Of course, now that he had her money, there was no reason for him to wager his gun or the old wedding ring.

Kipp had no cause to be jealous. Solomon Wolfe looked dipped in hard times from his shaggy hair that reached his collar to his black beard. There wasn't an ounce of softness stamped on his face except when he looked at Garnet, who clearly adored him.

Despite his constant winning, his goading of her, Cairo had not seen him smile.

Until he tormented her. Then his eyes were amused, crinkling slightly at the corners, as if he knew her to be an inferior player, one of the weaker sex who should be cooking and bearing babies and staying at home.

Then she wanted to rip him apart.

The emotion startled her; she detested showing emotion.

Cairo gripped her custom cue and realized her fingers were sweating. She methodically dried and dusted them with chalk. She would go to New York, dance at society balls, and ride a fancy carriage in the park. She would entertain the upper crust of society and live the life she had worked for, had planned for. Solomon Wolfe was not taking New York away from her. . . .

He had beaten Cairo again, taking the best of the twenty-one frames and expertly nudging the scoring beads with his cue stick. She'd bet rashly, determined to retrieve her losses. Since he had arrived, Solomon Wolfe had taken nearly twenty thousand dollars from her, almost her entire savings, her New York society bankroll. She refused to offer her jewelry or any fixtures of the elegant billiard hall she had purchased with night after night of hard work.

She eyed Solomon as he leaned over the table, banking his shot off the cushions and spinning one red ball against another. Angular, lean, and tall, he watched the balls shoot into pockets. He circled her prized table, a broad-shouldered, narrow-hipped, poorly dressed predator who could devour her dreams. She detested the smooth caress of his lean hand on the polished wood— *her* wood in *her* billiard hall.

He enjoyed tearing her pride away from her, scooping up his winnings in his dark, powerful hand and tucking them into his pocket. He'd wanted the money at first, but now he was taunting her, searching out her weaknesses.

"The least you could do with all my money is to buy

yourself new clothing. Your boots are shameful," she murmured, moving past him to smile at Kipp, who had just arrived.

"*Chérie.*" Kipp took her hand, kissing it. He looked at Solomon over the top of her head and the older man nodded slowly.

"Mr. Wolfe, perhaps you would like to change the pace. Have you ever played carom?" she asked, watching Solomon study Kipp. Kipp's hand rested on his gun.

"Fifteen-Ball is fine with me," Solomon said easily, his gaze locked with Kipp's angry one. Color rose in the youth's face and his fingers tightened on his gun. Cairo recognized Kipp's dark, narrowed look. Whatever he'd done today filled him with excitement, power, the need to prove himself.

She hoped he wasn't riding with the wild, young bunch who stole horses and sold them to the army. Or with the men holding up the stage lines—a stage had been robbed today, the driver's arm wounded by a man with a "lightning draw."

Cairo placed her hand on Kipp's ruffle-covered chest, soothing him with a smile. If she could stop him from whatever drew him to danger—"Dinner, later?"

Kipp's gaze slowly lowered to her and softened. He nodded curtly and moved slightly back, urged by her gentle push. "Shall we play, Mr. Wolfe?" Cairo asked, moving quickly to distract the crowd who sensed a gunfight.

Solomon played quietly, deadly, winning match after match, and Cairo murmured to him, "He's only a boy. Don't you dare hurt him, Mr. Wolfe."

"He wants you." His fierce black gaze shot to her face, lashing at her. "Does playing him along make you feel younger?"

For a full moment, Cairo could not move her lips. She

stood very still in the midst of her game with Solomon, staring at him. A froth of pink feathers slipped to quiver along her cheek. "What did you say?" she asked carefully, straining to keep her tremble of anger from showing.

The pink feathers quivered again and she knew she had failed.

Solomon shot in his hard, fast, instinctive style. He traced the balls skimming across the green cloth to drop into the pockets. "Five ball, side pocket. . . . You could cause him to lose his life. He's out to impress you."

"You're safe, Mr. Wolfe. Kipp knows that I don't allow gunplay here."

Solomon finished the game, winning again, and scooping up the fat gold poke she had placed on a wall shelf used for wagers. He took back his wager, a smaller poke that he had won the night before. "I'll be back."

Of course he would. He was dragging away her dreams, killing them, strangling them in his hard, scarred, too-competent hands. Cairo acted quickly. "I'd really like to try another game. You may enjoy it. Come early tomorrow night, before the parlor fills, and I'll teach you the rules." She also intended to ask him what it would take to stay away from her business.

"I want to know," she added as an afterthought, "exactly how and when you learned to play so well . . . although you don't seem to have a variety of games at your disposal."

"Beer halls," he drawled slowly, nettling her. "Low-down, cheap beer halls where men played and women served drinks." Then he took a slow, amused look around her elegant parlor and flicked a pink feather with his fingertip.

Instant rage surged through her, molten and ready to scald. She held her body taut, narrowing her eyes to shield her anger. But his pleased arrogance, just a drift of humor skimming through his hard face, mocked her. Solomon nodded his shaggy black head in that same quick manner as he did everything. "Tomorrow."

The man lacked grace.

He lacked gallantry.

He was a burr under her proverbial saddle, and he was hacking her dreams into shreds.

Then she looked down to the cracking sound and found that she had broken her best painted fan.

Solomon hammered the boards into place, repairing the old barn that would hold winter hay for his new herd.

Never far away, Garnet was napping on a blanket in the barn, curled beside her kitten. She refused to stay at the boardinghouse while Solomon played, refused to miss "one high-falootin' minute at Miss Cairo's," and she napped heavily during the day. In the early afternoon, her stomach was filled with stew purchased from the boardinghouse, fresh bread and butter and jam.

Solomon wiped his forearm across his brow, the sleeve absorbing his sweat. Since Garnet had found him talking to Blanche, the little girl had been filled with questions.

Solomon had more than a few questions that he needed answered. What did Blanche know of Duncan's betrayal? Had Blanche planned it?

Whatever had happened in the past, *Kipp was his son.* Solomon sensed the bond each time he looked at the youth. From Kipp's wild-eyed cocky look of last night, he was following in his father's footsteps. Cairo and Kipp weren't lovers. She treated him too lightly, moving away from him with ease.

Cairo didn't want to be owned. Beneath her silk and polish, she was a woman who knew what she wanted, and it wasn't the boy. She'd want another man, like her English lord, a lapdog and a meal ticket.

Solomon picked up another board, covering a hole in the barn with it. He stopped the hammer in midswing, sensing the shadows moving around him. He slowly put the tool aside and turned to face the young gun, who stood with legs spread, braced to draw down on him.

"Hello, Kipp," Solomon said, walking away from the barn. He wanted Garnet to remain napping while he talked with his son.

"Leave Cairo alone," Kipp said softly, rage trembling in his voice, a tone that could cost him his life, Solomon noted.

"I'm only taking her offer. It's her business. She knows playing and betting can end with a win or a loss." Solomon remembered Cairo's lips tightening, her honor and pride warring with her temper. He admired the way she had lifted her head and leveled an ominous look at him, her honey-brown eyes darkening.

"She's a woman on her own. No self-respecting man would take as much from her as you have."

"Does she know you're here?" Solomon doubted that Cairo knew of Kipp's visit; she was a woman who liked handling her affairs alone.

"None of your business. Stop making eyes at her. She's mine."

Solomon slowly unstrapped his gun belt and eased it to a wooden bench, letting Kipp know that he would not draw against him. The youth's eyes were squinting against the afternoon sun and Solomon had the advantage of studying his son's features, so much like his own. "Does she know that?"

Kipp's rawboned young face flushed with anger, his eyes narrowing. "I'm going to marry her someday and she knows that she's the only woman I want. That's enough. Cairo will come around. In the meantime, stop whatever you're doing to make her nervous and off her game. Let her win back what you've taken." Kipp nodded toward Solomon's gun belt. "Put that on. According to town gossip, you were fast when you were young. Let's see just how fast you are."

"I'm not drawing against you." The nerves in Solomon's body tightened; Kipp was riding a fine edge. One wrong move and Solomon's son would kill him . . . because Solomon would not fire back.

"Afraid? You're a coward," Kipp snapped, ripping his gun belt off and tossing it to the ground. "Maybe you can understand something else, old man."

Solomon dodged Kipp's first blow.

"Stand and fight." Kipp swung again and Solomon leaned to one side, the blow hissing through the air.

Solomon remembered how he had challenged Ole on his deathbed years ago, when he burned for Blanche and wedding vows stood in their way. "I don't want to fight you, son."

"There's not much you can do about that, old man. Because I'm going to plow you good," Kipp stated hotly.

Cairo leaned back against the headrest of her elegant porcelain clawfooted tub. Jasmine scents and soothing buttermilk floated softly around her. She stared at the fringe on her draped satin curtains. It was midafternoon now; later in the evening, Solomon would return and she would teach him how to play carom. The three-ball game demanded intense skill and trick shooting.

Solomon's style ran to hard and fast, and predictable; she'd never seen him use anything that might require the finesse of a trick shooter such as herself.

Soothed, wrapped in her plans, Cairo stepped from the tub and behind her hand-painted silk screen. She would take her usual nap, soothed by the tea Quigly left on her bedside table, and she would rest.

Cairo wrapped the sash of her robe around her waist, smoothing the embroidered silk dragon across her chest. She'd been far too caring, too gentle with Solomon Wolfe.

And she detested the dark humor, the amusement flickering behind his black lashes. *Delighted*, he had murmured.

"No one mocks me," she muttered, sipping her tea. She allowed the chamomile to calm her before she settled down on the pillow, relaxing, relaxing, slowly easing her toes, her legs, her fingers, back, neck, and, finally, her entire body. She floated into the high, soft, elegant bed, easing the tension from her.

She listened to the sounds of Fort Benton's afternoon, hammers pounding, new buildings being built, sternwheelers blowing their whistles, men, women, and children in the streets. June's warm breeze stirred her curtains. It was four o'clock now and she could rest for two hours before having an early light dinner and meeting Solomon. She shoved away the sense of excitement quivering in her, the sport and the romance of billiards tempting her. Facing Solomon required a cool head, and she would not lose more to him by missing out on her rest.

The sash cut into her waist slightly, and Cairo drowsily eased away the silk, letting the breeze flow over her nude body, letting it calm her, sweep away the tension. . . . When she closed her lids, she saw Solomon's mocking eyes, that cocky, arrogant line of his hard mouth, almost softened by his amusement.

Anger stirred in her just as it always did when she

thought of Solomon Wolfe. She refused to be anyone's amusement.

Cairo sprang to her feet, jerking on the silk pajama drawers that Quigly had fashioned for her. She knotted them impatiently, then drew on the matching embroidered jacket, tying the sash at her waist. She would not have a moment's peace until she destroyed Solomon Wolfe—made his life just as miserable as he had made hers. She intended to retrieve her cash and send him back down the river just as poor as he had arrived.

She threw a small flat cushion on the floor, bending to place her head on it. She pushed her legs upward to stand on her head. If she couldn't rest, her body tense, she might as well meditate, concentrate on the blood circulating through her brain. She braced her palms flat on the floor and began to hum a monotone chant, concentrating, focusing, wiping Solomon out of her mind.

The shadows stirred and she opened her eyes to view dusty, worn boots. Solomon Wolfe's boots. "You should have those resoled," she said calmly, refusing to give him the pleasure of her alarm. From her viewing angle on the floor, Solomon looked huge, arrogant, and amused. He traced her pajama-clad body slowly down to her stomach, then to her breasts. Cairo blew away the end of the silk sash, which had slid onto her nose. "The shoemaker here is excellent."

When she would have allowed her feet to descend from the wall, Solomon's single hand pinned her ankles to the wall. "Nice feet," he said conversationally. His thumb stroked her ankles slowly, maddeningly, just as he had stroked his cue stick and the wood of the table, admiring them. Cairo tested his grip, found it gentle but strong, and glared up at him. "A bit on the large size for a woman, but good straight toes," he said, continuing to stroke her ankle.

"Thank you," Cairo returned with clenched teeth. Solomon's tone might have been one he was using for pointing out a cow he might decide to purchase. "Would you mind . . . ?"

Her jacket was sliding down, the sash opening. When he released her ankles and stepped back, Cairo eased her feet down to the floor and stood. She quickly tightened her sash. Aware that the silk cloth did not conceal the outline of her breasts, she tried to breathe shallowly. "What do you want?"

His eyes locked on her unbound breasts and she folded her arms protectively over them. "You invited me here," he reminded her in a drawl that lifted the hair on the nape of her neck.

Cairo ran her hand through her hair, pushing the weight back from her face. "I meant downstairs, before the crowd came."

Solomon braced his weight on one leg, looking too masculine and angular in her flower-and-ruffle bedroom. He looked around the room, not shielding his interest. He studied Bernard's gilt-framed portrait for a moment, then the elegant china tea service. "Very nice."

"Very nice and expensive," she returned, regretting the snap to her voice. "If you'll just wait downstairs, I'll be there shortly."

His black, sharp gaze cut back to her face. "Why?"

"I . . . I thought we might talk about playing something else. I'll be happy to teach you the rules before we play in earnest."

Solomon looked down her body slowly; then before she could move, he caught the sash and pulled her to him. She breathed heavily, refusing to strike at him, refusing to show the wild emotions pumping through her. She clamped her lips closed against the threats leaping to them.

"You're tying that boy in knots," he whispered close to her lips. He stood very still, his heartbeat pushing at her breasts.

"Let me go," she ordered, lifting her face to his. The movement brushed her mouth against his, and Solomon inhaled sharply. His lashes lowered as he searched her face.

Cairo held very still in the storms circling her. Solomon's hand at her waist had flattened, smoothing the sash, following it around to her back, then slowly, slowly down the gentle curve of her hip. "You've never been on a man's leash," he whispered in that deep, quiet voice. "Or you wouldn't toss challenges out so freely."

She gripped his arms, arching back from him. Beneath the worn black shirt, Solomon's arms were corded, strong.

His hand reached to her back, flowing and opening low on the silk. Then he jerked her to him.

The collision of hard male angles against her body took away her breath. She resented looking up the inches into his face, frowning at him.

"I said let me go." She was too aware of his fingers smoothing her hair against her back, of the dark, rich excitement lighting his eyes.

"When I'm ready," he murmured, leaning closer, easing his hard-boned face against her temple and inhaling her fragrance.

Cairo closed her eyes, unprepared for the assault on her body. Her breasts touched his chest now, that hard flat surface beating rapidly against her softness.

Solomon trembled just once against her, his body hardening against hers, surprising her. . . .

Then with an impatient growl, he bent, scooped her up, and tossed her onto the bed. "You're good," he murmured, while she scampered off to the side of the bed. "No wonder that fancy man on your wall left you so well fixed."

He caught the blush pot she hurled at him. He caught the powder and, on his path to her, caught the vase and flasks of perfume and placed them on a table.

"How dare you!" Cairo hurled herself at him, not caring about his strength or size. "How dare you come here and—"

Solomon bent slightly, caught her body on his shoulder, and dumped her on the bed. While she panted, winded for the moment, he discarded his gun belt and followed her down on the bed. His hands caught her wrists, pinning her hands beside her head.

He lay very still, heavy, angular and solid upon her. His dark gaze trailed over her hair, spread across the lacy pillow and flowing over the side of the bed. When he looked at her flushed face, his eyes narrowed and met hers. She didn't understand the stillness in him, nor her response, the leaping awareness of her femininity. She looked away. "Your boots are dirty," she noted in her best aloof tone, aware that he continued to study her closely.

Solomon looked inside, near the bones and the fears scurrying around in her, exposing her . . . frightening her . . . stirring an excitement that she didn't understand. Beneath Solomon's hard, aroused body, Cairo blinked up at him, breathing hard.

"Is this what you want?" he asked huskily, moving upon her, easing his hard body higher, pressing against her intimately, separated by the silk.

"No," she managed in an uneven whisper. Her heart raced; her body softened and dampened. "Not ever with you."

Solomon eased open the white silk, his face dark and flushed as he studied her left breast, his fingers trembling, warm against her skin. Her nipple leaped to the brush of his fingertip. Unable to stop her high, keening sigh, Cairo closed her eyes, her body wrapped in pleasure she had only just discovered.

She opened her eyes to Solomon's harsh face, the intense fires beating against them both. "Wrap your legs around me," he whispered, lying hard between her trembling thighs.

"No. You're squashing me, you oversized ox, and your boots are very likely ruining my bed," she managed, shivering as his gaze slid down to her breast.

"My boots are off this bed. It's short," he returned, tracing the perimeter of her softness. His fingers moved on her skin, feathering across her jaw, along the rapidly beating vein in her throat, down to press against the softness of her breasts. She inhaled as his calloused palm massaged her gently, his fingers closing possessively over her. His fingertip lightly touched her nipple, just at the very peak, and she regretted her soft cry, the tightening of her body. . . .

Then his mouth was brushing hers, tantalizing, nibbling on her bottom lip, circling, nudging her upper lip. Solomon's beard chafed her skin as he opened his lips, breathing hotly against her cheek, his body tense above hers. "I haven't wanted a woman for a long time. If you mean to stir me, you're doing a daisy of a job."

She swallowed, aware that his lips found and traced the movement. His harsh, angular face was hot against the hollow of her throat and shoulder, and he breathed heavily. His hands bound hers to the pillow now. She turned to see their fingers locked, his hard palms against hers, his strong dark fingers intertwined with her slender pale ones. "Quigly will kill you. Or I will," she whispered, shaking now with the need to hold him close, to keep him tied to her with her arms and legs.

Then he kissed her, hard and full on the mouth, letting her know his passion, his heat. He fitted his mouth over hers and plied her lips gently, leisurely.

Nothing could have kept Cairo from arching up to meet the thrust of his long, hard body. To meet his mouth, his wonderful soft, beguiling mouth with hers.

Outrage trembled and died in her; Solomon had no right to look so hard, so tough, and to kiss so sweetly.

No one had ever kissed her so intently, finding the exact curve of her lips, tasting them. She shuddered, aware that her mouth ached for each tempting brush of his lips.

His tongue teased her lips now, finding the parting of her mouth and tormenting her. She opened her eyes, watching his frown as he tasted her mouth. Then he was rolling away from her, standing on his feet and tossing her robe over her.

Solomon breathed deeply, sucking air into his taut body as he faced the window. His look across the room to her sizzled, heated the air and caused her to quiver in places she hadn't realized she had muscles. She jerked her robe up to her chin, certain that her blush had consumed her entire body.

"Miss Cairo, I just found this brat—" Quigly stopped in midstride, Garnet dangling beneath one arm. He eased the girl to her feet, and she jerked down her new dress, smoothing it. She propped her hands on her thin waist.

"I know what's been happening here, don't deny it," Garnet stated, walking to Cairo's bed and glaring at her. "First it's that Blanche woman, wanting to bed my uncle Solomon. Then it's you, a woman who ought to know that he's too old to live through a good poke. You seem like a nice sort, Miss Cairo, but he's all I've got, poor specimen that he is, and between the two of you—that Blanche woman and yourself—there won't be enough left over to make half a man. There I'll be, out there in that damned wilderness, taking care of a brains-shot-to-hell cripple."

"Garnet, thank you for rescuing me," Solomon said easily as he picked up his discarded gun belt and lashed it on his hip.

Quigly stared at Cairo, who stared back angrily. The massive butler looked around the messy room and blinked. "Shall I take the child downstairs, madame?"

"Don't you dare," Cairo returned before she could stop the words. She didn't want to be alone again with Solomon . . . ever. "Rescuing him," she muttered. "I'd rather—"

Garnet's scrutiny stopped her. "You look all rosy and soft. You got scrape marks on your neck," the girl observed wisely. "Why are you holding that robe up to your chin?"

"I find this room is a bit chilly," Cairo stated with her best imperial tone, and shivered. Solomon had just tossed her onto her own bed, touched her breast, nuzzled her cheek and throat, and *he* looked like the abused, outraged member of the soiree. Cairo threw a frown at him; she had not invited his attention.

Garnet looked curiously at her uncle, who was holding his hat in front of his lower body and glared at Cairo.

"You got fire in your eyes and your face looks hot and why are you holding your hat like that?"

"Let's go, Garnet," Solomon murmured, placing his hand on her head and shaking her gently.

Cairo reluctantly admired his gesture of comfort to the girl. Garnet had no place in the storm between the adults.

She looked up at him. "Solomon, first it's that Blanche woman plopping out her udders at dawn, then here you are steaming up this one. She's thin—look at her. Nothing but skin and bone. You can't keep warm in the winter cold if she doesn't fatten up. Do I have to worry about everything?"

Cairo tried to find the words to scathe Solomon, to lash out at him, but she glanced at the child watching her and Solomon with adult interest. "Ah . . . Quigly?" Cairo hinted, and sought safer ground. "Perhaps you would like to serve . . . ah . . . something? Garnet must be hungry."

"Ah . . . yes . . . tea? Milk? Geranium cake?" Quigly asked politely as he replaced a perfume flask on Cairo's dressing table.

Garnet crawled up onto the bed beside Cairo and sat with her back against the headboard as the woman was doing. "I'd like some grub and I like this real fine," she said, bouncing slightly.

"Let's go," Solomon's voice was impatient, rough, his eyes dark and flashing as they locked with Cairo's angry ones. Solomon was angry, too, his mouth tight and his dark cheeks touched by a reddish tinge.

He'd wanted her. His body had hardened, thrusting at her though layers of clothing, and he wasn't happy about his desire.

Neither was she.

"Solomon, if you wish to wait downstairs," she managed in a tight tone, "perhaps Garnet would like to share a piece of cake with me." Garnet's "Blanche woman" might be Blanche Knutson, and if she was, Cairo wanted to know.

Cairo smiled lightly and met Solomon's dark, ominous threat. How dare he kiss her in that dark, soft, sweet, enchanting way, when he really wanted the lushly packed Blanche. While Garnet fiddled with with the fringes of a pillow, Cairo fluttered her lashes and murmured, "I hope Quigly doesn't forget the honey with the geranium cake. You know, honey has many varied uses, not all pleasant. Ants love it."

Solomon instantly caught her meaning. He inhaled sharply as she glanced downward to his masculinity.

He moved impatiently in the room's afternoon shadows, a long-legged, angular man with shaggy hair and an impassive face, and Cairo glanced at the outline of his body. He was aroused and uncomfortable.

Cairo allowed her smile to die. The image of Blanche wouldn't go away. She fought her curiousity and lost. Cairo heard herself asking "Did you kiss her?"

She immediately regretted the words slipping from her lips.

Solomon scowled down at her—the picture of a disgusted, elemental male in a ruffled, lace bedroom ... confronted with two females on the bed that he had just vacated.

"Nah. My uncle isn't a kissing man. He tried to stay out of her reach, though she got a good horn-hold on him," Garnet answered for him.

"Let's go," Solomon said abruptly, looking dark and angular and stormy in the feminine bedroom. Anger shot off him like lightning bolts.

"We want to girl-chat. Why don't you run along, Solomon?" Cairo murmured as she sniffed and played curiously with the little girl's hair. "We'll be just a little while. Amuse yourself at no cost at the table downstairs, why don't you?"

He nodded impatiently, ran his hands through his hair, glared at Cairo and walked from the room. Cairo smiled at Garnet. "Now, what was that you were saying about that 'Blanche woman'?"

"Well . . ." Garnet began thoughtfully. "She knows how and where to grab a man. But she sure couldn't make Solomon all hot and ready for bed like he was here with you. She's got big white melons that bounce when she rides her horse. Don't worry, you don't have that disgusting, jiggling fat problem," Garnet stated as she flopped to her back and wallowed in the soft pillows and featherbed.

"Thank you. I am grateful that I do not have jiggling fat." Cairo closed her eyes. "Hot and ready," she muttered, remembering Solomon's dark face over hers, his heat penetrating their clothing.

She shivered again. The thought of Solomon thrusting against her intimately—she pushed the image away.

Garnet touched Cairo's loosened curls. "In another minute, there would be screaming and shouting and the bed bumping the wall. I heard a man yell 'Glory' so loud once that—"

Cairo shook her head. "No. Mr. Wolfe was not—"

"Yep." Garnet bounced again on the featherbed. "Sure was. Hot and ready. I seen lots of men on the Barbary and I know. Never thought that my uncle would get himself worked up though. He's not the type. His man-works probably haven't been used in years. Well, at least not since he's got me to protect him. I've kept him pretty busy and away from painted women. He hasn't got enough money anyway—well, now he's got your grub-stake, of course. But the thought of my uncle getting a disease from a working woman just curdles my guts."

Cairo stared at the little girl, then forced her moving, silent lips to close. The thought of Solomon, a worn-out gunslinger with absolutely no gentle manners, as a potential lover was out of the question. He would not fit into New York. Or fit into any part of her life. She detested him, flat-out detested him, from his dirty boots to his shaggy, black hair and his taunting eyes and his sweet, enchanting kisses. "I'm certain he's . . . ah . . . been involved," Cairo murmured.

Solomon probably soft-kissed every woman he'd known, and Cairo detested him for that, too.

Detested him, she repeated mentally. But Garnet was here now, and available for Cairo's stealthy questioning of Solomon's weaknesses. No doubt he was a drunkard and a wastrel, from the way he and Garnet had arrived in Fort Benton. All Cairo had to do was to find and pry open his very entrails, and then she'd use her knowledge to— She allowed herself one frown. After she was finished, Solomon would not be caressing *her* billiard table or *her* cue sticks.

She rubbed her ankle against the other, remembering the smooth touch of his thumb on her skin. "Let's talk about Blanche, shall we?"

five

"You asked me if I kissed Blanche," Solomon murmured without looking at Cairo. He sank two balls and sighted on a cluster of three.

"I am not interested in where you put your mouth or your eyes, Mr. Wolfe. So long as it isn't on me. You're just lucky, because I haven't decided how to torture you," Cairo returned, not looking at him. "I have decided that I am going to ruin you. That I am going to run you out of town without the help of the citizens' tar-and-feather committee. Please make note of that in some legal document somewhere in case I have to raise the child. By the way, I think it's disgusting the way you . . . ah . . . performed with Blanche in front of Garnet. Think of the ideas you gave that poor innocent child."

He shot the three balls and they rolled into separate pockets. Unused to being ignored by the men in her parlor, Cairo dug her nails into her palm. "Don't ever . . . ever do that again . . . touch me," she threatened under her breath.

"Did you get all the information out of Garnet that you wanted about me?" Solomon returned easily in an aside as he circled the table.

She glared, then was forced to follow him so that the men wouldn't hear. She detested the movement, following him, and bumped into his back when he stopped suddenly. She took a step backward and smoothed the curls at her nape. "If you think that I am interested in your . . . your trysts, you are badly mistaken."

Solomon finished his shot and stood straight, looming over her and forcing her to look up the inches to his face. She met his dark frown with her own; then when he took a step closer to her, she was forced to move aside to let him pass to the opposite end of the table.

She detested moving aside for Solomon Wolfe. She detested accommodating him in any way.

"Kiss," Solomon murmured as the ball he just shot gently tapped another and the balls remained close together. Then he looked at her, his gaze darkening as it touched her lips. The term "kiss" was used in billiards, but Cairo did not doubt that Solomon was taunting her.

She tightened her mouth, her lips sensitive and aching from his damnable sweet kisses—her entire body tensed, trembled and heated, her knuckles turning white as she gripped her cue stick.

He dared to use her table and to mock her over it!

She knew ways to disable men with her cue stick, ways to leave them gasping and in pain and wanting to escape her. One thrust at Solomon and Blanche would be hard put to find the "horn-hold" Garnet had mentioned.

Cairo smiled tightly at Audey Mackey and noted Kipp entering the parlor. His right eye was black and the left corner of his grimly set mouth was swollen. He glared at Solomon's back and began winding purposefully through the crowd toward the table.

Solomon turned slowly when Kipp stood beside Cairo, his hand on her shoulder. She looked up at Kipp, noting his stormy mood, the bruise running along his jawline. "Kipp, what happened?"

"Horse threw me," he stated curtly, his black eyes locked bitterly with Solomon's shielded ones. Then Cairo knew that the men had fought. Though of a different nature, Kipp was wearing Solomon's marks the same as she. Her throat—beneath the dress's high ruffles—bore the tiny chafe marks.

Kipp squared his shoulders. "Or maybe I ran into the side of a house. Any objections to playing me, Wolfe?"

"I'd like that." Solomon nodded and continued to shoot in his methodical, fast way.

Kipp took a step toward him, his tall lithe body taut with anger, and Cairo stopped him with a touch of her cue stick. She refused to have her parlor turned into a tournament for hot-eyed, passionate males with herself as the sacrificial woman. "Not on this table," she stated unsteadily.

Cairo fought the gush of anger and the trembling running through her. Solomon moved quickly, instinctively, yet was methodical in everything he did. In contrast, when she acted impulsively, the usual result was disaster.

He'd tossed her onto her bed and had followed her down. Her body still remembered the impression of his angular, hard-muscled, corded one.

Wrap your legs around me. What right did he have to think that she wanted to play clinging vine to his tree?

She thought of him pressed hard and intimately

against her and tossed away the tree image. Bernard had taught her to be strong in her own right, not to need anyone. . . .

"Count to ten and hold your breath," Solomon said as he sighted another shot.

She rounded on him, this low-down, miserable soft-kisser, this hard-bodied, hot-eyed— "What?"

"You're mad as a wet hen. In another minute, you'll explode. If you want to calm down, count to ten and hold your breath," he repeated. "Otherwise you'll faint and I'll have to loosen those fancy unmentionables of yours."

"No man is touching her unmentionables but me," Kipp stated hotly. "I'll shoot the nuggets off any man who tries."

"Hush, Kipp. My unmentionables are not to be discussed by either one of you. I will not explode or faint, Mr. Wolfe. I have *never* lost my temper or experienced the vapors." She refused to rise to his bait and turned to Kipp, who was glowering at Solomon. "Kipp, come into the kitchen and the cook will give you a steak to help the swelling," she offered, touching his arm.

"A kiss would help," he murmured, his lopsided smile down at her appealingly boyish. She stood on tiptoe and kissed his cheek, his eye, and his mouth. She liked his friendly teasing, easing the taut moment. "Feels better already," Kipp said, his tense body relaxing. "How about later?"

She laughed, enjoying the play with her friend, and found Solomon's mouth curving, mocking her. "Anytime," he said in that deep, gravel-rough taunting tone. "Just place the two pieces on the table."

The crowd moved closer, sensing tension running between the two men. "I'll raise the bet two thousand,"

Cairo heard herself saying, rage and frustration hitting her like ocean waves.

Kipp stepped in front of her, his hand poised inches from his gun butt.

Solomon kept his hands on the cue stuck, leveling it in front of him. "This is between the lady and myself."

"I'm making it my business," Kipp returned between his teeth, and backed a step away. Solomon moved slightly to the side and Kipp followed, creating a circle. It was a deathly dance that no one would dare enter. "She's only a woman, and she needs protecting. I'm doing it. Put down the stick and let's call it."

Cairo stepped between the two tall men with equally black hair, one just as dark skinned and brooding as the other. "I will not have fighting here. It's my table and I'm playing the challenger."

"He's a hustler. You know what they do to hustlers," Kipp stated darkly. "Let me handle him, Cairo."

"I play a fair game. So does the lady." Solomon placed the cue stick on the table and Cairo discovered that his hands were on her waist. She tried to move away stealthily, but his firm grip prevented her. He tugged slightly and she was unbalanced, leaning backward, supported by him. His breath teased the feathers in her hair. She turned to frown up at him and discovered his eyes still locked with Kipp's.

"He's hiding behind your skirts. There's nothing more puke-disgusting than a coward," Kipp snapped.

"Take it easy, son. You've got too much temper riding you to be careful," Solomon stated evenly, his hands releasing her. "When you start calling a man a coward, do it when you're not riled."

Kipp's jaw tensed, his black eyes flashing dangerously. "Stop giving me advice, old man."

Cairo, caught between the press of the two tall men, knew that in another minute Kipp would be calling Solomon out into the street. She would not have Kipp hurt or jailed because of her. The thought of nursing Solomon—because if he was hurt, she would be the cause— turned her stomach. She pushed Kipp's chest gently, reminding him that she disliked fighting. "He's playing fair. Don't you think I'd notice? I handle my own business."

He stilled, looking down at her, and she saw the warmth return to his eyes. "I could change all that, *chérie*. You could be my business."

Because he was relenting and the tense moment had passed, Cairo smiled, wanting to smooth their friendship. She wanted to tell him that she understood his emotions, that one day he would meet someone who would love him, but that woman wouldn't be her. Deep in Kipp lived a man who would want children, and she wanted none of that cozy picture; she wanted balls and sleeping until noon and elegant grace, with an upstairs maid. Kipp wanted her now because she was not available. In a few years, he'd realize his mistake and dislike her for taking his youth. Cairo felt very matronly, patting his sleeve. "If you want to shoot something, come practice with me tomorrow. Cook will prepare a picnic lunch and maybe we could find a few wild birds for dinner."

Kipp looked at Solomon. "You won't always have that kid with you or a woman to protect you." The young man blinked and looked down. Garnet was tugging on his hand.

She grinned hopefully up at him. "You can come eat with me. The cook makes good stuff when they play. Want to? If you do, I'll let you look at my ma's locket.

Solomon says the pictures are of my grandma and grandpa."

Kipp's head went up and he grimaced. "Kid. Don't ever touch a man's hand when he's about to draw down. You've got jam or something on your mouth," he noted with disdain.

"I bet I can beat you at blackjack," Garnet returned, undisturbed. Her leer up at him was not childlike; clearly she adored Kipp.

"Move away, kid." Kipp almost shuddered and despite the emotion swirling around her, Cairo shielded a smile behind her fan.

"Garnet, go back to your table," Solomon said softly, picking up his cue stick. "It's that or the boardinghouse."

"Ha! There's not a window in that place that I can't slide out of." Then she flounced off to her table where she sat, elbows on knees, dour face propped on her fists, moping at them.

"The kid has a point," Kipp said, bending to kiss Cairo's cheek. He glanced at her throat and frowned slightly, edging back the high ruffled collar to inspect the red marks before she could conceal them. "Better tell Quigly not to put so much starch in your ruffles."

She moved away from him, certain that she had had enough of male concern and orders for one night. "Tomorrow?"

"Sure." He walked to Garnet's table and eased into a chair, delighting the child, who plopped her kitten in his lap. Kipp rolled his eyes and sat stiffly, stroking the kitten. He did not conceal that he would rather caress Cairo.

Because Cairo was angry now, frustrated that evidence remained on her of Solomon's touch, she picked up her cue stick and faced him. "I dislike you, Mr. Wolfe. Shall we begin?"

"I'd rather finish," he murmured softly, looking at the lace that was rapidly rising and falling on her bosom. "Looking at you upside down does things to a man."

She stared at him, then shivered, gracefully placing her spread fan over her bodice. She forced a warm smile to Archie Medlock and whispered unevenly to Solomon, "You are horrid."

He leveled a look at her. "And you can't kiss worth beans," he returned. "Are you going to stand on your head tonight?"

"Your bets last evening were disastrous," Quigly stated in his rich, bass monotone. He sat at the massive desk in Cairo's apartment. Dressed in his favorite African prince costume of a dark-red turban with a matching caftan, Quigly's impressive seven-foot height dominated the ornate, feminine room.

She'd loved him from the moment Bernard had won him from a gentleman of the South. Bernard had immediately given the former slave his freedom but welcomed Quigly to stay, if he chose.

Quigly adored Bernard and everything Bernard represented: class, distinction, and education. Together, the three had become a family.

Cairo had crossed her arms tightly across her chest, though she left her palms open and upright. On the floor, she sat straighter, her legs folded in front of her. "I am trying to meditate, Quigly. You are disturbing me."

He closed the account book and placed the new elegant pen into its holder. "Disastrous. Foolhardy to say the least. The first loss was two thousand. Four thousand the next. Even the merchant princes here in Fort Benton couldn't afford those losses. We are approaching thirty thousand . . . a fortune."

"I am just tantalizing him, setting him up for the kill and keeping the interest of my customers," Cairo said in her own defense. "I don't want to appear unbeatable, otherwise they would never bet me."

"Mmm." Quigly's tone lacked belief. "Just the same, our New York resources are dwindling rapidly while Mr. Wolfe's are multiplying. He has ordered a sizable amount of lumber and bricks. Enlarging his home, I believe."

"I really don't care what he is doing." Cairo's upturned palms slid to grip her upper arms. Solomon's long, dark fingers had grasped her New York money, and she needed revenge.

"He'll be back, Miss Cairo. I suggest you refuse to play him."

"I detest that man, and I will not give him the pleasure of seeing me run," Cairo stated flatly. "Please see that Cook has the picnic basket ready."

"Yes, madame. May I say that you look unusually tired. A bit bruised under the eyes as if you have not slept. Perhaps a nap this evening, before the customers arrive?"

"Of course I didn't sleep. Not after Mr. Wolfe invaded my bedroom," Cairo snapped. She frowned as Quigly grinned hugely. "I could sell you," she threatened, not meaning it. Bernard had freed Quigly, yet Cairo sometimes tossed it at him when she was irritated. Quigly took no offense and usually returned dire threats of his own, such as not lightening her hair.

Cairo eyed the massive man. "Maybe to outlaws in Canada. In the wilds, where there is no silk and where herbals are sagebrush and bunch grass. Your celestial embroidering women would not like a buffalo diet. Your sewing machine needles would break on the leather."

Quigly's massive shoulders shuddered; his sigh was

wistful and forlorn. "New York never seemed farther away."

"You won't be able to visit the milliners or the French courtiers. Think of all the fabulous silks and satins and ribbons and lace you'll miss. French lace, Spanish . . . beads and pearls."

"You are truly cruel, Miss Cairo. Poor Bernard. If he only knew what a terror he fostered."

Solomon paused, his knee braced on the board he was sawing. The smell of freshly cut lumber hovered in the late morning air and the sun warmed the framed addition to the house.

They'd been here barely a week and he could feel the old place becoming home again—

He stood very still, listening to the sounds around him. Garnet's swing creaking slowly on the tree near the house. The creek meandering through the cottonwood trees. . . . The birds had stopped chirping up on the knoll and the cows had stopped grazing, looking in that direction. A rifle barrel glinted in the sun, high-powered shots cracked through the morning air, and four cows dropped lifeless onto the prairie. Solomon picked up his rifle on the way to Hiyu Wind and swung onto her bare back. "Garnet, stay put," he shouted to his niece.

Dust rose in the morning wind, the rider traveling fast and away from Solomon's ranch. He leaned down, holding the rifle in one hand, ready to lift it and fire.

The big chestnut gelding with white markings was powerful, the rider whipping the horse's rump. Solomon paced Hiyu Wind, realizing that while she was fast in a short distance, the gelding probably had more stamina and was too far in the lead.

The rider eased the horse down into a coulee and

Solomon dismounted, waiting. In hiding, the rider would have the advantage while Solomon had none. He waited, experienced with bushwhackers and their impatience. After fifteen minutes, a blond youth led the gelding out of the coulee and mounted. Solomon swung up onto Hiyu Wind and the rider spotted him, racing once more, this time headed for the Knutson spread.

Solomon took his time riding into the ranch. Blanche leaned against a pillar of the front porch, her gaze following him as he swung to the ground and led Hiyu Wind to the water trough. He took a rag that was hanging on the corral and began to wipe away the Appaloosa mare's sweat, taking care not to let her drink too much.

"Solomon. How nice. I'm so glad to see you. You've come for lunch? You'll come inside, won't you?" Blanche murmured behind him, her hand smoothing the shirt across his shoulders. "Lord, you still sit ahorse magnificently, Solomon. So straight-backed and your shoulders so square. There never was a man who could ride like you. Except maybe our son."

"Hello, Blanche." He nodded to the lathered gelding that was still saddled in the corral, the reins fallen to the ground. He moved away from her light caress on his back. She'd dislike the sight of his scars. "That's a poor way to treat a good horse."

Her eyes flicked toward the horse. "Yes, well. I'll have one of the hands take care of it. Come in, won't you?"

"I want the rider of that horse," Solomon said, turning to face her fully.

She glanced down at the rifle in his hand, then up at his face. "Solomon, you're in a positive lather yourself. Your eyes are just like burning coals. You never could hide your temper from me. Maybe that is because we mean so much to each other."

"*Meant* so much, Blanche," he corrected, scanning the house. It looked the same—high, wide, and fancy—built to Buck's showy taste. "Your man just shot four of my cows."

Blanche inhaled, her eyes widening and her hand flattening over her stomach. "Not one of my men. I've given strict orders that cattle on the old Johnson ranch were to be left alone. Even sheep."

"Whoever rode that horse shot four cows," Solomon stated flatly.

"Take four of mine. They're the best Texas stock around. I'm certain they are better stock than what you had, Solomon. But come into the house and . . ." Blanche smoothed his chest and moistened her lips. "Relax. Cook makes a wonderful steak."

Solomon looked over her head to the man moving out of the shadows of the huge barn. *Duncan.* Older, harder, his blond hair mixed with gray now, Duncan limped into the burning sunlight. His gun belt was tied to his left side, his right thumb hooked into it. He came to stand by Blanche and she shot him an impatient, distasteful glance. "I can handle this," she said. "Solomon and I are just discussing livestock. You aren't needed, Duncan."

Duncan. The name pounded feverishly in Solomon's blood, etched in his mind.

Duncan's once-handsome face was harsh with lines now, his blue eyes just as cold as years ago. "The three of us go way back, Blanche."

Solomon breathed quietly, controlling the rage within him even as his gun hand dropped to hover above his weapon. He allowed his eyes to drop to the older man's permanently curled fingers, then to his leg. When he'd seen Duncan last, he'd thought the man was dead. Back then, rage had sent his bullets off their target, but the next time— "Duncan."

Duncan stepped to one side and Solomon faced him. The two men moved in that small deadly circle, each watching the other's eyes for one change of expression. "I can't match you for a draw now, Solomon," Duncan stated tightly. "Unless you've slowed down. Have you? Makes no matter. Kipp is faster. You've met Kipp, haven't you?"

The rage humming through Solomon, waiting to lash out at this man who had ruined Fancy's life, hovered. "I've met him."

Duncan's cold gray eyes lit, aware that Solomon knew of his son. The older man knew how to use leverage, how to aim for weaknesses. "The kid is young and hot for a rep."

Solomon breathed quietly, forcing his hand to lock on to his gun belt. If he wanted to change the course of Kipp's life, he couldn't do it by shooting Duncan. Then there was Garnet . . . if he shot Duncan, he'd hang, and there would be no one for Garnet.

Solomon glanced at an open upstairs window, the lace moving aside. A man's fist grabbed the curtain and jerked it down. The window pane broke and Blanche issued an unladylike curse. "Those boys are brawling again and costing me windows. It takes forever to get a pane of glass here in the wilderness."

"They're just playful, Blanche. Like we used to be. Right, Solomon?" Duncan said too silkily.

"Could be that we'll have another chance at it," Solomon returned just as smoothly. He was a man now, not a youth who grieved for his family, who had been tied to a cave wall and beaten. He recognized the quick flash of awareness in Duncan's eyes. He knew the difference between Solomon the youth and Solomon the man.

For once, Solomon decided his years of survival were useful. He knew now that Duncan's taunts had caused the misfire, but the shots had crushed bone, causing permanent damage. He studied Duncan's hand. "You've had an accident."

Duncan's harsh face tightened into an ugly mask. "Gunshot from a bushwhacker."

"He almost died," Blanche murmured, beaming up at Solomon. To goad Duncan, Solomon thought of touching her, of taking her off and bedding her; her face and body were taut with need, he caught her scent—

He remembered Cairo beneath him, hot and flushed and soft, and knew that once in her, nothing could draw him away.

Solomon slammed the door closed on his thoughts of Cairo. He noted a gun glinting from the barn loft and another from a shed. He held his rifle loosely and noted the distance to the water trough. "You go down with the first shot fired, Duncan," he stated, bracing his legs apart.

"Down?" Blanche asked urgently, looking anxiously from Solomon to Duncan and back.

"How's ranch life?" Duncan asked with a smile. "But you haven't been there much, have you? From what I hear, you've been too busy with Cairo Brown."

"Solomon is not interested in that low-down, medicine-show, billiards hussy," Blanche declared, glaring at Duncan.

"Isn't he?" he asked softly. "I hear there's lots of smoke in the billiard parlor every night. Kipp is gnawing at the bit, ready to see if he can take Solomon." Duncan rubbed his damaged right hand. "I owe you."

"What do you owe him, Duncan?" Blanche asked, frowning.

"Plenty," Duncan snapped.

"Likewise," Solomon said, watching Kipp step from the house onto the porch.

"What is happening?" Blanche called to Kipp, her tone distressed. "I told you boys not to break another window. You've broken more windows in your brawls than can be shipped up the river."

Kipp wiped his hand across his bleeding lip and walked toward them. Solomon noted that Kipp placed his back to the hidden guns while he faced his mother. Duncan's face was impassive as he said, "Kipp and his brother, Edward, sometimes get a bit on their high horses as boys will do. Kipp, here, has been a little sensitive since you've been sniffing around Cairo."

"Solomon is *not* sniffing around that woman," Blanche stated hotly.

"Why are you here?" Kipp asked Solomon, and the older man recognized the wary expression, the shifting of a subject too close to his heart. Kipp had learned how to survive in this house of intrigue and hate.

"Someone shot four of my cows. I followed a blond rider here. That's the horse," Solomon stated, watching Kipp closely. The youth's eyes swept to another boy who was lounging in the shadows of the porch.

"Duncan, if Solomon says he's missing four cows, go pick out the choice ones of the herd. Make that five for his trouble," Blanche ordered. With a ladylike gesture, she slipped her hand through Solomon's bent arm. On her other side, she slid her hand through Kipp's. "Why don't we all just go have a glass of my cook's fine lemonade while we're waiting?"

Solomon studied a youth slouched against a pillar, his

hand resting on his gun. The boy looked like a young Duncan, handsome and cruel. Blanche followed his gaze to the boy. "That's my son Edward. He's just sixteen and isn't on his best behavior today. Edward, come here and meet an old friend of mine, Solomon Wolfe."

Kipp glanced at Duncan's grim expression, then at the boy on the porch and at the hidden guns. "I'll show you the herd, Solomon. You can take your pick like Mother says."

Blanche beamed at Solomon, then at Kipp, her hands clasped to her lace bodice. "Yes. You do that, Kipp. Though I'm sorry about your cows, Solomon, I can assure you that no one here would have done such a thing."

Kipp looked down at the ground, then glanced at Edward with distaste. "Let's go. Did you ride your horse without a saddle all this way?"

"Had to move fast," Solomon returned as Kipp began saddling a deep-red bay. The mare was a good choice, likely to have stamina and agility.

When Solomon and Kipp rode out of the ranch yard, Edward came to stand beside Duncan.

Solomon traced the white rumps of antelope bounding across the prairie. Buck had gotten his second son, sired by Duncan.

Fancy had loved Duncan—*"Duncan told me he loved me. He sold me to a house in Butte first, then there were others. He had a man move me all the time . . . at first . . . when I was young."*

That was why it had taken Solomon eighteen years to find her, because Duncan had played games, and because of Fancy's shame.

"Thank you for helping me back there," he said, studying Kipp's young profile. He saw Fancy and Garnet in the lift of Kipp's cheekbones, the slash of his brows and the shape of his eyes.

Solomon's throat tightened with a need to reach out and hold his son. He smiled tightly, mocking himself. Kipp would be stunned and angry.

"I never liked a stacked deck. Sometimes Duncan and Edward get a little pushy, especially when Mother is involved. She likes you. Besides, you and I haven't played out our hand yet," Kipp stated.

"No, we haven't." He wanted to tell Kipp that if he ever needed him. . . .

Blanche would have to tell the boy soon.

"Don't think because I saved your hide that I'm happy about it," Kipp stated as they herded the five cows toward Solomon's ranch. "I just don't want anyone taking care of you but me."

"That's comforting," Solomon said.

"Yeah. Don't get any big ideas that we're going to be friends either. Cairo will marry me. We're pretty close now."

"I can see that."

"I'll help you get the cattle over to your place and dress down those cows. You'll probably need the meat. But then we're quits, understand?" He looked at Garnet, who was riding her pony over the hill, holding her kitten. "You ought to take better care of that kid. She's lonesome."

Garnet grinned up at Kipp. "Were you coming to see me?" she asked hopefully.

He frowned at her. "Back off, kid. You're crowding me. We've got man work to do here and can't do it with some little snot-nose hanging on us."

She grinned wider. "I just love men with big dark frowns. You look like Solomon when he's in a snit."

Solomon tensed; Garnet's childish perception dismissed years, his beard, and shot to the core of the father-son likeness. If she could see the resemblance, others would soon see it, too.

"Holy hell," Kipp muttered in disgust, and looked away, ignoring her.

Garnet urged her pony close to his, her eyes adoring.

Kipp slumped as if doomed. He rolled his eyes and shook his head, trying to ignore her. "Kid, did anyone ever tell you that you're a pest?"

"Not lately," she said cheerfully. "I've been sort of missing that."

Later, when the carcasses were hanging in a cool shed, Kipp nodded. "We're done."

Solomon washed his hands in the basin Garnet held and dried them. "Kipp, I'm asking that you watch Garnet for a few hours."

Kipp tensed. "While you mess with my woman."

"I've got other plans. Personal business not close to town."

Kipp leveled a look at Solomon. "Edward is my brother. You got off lucky today. Take my advice and don't ask for trouble. If you hurt him, I'll have to take you down for sure."

"It's Duncan. We've got personal business," Solomon stated grimly.

Kipp considered this for a moment, then said, "I saw that. It's all horns and rattles between you. He's a back-shooter. Take my word for it. A regular sidewinder. I liked how you handled yourself today, how you didn't turn tail when the odds were against you. But you might not be as lucky a second time," Kipp said, trying to shake loose Garnet, who was holding his hand. "Yeah. I'll watch the kid. You've got a few hours."

six

Solomon stepped into the cave. The Highwood
Mountains were a hard ride from his ranch. With
a little pressure, a Knutson ranch hand had told him that
Duncan was at his favorite hangout, "entertaining a lady
in private."

A terrified cry drew Solomon along the cave to where
Duncan was mauling a girl. "She's a little young, isn't
she?" Solomon asked, fighting the edge of fury riding
him. Fancy had been young once, beautiful, soft, loving—

Duncan tensed over the girl. Her terrified expression
hit Solomon in the stomach like a giant fist. Fancy . . .
Fancy . . . running through the wildflowers . . . then serv-
ing in bawdy houses.

"She's just a half-breed," Duncan said, easing himself
awkwardly to his feet. "I paid for her. Do you want her?"

The girl grabbed her clothing and ran past Solomon,
her face swollen and bruised, her lips bloodied. "Teaching her lessons?" Solomon asked, nodding at the girl and

aching for Fancy's pain. "Wait outside. I'll take you away."

Duncan strapped on his gun. "Remember this place, Solomon? Came back to visit, did you?"

"Your lookout is tied to a tree, Duncan," Solomon said softly, watching the man who had dishonored Fancy and who had taught him a lesson with a bullrope in this same cave. He glanced at the shackles on the rocky wall and remembered how his blood had run down his arms. Finally he'd tugged one shackle free. "This is between you and me."

"I'll kill you," Duncan raged. "You crippled me. But I got my revenge. Every chance I got, I took it out on that whelp of yours, Kipp. And I had your sister working the lowest dives anywhere."

"Fancy is gone now, Duncan. You put her in her grave."

"She loved me," the other man taunted. "But you got a kid, don't you, another female that I'll be waiting for."

Solomon's body chilled as he removed his gun belt. He drew a small rope from a box and began lashing it around his wrist; he would make the fight fair by tying one hand. "I want this to be fair—"

"Was it fair when you shot the living hell out of me?" Duncan yelled madly, and charged at Solomon with a board.

Solomon pivoted, jerked the board from Duncan, and tossed it aside. Then Duncan ran at him again, and Solomon began a series of methodical punches that brought the other man to his knees.

While Duncan swayed on his knees, Solomon held his hair. "Remember this, Duncan. You're lucky to be alive. But you come near Garnet and I'll kill you."

"Then . . . you . . . better . . . kill me now," Duncan managed unevenly as Solomon dragged him to the shackles and fastened them.

He poured a bucket of water over Duncan's head. "I want you to hear what I'm saying. You hang here for a while like I did and maybe you'll cool down."

"I'll . . . kill . . . you . . . and the whelp and the brat, Garnet, for this. . . . Then I'll fix . . . your hands . . . good. Gunman's no good without . . . hands. You'll be begging . . . for someone to end it. Maybe I'll . . . do it myself."

"You touch the boy or the girl and I will finish you," Solomon stated coolly as the other man slumped, unconscious.

Cairo leaned back in her foamy, scented bathwater and let Quigly apply his new moisturizing-cream concoction to her face. After two weeks of Solomon mauling her life, the third week of June was perfect . . . and calm without Solomon Wolfe. She'd used the respite to collect her temper, and now she felt up to any challenge. "Mmm. That feels so good," she murmured, allowing herself to indulge in the scents of her steamy bath and the herbal cream.

"Beeswax and lanolin, a bit of cocoa butter and calendula oil, glycerin, borax, and so forth," Quigly informed her in his absorbed, studious tone. "I made several jars of it. Lift your hands and I'll use the moisturizing concoction on them."

"Quigly, you're marvelous," Cairo exclaimed, meaning it, as he gently massaged her hands and wrapped them in warm towels to absorb the oils. She lay back, enjoying the quiet and the luxury that had not always been hers.

She savored a whole week without her local predator. She realized she was speaking aloud when Quigly chuckled.

"Your local predator, Miss Cairo? Now, I wonder who that might be?" he asked in a rolling, deep amused tone.

"Solomon Wolfe. Don't torment me or I'll wrinkle every scrap of silk I can find," she shot back as he adjusted the towel turbanned over her hair. She eased her toes out of the water, propped them on the side, and Quigly gently massaged the oil into her toes. "The rest is doing wonders for me. If he stays away just a bit longer, I'll be back to full playing power. . . . Not that I ever had difficulty, Quigly. I'm as good as I ever was. But the man did nettle me and I hurried my strokes."

"Yes, madame," Quigly murmured too agreeably. "I understand that he is building onto his home. Several of the farmers who knew a man named Ole are helping. Perhaps he's preparing to take a wife to help him with his child."

"Garnet is his niece. She told me. Apparently Solomon rescued her from the Barbary in San Francisco. That poor baby." Cairo enjoyed the girl—she was tough and sweet and no one's fool. Garnet reminded her of Ethel, the horse trader's daughter, scurrying to survive . . . to scavenge food for her family and keep her father's nags alive until he sold them.

Cairo wanted to protect Solomon's fierce little charge, just as someone should have protected Ethel. Cairo considered the warm thought and dismissed it; she had no maternal instincts. She'd used them up all before she was ten, caring for her mother and younger brothers and sisters.

Despite having sons, Blanche's mothering instincts were shallow. The pain in Kipp was too easy to see.

"Humpf. That baby can pick pockets with the best of them."

"She's a survivalist, Quigly, just like you and me. Bernard would say that all she needs is a little diction training and more rounding of her vowels."

Quigly snorted loudly. "Diction? That rapscallion will never make a lady. Not in two thousand years. I cannot say that I adore the child, madame. She uses gutter language that even I have not heard."

Blanche and Solomon Wolfe suited each other. The viper and the dragon.

Cairo shivered, smoothing the warm scented water over her. Lying heavy and thrusting between her thighs, his face warm against her throat and his breath flowing across her breasts, Solomon was just like any other man . . . ready to take what he wanted.

Or was he really like other men? What made her skin leap to his touch, her body dampen and soften?

Cairo squeezed the bath sponge and studied the sudsy water for answers to her response to Solomon Wolfe. She was inexperienced sensually, of course. And Solomon had used tricks she hadn't expected from a hard-looking man. "He is a soft-kisser," she muttered, disliking the memory of his hard "horn," to use Garnet's word.

Cairo considered the way his eyes lit when she threw her bottles at him. He reminded her of a boy at play. Except when he lay between her legs where no other man had been. He was too hard and too big and probably too familiar with women. With how to make their thighs tremble and how to look at their breasts as if he wanted to—

She clamped her thighs closed. Solomon's well-used beastie was not enjoying the comfort of her private lair—ever.

Beastie. She remembered how Bernard had gently introduced her to the word, to spare his gentlemanly ears from Ethel's gutter language. Bernard had explained to her about her father and why he wanted her to touch him intimately and how it was not intended or proper for little girls to serve their fathers. How Bernard had shuddered and stumbled to find explanations and had described to her the coarseness of such a man, ruled by his animal instincts, his "beastie."

She pushed away the acrid memories of her father in that other place, that other time, and allowed Solomon's image danced into her thoughts.

Cairo swallowed tightly. Solomon probably had littered the West with his spawn and not been responsible for their safety or comfort. Black-eyed children who looked like Garnet. Cairo studied the loofah sponge in her hand. Kipp's eyes were just as fierce, just as black.

She squeezed the water from the sponge just as she forced away the thought that Blanche's son could also be Solomon's. *That blood ran between Solomon and Kipp wasn't possible.*

"I'll miss the girl. If not her uncle," Cairo murmured, giving herself to the scented bath. She wallowed in the luxury and the sense that her New York dreams were returning, oozing back into her grasp. "I'll want escargots for our first meal in New York, Quigly. What about you?"

"Escargots would be lovely. I can't wait for my herbal greenhouse, where I won't be at the mercy of the seasons."

"You'll have the biggest, best greenhouse money can buy and a dress designer's studio, and I'll have the fanciest parlor to entertain New York society. You'll have to hire a staff, Quigly. Just think of it."

"*If* Mr. Wolfe keeps his hands off your accounts." He

paused when she frowned at him. "You might change the rules."

"I tried that. You know the challenger always chooses the game and that man can play excellent Fifteen-Ball. He was getting better—"

"Without practice, he'll be easy prey for you."

"Yes, I like to think of him that way . . . as my prey. Do you have the lemons ready to rinse my hair? I'll need to sit out on the porch for the best sun to lighten it."

That evening, Cairo laughed aloud at Sam Johnston's tale of his wife's attempts at cooking. Poor Betsy Johnston had just passed by, entering the women's entrance of the restaurant and glaring at her husband through the windowpane. Sam had raised his glass to her, toasting his independence for an evening and his delicious steak dinner at Cairo's.

Cairo glanced at the long mirror over the bar, studying her sun-lightened hair. Without Solomon Wolfe at her heels, life was once again rich and waiting for her.

Cairo smoothed her elegant gloves that reached to her upper arms and decided to change them. The male customers enjoyed the long, slow removal of her scented gloves, the delicate stripping of each finger and the slide down her arms.

She inhaled the flower scents, motioning to Henri, the bartender, for her glove box. He dipped behind the bar and handed her an elegantly designed box, imported from Chicago, and Cairo smiled at George Bumstead as she selected a fresh pair of gloves—lilac, to match the lighter shade of her dress. She smelled them delicately, enjoying the luxurious cloth and scent before she began to slowly, artfully work one onto her hand and her arm.

She studied the practical, buffed nails of her right

hand. Then she removed her ring, the large, single pearl had once graced a gambler's stickpin. She eased on the second glove, then replaced the ring over the fabric. The pearl was as smooth as her future.

The male banter rumbled comfortably around her, the room scented by expensive, house cigars, bay rum, and money that was hers for the taking. Cairo smoothed her evening gown, one of Quigly's best designs. The high lilac lace collar eased into a deep V at the bodice, a swath of satin circling her hips, back to the bustle. The skirt was of striped satin and silk, dark purple to lilac shades, and the dark purple slippers looked wonderful just below a ruffled lilac petticoat. She inhaled luxuriously and smoothed the well-polished bar, which she fully intended to take with her to New York.

Cairo allowed herself a small, pleased smile and studied the men in the mirror. There were Tex and Roy, two Texans without last names, probably outlaws, but gentlemen down to their Mexican spurs. Then the bald head of Thomas Endive, a widower and lately of Boston, living on the remnants of his wife's family money. Big, raw-boned Alek Erasmus of Jewish-Russian descent and his small dapper friend, Petey—

The face looming over Petey's and finding her gaze in the mirror caused her to grip her discarded gloves and strangle them. Solomon Wolfe nodded to Quigly, and Garnet flounced between the men to her appointed table.

Cairo straightened her shoulders, pressed her hand flat against her churning stomach, and forced herself to smile lazily at Solomon. She nodded to James Harrington as she passed on her way to the man who stood in the center of her parlor, looking big, rough, and immovable.

She distrusted Solomon's appearance now, after a

week of his absence. He wanted more—he wanted to take her dreams of New York and suck them dry.

She disliked the way his eyes followed her slow, meandering path to him—like a wolf watching its prey.

She detested the tightening of her nerves, the hair rising on her nape, and the instant tensing of her body.

"I thought you'd had enough," she murmured, touching his shoulder with her fan.

He stood, unmoving, looming over her. Her angular, broad-shouldered, hard-as-nails predator had returned. He smelled of soap and leather and a deeper intimate scent that caused a reluctant excitement scurrying through her, flicking at her senses and her nerves. She snapped open her fan and closed it, killing whatever memory she had of Solomon pinning her to the bed. Cairo regretted her taut nerves and the slight tremor that coursed down her body when Solomon glanced at her mouth. "Well?" she asked impatiently, waiting for him to speak. "What do you want?"

Two hours later, Cairo gripped the table behind her with damp palms. She pushed back the tiny tendrils clinging to her hot cheek. She forced herself to breathe quietly and gripped the cushion tighter, using it as an anchor to prevent launching herself at the man who had just taunted her into betting the last of her cash reserves. "I will not place the two pieces of my cue stick on the table," she snapped at him, answering his suggestion.

She would never submit to this man.

"Can you cook?" he asked without interest as he moved past her and she grabbed her skirt, jerking it aside.

"I play pool," she stated, too harshly, angry that her skills, her table, and the red balls had betrayed her. "I am a businesswoman, a professional billiardist."

Solomon turned to face her. He leaned back against the table where he had won all of her cash and studied her. "I'll wager this cash of yours and the promise not to play you again against—"

Cairo stopped breathing. The male crowd stopped moving, stopped talking and stared at Solomon. The customers edged closer to the tense scene between Cairo and the man who could beat her. "Against what?" she asked when she could whisper, her throat almost closed with tension.

Whatever Solomon wanted to wager, she had to meet him. She had to win back her savings. . . .

"This," he said slowly, taking the old wedding ring from his pocket and rolling it onto the green material of Cairo's billiards table.

She stared at the small gold circle. It had little value and they had been playing for thousands. "I don't understand."

He locked his legs at the knee, reminding her of his gunfighter profession. The hard mask was down, his eyes too alert, too knowing. "Marriage. To me."

"No." She turned to him, gripping her cue stick in both hands. "I detest you."

"Didn't ask you to like me," he stated in a logical tone.

"You're serious!" she exclaimed, incredulous that he would conceive of marriage to her.

He nodded. "Garnet needs a woman's touch. Just for a year. You're not much, but she seems to like you. You might be able to shave off her rough edges . . . at least enough for another woman to manage her."

"You must be jok—" Cairo's skin heated, then chilled, and she stood very still. She gripped the table that had been her anchor through the years, solid and dependable, even when it was dismantled for wagon transport. "You are serious!"

"You lose and you marry me. You'll have to do until a better wife comes along, or until the year is over. That should be enough time to put my ranch on its feet," he stated easily, and then began shooting practice balls. He glanced at her. "I don't have all night."

Beneath Cairo's trembling fingers, the pulse at her throat beat wildly. "No," she murmured slowly, watching Solomon lean over the table to sight down on a shot.

His trousers tightened over his backside and the cloth over his thighs lifted with hard muscle as he shot. "All you have to do is to place the two pieces of your cue stick on the—"

Cairo plopped down the huge pearl ring on the green material. Then she slipped off the black pearl necklace with the ornate diamond pendant and tossed it to the table. "I'm certain that will cover a portion of your wager. The rest of my jewelry goes with it."

She closed her eyes. Bernard had taught her that a lady never gambled with anything but cash; Solomon had chopped away at her foundations, nudging her into the distasteful wager. . . . She hated him down to her bones and in her entrails and in her blood.

She wanted to maul him, just as he had mauled her New York dreams.

Solomon moved close to her and she realized too late that his hands rested on either side of her, pinning her to the table. She glanced at the crowd watching with interest and dismissed everything but resisting Solomon Wolfe. She resented leaning back, arching her body away from his. She realized, too, that his thumb was lazily stroking her knuckles. "I don't want your jewelry. What's one more man?"

"I lived with *one* man, though it's none of your business, Mr. Wolfe. And dear Bernard was a gentleman."

"Mmm." His dark gaze trailed across her lips and she realized she had just moistened them with the tip of her tongue. "The English baron? He kept you?"

"My, but you've been busy gossiping, haven't you?" she tossed back, resenting the hard press of his chest against her silk bodice. She resented the rapid beat of her heart, racing against the material.

"Are you married now?" he pressed, surprising her.

"Of course not!" She edged her hand away from his thumb and found the toe of her slipper pressed by his boot. "Remove yourself from my personal area, Mr. Wolfe."

He studied her hair and inhaled. "Single women are hard to get in these parts and you qualify for a wife right now. Garnet needs a woman like you—for now. The baron may have been a gentleman. Don't count on it from me."

"You and dear Bernard do not fit into the same breath. I realize you are not gallant. Do we play or not?"

"You're not my choice pick. If there were more women here or any other woman who could handle Garnet, you wouldn't be considered—"

"As your wife? How lucky I am," she exclaimed with false delight.

"I'm walking out of here tonight and leaving my ring. I'll be back, and I'll wager everything, my ranch included, against you wearing my ring as my wife."

Then Solomon placed his hand flat on her waist and pressed her gently. "Never figured you for a coward, Cairo," he murmured, his gaze mocking her before he walked over to Garnet and picked the sleeping child up in his arms.

Cairo rubbed her lurching stomach and traced Solomon's path out the door. Garnet sleepily waved goodbye, then snuggled to her uncle's shoulder. While he had the child's affections and trust, he would never have Cairo's. "Never, Mr. Wolfe," she said between trembling lips. "Never."

The next night, he sat with Garnet at a table, eating dinner and watching Cairo play her customers. She tried to ignore him, tried to fight the need to wipe that mocking curve from his lips. When she came close, Solomon stuck out one long leg, blocking her path. "You're running pretty fast tonight, Cairo. Your color is high."

She edged her silk flounced skirt away from his boot. "I'll get your ring."

"Keep it for now. My wager holds. Though my opinion of your sporting blood is lowering. You look like you might pack up and run before morning." He shrugged slowly. "I'd expect that from you. You aren't a real daisy in the bride department."

"Do you think I care what your opinion is of me? I will never be your wife, Mr. Wolfe. Not even for a year— or until someone more suitable comes along."

He looked slowly down her elegant embroidered pink silk gown, then back up. "You're a poor specimen, for certain. Probably useless on a ranch."

"Yes, I am," she returned tightly, removing her skirt hem from his trouser leg. "I am not suitable material for your quest."

Then he smiled, slowly, leisurely, tauntingly. He drew on her best house cigar, the Sultana, blew a smoke ring, and studied it. "Lady, you are a coward."

She slashed though his rising smoke ring. "And you, sir, are no gentleman."

"Never claimed to be," he returned easily, and blew

another smoke ring. "But then, I've always worked for a living."

She slashed at the smoke ring, destroying it, just as she wanted to destroy him. "So have I."

He lifted a questioning eyebrow, recalling his opinion of her as Bernard's lazy, kept woman.

That night, Cairo awoke in a cold sweat, her hands crushing a pillow and her blankets tangled around her legs. The dream gripped her in its cold shroud—her mother screaming in childbirth, her wedding ring gleaming on thin, blue-veined, rough flesh. "A woman is a man's property," her mother said between her white, bleeding lips. "She does what a man tells her to do, and if that's birthing and slaving in the fields and—"

Cairo shook, sitting upright, remembering how a frightened, hungry little girl watched the agony of a woman in childbirth—

"Marriage means you do what your man says, girl," her mother cried out from the past. "You're his property when you're a wife."

"Never . . . never . . ." Cairo whispered shakily. "I will not marry Solomon Wolfe."

"The only thing that's keeping you alive, pilgrim," Kipp's voice said quietly in the doorway of the saddlery shop, "is Cairo."

The afternoon customers eased out of the shop and the saddle maker glanced worriedly at the gleaming saddles. "Sure would appreciate you taking any disagreements outside," he said hopefully.

Solomon hung the harness he had been looking at on a peg. He'd wondered when his challenge to Cairo would reach Kipp; it had taken longer than he expected, and now it was the last week of June. He'd been in Fort Benton one month and he intended to harness Cairo before the last day of June went down.

With his ring on her finger, she wouldn't be marrying Kipp. He'd meant what he said about her being the only woman to tame Garnet. Cairo seemed to know instinctively how to gentle the girl's thievery and rough language.

Then there was the other: the hot need to take her, the soft need to linger, and the excitement racing between them. They were fighters, going toe-to-toe, and he wasn't ready to let that game go just yet. Not until he understood why in the hell Cairo Brown interested him when no other woman had stirred him since Blanche. It was sheer, cussed orneriness that made him want to marry her; some devilish backward need to torture himself—he struggled for a word he'd heard and found it. Perversity. The unnatural need to take the most difficult path, and Cairo purely fit that need. She was prickly as any wild rosebush. A man would have to be crazy to want to tangle with her.

But that he had purely done, locking horns with a useless gambling woman and wanting to capture her like his own juicy Sabine woman in that Roman story. Solomon admitted to himself that when it came to Cairo Brown, he was not a logical man.

He faced his son, who was wearing the same slap-leather look he had worn as a youth. "Hello, Kipp."

"The kid is at Cairo's now. Seems that Cairo has taken a shine to her. I won't mind raising her," Kipp stated, his hand hovering over his gun.

"That's generous of you."

"Let's have this out. There's no worn-out old man

taking my woman away from me," Kipp said, breathing too evenly. "The word is that you want to wager her into marrying you. The only man Cairo is marrying is me."

Solomon held his hat in his hands, making certain that Kipp knew he would not draw. "She's got choices and all she has to do is not to play me. That or win."

"You'd dare plop a fine lady like that down on a two-bit dry-water spread?" Kipp asked, not bothering to shield his temper.

"The ranch has a creek and the lady can say no," Solomon said evenly, and wondered how his son had survived among Blanche and Duncan and Edward.

"Pack up and get out or you're a dead man," Kipp said, his black eyes burning.

The crowd peering in the windows and hovering at the doorway began whispering. Dressed in a pink ruffled dress, Cairo stepped into the saddlery, her pink parasol gripped in one gloved hand and Garnet's small one in the other. "What's going on in here?"

"Gunfight," Garnet stated too quietly and too wisely for a six-year-old girl. "Kipp, you won't shoot Solomon, will you?" she asked shakily, tears dripping from her lashes.

"He's not shooting anyone. It's just a thing men seem to enjoy, threatening each other. It's something bred into them, a pushing, shoving thing that has absolutely no purpose." Cairo bent to pat a handkerchief across Garnet's eyes, then held it to her nose. "Blow."

Garnet blew but didn't take her eyes from Kipp as she finished. "Don't, Kipp. He ain't much, and he's old, but he's all I got," she begged.

Solomon reached to place his open hand over Garnet's hair and noted it was slightly damp and soft as if it had just been washed. He shook her gently and she reached to cling to his waist, peering up at Kipp. "You look real pretty," Solomon said to the little girl, trying to ease her fears.

"I held my breath underwater and Cairo built soap castles in my hair and showed me them with a mirror. Then she made points and called it my 'princess crown.'" Garnet shivered and hugged Solomon tighter. "Kipp?"

"Kipp isn't shooting anyone, are you, Kipp?" Cairo asked firmly, the tip of her parasol placed firmly on his chest.

Solomon noted the cool steel in her soft tone. She was a woman who had faced trouble before, and he reluctantly admired her. The novelty of having a woman with a pink, ruffled parasol fend off a younger gun distracted Solomon.

Unused to emotions, he decided that Cairo had the ability to amuse him; he'd never been protected by a woman.

Solomon glanced at her bodice, the high proud line of it lifting into the sunlight, and knew that he wanted to taste her.

To put his mouth on her . . . anywhere . . . and taste her.

He shifted restlessly, uncomfortable with his emotions.

The youth flushed. "I thought I'd nick him in a few places. Just to give him an idea that you're my girl. It's not like it's the first time he's worn a bullet or two, from the looks of him."

"I have worn them," Solomon admitted carefully, and prayed his son would never know the agony of lying near to death. "When a man plays a hard game, he can expect pain."

"That's enough, Kipp," Cairo stated. "I won't have you hurting anyone because of me. Not even—she glanced at Solomon and frowned in distaste—"Solomon. Nor will I have you making decisions about who I play or my wagers. I've never allowed anyone to do that.

Solomon nodded. He reluctantly admired this fierce woman, chosing her own path, her own dreams. "I appreciate the rescue, Cairo. I was a goner for sure. That's a nice piece you're wearing, Kipp. Takes a good man to pull through that trigger."

Kipp glared at him. "Colt. Model Thunderer. Better than that Lightning model you have. Damn right you were a goner—uh!" He grunted, rubbing his chest where Cairo had just jabbed the sharp tip of her parasol. She frowned meaningfully at him, then glanced at Garnet. Kipp understood his trespass. "Uh . . . sorry, kid. I forgot you got tender ears and all."

"Damn right I do, you low-down backside of a mmm—" Solomon's hand muffled Garnet's mouth.

"Garnet and I were just going to have a lemonade at the dry goods store, Kipp. Why don't you come along?" Cairo asked lightly, easing her ruffled hem from Solomon's leg. She shot him a sidelong glance. "You are not invited, Solomon. I'm certain you can find something else to do in the meantime."

"You'd better rethink the bet you just made. If you lose, you'll probably back out of the promise to marry me, taking care of Garnet until a suitable wife comes along," Solomon murmured as Cairo passed him to line up for a shot.

The deep, lazy drawl nicked her tense nerves. She flashed a hot look at Solomon. "Yes, of course I will marry you, if I lose. But it's an even match so far, isn't it? I will not lose to you, Mr. Wolfe. Count on it."

"Mmm." His tone was doubtful. "Dear old Bernard probably made things easy for you. Ranch life is hard. You might have to lift a finger to get what you want."

She leveled a glance at him and inhaled sharply. There he stood, all six feet four of him, rangy, worn out, with nothing to show, while she had clawed her way out of poverty . . . worked for her skill until her body ached and her mind blanked. "I worked for everything I have," she tried to say quietly, her nerves screaming.

"Uh-huh," he returned lightly, studying her face and then her body, a bold taunt.

Furious with Solomon's lingering gaze on her lips and her bosom, Cairo quickly lined up her shot. She'd exorcise him with this frame, tear him from her life and shred him into pieces. If he thought he could possibly take everything she'd worked for, planned for— She shot too fast, the spin on the ball less than needed, and it nudged the target ball weakly. Both balls nestled together on the green cloth, when one of them should have been in the corner pocket.

She frowned deeply. She never missed that simple shot. It was hers. But it had gone wrong, because the target ball rested firmly on the table. She blinked, hoping for a miracle.

Cairo swallowed, her body chilling. As if in a dream, she watched as Solomon finished the deciding frame and took the match. She tried to rally, to paste a champion's conceding smile upon her lips, and failed miserably. When Solomon turned slowly to her, her congratulations came out in a helpless groan.

She couldn't have lost. The shot was too simple. She

glared at Solomon, not ready to accept that the miss had been her fault.

She shook her head, trying to dislodge the nightmare. She stared at her fingers, her white knuckles as she gripped her beloved, beautiful, faithful cue stick.

She closed her eyes and relived the losing shot. Too fast, too light, not enough spin.

While she stared blankly at her beloved mahogany table, someone tried to remove Cairo's cue stick from her hand. She gripped it once again tightly, as if it were her anchor to New York, to the dreams Bernard had given her. Then she allowed the stick to slide away—

She had just lost the game to Solomon.

She replayed the scene, hoping that it would dissolve like a nightmare upon waking. She had rashly agreed to marry him if she lost. That was just after he'd implied that she'd never lifted a hand to earn everything she owned, that Bernard had kept her—

After Solomon Wolfe had stared brazenly at her face and then her body.

Her customers were hovering uncertainly around her and she forced a bright smile at them, unable to speak. Quigly said the words she couldn't utter: "Drinks and cigars on the house."

She'd bet her freedom. She'd placed her life on the fast green material and spun it away.

Solomon stood next to her, watching her with that dark, solemn expression as if waiting for her to ask for mercy . . . to ask for another game.

She wouldn't. She had lost well and good and now. "How do you want to do this?" she distantly heard herself ask.

A brief gleam of admiration lit his dark eyes as he nodded. "The preacher is right here."

"Fine," she said lightly, carelessly as if she were purchasing new cloth for a handkerchief. Her stomach lurched. Just fine. A whole year of her life wasted, lashed to a low-class lout with the scuffed boots—she looked down at his boots, then slowly upward to the worn black trousers, the black worn shirt, to his shaggy, uncut hair.

Her New York society debut would be in the shack of a run-down ranch. Sarah Bernhardt would be giving performances without her.

Cairo ran her fingertips over the lace on her bodice, seeking the small hard lump between her breasts. "I've never taken knockout drops, but tonight might be a perfect time," she murmured aloud, finding her pale face in the bar's mirror. "This must be a nightmare," she muttered to herself.

"This ain't no dream, Miss Cairo," a man said, and she recognized him as a minister and a traveling judge.

"Hello, George. So nice of you to come," she forced herself to say politely, then noted distantly that a photographer was positioning his camera for a shot.

"You may kiss the bride."

"There's no need for that—" Cairo began, her sentence stopped by Solomon's lips.

He slid his arms around her, looked down into her eyes, and pulled her tighter against his tall, hard body. Then his eyes closed slowly . . . or were her lids closing? His lips were on hers, teasing softly, sweeping gently over hers for a firm, tight fit.

She breathed his scent, or was it the fresh prairie air?

He was breathing now, slow deep breaths sweeping along her hot cheek, his lips molding softly, so softly, opening her lips to his. He was cherishing her in a way that no one had, tasting her and treasuring her and tempting her.

She would faint, she who had faced everything—

She would taste and hunger and take—

His tongue touched hers, playing, tormenting, suckling gently.

Cairo opened her mouth for his pleasure, taking him into her own and delighting in the play.

His hand opened on her back, supporting her. His body bent over hers and she caught his shirt—reached to hold him tightly, her arms sliding around to his back.

Everything was gone, she was drifting away, becoming a part of something warmer, anchoring herself to that warmth and safety. . . .

Then Solomon gathered her so close, so close, tasting her more deeply and Cairo surged up to meet him, her fists locked in his shirt, her mouth hungry for his, her legs softening, weakening.

Hot. Very hot. Hungry, aching, wanting all the layers of clothing separating them torn away.

His mouth moved slightly away and Cairo followed it hungrily, lifting, arching into him, needing Solomon's hard body against her own.

His eyes were dark, promising, his hands trembling on her waist, caressing her. "Mrs. Wolfe," he whispered softly before she felt the world spin away.

She awoke to find herself stretched out on her beloved table. She gripped the fast green cloth with her fingertips—this table that had been dismantled and re-formed during the tours across the West. The Italian slate beneath her palms was real; the nightmare that she had just married Solomon Wolfe was not, spinning around her like the little red balls inches from her head. The damp cloth on her forehead was cold. She blinked, grabbed the rag, threw it away, and gathered her skirts. She slid over the edge of the table and smoothed her skirts with shaking hands.

Then she turned, checked the beautiful cloth of her beloved table, and noted a wrinkle.

She smoothed it quickly, her hands shaking, then looked for the biggest wrinkle of her entire lifetime.

Solomon stood at the bar, a worn boot braced on the brass bar. He toasted her.

She raised her hand to smooth her hair and caught the glint of gold.

Solomon's wedding ring circled her finger. She stared at it. She remembered how he had placed it on her finger—efficiently, quickly. A thorough man who took what he wanted, including that devastating, humiliating kiss.

Cairo kicked her skirts aside, curled her hands into fists, and began stalking straight toward the source of her humiliation and mortification.

Quigly stepped in front of her. "Hors d'oeuvres?" he asked, extending a tray of food to the men who munched and watched with interest as Cairo looked at the ring on her finger, then up at Solomon, then down at the ring.

"No," she stated hoarsely. "This is a nightmare."

"Mrs. Wolfe, if you would just step next to Mr. Wolfe, I can take this picture," the photographer instructed, thrusting his head beneath a black cloth and positioning his camera.

Solomon's arm encircled her, drew her close, and before Cairo could move away, the photographer's flash blinded her.

"Mrs. Wolfe, I truly enjoyed the evening," Solomon said, placing his worn black hat on his head. "Truly, I did. But it's a hard day tomorrow at the ranch and I'd better get back. Take care of my bride, boys," he said, nodding to the crowd.

Then the men parted ranks as he walked toward the door and out of it, without a second glance. In every man's face glowed sheer admiration; Solomon had conquered the untouchable queen and had branded her for his own.

"Congratulations, madame," Quigly stated as he waved the bartender to set up drinks on the house. He glanced meaningfully at Garnet, who was sleeping, her head on a table. "Where shall I put the child?"

Cairo tried to move her lips and couldn't. She plopped into a chair, careless of wrinkling the costly material draped between her spread knees, and stared at the ring on her finger. In the distance, she remembered herself say something that may have sounded like a "yes" and an "I do."

She remembered Solomon's deep, certain voice repeating his vows. She remembered . . . she forced herself to breathe . . . she remembered every single shot Solomon had performed without giving her a chance to take control. . . .

Married. The word rang of a funeral dirge.

Married to Solomon Wolfe. Ungallant, tattered, worn-out gunslinger, who didn't have more than one shirt and one pair of trousers to his name.

Solomon Wolfe with his broken-down ranch, his poorly bred cattle, and nothing but hard times ahead of him.

She was Solomon Wolfe's wife.

"The child?" Quigly pressed, holding Garnet's head in his white glove. He looked down at her with disdain. "She is drooling on my glove. Where may I put her?"

Cairo blinked. Solomon had walked out of the parlor, leaving his charge behind . . . to his wife's attention. "I . . . I . . . take her to my bed."

Quigly winced. "Of course. On top of the covers, I presume."

"I'll take care of her."

"As you wish," Quigly returned, picking up Garnet and ascending the staircase.

"Out," Cairo ordered the crowd of men and nodded toward the door. They weren't hers anymore, they were his, admiring Solomon's raid. She didn't want to toy with them, to perform and to flutter her fan, fascinating them. She wanted to follow Solomon Wolfe out into the night and call him out. Dueling pistols were too good for him. She'd prefer to attack him with her cue stick. No, she wanted to tear him apart with her bare hands.

"Congratulations, Miss Cairo," the men said one at a time as they shook her hand and passed out the door, smoking one of the cigars that Quigly had provided.

Cairo dismissed the bartender, who extinguished the lamps; then she sat in the darkness of her beloved parlor.

She spread goose-liver pâté over a cracker and stuffed it into her mouth. Then another.

Then she picked up the silver tray and launched it at the door through which Solomon Wolfe had passed. She pelted the door with billiard balls.

"Yes, madame?" Quigly asked from the shadows, picking his way through the rolling balls to bring her a china cup filled with chamomile tea. "Are we distressed?"

"We?" she asked, outraged. "We, Quigly? Are *we* married to Solomon Wolfe? Did *we* just get mashed and crushed and had the living breath sucked out of *us*?"

"You played the role outstandingly well, Miss Cairo. Until a moment ago, one would think you were a well-warmed bride."

She glared at him, hovering on the idea of pitching the tray of liver pâté at him. "Bride?"

"Yes, madame. That's what you are now. A bride. Mrs. Wolfe, spouse of Mr. Wolfe."

"You know what happened here, don't you, Quigly?" she demanded in a low, hushed shout as she kicked off her slippers. Then she threw them at the place where Solomon had toasted her. "That man—that man pushed me—taunted me into—this impossible circumstance. The men, my customers, all worship him. That swaggering, down-on-his-luck—"

"I will kill him," Quigly offered smoothly and without sincerity.

"Leave that to me. Do you realize . . ." she asked quietly, her hands on her hips after launching a bottle of her finest house brandy at the door. "Do you realize that Mr. Wolfe just married me tonight—and walked out of here—*on my wedding night?*" she asked, outraged. "And how they adored him for it."

"Most unromantic," Quigly soothed. "Sot. Misbegotten son of a gila monster."

Cairo strode back and forth, tearing the ribbons and feathers from her curls. "Solomon Wolfe is a—"

Quigly raised one firm white-clad finger. "Ah ah!"

"Mr. Solomon Wolfe has just shown the entire town of Fort Benton that I do not interest him as a woman."

"Mr. Wolfe is a blackguard, a dolt—"

"The least he could have done was to have stayed the night. Oh, not in my bed, of course. There are just things a woman cannot permit, Quigly. And one outstanding crime upon a woman's honor is a husband leaving her on her wedding night. That insult goes straight to the heart. This calls for revenge."

seven

Solomon rode through the moonlight spreading over the plains and thought about the woman he had just married. There was enough fire in Cairo tonight to melt gold dust into bricks.

She had the wild, hot look of a woman who needed to be loved. Solomon listened to the hoot owl, its great wings sweeping against the moon, and he shifted uncomfortably on his saddle.

Garnet wasn't the entire reason Solomon wanted to leash Cairo Brown.

There was just enough pure orneriness in her thin body to accept Kipp's marriage offer. A young hothead around a woman like Cairo would call out every man who looked at her.

But the damnable need to claim her was his own, Solomon admitted moodily.

Women had never been a part of his life—other than to feed his body's needs when he was younger.

She'd have to bend that high-wide pride of hers and come to him.

Or she wouldn't.

Solomon reluctantly admitted that he admired Cairo's honor.

Beneath those fine feathers, lace, and silk there was a hot-tempered, passionate woman. Solomon pushed away a smile. He was acting like a boy.

He closed his eyes against the sight of her pale breast when she lay beneath him. He clamped his lips closed against the groan that almost escaped into the night air. In another minute, he'd be howling at the moon.

If his body had to rediscover the need of a woman's heat after all these years, why did he ache for a high-and-mighty, fiery, worthless, bony woman like her?

Solomon inhaled the night and remembered Cairo's womanly scent swirling around him.

He heard his curse, startling himself and his horse. Now he was saddled with a woman who had trouble written all over her.

He straightened, sighting a shadow next to the old barn. He rested his hand on his rifle, realizing that he made an easy target in the silvery moonlight.

"Wolfe?"

"Jacob?" Solomon swung from his horse and walked to meet the other tall man emerging from the shadows. "Jacob Maxwell," he said quietly, watching the gunman stand, legs spread in a gunfighter's stance.

"It's been a long time, Wolfe," Jacob said slowly in his southern drawl, his black eyes slits in the moonlight.

"A long time. Back in Dodge."

"I'd just taken a slug in the leg and another in the arm. If you hadn't been taking care of my back, I'd have been a goner."

Solomon extended his hand. "I've never thought highly of back-shooters."

Jacob looked down at Solomon's hand. Then Jacob slowly extended his own gloved one for a firm handshake. "Can I come in?"

"Are you here on business?" Solomon asked as the two men shared a bottle of whiskey.

Jacob leveled at look at Solomon. "You've got some big enemies here. The word is out that they'll pay well for a fast gun to take you down. When I caught the name, I thought I'd mosey this way a bit and see if you needed help. There's lots of folks that will come if you have need—like the parents of those kidnapped children and a whole crowd of others you've helped along the way. All of them want to repay you, especially those who you wouldn't let pay in cash. I rode over to the Knutson spread to get a handle on the situation. There's a foreman there, Duncan's the name, who's got an uncommon need to see you six feet under."

When Solomon shook his head, Jake continued, "Didn't think you'd want my help or talk of repayment from those you've helped. Just thought I'd pay my respects before moving on. I see you're wearing a Lightning model Colt. Doesn't pack the power that a Peacemaker does."

Later, seated at Solomon's table, Jacob twirled Solomon's Colt through his fingers in an expert display. "Light. Too light, and it only takes a .38 caliber. Bo MacCallister says to tell you to keep the sun at your back," he said, the old gunfighter's warning given with affection. "He's still bragging about how you paid for his small spread and gave him a place to end his days. He said for you to come back when you want."

"Bo deserved it. He is a good man." Solomon flipped

the gun through his fingers in the showy way that sometimes lessened trouble. "The trigger pulls a bit hard, but you get used to handling it. The weight on the Peacemaker was slowing me down," Solomon returned, leaning back in his chair. "Jacob, when you need a place, come back here."

"You bought two small spreads for two old guns down on their luck and next to dying. Gave Bo and Ephraim each a reason to live, never mind the old drovers you staked. You did jobs for free, protecting the innocent and living for the romance of it. But there aren't many angels like you, Solomon," Jacob said slowly, twirling the unloaded gun. In the lamplight, and dressed in his ruffled shirt, he looked like the perfect spawn of his French aristocratic ancestors. "But I'll remember. You've always been smart, figuring out ways to do things no one else thought could be done. You'll be an old man sitting on your porch when the rest of us are gone."

Solomon told him about Fancy and Garnet. Jacob understood, a man who shared no family, no ties, but a bond between brothers of the gun. "A man has to stand for what he believes," Jacob said. "And with you, it's your word and your honor."

"I got married tonight," Solomon stated slowly, remembering Cairo's soft, welcoming lips beneath his, her body pushing fiercely against him, taut as a bowstring with the hunger humming between them.

But he knew that if he had not walked out, had not left Cairo tonight, nothing could have stopped him from taking her.

Jacob lifted an eyebrow and grinned. "Strange way to spend a wedding night, Solomon. You should be licking champagne from the soft, delicate skin of your bride," he said, reminding Solomon of his grand drunken speech that night out on "the wide lonesome" with Jacob.

"The lady hasn't decided she wants me. She's good with Garnet; most women aren't. We bet. She lost."

Jacob laughed outright and Solomon found himself grinning.

"She must be something. You've never come close to wanting a woman that bad, so far as I can remember. Unless it was that time you were skunk-drunk and mooning about how you wanted romance and to write love letters to your sweetheart. Never saw a cowboy bay at the moon and call for Aphrodite to come sailing down on a moonbeam. Son, you actually said you wanted to grow tulips for your sweetheart. You, Solomon Wolfe, top gun."

Jacob grinned and caught the apple Solomon threw at him. "That Blanche Knutson—now there's a woman who needs reins and a man with a good, firm grip. *Mais oui*, you take that woman and you don't need no pepper with your crayfish, son. I always like a chili-woman. If I stayed around here, I'd be that man, don't you know," Jacob said slowly, allowing his Louisiana background to surface. "But I'm moving on."

Jacob winked at Solomon. "Has your sweetheart put her pretty little tongue into your ear, boy?"

"It would not be wise to explore that thought, for I truly believe a man's ears are a private matter," Solomon returned the tease easily. Then Jacob began to chuckle and then to laugh, because the night Solomon had become drunk, he was outraged that a saloon woman would touch his ears so intimately. She had shocked him down to his boots and jerked the righteous manhood right out of him.

"There you were fifteen years ago, digging a hole in

the frozen ground and mourning your nag," Jacob continued between roars of laughter. "Drunk with swill and trying to write letters to your ladylove while you buried that horse. By sweet heaven and Gabriel, then I knew I had a friend who would stick with me. Because you sure stuck with burying that nag and all the time harping about not being able to write like Shakespeare and having your ears defiled by a hot-tongued woman and wondering if Lady Godiva got cold."

"Sally was a good old horse." Solomon found himself chuckling. "We gave her a funeral to be proud of. You standing out there in moonlight quoting Latin and craving crawfish and swilling rotgut was a sight to remember."

Jacob placed his hand over his heart melodramatically. "*Et tu, Brute*." He tossed a silver flask to Solomon. "Before I must depart, let's proceed with our reunion, and toast this woman who has shackled you and who has yet to defile your ears. Now, tell me just what this woman has that no other woman has."

Solomon thought about Cairo. "She's just ornery enough to get me through this time with Garnet, who can be sheer hell around most women."

He looked at Jacob's grin and added philosophically, "You see, son, it's the sport and the romance of capturing a woman who will go toe-to-toe. And Mrs. Wolfe is purely a fighter. Didn't know if I could do it at first, but then I got to liking the idea. She's a betting woman and I needed the cash to get started. Now it's more than that. Other than the scarcity of women, I suppose it might be the way she gets to me. . . . Makes me want to pack her up and toss her over my shoulder and find the nearest place where we can fight it out. I purely love getting her riled, watching her getting all tight like she's getting ready to jump on me and tear me apart or burst right into fire before my eyes."

Jacob was nodding sagely. He had a faraway look in his eyes as if thinking of a woman in his past as Solomon sipped the fine whiskey and contemplated his new wife. "Never saw a woman stand on her head before. Now, that will purely do things to a man, Jacob Maxwell—looking at a woman in her silk pajamas who is standing on her head. It turns a man's logic real quick."

After a day of curious stares into her parlor's windows and hours of playing billiards, shooting the massé, and every other draining trick that Bernard had taught her, Cairo still wanted to rip Solomon into shreds. Fort Bentonites worried about President Garfield, who had just been shot and lay unconscious; then they wondered about when The Champ would make her move.

July's heat shimmered on the prairie and added to Cairo's dark, volcanic mood.

His taste remained on her lips; memories of the hard press of his chest against her and the slight chafing of his beard leaped to life at the slightest provocation.

He had suckled her tongue and ignited some . . . spark of heat in her, she brooded darkly.

Solomon Wolfe was the reason the Palace's red doors bore a "Temporarily Closed" sign and the reason the velvet curtains were drawn over her windows day and night.

Bernard had taught her that a lady never wagers personal items—such as she'd done in desperation with Solomon—that a lady always places cash or coin on the billiard table. With Solomon holding her cash, and her credit extended at the dry goods store, Ah Sing's laundry, and the livery, Cairo did not have anything to wager, and Solomon Wolfe was the cause.

She wasn't ready to face Kipp or the town's gossip. She dressed in her muslin camisole and knickers, and her long, flowing dragon-decked silk robe while she taught Garnet how to play billiards and how to brush her hair.

To distract herself, she'd begun to tell Garnet stories about King Arthur and his gallant knights and Lady Guinevere. With a child's insight, Garnet had quickly identified Lady Morgan Le Fay with Blanche. Both were beautiful and dangerous women.

Cairo sighed longingly. Bernard had introduced her to fair damsels in castles and white knights, and she longed for his wisdom.

Her nails delicately brushed her prized table as she thought of Solomon Wolfe, who wouldn't know gallantry if it smacked him on top of his shaggy head. Solomon would never be any woman's white knight.

Quigly had pounced on Garnet at once, measuring her for dresses until the little girl acted like a hunted animal. Because she would not have a child in her care looking uncared for, Cairo ordered Garnet shoes from the shoemaker. She added black shiny slippers with brass buckles just like those she had always wanted as a girl.

Quigly had begun nudging her about starting a milliner's shop in *her billiard parlor*. He contemplated areas of the bar and the room as if visualizing displays and sewing machine space and shelving for cloth.

Cairo glanced around her beloved lush, gleaming, perfect billiards parlor. It was really her first home; the luxurious apartments overhead had been meticulously furnished with the best of furniture shipped from Chicago.

The second night Cairo lay beside the sleeping girl and plotted how she would deal with Solomon.

Cairo placed her arms behind her head and stared at

the light from the streetlamps on her ceiling. She'd have to devastate him in front of the whole town.

She clamped her thighs together and wished she had disabled Solomon when she had him in her clutches.

He'd left her after the wedding. She was a bride without an interested bridegroom.

He'd struck at her pride, wounded her, and walked his long legs right out of her door—after that damnable kiss.

Solomon Wolfe would pay for that dearly.

On the third day, she forced herself to walk down the street to the post office and tried to ignore the snickers as she passed.

Before dawn on the fourth day, while Quigly muttered and objected to watching Garnet, Cairo rode to the Wolfe ranch. Without an audience, perhaps he would see reason.

She knocked at the ranch house door, glancing at the new lumber and bricks stacked beside the house. Dawn spread pink color over the fresh boards on the new addition to the old house. When there was no answer, she knocked again, this time sharply.

Then a man's hand shot past her and lifted the door latch, and another hand pushed her into the house.

Cairo pivoted to glare at Solomon, who was studying her ornate hat. A tall black plume had been broken when she was propelled through the door, and Cairo snatched it away. He touched the hat's tiny blackbird before she could dash his hand away. "Don't touch. You've just caused me to break an ostrich plume. They are very expensive. Like me," she added, reinforcing the difference between them. "You're like jerked beef to my caviar."

Solomon didn't button his shirt, but tossed his hat onto a nearby chair and ran his hand through his shaggy, wet hair. He shook it and a spray of droplets landed on her face and her bodice, causing her to gasp.

He unstrapped his gun belt, rolled it neatly, and placed it on the scarred board table. "Did you come to cook breakfast?" he drawled in that deep, amused tone she hated.

"Of course not. I don't cook."

"Why are you here?" Solomon asked softly, taking two steps toward her, his gaze fastened to her lips.

She slashed out her hand and pushed away the uneasy sense that she had lured a dragon from its lair. She stood very straight. "You can't just marry me, leave me with Garnet, and walk away, Solomon."

"Why not?" he asked, slowly taking in her black riding dress and boots. Cairo tugged up her black kid leather gloves. She resented the color moving up her cheeks and the leaping awareness of Solomon's freshly bathed body as he came closer. "That rig looks like an outfit a widow would wear—widow's weeds. Since I'm still alive, you must be mourning your dearly beloved Bernard."

"Do not talk about Bernard. You have my cash and, therefore, Mr. Wolfe, you have the means by which I earn my living," she threw back, taking another step backward as he advanced. In the small enclosure of the house, Solomon looked even larger than he had at her parlor.

"A man usually takes care of his wife—sees to her needs," Solomon murmured.

She tried to keep her eyes above his shoulders. The temptation to glance at his chest—which had recently pressed hard and warm and rough against her breasts. Cairo sniffed delicately, haughtily. "The whole town is talking."

She glanced down at his chest, at the droplets clinging to the black hair and the wide expanse of tanned skin. The mat of black hair narrowed, flowing down into the trousers that had not been fully buttoned. "Button your shirt. Button your trousers. Only a—"

"Villain?" he supplied with a lifted eyebrow. "Blackguard?"

She refused to rise to his bait. "No gentleman would act as you do. I demand that that you button your shirt."

"I prefer that you unbutton yours," he murmured softly. "We'll start with this," he said as he jerked out her hat pins and ripped away her hat. He sent the elegant affair sailing to a chair.

Cairo disliked his close inspection; she regretted the flush moving up from her throat. "How's Garnet?" he asked conversationally.

"Step back, please."

"Kiss me. Just once to show me you know how to," he invited softly. "Or did you give them all to Bernard?"

The tension between them had shifted, stilled, and changed. Solomon was hunting her now, pushing her to the limits, forcing her to a duel she didn't understand. "I don't know why you insist on tormenting me about Bernard. He was a dear man. I know how to kiss *gentlemen*," she stated slowly.

"So you've come after me and you want me," he drawled slowly. "Makes a man feel good to know that his bride wants him."

She grabbed his hand as he began to flick open the buttons on her bodice. Then his hand was on her breast, caressing her lightly, and she was trembling. She stared up at him, barely breathing, her body quivering against his and the strange, aching heat sweeping through her.

Solomon nuzzled her cheek. He nibbled her ear, his breath uneven. Cairo stood still, stunned by the sensations twining around her.

His hands trembled when he eased hers aside to open her bodice. He unknotted the laces of her camisole and all the while Cairo watched, fascinated by the striking bones of his angular face, the warmth of his eyes upon her body.

He trembled, then placed his hand over her breast. Shaken, Cairo glanced down to see his dark forefinger gently circle her nipple. She closed her eyes and bit her lip, the exquisite delight of his touch sweeping warmly into her.

Solomon's gaze smoldered down at her. "This won't get you out of your wager, Mrs. Wolfe."

"You think I've come to . . . to pay you off?" she asked incredulously after a heartbeat.

Lace tore as his hand closed over her breast, lightly, possessively. "Sure do. But I'm not buying. You made an agreement. Are you backing out?"

"Of course not. I am a woman of honor," she returned, trying to ignore the gentle rolling of her nipple in his thumb and forefinger.

"You've lived with a man before," he said, watching her.

"You are very different from Bernard," she stated flatly.

"Count on it. You'll have to come to me, if you want it to look like you're keeping your marriage vows, Mrs. Wolfe," he whispered against her hair as his hands smoothed her waist. "Or I'll give the money back to you and you can go on your way."

She considered the thought and her pride. "That

would look like you pitied me and worse—that I couldn't hold up my part of a wager."

"It would look like that. But you're only a woman and women can't be expected to know what's best for them. Women need their thinking done for them."

"Are you saying—" Cairo began unsteadily. "That I was unbalanced and gambled recklessly . . . because I am a feeble-brained woman?" She tried to force the outrage from her tone. "Are you saying that if I were a man, you would expect that I knew what I was doing? That if I were a man, I would honor my commitment, my wager to marry you?"

"Not likely. Men don't make good brides," he said slowly with a hint of humor against her hot cheek. He smoothed a curl away from her ear before he bit it gently. A tiny, fierce portion of her anger melted instantly and her body tightened, alert and hungry for more as Solomon continued, "You've got nice ears. You'll have to come after me and show the whole town that you want me."

"I don't like the sound of that," she said slowly. She stated the thought that had burrowed into her mind, lodging deeply. "If I . . . live with you, you will not place your beastie within me," she said very tightly.

For a moment, his frown was puzzled; then his eyes began to take on that amused light he seemed to reveal just for her. "Beastie?"

"You know . . . a man's b-body. . . ." she stammered, flushing wildly. Bernard had explained that when a man was in need, he resembled a beast and in the Englishman's gentle way, he explained the anatomy of the male and female.

"Beastie?" he repeated, incredulous humor in his deep voice. "As in a man's co . . . a man's . . . ?"

"Anatomical male area," she finished for him. "You know very well what I mean."

"Oh hell, I do," he murmured huskily, searching her flushed face. "I purely do know what you mean."

Then he began to grin and the grin became a chuckle and the chuckle became roaring laughter.

The sound stunned her for a moment; then Cairo pushed back from Solomon. She swept trembling hands over her mussed clothing and tried to tighten her camisole and button her bodice. She stripped away her gloves and glared at Solomon, who was grinning boyishly at her. She wanted to launch herself at him. "You. You've ruined my lace. Torn it terribly. Do you know how much good French lace costs?"

He stepped nearer and Cairo found her back to the wall. Solomon smoothed her throat with his hand, smoothed her chest, and placed the flat of his hand between her breasts. "Pack up and move out here. Where we can see who's really the best at this game."

"No," she returned shakily as he smoothed her breasts.

"It's up to you."

"I know this game. You are challenging my honor. The best I can do is offer that you have an attorney name me as Garnet's custodian."

"Mother," he corrected with a kiss to the sensitive corners of her lips. She refused to answer his challenge as he looked down at her breasts and continued in a husky, deep tone, "I adopted her. This place would be hers if anything happened to me. As my wife, you're her mother."

While Cairo struggled with her pride, Solomon stepped back, then poured coffee into a granite cup. "You owe me a year," he said. His unbuttoned shirt slid aside and the sun from the window glistened on the hair covering his chest. "Or until a good woman comes along who knows the wifing business and how to keep a home."

"Billiards is my business." Cairo tried not to look at his chest. "Wifing business? Do you honestly think that I would want to live here?" she asked desperately.

He shrugged. "A wife belongs with her husband."

"I'll do anything! You could agree to an annulment," she offered desperately. She hated the word he forced her to add with the lift of one black eyebrow. "Please?"

"Garnet needs you. There isn't another woman around who can manage her, and I've got to be about making a living for us."

"I'll give her a home. With me. I'll buy a house. She can go to the new school," Cairo threw at him desperately. She didn't like the set of his jaw, nor the look he leveled at her. As if he expected her to run from her wager at any moment.

"This is her land. Where her mother grew up. I want her here with me . . . and my wife. You can teach her."

When Cairo shook her head, the loosened curls at the back of her head came free; they spilled over her shoulder. She ripped away the cameo-studded combs that had supported her hair. "Bondage. You are a primitive wanting slavery."

"Either you'll hold to your end of the wager . . . or you won't," Solomon stated firmly, his dark gaze challenging her.

She inhaled and tightened her lips, disliking what she was forced to say next. "I have accounts that must be paid, and you have all my cash."

"Tell me who and how much, and I'll pay them."

"With my cash," she stated carefully, holding her temper.

"It won't be any different than when Bernard paid your bills."

Cairo felt the angry heat rise in her, warming her ears. "You are forcing me to depend upon your goodwill. You realize that marriage is a . . . a serious matter. There are ah . . . certain restrictions for husband and wife."

"While I'm married to you, I won't be bedding another woman. Because I'll have my daisy waiting for me at home," he murmured, and she distrusted the slight curve of his hard lips and the wrinkles deepening beside his eyes.

"Don't think of me as your daisy. The thought curdles my blood . . . and don't mock me."

He eased his finger inside a long curl and tugged it slightly. "You can always back out."

Fully clothed, Solomon ran, dove into the cold running stream, and came up for air, his body still taut with desire for Cairo. He swam, pitting himself against the stream. Then because he knew it was not safe to be without his gun belt, he quickly walked to the grassy bank and strapped on his gun.

The old lone buffalo bull watched him as he passed. "Beastie," he muttered to the sunlight. Solomon grimaced, remembering the delicately fashioned word.

He had been very careful with his body, and his last sexual release was too long ago. His desperation for a worthless, bony, spoiled woman named Cairo was proof of his pitiful condition as a man.

At the house, Solomon picked up a saw and ripped it across a board. He sawed rapidly, lost in his thoughts of the woman who was his wife. Cairo, a woman of experience, knew how to play men, and he was only one of many. She made grown men swoon as she passed, touching them with her fan. His son was in love with her.

Solomon discarded the saw and picked up a hammer. He slammed it against the square nail, pounding it into the new lumber with two blows. All he needed now was to lose his head over a female who knew how to jerk men's reins.

He glanced at the lone bull on the lush grass near the stream. Until lately, he was just like that old buffalo, knowing what he had to do and realizing his deathly future.

Cairo tasted like nutmeg and silk and honey, and having her as his wife meant a mother for Garnet, and it kept her from ruining Kipp's young life.

Cairo Brown was his burden to bear, a worthless female who made her living off men.

The old bull watched him from the distance as if he understood the need humming through Solomon's body. "Old boy, I'm not too happy myself," he said, pounding another nail.

eight

"Solomon's *wife?*" Blanche demanded in an outraged hiss as she circled the stacked cans of condensed milk in T.C. Power's dry goods store to face Cairo.

A steamer's toot matched another's whistle as the two racing boats neared Fort Benton's wharf. The steamers' whistles reminded Cairo of Blanche's taut expression, pumped full of steam and ready to burst.

Cairo looked up from the cotton goods she was considering for Garnet. She placed the basket she had been carrying on the bolts of cloth. She decided from the fury in Blanche's expression that the toy china set, just like one Cairo had always wanted, could be broken. Cairo adjusted the student's slate and paper tablets around the china to protect it.

Dressed in a striking indigo blue day dress with an elegant hat crammed with feathers, roses, and tiny elephants—the latest fashion, according to the newspaper—Blanche gripped her parasol tightly. The tiny elephants quivered as Blanche demanded, "Tell me it isn't so. No righteous woman would have wagered herself. But then you aren't righteous, are you?" Blanche asked tautly.

"Perfectly righteous." Cairo noted that Garnet was well away from listening distance, absorbed in the huge jars of candy on the store's counter. Blanche looked unladylike now and Garnet's bawdy but pointed comments could start more trouble.

"Solomon Wolfe is a man—" Blanche clamped her lips closed against what she obviously intended to say. "He came back for me. Somehow you finagled, plotted to get him—maybe drugged him. The undesirables—those China celestials—have potions to make a man do things he doesn't want to do. That's it—you slipped him rhinoceros horn or some such animal part. Or you put something from the demonical dens into Solomon's Sultana cigars."

Cairo smoothed the bolt of cornflower blue calico cotton. She noted that Blanche was indeed as "well stuffed on her fore" as Garnet had noted. Cairo remembered Solomon's mouth on her breasts, tugging the very cords from the most tender depth of her. With his need to taste and lick and nibble, no doubt he had enjoyed Blanche thoroughly. Cairo forced her nails to stop digging into the soft cotton.

"Release him from whatever hold you have over him," Blanche ordered dramatically. The tiny elephants danced and the gigantic blue rose petals on her hat quivered with her anger. "If you don't, I will ruin you. Solomon is mine."

"Does Duncan know that?" Cairo asked smoothly, realizing how much she disliked being attacked, threatened, and forced into situations. Since her ride back to the Palace, trying to look very proper with lace torn by Solomon's hands, Cairo had needed revenge.

Cairo smiled leisurely. Blanche always got what she wanted, and now she wanted something that was legally Cairo's. Solomon was hers until she got rid of him—somehow managed to discard him.

Blanche waited impatiently. "What will it take to buy you out? Kipp says you'll go to New York one day. Go now," she ordered. "I can have the funds in your accounts within the hour."

Cairo watched with interest as Blanche struggled for control; then she asked, "How much did you pay the last woman Edward forced and beat badly?"

"What?" Blanche frowned. "He has daughters of Eve—I cannot abide the word for what those women really are. They probably enjoy a man being a man."

Cairo thought of the young girl, battered and shamed by Edward, and the money that had arrived at Sarah's boardinghouse to keep the girl quiet. "It took a solid week of trying to get the last girl to say anything, to stop staring at the wall, Blanche. Heaven only knows what horror she was wrapped in."

Blanche shifted and glanced away, and Cairo was grateful for that uncomfortable show of caring womanhood. She suspected that Blanche didn't know how to handle either of her sons. Blanche turned back to her. "Edward, out of the goodness of his heart, saw that one girl had money, though he had no part in what happened to her."

"He's his father's son, isn't he?" Cairo asked, catching the widening of Blanche's eyes, the stark white of her face. "Duncan is Edward's father, isn't he? The same blond hair?"

"Duncan is my foreman. Edward is my son. Buck's

son." Blanche looked as if she might launch her brilliantly clad body at Cairo at any minute.

"The women they abused all noted a peculiar birthmark on each man's thigh. The exact birthmark, Blanche. One on Edward's right thigh, quite sizable, and a matching one on Duncan's. I was quite careful to ask the size and shape of each mark. The only reason I don't expose Duncan's relationship to your son, Blanche, is because I value Kipp. He has qualities that he obviously didn't inherit from his mother—like caring and gentleness and the ability to laugh and enjoy genuine friendships."

"Kipp is a hot-blooded boy, naturally wanting to try everything in skirts. You're just his fascination at the minute," Blanche shot back.

Cairo spoke tightly, not shielding her anger from Blanche. She kept her voice low, so that Garnet would not hear. "The last girl crawled to my back steps. Edward had made a fine penny by selling her again and again. She lost a baby that she and her husband wanted badly. She killed herself because her husband couldn't deal with what had happened to her. Then, because he loved her, her husband sought out Edward. Duncan and his men humiliated him. The boy took his life. Because of Edward."

Blanche paled. "That's only gossip. Just tell me how much you want to leave here, to release Solomon from his bondage to you, and our business is finished." Blanche drew herself very straight. "If you don't take my offer, I will destroy you."

Cairo slowly drew away her glove to study her neatly trimmed nails; she allowed the sunlight passing through the window to touch Solomon's wedding ring. "His mother's. And now it's mine."

"He's not living with you. The whole town is talking about how he walked off after that heathen ceremony at the Palace and left his new bride standing there. That . . . that . . . kiss . . . that sinful kiss," Blanche sputtered, "only showed how little he cares. No man would treat a lady like that in public. That little exhibit only proved that you do not have his high regard."

"Apparently you have all the details. How nice of you to be interested," Cairo said smoothly.

Blanche's gloved hand rose to her throat, then she forced it to her side. "I paid to keep the Johnson place for Solomon. I repeat—If you do not remove yourself from marriage vows with Solomon, I will make your life unbearable."

"I can't wait," Cairo returned in a bored tone.

"Your ruin is upon *your* head, not mine," Blanche continued unevenly, the huge hat quivering above her furious expression. She glanced to Garnet, who was skipping around a barrel toward them. "Garnet. My dear child. How are you?" Blanche exclaimed with obviously staged delight.

"My pa is married now. You'll have to keep those melons in your shirt," Garnet stated wisely around a licorice stick.

Blanche's hand flew to her heart. "Pa?"

Garnet ran through the tables toward the door, which Solomon entered. "Pa!"

She leaped up into his arms and he held her on his hip.

He stood very still, outlined in the doorway, facing the two women studying him. Solomon looked as if he'd been caught raiding the candy jar—there was just the hint of the guilty little boy clinging to him. His expression said that he wished he were in front of a stampeding herd of buffalo rather than the two women. Then he locked his legs at the knee and settled into a determined, wary stance. Cairo couldn't resist—the temptation to pay him back was too much. "Pa. I'm so glad you could come into town," she murmured as she moved toward him.

Solomon swallowed slowly and his wary look lifted Cairo's battered pride. She had him now at the tip of her sword. "We were just discussing you, *Pa*," Cairo said when she stood near him.

"Ma!" Garnet exclaimed happily as she wrapped her free arm around Cairo's neck and hugged her.

Blanche daintily brought a handkerchief to her eyes and sniffed. "Oh, Solomon. Tell me this isn't true. Tell me you haven't entered matrimony with this medicine-show woman, this woman who traveled and lived openly with a man who wasn't her husband. I beg of you, dear Solomon."

"True enough," he said, around the bit of licorice Garnet had just stuffed into his mouth. He glanced outside to a team of draft horses passing on the street and murmured, "Now, that's a fine big beastie."

Cairo caught the mockery in his expression. She flinched, then fought the color rising up her cheek. Solomon wasn't helpless in verbal swordplay.

Blanche wound around the tables, gliding toward him. She placed her gloved hand upon his arm, her beautiful eyes adoring him. "She drugged you. It's all over town that her slave went down to Chinatown, purchased something from the demonical dens, and made you marry her. Under the circumstances, no one would hold you to this marriage, dear Solomon."

Blanche lightly skimmed the angular contour of his shoulder with her glove. "I'll bring up your child, Solomon, just like my own. I am an experienced mother, you know," she murmured, sending him a knowing gaze. "Just rid yourself of this—this medicine-show woman and everything will be just like it was before."

Garnet smelled one of the blue silk roses on Blanche's hat. "Pa is hot for Ma. Hard to miss the horn he's wearing when he rolls around in bed with her."

Solomon frowned. "Garnet, hush. *Now.*"

Then he studied Cairo's blush. "Ma?" he asked slowly, a humorous tone in his deep voice. She whipped her fan in front of her flushed face. Solomon never lost an opportunity to challenge and torment her. She had no plans to play "Ma" to his "Pa."

Blanche shifted restlessly, but Solomon's eyes remained locked on Cairo.

Garnet grinned, bursting to tell Solomon what had passed before his arrival. Her tone held pride as she loudly whispered in his ear, "Catfight. Low-down, quiet hissy affair. Ma did fine. Held her own real good."

"Yes . . . well. . . ." Blanche cleared her throat and bent to kiss Garnet's cheek. The little girl winced theatrically and wiped her sleeve across her face. Blanche recovered quickly. "Come see me, Garnet . . . Solomon. I'm certain you'll discover your mistake soon enough. Anytime, Solomon. Night or day, I'll be waiting," she added as she sailed out the door.

Cairo fought her temper and lost. This was the man who had broken her black ostrich plume and had . . . had feasted upon her body only this morning. He stood there, hat tipped back, Garnet on his hip and chewing licorice as if he were innocent of arousing her . . . passions, she spat out mentally. She wrapped her gloved fingers in the worn black shirt covering Solomon's chest and jerked. "She says you owe her money. Do you?" she asked tightly.

Solomon's expression changed to impassive. He

placed Garnet on the floor. She gripped his hand and took Cairo's, looking up at them worriedly.

"She paid the taxes on the ranch while I was gone."

"Solomon Wolfe, you are to retrieve enough money from the funds you are holding—my wagering money— and you are to pay her the exact amount. I will not have you owing Blanche Knutson—not while you are . . . temporarily married to me."

"Can't."

"Why can't you?" Cairo demanded after a full moment.

"Can't have my wife paying my debts."

Cairo punched his chest with her finger. *"It's my money."*

Solomon spread his hand over Garnet's head and shook her gently, because the little girl was obviously frightened by the storm brewing between the two adults. Then Garnet grinned widely. "She does sound like a wife and a ma, doesn't she? They nag and boss just like her. Ain't she a daisy, through and through?"

"I do not nag." Cairo hit his broad chest with the flat of her hand. "You will do as I say, Solomon Wolfe. I will not have you owing that woman anything. Not while . . ." She floundered a bit, wishing she had not risen so sharply to the desire to wrench Blanche's tentacles from Solomon.

"Yes, Ma," he said too easily. "But I'll consider it a loan from you. It's good to see my new bride protect our family honor."

Cairo sent him a dark, furious look and hoped she could contain the steam rising in her. In another moment, she'd explode. "Oooo," she said beneath her breath.

Then he bent to kiss her. Right on the perfect "Oooo" of her lips.

Cairo reeled with the teasing delight, with the soft, warm brush of his lips against hers. Heat reached out and swirled her into a storm right there in cotton goods. She found her lips pushing against Solomon's, meeting the flick of his tongue with her own. She tasted licorice and hunger that she wanted to dive into, to challenge and to—

Then she stepped back, knocking over a stack of tin cups. They clattered noisily to the floor, and the clerk ran from behind the counter. "Is everything all right?"

Cairo swallowed and glared at Solomon, who was grinning broadly, his teeth shining whitely against the dark contrast of his beard. "Nothing is right," she snapped before quickly sorting through a stack of shirts and holding one up to Solomon for fit. "Put it on my account. I cannot have my—"

"Husband?" Solomon supplied, looking too innocent.

"Whatever," she snapped, dismissing his term. "You look ill-kempt. You are besmirching my ability to fulfill whatever role is currently mine."

Garnet shook her head. " 'Smirching, 'smirching, 'smirching. All I hear all day long from Ma is this 'smirching business. She's in an awful fit about something, Pa."

Then she beamed up at them. "Now I got me a ma and a pa. With a cat and a bull and a buffalo, and chickens, I got me a real family."

She frowned as Blanche's voice sounded at the door of the store. "Kipp, don't—"

"I don't care how big Wolfe's rep is. He's taken my woman," Kipp stated darkly, and stepped into the store, tall, rangy, and deadly. "A man has to keep what is his."

Solomon stood very still, his back to the door. "Take Garnet and move away from me," he ordered Cairo softly before he turned. "Hello, son. You wanted to talk with me?"

"Outside, pilgrim. Now. Let's call it." Then Kipp stepped into the sunshine on the street.

On Front Street Blanche protested worriedly. Kipp snapped, "Mother, keep out of this. This is men's business." He faced Solomon, who walked to him. "Back up, old man."

Zac Studeman, a bystander, glanced at Cairo as she motioned to borrow his gun. A longtime customer of hers, Zac nodded in agreement and slipped her the weapon. She pressed the gun between her skirts and moved quickly.

Kipp glanced at Cairo, who now stood between Solomon and himself. "He's not hiding behind your skirts this time. You'd better spend your time picking out cloth for widow's weeds." Then his mouth tightened, his eyes accusing her. "I gave up chewing tobacco for you. Do you know how that costs a man with his gang?" he demanded tightly. "Then you go off and marry this—"

She touched his gun hand, praying that Kipp would not draw on Solomon. She had no intention of letting either man fight for her. A slug in the dirt might be necessary to cool them down. If their toes suffered, it was their fault. She'd seen Bernard get the attention of more than a few combatants with that ploy.

"How good are you with that?" Solomon asked lightly, nodding toward Kipp's revolver.

"Good enough to take the fastest gun, let alone an old man like you."

"That's a good choice of gun. The Lightning model is a shy better."

"The Thunderer model Colt suits me," Kipp returned warily. "Newer than the Lightning. More power."

"See that lightning rod?" Solomon said, slowly drawing out his revolver and indicating the rod on the rooftop of the Choteau House, a hotel on Front Street. He aimed and fired, sending the ball at the end of the rod into the air where he kept it by firing successive shots.

Kipp picked another lightning rod, drew from his holster, and fired. Solomon hit the next one, then Kipp the next. "Nice draw. . . . I'd say the Lightning and Thunderer models are a close match."

"Depends on who is holding 'em. Good shooting, Wolfe," Kipp said begrudgingly. "Is that a rosewood handle?"

Solomon held the Colt out to Kipp for him to examine. "Made from one piece of rosewood."

Kipp handed Solomon his Thunderer and Solomon considered the elaborate ivory grips. "Little bit of weight here that could cost you. You might think about something lighter."

Kipp considered the thought. "You could be right. I'll consider it."

Cairo looked from one man to the other. They acted as if they were discussing brands of tea. A large crowd had gathered on the sidewalk and they were nodding toward Cairo, the original object of the two gunfighters' attention. Kipp raised Solomon's Lightning model to fire at another ball, sighting it carefully.

"Stop. You will not fire another shot. I will not be the reason Sheriff Healy arrests you," Cairo said, lifting Zac's revolver in her hand and leveling it at the small flag on the upper deck of a sternwheeler. She shot; the small flagpole cracked and fell. She glared at both men and handed the gun back to Zac. She smoothed her skirts and straightened her bonnet. "You are embarrassing me, the both of you. Now get off this street and go do something together that men do when they are settling their differences . . . some male peacemaking thing. . . . Because I will not tolerate either one of you acting like this about me!"

"What makes you think this is about you?" Solomon asked very slowly after a tense minute, eyeing her from his lofty height.

"This is men's business, Cairo," Kipp added from his equally tall height, frowning at her as if she had intruded on an area of male domain that she did not understand.

Blanche grabbed Solomon's arm, holding it to her abundant bosom and gazing adoringly up at him. "She's never understood *real* men."

Then Cairo felt the taut tether snap within her. In another minute she'd lose whatever decorum Bernard had praised in her and run screaming into the Missouri River. She squared her shoulders, took Garnet's hand, and smiled with the last bit of control she possessed. "Yes, Pa. You're absolutely right. This doesn't have anything to do with me," she murmured; then she stood on tiptoe, kissed his cheek, and walked back to the darkened sanctuary of her billiard parlor, leaving Kipp, Solomon, and Blanche staring after her.

She couldn't abandon Garnet to Blanche. Kipp needed a thrashing and Solomon would have to fend off Blanche's tentacles by himself. "Come along, Garnet. It's time for our game," she called.

Garnet, who was uncertain and hovering close to Solomon, holding his hand, let out a whoop and raced after Cairo. "This is my new ma," she announced to a boy rolling a hoop down the street with a stick. "Ain't she grand?"

nine

"Solomon has ruined me. It's only the first week of July. By December, I could be begging for coins on the street," Cairo muttered to the dark shadows of her elegant billiards parlor. "He's taken what I've struggled for and crushed it, just like he broke my black ostrich plume," she added miserably. "I loved that plume and I loved my edge, Quigly. When girls my age were dreaming about marriage and courting and sewing pillowcases for their bridal beds, I was perfecting my edge. Poor Bernard, Quigly. He is probably turning over in his grave."

"We buried him well. You had just had a big win from a Chicago player. He really did not like losing to a woman." Quigly continued an intricate stitch, repairing her torn underwear.

Underwear that Solomon had ripped away from her, just like he was shredding her pride, Cairo brooded. "He's got my New York money and he's walking around town in the same worn clothing he arrived in. Do you know where the responsibility for a man's clothing lies,

Quigly?" she demanded glumly, smoothing her beloved cue stick. "With his wife, that's who. It's 'wifely business' along with other duties."

"You take very good care of Garnet, Miss Cairo," Quigly soothed as he frowned and shook his head, examining his stitches. "She's sleeping nicely upstairs."

Cairo inhaled and exhaled slowly. "He's not even really interested in billiards, and he's taken my honor and my edge. Oh, how I loved my edge," she mourned again whimsically.

"The bar's mirror would make an excellent place for the ladies to model their new bonnets."

"No." Cairo sat upright and glared at him. "It would not. That bar came up the river and cost a fortune. It was made for betting men to appreciate." She propped her knickers-clad legs on a chair. She wiggled her bare toes and mourned her freedom, her dreams. "Mr. Wolfe has shown the town that he doesn't give a fig about the woman he married. He left me, Quigly. He isn't in his *bride's* keeping. Nor does he appear interested in any way. The least he could do is make an effort at this marriage business."

Quigly studied her torn camisole. "There appears to be moderate interest. Perhaps you could offer him a partnership."

She scowled at him. "He is not getting his fingers in my business. Did you send that ad to Chicago and not New York?"

"Yes, madame. You have told me exactly how you would tar and feather me if I sent an ad for a suitable wife for Mr. Wolfe to New York. It is your aspiration to wallow in New York society and you do not want any rumor that you needed help in this venture to—ah . . . find a suitable wife for Mr. Wolfe."

"A Chicago woman is fine. Or San Francisco. Preferably someone adequate to his specifications, but the rural women would probably suit him better. Ones who know about cows and housekeeping, that sort of thing. Did you remember to add 'able to read and add sums'? I want to make certain that Garnet continues her education, and traveling to the town school isn't possible in the winter."

"Yes, madame. And I did as you instructed and used my name for the address. As you said, you do not want the locals to know of your plans."

"Once I find my replacement, Quigly, we're off to New York. Now, I want a billiard game."

"At three o'clock in the morning?" Quigly protested wearily.

Cairo glared up at him. "You know what he's doing, don't you? In order to save whatever reputation as a woman that I have, as a lady, he's forcing my hand. I have to claim him. The whole town is laughing . . . I am the butt of jokes and gossip. Me! Cairo Brown, elegant professional lady billiardist, desired by men. Solomon Wolfe is my husband and I have to claim him or I won't have any standing as a lady at all. What kind of a lady can't keep her husband from wearing rags and . . . can't keep her husband?" she repeated, outraged.

"She called him *Pa*!" Blanche snapped. She ripped her elegant hat from her head, threw it to the floor, and trampled it on the expensive Oriental rug. "*Pa* as if they were married—with a family between them."

"They have the kid," Duncan murmured, watching Blanche from her bedroom doorway. "And Kipp."

Blanche glared at him. "Get in this room and shut the door. I don't want anyone else to hear what happened today. And they do not share Kipp. He is *my* son and Solomon's."

She kicked the abused hat away and began tearing at her clothing as soon as Duncan closed the door. "Solomon is mine, do you hear me, Duncan? Mine. I've waited for him."

Duncan rested his broken hand on his gun belt. "You and me can get married, Blanche. We've got a son between us, too. It's time you let me take my rightful place as your husband."

Blanche turned to look at him. "I want you to get her out of the way. She's an inconvenience I dislike."

"She's an uppity bitch, but a fine-looking one."

Blanche's anger welled up inside her and burst free. "Offer her money and put her on the fastest steamer out of here. If she doesn't want to play our way, pay someone and send her anyway. Do something that makes it look like she ran away."

She glanced at the bulge in his trousers and placed her hands on her hips, smoothing them. "You'll do that for me, Duncan. Won't you?"

"I could. If I wanted to."

"You will. Make certain that you don't hurt her big Ethiopian. I want him here. He's the fanciest servant anywhere." She considered Duncan slowly. "You always do what I want, don't you, Duncan?"

Duncan would never have her ranch and that was what mattered—because she was saving it and her marriage vows for Solomon.

"Go," she ordered Duncan, hating him passionately and hating her dark, willful side. She'd wanted and she'd taken; Buck had spoiled her, forged her into a woman she disliked. Duncan represented that part of herself she wished had never happened. Through the years, he had worked on her senses, her pride, eroding whatever good might have grown. He'd locked her with him in the dark quagmire of intrigue, doing for her, but taking in return—blackmailing her. She'd become loathsome, and only Solomon's touch could save her.

Over her, Duncan's harsh face became ugly. "Someday, Blanche. Someday, you'll—"

"You threaten me and I'll see that Edward never comes close to inheriting his share," she tossed back. She remembered Duncan's fiery birthmark, a match to Edward's. It was true then, the shared brutality of the women.

Her stomach lurched and she felt the steady crawl of bile up her throat. She loved each of her sons desperately, but Edward had been groomed by Duncan and she knew that eventually her love for Edward could be her doom. She'd always survived, and if she had to cut Edward free, she would do it. She placed her hand over her heart, remembering how she had given away one baby to survive. Where was her second son now? She hated Buck passionately for forcing her to take her son to an Indian woman. But she had kept the baby alive. She hated Buck and she hated Duncan, because he knew the blackness that painted her heart. "Now get out of my bedroom."

After Duncan left, Blanche shivered and forced away tears. She was frightened. Cairo seemed so strong and fierce as a woman alone in a world of men. But Blanche needed strength around her; she needed Solomon for her anchor to hold her to what was good within her . . . just as it should have been all these years.

Near his house, Solomon stroked the paint pony, examining it, then moved on to Hiyu Wind. She nuzzled his hand and nickered softly before moving away to join the two other mares in the corral. Gretta, the big draft Percheron mare, was blind in one eye, but gentle and worth the trade of one of Blanche's prime Texas longhorns. Pansy, a smaller buttermilk mare, was frisky, a good cutting horse with the endurance to run long distances.

Solomon leaned against the corral and looked toward Fort Benton. With dusk settling around him, Solomon considered his current life. He had a son and a wife and the closest thing to a daughter—Garnet. He smelled the night air, picking through the freshly tilled garden, the new lumber, and the animal scents.

Kipp. Too hard for his eighteen years, seasoned by Blanche's plotting and by Duncan's wiles.

Solomon rubbed his wrist, an old wound aching slightly. He remembered the old gunfighter crumbling in the street, felt the burn of the bullet scraping across his scarred wrist and the acid bitterness in his mouth. He'd known then that he was forging his own path, and all he wanted now was to raise Garnet well and to help his son.

He'd looked at Kipp, filled with himself, standing on the street, ready to kill, and saw himself so many years ago. The boy could be one of the wild young bunch raiding horses from the North-West Mounted Police, robbing stages and the wealthy foreign nobility who thought the Montana wilds offered exciting pastimes.

Yet his son had shown a high sense of honor, and Solomon counted on that.

Cairo. There was no reason to want her. She was like every kept woman Solomon had ever known. Vain, concerned with her bankroll, and totally useless.

Except in bed.

There, lying beneath him, issuing surprised little gasps as he tasted her, Cairo could rip away a man's heart and soul into her cold little fist. She tasted new, but Bernard probably hadn't been the first man to experience the excitement that lithe body could arouse. Bernard, or the men before him, must have taught her ways to excite a man, to make him feel as if she actually wanted him, as if he was the first man to touch her pale, soft body with the delicate muscles moving beneath her silky skin.

No wonder Kipp was hot for her, Solomon thought grimly. Sweet, innocent lips that begged for a man's. Heat pouring out of her, filling her cheeks, dampening her drawers like sweet dew as he touched her.

A woman who exploded like that when a man touched her knew exactly what she was doing . . . and usually how to control it.

Why did he claim a woman with a heart like a stone? Garnet liked Cairo—that was why. He wanted a sensible woman who knew how to grow a garden and raise chickens and teach Garnet to be a kind, gentle person.

Despite her trappings, Cairo was not a gentlewoman. There was enough savage in her to fight him.

He enjoyed sparring with her, tormenting her and watching her light with fury . . . and with passion. The only woman he had ever tormented was his sister. Yet each time he saw Cairo, all decked out and looking perfect, he wanted to watch the color rise in her cheeks and her honey-brown eyes darken. Solomon stared at his hands, locked on the board.

No man his age should feel as if he wanted to run a woman down and kiss the daylights out of her. That was exactly what he'd wanted to do when Cairo's elegant skirts swayed away from him.

He traced the movement on the horizon, the hairs on the back of his neck rising slightly. A gunfighter had an extra sense of danger, of knowing when he was being watched. The mares moved restlessly in the corral, unused to being confined.

Whoever was circling his ranch would have to come get him, Solomon had decided. He patted Hiyu Wind's mottled rump and traced the movement in the shadows. "Blackfoot raider. He's probably after you, Hiyu," he murmured, walking away from the corral into the shadows of the house to wait.

An hour later, Solomon warmed the food that Blanche had sent that morning. While the gesture was neighborly, the note enclosed bore the scent of lavender and an invitation for hotter fare—that of Blanche's well-warmed body. Solomon had pitched the note and kept the food.

His wrists tied, the young fierce Blackfoot warrior glared at Solomon.

"White man's food," the young Blackfoot warrior spat as Solomon placed a filled plate in front of him. The youth sat tensely; he tested the bonds around his wrists, tied behind his back. "Where is the woman to cook this meal? Are you a woman?"

"I caught you, didn't I?" Solomon asked gently.

"I did not want your worthless horses. I was passing to Canada." The boy was younger than Kipp.

"Uh-huh. You were circling my corral and had your hands on my best mare, ready to ride. You were very good though. Quiet. Like a fox crossing in the night. You must have stolen many horses."

"Many horses," the boy stated with pride. His head went up and Solomon noted his fierce blue eyes. He'd seen blue eyes like that before—

"Who are you, white man?" the boy asked, staring hungrily at the antelope steak Solomon had just fried for him. He bent to sniff at the apple pie Blanche had sent to Solomon. He didn't like her interference but had placed the food on the table for the too-thin youth.

The boy's name was Joseph. After eating ravenously, he dropped into an exhausted sleep while Solomon studied his youthful face. This Blackfoot raider had white blood and striking blue eyes—just like Blanche's.

The next day, Solomon tied the youth to the corral. "You like horses. You can keep them company while I do my chores."

The youth regarded him with a sullen, aloof stare. He touched the eagle talons on his necklace. "I am an eagle, a warrior. Without your gun, you would fall at my feet. I would dishonor you—man without a woman."

The youth wore bitterness like a cloak. A half-blood, he'd probably been hurt more than his share. Solomon untied him and stood back as the boy crouched to fight him. "Take that horse," he said, indicating the buttermilk mare. "She's fast and long-winded. You can make Canada today."

The boy straightened slowly. "You shame me? You would *give* me a horse?"

"Your people have had too much pain. The mare is a gift from me to you, because I have a son a bit older than you. Someday, I'd want someone to help him out."

"You do not spit on me because of the color of the sky in my eyes?" Joseph asked warily.

"You are of Indian and white blood. There is pride in that, and there are many like you here. They are respected."

"My mother gave me away. It is said she was white," Joseph stated darkly. "That from her, I got my eyes."

"You've got a place here with me, so long as you want to stay. I need help bringing in and breaking the horses that I traded from a farmer. There's maybe five mares and a stallion. He's a killer, mean and tough. The two of us might have a chance." For the horses, Solomon had traded a week's work at threshing time to Audy Fitzpatrick, a neighbor.

Joseph's head lifted with pride. "I can bring in the herd alone. If I chose to. Or I can take them to Canada. To my people."

"You could." Then Solomon shoved the boy's knife back into his scabbard and turned away. The knife sank into the dirt at Solomon's boots and he paused, turning slowly to face the youth. "I'd like to have those horses in my corral by nightfall, Joseph. But I'll have to keep my horses in the barn to keep them safe from that stallion. That means using a hammer and nails for a good part of the morning. We'll start out after lunch."

"You trust me?" Joseph asked warily.

"I do and I need a good man riding with me. You can have your pick of the horses. I'll write a paper saying so."

Joseph eyed him thoughtfully. "You give me a gift. I cannot write. How do I know that what you write is what your lips say?"

"You'll have to trust me," Solomon returned evenly. "Remember. My son's name is Kipp and if he's in trouble, I'd appreciate it if you would tend him."

"What does he do, this Kipp?" Joseph asked warily.

Solomon found himself smiling. "I don't really know. But he could be in the horse business, just like you. And the both of you better think about the reward the Stockmen's Association is offering—word has it that anyone turning in information about horse thieves in the area will collect a good-size bounty. It's a standing offer posted by the association."

* * *

"It's even worse than I remembered," Cairo muttered dismally as they drove the wagon filled with her beloved, elegant furniture toward the old ranch house. A freighter followed with her billiard table, carefully dismantled, and wrapped for bruises. The hired bullwhacker's oxen leaned into their harnesses, pulling the ten-foot one-thousand-pound table with its six-hundred-pound slate top. Garnet ran ahead, calling to Solomon. At dusk, the house nestled in the shadows of the smooth knolls, the meandering creek and cottonwood trees behind it. "Oh, God. A buffalo lying right there by the creek. The barn looks as if a good wind would cause it to collapse. Look at that windmill . . . it's no better with missing blades. But the house . . . Quigly, the house . . . Just look, part of the roof is gone—"

While Baroness Burdett-Coutts-Bartlett, Sarah Bernhardt, and the Russian Romanovs were living in style, Cairo would be living in this hovel.

"If Mrs. Brody had not looked at me with pity, and Mrs. Stevens had not queried lightly if there was some reason my husband did not want me, I would not have been forced into telling that lie—that Solomon was making his home livable in our separation," she muttered.

"There are new shingles nearby and a large room has been added to one side. There appears to be another room planned on the opposite side," Quigly stated cheerfully. "There are cattle in the field and horses in the pen. All it needs is chickens, sheep, and a pig. Look there— Mr. Wolfe is plowing a garden," Quigly noted, nodding to Solomon, who was following a big draft horse with a plow.

"Oh, please, Quigly, don't try to pull Bernard's rosy-picture act—head up, stiff upper lip—with me. This is a nightmare," Cairo muttered, gripping her shawl around her shoulders. She closed her lids and wished Solomon Wolfe to fly to the moon. "Until he signs back my money to me," she muttered. "Do you realize that I am dependent upon Solomon, after everything I've been through— *we've* been through?" she demanded, not shielding her outrage and frustration.

After avoiding marriage offers of every kind, and dreaming of New York and socials, she was now married to one Solomon Wolfe, worn-out gunslinger with a future of hard times painted all over him.

"The only hope for my salvation is that no one hears of this. I am hiding for the duration and praying that some woman will sacrifice herself to rescue me. When I had to leave most of my furniture, I felt as though a part of me was being ripped away."

"We'll brew a good cup of tea," Quigly consoled her.

"He plows in *suspenders*," Cairo found herself repeating as Solomon scooped Garnet up to his bare shoulders and came walking toward the wagon, which had just stopped in front of the house.

He stood there looking up at her and waiting, making her come all the way to him. Garnet's beaming grin above his black wind-rumpled hair softened his hard image. "My pa missed me," she stated proudly.

Cairo nodded to Solomon while Quigly stepped down and began unleashing the ropes of the packed wagon. "Cairo," Solomon said, nodding his head just once.

"Solomon," she returned stiffly, looking straight ahead and fighting his rugged, lean, tall workman's image. She closed her eyes against the urge to push away the damp hair on his brow.

He swung Garnet to the ground and she ran to the corral, standing on the posts and talking to the horses.

Solomon braced his weight on one long leg, hooked his thumbs into his waistband, and looked at Cairo. Solomon's suspenders only added to his rugged male stance; the seasoned pads and cords and flat stomach of a lean man, not the smoothly contoured body of a boy, excited the dark, feminine sexuality within her.

She pushed back that excitement. This man had taken away her New York. "You're dirty and sweaty," she said tightly.

"A man gets that way when he plows." He said it slowly, huskily, as if he was thinking of—

Cairo swallowed. Surely the strenuous efforts of making love and plowing couldn't be the same. "Please put on a shirt, then help Quigly unload my things," she ordered, not willing to say the words.

"So my bride has come to collect me," he said quietly as he slid off his suspenders. He drew on his shirt, but didn't button it as he tucked it into his trousers and replaced the suspenders.

"In a word, yes—" she began, stopping when Solomon reached for her waist and swung her to the ground. Then his hand cupped the back of her head, sending her bonnet askew, and his mouth found hers, sealing it perfectly.

He tasted of hunger, and . . . he tasted delicious. Cairo sank into the light, teasing kiss, which roamed her lips, tasting them. She found her gloved fingertips latched to his shoulders.

Then Solomon reached behind her, and crushed her bustle on his way to find her backside and press it. While she dealt with this intimacy, Solomon began helping Quigly lift a fainting couch and carry it into his house.

Cairo followed, careful to keep her gown from touching the door and mulling over the pressure she'd felt on her backside. Surely he hadn't sought her, and that wasn't a fond parting pat that he'd given her. She pushed her mashed bustle back to its center mooring and decided to ignore the event. Because now she could deal only with the sight of her new home. It loomed before her. This lair of Mr. Solomon Wolfe, dragon extraordinaire.

"My billiard table had to come," Cairo stated, glaring at Solomon. "You'll have to pay the freighter, Solomon. You will not allow him to handle the slate top and it is not my dowry to you. It and the table remain in my custody for the duration." She willed Solomon to start a brawl with her over her beloved table; then she would return to her parlor and start betting her jewelry, because nothing was keeping her table from her. Not even the man who was ripping away her New York dreams.

Solomon nodded and opened a double door to a new large room. Cairo followed him in, gripping her merino wool shawl as she stared at the barren, board-lined wall, the open window frame, and the sawdust on the new flooring. "My room?" Cairo asked tightly.

"The table goes in here. You might want to sweep it before we carry in more furniture."

"Sweep? Me?"

She hovered around the men as they eased the slate from its upright position, carefully wedged in its braces. She cried out when they gently slid the massive stone downward from the wagon and onto a skid wagon. She threatened murder when they moved it into the house, gentled it with ropes running beneath it and shoulders to support it. She prayed when they slowly eased it onto the table, raising and sliding it into place.

Because she had strained along with the men, pushing her own weight and muscle to secure the huge flat slab, Cairo was drained. "Pay the freighter, Solomon," she said, leaning against the wall and closing her eyes.

When she opened them, she was looking into Solomon's dark amused ones and they were alone. "If anything had happened to it, I would have buried you under the pieces of Italian slate."

Solomon ran his fingertip along her hot cheek. "So you do sweat. Can't say that I've ever seen a lady so hot."

She glared up at him and swatted away his hand. It rested gently on the damp cloth between her breasts before moving away. "It's the middle of July. It's hot and I have been under stress."

"You've got a mouth on you," he murmured. "Didn't know that ladies knew so many different ways to kill a man. If you cluck and nag and worry over Garnet half as much, she'll be safe, too."

"I do not cluck, Mr. Wolfe," Cairo returned breathlessly, realizing how large Solomon was, looming over her. She felt herself falling into his steady gaze.

"You're a daisy. A fighter for what you want. That's good for Garnet. I'd appreciate it if you taught her a bit about it before you leave," he said approvingly, then dipped his head for a quick hard kiss that took her breath away.

Two hours later, Cairo flung herself onto the bed she had just made with Garnet's help. "I'm dying for a bath," she muttered tiredly, blowing a curl from her cheek. "Quigly, I must have a soak. I'm afraid I just ruined my best Parisian gloves."

"Yes, Miss Cairo. I understand perfectly," Quigly agreed, looking with disdain at his ruined white gloves.

Garnet burst into the room, circled the billiard table at one end and danced over to Cairo's walnut clothes wardrobe, touched it, then over to the dressing table where all the bottles and powders stood neatly in a row.

She smoothed Cairo's hair and grinned at her beguilingly. Unable to refuse, Cairo hugged and kissed Garnet, and the little girl beamed. "It's okay if you kiss me. 'Cause you mean it."

"Little girls need kisses," Cairo stated, smoothing Garnet's hair. They needed food and shelter and so much more, she thought, aching for little Ethel and her family. She hugged Garnet again and wished she could have done more for her own mother and family. She didn't ever again want to be tangled in the responsibility for others, but for Garnet she would try to be a proper "ma."

"Pa said he's got water heating and Quig needs to help him haul more from the creek." Then Garnet leaned out of the windowless hole and yelled, "Pa, Quig will be right there."

"That man," Cairo muttered darkly, locking her glare with Quigly's. Quigly pressed his lips together and nodded.

Later, Cairo soaked in her tub behind the closed doors. She gazed at her four-poster bed and counted the minutes until she could pour herself into it. She dried, wrapped herself in an elegant bath sheet, and lay stomach down on the bed. "Quigly. I'm ready."

They talked about everything but the ranch as she lay on her stomach, wrapped in her sheet. Quigly's giant, knowledgeable hands worked out the tension slowly, and she gave herself to the pleasure. He had found the tight muscles at the backs of her thighs and was muttering about the tiny cooking stove; then the double doors opened.

From the corner of her eye, she saw Solomon's long legs and bare feet. He stood very still as Quigly began to knead her calves. "That's enough," he said, too quietly.

"*I* say when it's enough," she returned as Quigly hesitated and then straightened.

"A husband has rights," Solomon stated slowly. "And saying when is one of them. I'll do the rest."

"Quigly is very good. I'm certain you wouldn't know about how to use the oils. They are very expensive . . . like caviar," Cairo said over her shoulder. There was a raw edge to Solomon's deep voice, like that of a mountain cat's warning growl. The sound raised the hair at the back of her neck.

"I'll learn. Quigly, until the new rooms are boarded in, your bed and Garnet's are in the barn as you asked. She's looking forward to telling you bedtime stories."

"Oh, goody," Quigly muttered gloomily, and left the room with slumped shoulders, a man facing his doom.

"Garnet is sleeping with me and Quigly will take the extra bed," Cairo began after the doors closed. "I'm afraid you'll have to sleep in the barn."

"Not tonight." Solomon unstrapped his gun belt, slid his suspender straps from his shoulders, stripped off his shirt, and stepped out of his trousers. He stepped into the bathwater, scrubbed his chest, washed his hair, sluiced water over him, and stepped out of the bath.

Cairo closed her eyes. The image of Solomon's hard, corded body gleaming in the lamplight remained behind her lids. "That entire process must have taken ten minutes. No doubt you've missed a corner or two. Your new clothes are on the chair. I can't have a husband of mine dressing like you do. You can take them with you and tomorrow we'll discuss my rules for living here."

"Thank you, Mrs. Wolfe," he returned formally. Cairo kept her head propped on her forearms; she would wait until he left before she crawled between the blankets and sank into sleep. But first she'd call to Garnet—Cairo's body went taut as she realized that Solomon was continuing Quigly's massage.

Solomon's big, rough hands were slick with perfumed oil as he kneaded her thighs, parted them slightly, and began working his fingers upward into the tight muscles of her back and shoulders. She held her body very tightly as Solomon's calloused fingertips brushed the soft, sensitive perimeters of her breasts. "That's enough," she said tightly, drawing the bathing sheet closer to her.

Solomon leaned down, eased the hair from her nape, and whispered against her skin, "Mrs. Wolfe. While you're married to me, there will be no massages from other men."

"Quigly has been tending me for years—"

"Not anymore," Solomon said very slowly, turning her over and lying over her very carefully.

Cairo blinked, too aware that her naked body was lying beneath Solomon's very long and hard body and that he wanted her. "No," she whispered tautly as his large hands slid under her hips to her buttocks and caressed them. "This won't do."

"Comes with the territory," Solomon said, smiling, as he continued kneading her bottom.

"Exactly what—" When Solomon's hands each gripped a soft buttock possessively and gently lifted her to him, Cairo cleared her dry throat and swallowed. "Exactly what do you have in mind?"

"Billiards," he said huskily, tracing her lips lightly with his. "I've missed playing you."

"Oh . . . oh, I see," she said when she could talk. "Yes. I know how a sportsman feels when he—or she— hasn't played. There's a certain restlessness involved." His chest moved slightly on her breasts as he settled more comfortably on her, nudging her feet with his.

The movement was playful, and strangely unsettling.

"You've got nice big feet. That's good for a farmwife," he said, rubbing his chest against her breasts, which had become very sensitive.

"Don't you think a bat or a bird might fly in this open window?" she asked in a voice that seemed too husky for hers. The question was the only one she could dredge from her brain. "A screen would help."

Solomon closed his eyes and shuddered, his face very taut in the dim light. "What else does Quigly do for you that I should know about?"

"Absolutely nothing that would concern you."

Solomon slowly looked down to her breasts, groaned, closed his eyes, and rubbed his chest side to side on her softness.

Cairo went very still, aware that the mood had shifted and that he was lying very aroused, very hard and male between her thighs. She tossed away Bernard's word, "beastie," and thought of another—manhood . . . or male need . . . or a very warm, hard, compact, interesting piece of male anatomy. She had dampened and warmth seeped from where his body touched hers into a deep intimate place within her. Solomon breathed heavily, closed his eyes, and lowered his lips to hers. The hot, feverish kiss took away her breath.

"The cow will need milking before light. You can plant the garden later. If we have a late Indian summer, we just may get chicken lettuce or spinach. Maybe beans," he whispered into her ear. "Do you want that game of billiards now or later?"

"Cow? Garden? What do you mean, now or later?" she managed as he stroked her breasts, caressing them leisurely. She trembled, barely keeping her feet from thudding the bed in frustration.

Above her, Solomon looked rakish, devilish. She pushed at his shoulders, felt them tense beneath her fingertips, and knew that Solomon wanted her. "Exactly what do you want from me?" she asked shakily.

Solomon stood, jerked on his new trousers and an unbuttoned shirt, then walked toward the billiard table. He chalked a cue stick and began shooting practice balls as if the intimate moment had never passed between them.

"What do you want from me?" she asked more loudly as she drew on her black silk dragon robe, jerking the sash closed and striding toward him.

Solomon concentrated on a difficult shot. "I thank you for stopping a bit of Garnet's colorful language. And for the kisses and hugs. She's been needing them from a woman."

"She needs them from a man, too. You can kiss her now and then, you know. Especially when she goes to bed. To make her feel secure when you tuck her in. Bernard did as much for me."

When he snorted, Cairo grabbed her cue stick and chalked it briskly. She refused to place Bernard and Solomon in the same mental depot, other than they both cared for little, lost girls. "You need a domestic woman. You have my money. You can hire one for forty a month if you're lucky."

"Women are scarce hereabouts," Solomon noted, considering another shot. "That's too much money, even for a good woman. That's why you'll have to pull your weight."

"Like a horse in harness?" she asked tightly.

"Something like that. I want Garnet to have a good home." He paused, looked directly at Cairo, and nodded. "I'll try to give her those kisses. She hasn't had much tending in her lifetime. That's why I got you the milk cow. Garnet needs milk and good food. Make up a list of goods that you want for cooking and I'll get them. I'd appreciate it if you'd write down any advice for the woman who takes your place."

"Cook? Me?" Cairo asked, shaken. "But . . . but Quigly will cook."

He sank the shot into the pocket and began to place the balls into the triangle. Cairo burst the pyramid without the usual first shot to see who goes first. She passed Solomon on her way to align her next shot and he caught her sash, holding her. "You've been with a man before. You know that a woman plays her part."

She moved her cue stick between them. "I know that I could disable you right now and walk out that door, while you rolled on the floor in pain."

"I don't want a late-sleeping, worthless woman taking up space and time."

Cairo pushed back a heavy fall of curls and placed her hands on her hips. "Listen, you . . . you—"

She staggered back against the table, bracing herself against it, after Solomon left to check the stock. She tasted his parting kiss with her tongue, her lips sensitive and swollen.

"I am a professional billiardist," she stated in a hushed scream. "I have faced the best players and won, not to be stranded in this broken-down, miserable excuse for a—farm or ranch or whatever. Not to be told that I can't have my massages by Quigly, and not to be tormented at every turn," she said, remembering the dark humorous glint to Solomon's eyes, as if he enjoyed tormenting her to the limit before he made his escape into the night. She hurled a billiard ball at the door through which Solomon had just passed. "In the morning, I will resolve everything and make certain that Mr. Wolfe knows the boundaries of his ties with me."

ten

Solomon leaned against the corral and found the old buffalo bull watching him in the distance. Coyotes howled in the moonlight, the sound eerie.

He'd expected Cairo's dark, surly mood, but he hadn't prepared for seeing another man's hands on her white skin. Or for the quick gush of jealousy slamming into his stomach. Cairo looked drowsy, soft, and he'd been aroused instantly at the mere curve of her breast pressed to the sheet.

He shifted restlessly beneath the old bull's steady gaze. Solomon wanted Cairo; his instincts told him that he should sink into that lithe, pale body and take what he wanted . . . she'd known men before, been kept by them. He was no different.

The outrage in her eyes was nothing compared to his emotions when he discovered Quigly massaging her thighs.

"I'm too old for this," he muttered to the bull. "She's not what I want in a woman, much less a wife. But she's all I've got right now and damned if I don't enjoy teasing her."

"What are you doing?" Cairo demanded, awakening to find Solomon sliding beneath the sheet and lying beside her. She slid out of bed, the top of her silk pajamas coming open because Solomon was lying on her sash. She gripped the cloth and hoped that she was caught in a nightmare.

She had been dozing, forcing away the day of her defeat and conserving her strength to battle Solomon in the morning—when she would set her rules.

The moonlight passed into the room, lighting Solomon's rugged features and glistening in his beard. The silvery light spread across his chest and low on his hips where the sheet—her best cotton sheet—covered the rest of him. She noted that his . . . beastie seemed temporarily at rest. He pulled the pillows up behind him and sat, arms behind his head, regarding her with a devastating, boyish grin. "Dawn comes early. I'm settling in for the night."

"Not in my bed, you're not," she stated, flipping back the long braid that ran down her chest.

"I have to sleep somewhere."

Cairo fought the anger rising in her and lost. "Get out or I will remove you myself."

"Call it, little daisy," Solomon drawled slowly.

His widening grin cut her emotional tethers and she grabbed a cue stick with her free hand. She gripped her pajama top with her other hand and walked toward him. Solomon lifted an inquiring eyebrow, pursed his lips, and blew her a kiss.

"Out," she repeated, lifting the cue stick.

Solomon grabbed it and tugged her into the bed. "Come here, you," he said with a rakish, playful grin.

She squirmed beneath him, her wrists trapped in his hands. "I suppose you think this is funny."

Solomon's grin widened. "Could be."

Then he buried his face in her throat and shoulder and rubbed her skin teasingly, abrading it and making hungry bear noises.

Cairo fought giggling and lay very still. The rich tingle of pleasure his beard caused matched the excitement racing through her, created by the hard press of his body. "Exactly what are you doing, Mr. Wolfe?" she asked cautiously.

"Tasting you. You're buttered up like new baked bread."

"You obviously have me at a disadvantage. I am defenseless, crushed and mashed beneath your greater weight. You appear to be a brute taking what he wants," she stated carefully, trying to ignore the caress of his thumbs on her inner wrists.

Solomon lay very still, then he said, "True, all of it," and rolled away, his back to her, drawing the sheet up over his shoulder.

Cairo lay very still, then she slid from the bed, eased a pillow away, and tiptoed to the door. It wouldn't open. She tugged it slightly, rattling it, and held her breath as Solomon looked at her in the moonlight. "It won't open. How do I get it open?" she demanded, hating to ask one thing of him.

"You're not going anywhere," he said slowly.

"Oh yes I am. I refuse to be mauled or trapped," she returned, walking toward the window. She tossed the pillow outside and slid one leg through the opening.

"What makes you think I'd want you anyway?" Solomon drawled behind her.

"You have been showing signs of being amorous, Mr. Wolfe," she returned, her fingers tightening on the window. "You crushed my best bustle to maul my backside."

"Ha," he said, mocking her.

"Just what do you mean, 'ha'?" she asked, slowly withdrawing her leg from the window. She stood inside the room, studying Solomon's tall body, the shadows lying upon his hard-boned face. "After all, I am your bride," she pressed when he remained silent, watching her. "I demand that you desire your bride," she stated righteously. She shuddered under the impact of her outrage. She was just as womanly as the next bride; what was the matter with Solomon? He'd certainly risen to the occasion earlier in her billiard parlor.

"Can't," he stated after a long yawn.

Cairo inhaled. "Why can't you?"

"I'm not in the mood."

"Not in the mood," she repeated. "Oh. Well. That's good to know." Then a battery of thoughts hit her. Solomon's scarred wrists could reflect damage on other parts of his body. Other significant parts to do with the husbanding business. "Have you been injured . . . ah . . . in an area that might cause you distress?"

"I don't want to talk about it," he murmured, then turned his back to her and drew the sheet over his shoulder again.

Cairo battled her curiosity and her frustration. She took a few steps closer to the bed. "You started this. Now you will explain to me why you are not 'in the mood.' If you are . . . disabled as a husband, I need to know. I won't tell anyone."

Solomon was silent. Cairo eased to the bed. "Solomon, if you hurt yourself since we last . . . ah. . . ." She floundered. "You must tell me. Perhaps you need a doctor."

"It isn't a doctor I need," he murmured drowsily.

A new thought struck her. She'd known vain men, who could be as devious about their bodies as women. "Or . . . you're not one of those men who wear . . . who wear devices to insinuate that they are formed . . . ah . . . rather well, are you? You know, a codpiece? I've read about an Italian device that . . . uh . . ." She didn't know exactly how the device worked, but a Frenchwoman had told her that, and that men liked . . . She refused to think about the Frenchwoman's reference to men's tastes.

He gave a disgusted snort, then sighed sleepily, and Cairo's desperation tugged at her. If he fell asleep now, she might never know why he wasn't in the mood for his bride. "Solomon?"

She pushed his shoulder gently. "Mr. Wolfe? Are you sleeping?"

"Trying to," he murmured after another yawn. "Go lift the latch if you want out. I put one up high for my privacy when Garnet is about. While she's seen men in the all-together, I don't take kindly to the idea."

Cairo scooted closer to him and nudged his shoulder again. "Do you mean that after forcing me to marry you, after mashing me on my bed at the parlor, and after those damnable hot kisses, you are not interested tonight—on the night that I have come to you?" she demanded, then paused because she had discovered his toes playing with hers.

She eased her foot away. "You will not distract me by playing with my feet," she stated, leaning closer to him. "I demand to know why you are not in the mood."

Solomon turned slowly to look up at her. The movement slid her hand to his chest. He trapped it on the warm, hairy surface with his own. His heartbeat was steady beneath her palm and her fingertips moved slightly, drawn to the interesting textures of his chest hair, his skin, and an interesting flat nipple. He jerked slightly when she touched the nub. "You can't kiss worth spit," he said in an uneven deep tone. "It takes a real kiss to stir a man."

"Ha. You're just using that for an excuse. There is nothing wrong with my kisses."

He rolled back onto his side and presented her with his back, the sheet covering him.

"I can kiss just as good as the next woman . . . bride," Cairo stated indignantly. When he didn't say anything, she grabbed his shoulder, pinned it to the bed, and bent over him. "Here. Take this."

Then she kissed him with every ounce of her experience and rose to look at him. "Are you in the mood yet? I demand to know if you are stirred."

Solomon yawned and closed his eyes.

Cairo flopped down on the bed beside him, her arms crossed tightly over her chest. She fought the huge tears that burned her eyes—and lost.

She sniffed. Just once.

After a long silence, Solomon asked huskily, "What's wrong?"

"I've had a bad day," she wailed, grabbing the sheet to dry her eyes. "I'm supposed to be a bride. I've never been one before and nothing is going right."

"Bad day," Solomon repeated in a disgusted tone. "Come here."

Because she was in no obvious danger from Solomon, Cairo allowed herself to be drawn into his arms. She let her head rest on his shoulder. All she wanted out of him was the admission that he was in the mood, and then she'd disable him and toss him out of her bedroom. "Why aren't you in the mood?" she persisted after another sniff.

He snorted in disgust. "You should know why."

"I do," she lied, then reached to place another kiss on his lips. Any minute now, he'd admit that she kissed very well.

Solomon's lips answered hers lightly, his hand slid to her thigh, squeezed gently, then moved to her backside. "It's an awful thing to do to a workingman, kissing him when he's worn out from plowing," he whispered in a raw, husky tone. "If you feel a wifely obligation, a pat on the cheek would do tonight."

Because he tasted magnificent, because she wanted to scrape away his arrogance, Cairo forced another kiss upon his lips. Her fingertips moved slightly in the hair on his chest, rummaging through it. "You're very warm," she whispered, excitement leaping in her as it always did when she was presented with a challenge.

"Very warm. Hard day in the fields. Hot sun," he whispered, nibbling at her lips. "I'll probably fall asleep at any minute."

Cairo closed her eyes, capturing the excitement racing through her. Solomon lay next to her. There were other games to play, and she would master him this time. She carefully slid her thigh over his and locked him in her grip.

Solomon—her prey—lay very still, watching her.

She tightened her fingers in the hair on his chest. She had him. She'd cornered him and run him into the ground.

His hand moved along her back, slowly eased aside her pajama top, and Cairo tensed.

She wanted Solomon as she'd never wanted any other man.

When his fingers caressed her breast, one just resting on her nipple and tapping it gently, she inhaled.

He kissed and nibbled on her throat, and she fought to breathe. "You've got to concentrate more on getting in the mood," she whispered unevenly when she could.

He kissed her breast and every cord in her body hummed tautly. Solomon nibbled gently on her softness, tugging the tip into his mouth. When he caressed her other breast, Cairo realized that she was very warm, her thigh moving restlessly against his hard one.

Then Solomon was kissing her, and she was returning the wild, feverish kisses, gripping his head to hold him, to make him hers, to cradle him to her breasts where he delighted her and drew her further into a huge, aching fire. . . .

Slowly, so slowly, the world seemed to turn over as she experienced every touch, every kiss, every caress so vividly. Solomon lay over her, his weight braced by his arms, and he caressed her face, his thumbs parting her lips for his kiss.

So hard and warm, Solomon was hers, his kisses delighting her, heating the dark cords racing deep inside her.

She held him to keep him with her, to feed the hunger growing in her.

"Wrap your legs around me," he whispered unevenly in her ear, the tip of his tongue causing her to tremble.

Cairo clenched her thighs together, shivering with the emotions running through her. "Solomon . . ."

"Shh," he murmured. His hands ran down her sides, cupping her bottom, lifting her. Then his knee pressed between hers, wedging space for his body.

He lay within her thighs, warm and hard and thrusting against her. Cairo gripped his shoulders as that part of him found her softness, sliding a bit into the dampness.

"Yes . . . or no?" he whispered, breathing deeply, watching her.

"I . . ." She bit her lip, wanting him, aching for him. He lowered his lips to hers, kissing her so sweetly, so hungrily that her hips raised, wanting him, her heart pulsing for—

She caught him with her legs, trapping him so that he couldn't leave her, not now. "Yes."

Cairo grasped his hard buttocks, keeping him with her as the kisses became hotter and deeper and sweeter and—

She cried out, the slight pain startling her amid the pleasure.

Solomon held very still, his body lodged full and hard within her. He turned to look down at her slowly, studying her face and her tears. "Lady?" he demanded roughly.

She couldn't stop trembling, her hands pressing him down deeper into her. He resisted, continuing to study her. Then Solomon very carefully lay down upon her, holding her softly in his arms, stroking her. His heart slammed against hers and his corded, lean body trembled in her arms, like some magnificent beast that had come to her for keeping.

She kissed his damp temple and smoothed his back. Her fingers found deep scars, slowly tracing them. "What happened?"

He moved within her, sliding away slightly, and she lifted her body, trapping him. "You're not going anywhere, Mr. Wolfe."

"I'm winded," he muttered darkly, like a little boy who

wanted a treasure and whose pride wouldn't let him ask for it. The tone endeared him to her, because she'd peeled away Solomon's hardest layers to touch something deep within him, just as he had touched her. He held very still and seemed shaken to his core, which intrigued Cairo and endeared him more to her. "I haven't had a woman for six years . . . haven't had to stop . . . ever. And by God, I have never in my life had a virgin."

She had devastated him, shocked him down to the core. He looked shattered and she found herself soothing him. "Well . . . then this is a new game here with me, isn't it?" She smoothed his hair. She rested beneath him in a quiet, good, comforting way, his lips pressed against her throat and kissing her gently.

She fought the restlessness within her, the barely leashed need to—

Then suddenly, he was above her, pressing deep inside her, a fierce warrior taking, and she would give to him—

"Call it. Say it," he ordered, trembling above her, the silvery light of the moon lying across his tense shoulders.

"Yes," she whispered, desperate for him.

Solomon gathered her closely, gently, softly, and began to move within her, filling her.

She ignited, caught him close, and soared. He was a part of her now, *hers*. The fire flashed and hurled and burst and Cairo hovered on the tip of that honed, exquisite sword, crying out in surprise, her heart bursting from her. She dug her nails into Solomon's taut shoulders and held on to him for safety as she hurled through the universe and came gliding softly home to her dragon's lair and nestled beside him.

She awoke to the strong beat of Solomon's heart beneath her cheek, to the sense that he was caring for

her, covering her bare shoulder with the sheet and rocking and caressing her. The tender, awkward movements
endeared him more, for if ever a man was treasuring her,
it was Solomon Wolfe.

Cairo snuggled to his warmth and care; it was enough
for now, she had run her race and found what she wanted.

She held Solomon tightly; he was her prize, because
as little as she knew about the lovemaking process, he
had truly been in the mood. His great warm body was
her prize, her trophy; she had challenged him and had
won. She slid into sleep, stroking his damp chest, touching his flat nipples, and smiling against his shoulder.
She'd finally beaten Solomon Wolfe, run him into the
ground and taken him, conquered him. She moved her
thigh luxuriously across his. He was just a mere shell of
what he'd been before she'd won the battle. She'd taken
him and laid him low. . . .

The sunlight blinded her.

Cairo eased beneath the sheets.

She ached in muscles she didn't know she had.

Her thighs felt soft, her body drowsy and boneless. Her
breasts ached, her nipples hard.

She groaned, aware of the evidence of Solomon's hard
body flowing into hers.

"You'll have to come out of there sometime, even
clams do," Quigly's bass voice boomed over her head.
"This room is a disaster. Clothing everywhere. I do hope
he hasn't ripped any more clothes. The man does not
know how to tear with the seam."

"Go away," she ordered, unwilling to see anyone in
the bright, condemning light of day.

"Ma, Quig and me got your breakfast ready," Garnet
stated happily. "Pa said you'd want to sleep late, so's we

had plenty of time. Pa looked all worn out and hassled this morning, but making our baby probably tuckered him out. He's old, you know. But when he said you'd probably sleep late, I knew he'd given his all to the loving business and that our baby would be along shortly," she said very seriously before continuing, "Quig burned the bacon and started a fire on the floor. My kitty ate the bacon and the pig came in the door," Garnet informed Cairo merrily, clearly happy with the events. "Pa said he milked the cow but that you should try to plant a few seeds before supper. I reckon he sure did plant his all right."

She placed her small hand on Cairo's stomach over the sheet. "Our baby. Just think, Quig. Now I got me a kitty, a buffalo, cows, horses, a pa and a ma, a great pig, oh—and you. And pretty soon, I'll have me a baby to take care of while Ma and Pa make another one."

Cairo crossed her legs slowly, then eased her head out of the blankets. "Where is he?"

She wanted to say "blackguard," or worse, but after her preaching to Garnet about swear words, she clamped her lips closed against words too good for Solomon Wolfe. She wished she had him in her clutches so that she could devastate him again and this time with a cue stick. Didn't he know that husbands were supposed to comfort brides on the morning after?

A gentle word or two before he started demanding that she milk cows or plant seeds might have soothed her urge to kill him.

Quigly inhaled. "Off to do something with a grain farmer. I believe he mentioned animal fodder. Mr. Wolfe is paying his way. It appears that we have married a workingman, a common laborer."

Garnet cuddled close to Cairo and kissed her cheek. "Morning, Ma," she said softly, shyly.

However Cairo felt about Solomon, she couldn't refuse the hopeful expression on Garnet's face. "Good morning, Garnet."

The girl bounced off the bed. "I'll go pour hot water for your morning tea. You should rest in bed so our baby gets a good grip in your belly—"

"No!" Quigly placed Cairo's cue on the table. "You will not. Tea has to be prepared in a special way. You'll be burned."

"Catch me," Garnet crowed, leaping from the bed and running out the bedroom door.

"Oh, dear," Quigly muttered, then stopped at the bed, staring down at the sheets. "Blood is especially hard to remove," he stated loftily. "That man is an outlaw when it comes to destroying good cloth."

In the stream, Solomon soaped his hair and his body, washing away the sweat and grime of the day's plowing. He ached in every muscle, fighting the oxen team of Johansen, breaking the new sod for planting. Throughout the day, he'd brooded about taking a woman who didn't want him, who was a virgin until they'd made love.

Cairo was right; it was a new game and one that broadsided him. He hadn't cared about his seed, flying from the depths of his soul and pumping into her soft, tight, damp body. He'd gone blind then, lost in the heat and a strange tenderness, his body locked to hers to the very end.

He'd never lingered in a woman's body, felt her heart beat wildly against his, then slow. . . .

Solomon ran his fingers through his hair. The last

woman he'd given his seed to had been shocked by the stickiness. As a girl, Blanche had been fastidious.

The memory had dulled, Cairo's flushed excitement catching him.

During the workday, he realized he was standing still several times. He'd been locked in the image of Cairo beneath him, her maidenhead giving way to him, and the incredible pleasure of watching her burst and tighten and drawing him deeper. Then he'd worried about Garnet, and how he would pay for the winter feed for his stock, and how to keep them all fed.

Then he went back to being randy and starved for the night and his bride. Solomon wanted to sink into Cairo and stay there, to tease her until she flamed and kissed him with her untutored lips.

He thought about those lips capturing his tongue and her sucking it and every nerve in his body jolted painfully.

He should have cleansed her, taken time to awaken her this morning, but he was afraid if he touched her that he would want her again. And her body might be hurt even more. He'd torn through her virgin's flesh, hurting her.

What if he'd known? She'd winded him and she was pleased about it, smiling in her sleep like a kitten who had licked the cream bowl dry.

Solomon tightened his muscles against the slam of desire.

He glanced at the horizon, at the dying day, and wondered when Kipp would arrive, all steamed and ready to draw down on him.

Or when Blanche would unleash Duncan and Solomon would have to watch for bushwhackers. He was used to taking care of himself, but now there was Garnet and a woman who'd rather kick his backside than look at him.

He raised his hand to his cheek—to the spot where she had kissed him last, tucking him in carefully in a soft tangle of arms and legs. It was a kiss given to a child, sweet, dewy, and affectionate.

The tenderness in her had stunned him no more than her fierce demand to have him.

The old buffalo bull chewed its cud and watched Solomon, then lifted his nose to the wind, sniffing it.

Cairo, dressed in a green silk gown, twirling a parasol to match, and carefully lifting her skirts over the rough ground, picked her way toward the stream. The late-afternoon sun caught her curls beneath her green bonnet.

Just the sight of her, his reluctant bride, all steamed up and sailing toward him, lifted his spirits.

Solomon sat on a branch beneath the water and continued soaping his arms and chest. He wasn't happy about his body hardening at the first glimpse of Cairo. She'd taken everything from him last night, on her first night without her virginity.

He'd taken that from her, he thought darkly, and one of his lifetime rules was never to take a virgin.

She stood at the streambank, the image of a virgin bride, all hot and ready for more, fire flashing in her eyes, her cheeks flushed. Solomon settled lower in the stream, protecting his arousal from her sight. She'd love that—to know that he went hard at the sight of her. To know that a tiny corner of his hardened heart softened just to look at her now.

He closed his eyes, sluicing cold water over his head and trying to forget how sweet and soft and slick and damp and tight she was, holding him with every ounce of her body and wringing emotions from him that he didn't want to yield.

"So. You're back," she began tightly, snapping her parasol closed and standing on the bank with her hands on her waist. "I want to know exactly what you think you are doing, accepting foodstuffs from Blanche," she demanded hotly.

He thought about the basket of food that Blanche had sent. It was the only food in the house, because he'd been too busy building the new room and repairing the barn and corral and playing billiards. "You're on the warpath," he said carefully.

"We're stuck out here with nothing to eat. I kept enough bread for Garnet to eat with jelly, but a child needs regular meals. The pig liked Blanche's pies and her bread. Garnet's cat ate the fried chicken. The kitten hasn't died yet and Quigly has been muttering for hours, sitting and staring at that tiny stove. If you don't get a window in . . . *my* bedroom, my velvet curtains will weather and fade. The cloth came from Chicago."

"Did you milk the cow tonight?" he asked, admiring the proud, uplifting line of her bosom as it rose and fell rapidly in the dying light.

"You will not accept food from that woman. Or anything else. I will not have you shaming me as a woman."

"What did you cook for supper?" he asked, standing up and walking toward her, not shielding his desire.

"Why, you arrogant, narrow-minded— You know I never cook. Quigly always does—" she began, then glanced down at his hardened body. Her eyes widened, then the flush on her cheeks deepened and she blinked, forcing her gaze up to his face.

She was shy of him, and the tender thought looped

around Solomon's heart, snaring him. He stood in front of her. He shoved away his loneliness, his fear that she would look at his scars and find him repulsive. "Come here."

She looked away from him after a curious downward glance that raised his spirits more. "You'll catch cold."

"Warm me."

"How?"

The need to tease her leaped in Solomon, making him feel young and light. "Like you did last night. Clutch me close to your bosom and hug me and stroke me and take me deep inside you where it's warm and tight—"

She paled and took a step backward, bumping against a cottonwood tree. "Oh, sweet heaven . . ."

"Yes, ma'am. That it surely was—sweet heaven," Solomon murmured. "All the way to the top, daisy-girl."

"Shh. Don't talk that way," she whispered urgently, but the softness was in her eyes, warming him. Her gloved hands rested on his damp chest and Solomon bent to taste her parted lips, finding them just as sweet and soft and tender as he remembered. Until she grasped him closely, her mouth open and hot on his—

"I've never had a woman hold me all night as if she was afraid I'd get free," he murmured against her cheek. "Never had a woman latch on to me with teeth and nails and everything else, just as tight as she could."

"Oh, dear God," she whispered unevenly.

He couldn't resist tormenting her. After all, he'd thought of nothing else but her all day long, no matter how hard he tried to pull his mind away. She was sweet and flustered and he kissed the tip of her nose. "If you weren't in this rig, I'd like to get in your drawers right now, just to hear you cry out like a little kitten, or a wild bird coming home to rest—"

"Oh!" She looked at him with wide honey-brown eyes as Solomon eased her bonnet from her head and tossed it to a limb.

He began unbuttoning her bodice, the tiny button-holes tearing in his hands, despite his caution. "These wouldn't tear if you'd stop swatting my hands. Tell me exactly what Bernard was to you," he murmured between kisses. "Because sure as the sun comes up in the morning, I'm your first man and that purely pleasures me. My bride came to me fresh as a daisy."

She arched her throat, the warmth pulsing from her, the feminine perfume tangling erotically in his senses. "You'll catch cold," she repeated as he lifted her dress from her gently and laid it on the ground.

He unknotted her petticoats and helped her step out of them, also laying them on the ground.

"Solomon," she said so quietly that the shimmering cottonwood leaves above them seemed to stop moving. Her gloved fingertip trailed across his back, tracing the deep scars. "What happened to your back?"

"A bullrope, a quirt, a whip. In that order," he answered, tightly, the old pain surging through him momentarily. He turned to her, facing her. "Maybe I owe you an explanation."

"Not if you don't want me to know," she said quietly. "Sometimes there are things too deep to tell, too painful. Whatever is between us now, I don't want anything that does not concern our . . . situation."

Solomon looked at her in the dappled shadows, standing straight and new and shy of him. She had her secrets, too. Bad ones, so deep she didn't want the wind to know. Then she took his scarred wrist in her gloved hands and raised it to her mouth for a kiss. "And this, too, this happened at the same time?"

"Yes." He wondered about her past. Why was the smallest item of Garnet's care, and the child's joy and safety, so important to her?

"I see," she said slowly. Then she looked down at her clothing on the ground. "You know, a lady never stands in her unmentionables where anyone can see her."

He wrapped his fingers around her gloved wrist, unwilling to be distracted. "Tell me about Bernard."

"You have your past. I have mine," she stated.

"I'm sorry I hurt you," he said, meaning it, and found her shy blush enchanting.

"It was a small wounding, a minor skirmish. But remember that I won the war, sir," she murmured, her blush deepening. "It was I who vanquished you."

"You truly did," he conceded tenderly. "You were magnificent. All hot and ladylike and damn near enchanting as Aphrodite sliding down on a moonbeam. I could only surrender to your charms."

She shivered slightly and cleared her throat. "Ah . . . that's a lovely thing to say, Mr. Wolfe."

"It's true enough. You were pure glory, daisy-girl." Solomon looked down slowly to her breasts, lying within the confines of lace, then he bent to kiss her softness, tasting her with his tongue. "Did Quigly massage you today?" he asked, shoving away the image of another man's hands on her, this woman who had been a virgin until he'd taken her.

"Of course not. You might burst in like a—"

"Husband?"

"Madman. Massages are therapeutic, restful— Oh!" she exclaimed when he eased away her corset cover, her corset, then suckled her breasts through her camisole.

"You cannot . . . lust after me in plain daylight," she said shakily, pushing him away.

He reached for and grabbed the knotting of her drawers, circled her waist with one arm, and stripped them from her with the other. Then he kissed her deeply, caressing her tongue with his, as he slowly tore away her camisole.

He held her away, taking in her tousled long hair, the flow of it over her breasts—the small rose-color tips peeking at him—down to her soft stomach and the triangle of light-brown curls. Her thighs were white and soft, shielding feminine muscles, circled by the garters of her hose. He admired the shape of her calves, the strength flowing through her, and her slim ankles. "If you say anything about my feet now, I'll kill you," she stated tightly.

"Take off your gloves," Solomon ordered, uneasy with the desire pushing at him. He'd never wanted another woman like he wanted Cairo now and was desperate to see if what had passed between them in the night was true. The fire hadn't become ashes; it had deepened and softened and whirled around him like magic fairy dust.

His body, already hard, lurched at the sight of her peeling away the long gloves, slowly revealing her fingers. He wanted her to touch him—

With a frustrated cry, Cairo launched herself against him, her breasts warm against his chest, her arms locked around his neck as she kissed him hungrily.

Solomon allowed her to bear him down, then turned to lower her to the earth, on top of her clothing.

He slid into her easily, welcomed by her moist heat wrapping tightly around him. She held him fiercely, her arms locked around his neck and her legs capturing his. She trembled in his arms, arching against his hands cupping her breasts.

They lay very still, locked together, hearts racing, bodies taut and trembling.

Solomon fought the sense of coming home, of being clasped by someone who cared for him. Then he knew, he had longed for this. . . .

"You are absolutely disastrous," Cairo muttered against his ear. "Anyone could see us. That hard backside of yours must be shining in the sun. It's very white, you know."

"So are these. White as a dove's breast, soft and tender and sweet, too," he returned, rubbing his chest against her breasts. He lifted slightly from her and studying her flushed face amid the tangle of her hair.

She stroked a strand of his hair back from his brow. "You've ruined my coiffure. Quigly worked so hard on it. It was his therapy for being uprooted from his precious stove and sewing machine," she whispered with a shy conspirator's smile.

Solomon smoothed her curls against the crushed green silk. "Are you going to conquer me like you did last night?" he asked huskily, then kissed her slowly. "Ambush and devastate me?"

She arched sumptuously against him. "You're a beast, Solomon Wolfe. An animal. Are you in the mood now?" she asked teasingly as she tightened her legs, drawing him deeper. "I've got you. You are my prisoner. I've won. Say it."

Solomon reacted instantly, finding her lips with the hunger that had been humming through him, waiting for the moment to explode.

"Goodness," she whispered later as he lay over her, his face buried in her throat.

While he lay upon her, wondering what had happened, wondering why he had opened himself to her so quickly, so greedily, Cairo stroked his back gently and asked timidly, "Solomon? Are you . . . are you all right?"

He moved within her, still hungry, and she tightened around him, the tiny feminine muscles drawing him deeper until the fever caught them again and Solomon kissed her with the hunger running through him. Her cry sailed through the evening air; she held very still, her expression stunned, when she finally lifted her lids to look up at him. Cairo panted delicately and the movement of her body beneath his pleased him. "I regret that you have been hurt, dear Solomon," she whispered gently, kissing the corners of his mouth.

He stilled, unwilling to let the dark past into this moment, or Cairo into his life. "This hasn't anything to do with that."

She smoothed his beard. "I know. But I regret your pain."

He was uneasy with the tenderness he read in her eyes. "You need a bath, Mrs. Wolfe. Will you allow me?"

Then Solomon eased from her, scooped her into his arms, and walked into the creek. Cairo clung to his neck. "You wouldn't dare—"

She sank beneath the water and came up gasping for air. Solomon sealed her lips with his and sank beneath the water with her, kissing her. Cairo struggled free and stood up, glaring at him, her hair dripping around her pale body as she pushed it back. "You beast! You absolute beast!" she said in a hushed, indignant yell before she pushed his head under the water.

Solomon nudged his head between her legs and nuzzled her intimately before standing with her on his shoulders and walking out of the stream to their clothing. In future loving, he planned to do more than to nuzzle her there in that sweet place. For in his lifetime, he had never done more than to take a woman quickly.

Cairo grabbed a limb, slid agilely from him, then dropped to the ground. She jammed her fists into her waist and glared at him, wet, taut with anger, and glorious, dressed only in her garters and hose. He admired the sight of her until she blushed furiously and he thought how sweet she was.

While he dried quickly with his shirt and then began dressing, her lips moved as if she was trying to speak. Then she muttered, threw up her hands, and began jerking on her clothing. "You'll have to help me with my dress," she stated tautly, slamming it into his chest when he stood dressed in front of her.

"Yes, ma'am," he said, taking in the outline of her nipples beneath the damp cloth. "It would help if next time you came after me, daisy-girl, you didn't wear all that rig."

"Mmmft. . . ." She glared at him when she emerged from the folds of the dress. She quickly smoothed the wrinkled dress as if trying to wipe away what had happened. She paused at a grass stain and glared up at him. "You" was all she said in a dark, condemning tone that said she would like to assault him.

She stood there in the twilight, looking rumpled, frustrated, damp, and ready to throw herself at him at any moment. Then she glanced at the flattened grass where they had made love twice and flushed wildly, beautifully, her hands trembling as she drew on her gloves. She picked up her parasol and opened it despite the dying sun, as if she needed something familiar around her to comfort her.

Solomon bent to kiss her with the tenderness he was feeling, and she leaned slightly against him as he buttoned her dress. His fingers trembled slightly and he cupped her breasts with both hands, pressing her gently. She shook her head wearily against his shoulder. "I can't believe this just happened."

He rocked her against him as she studied her bodice. "You've ripped my buttonholes and loosened my buttons," she exclaimed indignantly. "I thought gunfighters had a certain dexterity."

He kissed her forehead, not wanting to admit how eager he was for her, how shaken he had been by his softening emotions toward her. "I'm new in the husband business."

Cairo sighed tiredly and allowed him to caress her back. She was good and warm and soft against him, and Solomon closed his eyes, keeping that tenderness within him. "Well," Cairo said after a few moments. She stepped away from him, then pointed her parasol at his chest. "You will not accept foodstuffs or anything else from *that* woman. Or any other woman while you're in my—"

He grinned at her and wondered at the boy lurking inside him, ready to torment her. "Too late. Mrs. Johansen sent a pail of her chicken and dumplings and her best apple dumplings. She sent her regards to my bride and said she'd be over to help you as soon as the crops were laid in. The quilting circle would like you to join them on Tuesday."

Cairo stared at him. "What?"

Solomon shrugged, enjoying her black look. "Seems like they think that now since you're a proper farmwife, maybe you might just be up to their standards."

"You know what this means, don't you? As your . . . your—"

"Wife? Bride?" Solomon enjoyed the quick leap of anger in Cairo's expression.

She threw out her hand in a careless gesture. "Whatever. I am obligated to return the favor by cooking something for her family. I do not relish indulging in chitchat about how to bake an egg, Mr. Wolfe. Oh, I know the housewife protocol, but I do not relish being enlisted by you."

He lifted an eyebrow, waiting for her to continue. Cairo glared at him, sniffed, then began picking her way around the old bull's dung to the house, her parasol aloft like a battle flag. She turned once, opened her mouth, then closed it. She closed her eyes as if wishing away a nightmare and shook her head.

eleven

One by one, Kipp slowly released his fingers from his new, rosewood pistol butt. He stood, legs spread wide, waiting. He'd come to see if Cairo needed him and discovered her leaning against Solomon in the shadows of the cottonwoods. It was a tender, intimate embrace, the softness of the woman leaning against her lover—the cords around Kipp's heart drew painfully tight. Solomon held Cairo against the protection of his body and a new shaft of pain shot through Kipp.

If only Solomon had treated her differently, just one wrong move, and Kipp would have ridden down on him.

Kipp swallowed tightly, noting that as she walked away, Cairo held her bodice buttons. His heart tightened painfully. "My daisy in the dawn," he muttered mockingly, his body rigid.

He was old suddenly, empty inside, as he was before Cairo and her fancy manners snared him.

What good was it—any of it? He'd tried so hard, to read poetry, to read about high society in the newspapers—so that he could talk about Cairo's magical world, one she longed for and one Solomon Wolfe had snatched from her. Cairo was the first friend he'd had in his life, the first woman to make him want to make something of himself. She brightened his life and hurled away the bitter past, a lifetime of living with his mother, Duncan, and Edward.

Kipp's stomach rolled unsteadily, his body cold in the summer night. He'd seen himself as Cairo's white knight, sweeping her away from the hardships of working in the billiard parlor. He'd planned to take care of her, to see the sights of New York at her side.

He reached into his saddlebag and jerked out a book on ballroom dance, tearing away the pages and grinding them into the Montana dirt. "*Language of the Fan*," he muttered, tearing up another small book.

Solomon had raked away Kipp's dream. In another two months, Kipp and the gang would have had enough money to— His gloved hand gripped his saddle horn, and the slight evening breeze turned the trampled pages of his dreams like dying birds, fluttering in the dim light.

The old windmill turned slowly in the evening breeze and the moonlight spread over the smooth prairie night.

Just then the door of the house opened and Garnet burst out, running to hug Cairo. Cairo's laughter rippled along the breeze and Garnet took her parasol, twirling it and swinging her slight hips. Then Cairo bent to hug the girl and they ran to an open window in the new section of the house. Cairo stepped up onto stacked lumber, then eased into the house. The child followed.

Quigly's massive body stood outlined in the door and he scratched his head.

"Games," Kipp muttered. In the Knutson house, the games were deadly and painful. Each barb carefully placed; plots to hurt and twist ran through the house like venomous snakes.

He listened to the steady sound of boots hitting the fresh earth, to the approach of a man heavier than himself, one who purposefully made noise. "Who's there?" Kipp asked into the night, spotting a man leading a horse toward him.

"Son." Solomon's greeting was soft and certain.

"Pilgrim, don't call me that," Kipp returned just as softly, resting his hand on his gun butt. No one had ever called him "son" as if he were tied to them, as if a deep bond lay between them. He fought the pain surging through him. "I could kill you now and no one would know."

"You could. I won't stop you."

"I could protect Cairo, now that you've ruined her— taken her down to this shack. And the kid, too." The angry cords humming through Kipp demanded that he fight this man who had everything he had wanted.

Solomon's hat shielded his face, the moonlight lying along his wide shoulders. "You're welcome to stay for dinner."

"You think I'd eat at your table, old man?" Kipp demanded tautly. "After you took my woman? You took away her protection. When she was alone, men respected her as a lady. Sometimes widows don't fare as well."

"I'll take care of her. Tell me about you."

"I'm Kipp Knutson. They've been calling me 'Kid' since I was fifteen. I want to know about you and my mother—what happened between you? Why does she want Cairo taken care of—"

"What do you mean?" Solomon demanded in a fierce taut way, echoing Kipp's fear for Cairo's safety.

"I'm taking Cairo away from here. Before Mother sets Duncan and Edward on her. She's goading them now."

"Tell me about you," Solomon repeated softly. "And your mother, and Duncan and Edward."

"It's Cairo I'm worried about. You think about her. I've always taken care of myself, just like I can take care of Cairo and the kid."

Kipp slowly drew his gun and leveled it at Solomon's heart. "Old man, say your prayers."

When Solomon didn't move, Kipp lifted the gun to Solomon's forehead. "I'm going to blow the top of your head off."

Solomon didn't flinch; there was no fear leaping in his eyes, only a soft regret. Kipp's stomach clenched. "I've been down that gun trail, son. It's a cold one. You get old quick. But I'm not stopping you."

"I haven't killed anyone, just nicked a few. Because I'm that good. Quick," Kipp stated tautly. "An old shootist like you isn't much, but taking you could add to my rep."

"I'll protect Cairo," Solomon said softly. "But two men would be better."

"What do you mean?"

"Cairo needs us. Duncan won't do his dirty work alone."

A sudden icy wind swept through Kipp; Solomon was right. Duncan's tentacles slid to men who would butcher Cairo, then sleep well. "I'll kill him now and remove the problem. Or I'll take Cairo with me, while you're rotting out here under the stars. What is my mother to you?" Kipp demanded rawly, sliding his gun abruptly into his holster.

"She'll tell you when she's ready. Come to supper.

Cairo will want to talk with you," Solomon offered gently.

Kipp thought of Cairo waiting for Solomon, and a sense of hot lead pouring into his raw, gaping wound caused him to leap into the saddle and race away. Solomon had a family waiting for him, while he had nothing.

At the small knoll, Kipp reined his horse to a full stop, glancing back at Solomon, who hadn't moved in the moonlight.

A strange bond ran between Solomon and himself that he did not understand. When Solomon's quiet gaze held Kipp's, there was a loneliness that reached into the youth. No one had ever looked at Kipp in that way— with softness and pride—no one except Cairo.

Buffeted by his emotions, Kipp reared his horse and shot into the stars; he had to put a bullet somewhere.

Solomon's answering shot into the night surprised Kipp, who shot again.

As much as he hated Solomon, Cairo needed them both.

And the kid, Kipp added reluctantly, racing his horse into the night. The kid liked him and loved Solomon. "Pretty hard to kill a pilgrim when his kid loves him. Maybe I'll let him live awhile longer," Kipp muttered, riding toward his gang's hideout, where he intended to drink until nothing mattered.

Solomon watched his son ride through the moonlight. Kipp was too rash, too quick-tempered and unseasoned to live long as a shootist. Years ago, Solomon had faced an angry youth who threatened him with a gun. He'd reacted immediately, bringing down his gun butt on the boy's head. The small gash was better than the loss of the youth's life. Solomon could have easily done the same to Kipp, but he wouldn't. There had been enough pain and distance in their lives; he would not hurt his son.

His son. He'd seen other men with their sons and daughters and had thought the time was past for him. To discover he had a son was "pure gold," Solomon found himself saying. "Because making a child is the best thing a man can do in this life."

Tender emotions stirred within Solomon, soon pushed away by fierce pride; Kipp was his blood, his child, a part of his parents and Fancy and Garnet. There was a line that would go on, blending the past with the future.

Kipp deserved a home and a family, someone to give him warmth and comfort. "Take care, son," Solomon murmured to the night wind.

Quigly pushed the chicken and dumplings around on the elegant china plate decorated in gold. He lifted the expensive wineglass to the lamplight and studied it with a lost, soulful look. "No fresh parsley. No oven," he mourned finally with a sigh. "Just a tiny little woodstove. No hot water reservoir. No warming ovens. No crêpes. No chocolate-dipped strawberries."

Cairo patted her lips with her Irish linen napkin, then placed it over her lap. She sat very straight on her cherrywood chair and nodded encouragingly to Garnet, who was miming her ladylike manners.

Quigly rose to his full height, placed a delicate tea towel across his forearm, and removed the plates with all the warmth of a frozen stone. "Apple . . . dumplings. Warmed in a black skillet and served with bovine cream," he announced elegantly, placing a china dessert bowl in front of each person. He sat heavily, stared at the dumpling in his plate and muttered, "Baklava. Delicate layers of pastry. French pastry . . ."

Cairo struggled to present a proper dinner conversation. She removed her slipper from Solomon's encroaching boot toe. He enjoyed teasing her and his dark quiet looks stirred her unsettled emotions. Sitting near the man who had just made love to her so heatedly presented problems. For one thing, she wanted to curl upon his lap and bring his head to her bosom and hold him close. She flushed and choked on a small bit of cinnamon-flavored apple when she remembered how he had spread her out and—she shivered, straightened her shoulders, and asked unevenly, "Ah . . . just what are you intending to do for a livelihood, Solomon? I mean . . . are you planning to work for other people, or develop a cattle ranch? Surely there can't be much money in laboring?"

"Sheep. Merino," he said, holding Garnet's small hand on the table. "I've been a cattle rep before—checking for brands for several spreads and returning them to their rightful owners. But that would take me away from home for weeks, and Garnet might miss me. She needs me to tuck her in every night, so she can sprinkle me with fairy dust." He bent to kiss the girl's cheek, then lifted a mocking eyebrow at Cairo.

"There's nothing wrong with fairy tales," Cairo informed him primly. Because now he knew that she'd been telling the girl fairy tales. Garnet needed a bit of golden fluff in her life, a bit of what Cairo had missed. "Or dreams. Everyone has them."

"I got me a dream." Garnet grinned widely, looking at Solomon then at Cairo.

Cairo knew Garnet's waiting-to-pop look. At any moment, she'd spew a ma-and-pa anecdote or gutter language involving sex. The child had absorbed the

Barbary's worst scenes, from abortions to sex orgies. An unlikely encyclopedia of colorful stories about pimps and prostitutes, Garnet had peered through keyholes and knotholes at every chance.

"Do not talk about what we said not to talk about," Cairo ordered her tightly. Elated by Solomon's tired look, which she supposed came from working hard to make "our baby," Garnet had not stopped talking about a baby all day.

"Sheep?" Cairo repeated cautiously, turning the conversation away from Garnet's grasp.

"Or cattle. But probably grain, later on. Flour mills are coming to the country soon," Solomon stated. He studied their wedding picture, which the photographer had sent by way of a passing cowboy. In an ornate gilt frame on a huge cherry buffet with claw feet, Cairo looked dazed and Solomon looked unreadable. "The house looks homey."

"That's because my furniture belongs in an elegant apartment. Of course, it's not there, is it? It's here and some of it is stacked in a corner," Cairo said flatly, staring at him. "Grain. Sowing, plowing, threshing in August heat—grain?"

Solomon met her gaze evenly. "I have to learn the trade. It will take some time. Meanwhile, I know cattle and I can hire out."

"Grain. One hailstorm could wipe you out," she stated flatly. "There's mold and weather and fire. What makes you think you could make a living as a farmer?" she demanded. Then she carefully asked the question that had been swirling through her mind. "Solomon, do you really intend to work as a common laborer? A hired man?"

"I don't have enough sheep or enough cattle. Hiring out this year makes sense. I'm breaking ground and sowing winter wheat in August. The grain men said they'd help me get started next year." Then he nodded curtly. "Everyone has dreams, isn't that what you said?"

"Madame, we have more than enough dirty laundry to send to Ah Ling's laundry. Do you want me to take it into town?"

Cairo breathed very quietly, remembering the slight pain and the heaviness of Solomon's body filling her, locking his body with hers. The stains on the sheet would cause the entire town to gossip. "I'm certain we can wash the sheets here. Just this once," she murmured.

She flushed and regretted her tumbling emotions. She regretted her fascination with a tough gunslinger turned hired laborer and potential grain farmer. If anyone in New York society discovered that her ex-husband had been a common laborer, she'd be doomed.

She ached in tiny feminine muscles and had decided that Solomon would not have her again, not until her thoughts were clear.

Right now two thoughts warred for top billing.

She had married a common laborer, while Sarah Bernhardt held magnificent engagement parties and built Italian villas and waltzed through entire nights. Then Cairo thought about her own approaching night and sleeping arrangements.

She eyed Solomon as he sipped his coffee and talked with Garnet about her day. Garnet was especially proud of helping Cairo frame the wedding picture and choosing a proper place for it. Cairo decided that at the first opportunity, she would have Garnet's picture taken with her. She wanted to leave the girl something of her second "ma," because she herself had nothing but a locket from her own mother.

Garnet longed for a home, for a family, and Cairo knew those emotions.

While she had had Bernard, Garnet had Solomon, who didn't show affection. He was affectionate last night, almost tender. At the stream, Solomon had been playful.

Cairo frowned at her untouched apple dumpling. She craved a really good fight with him. A no-holds-barred, out-and-out, see-who's-best, low-down dirty fight.

She bit her lip slightly and inhaled. Every part of her was sensitive now, swollen, aching, and tender after his lovemaking.

She remembered her teeth almost biting his shoulder, while he moved within her, so deep and full that she thought there could be no more . . . and yet there was.

He had reeled her into his arms last night, challenged her champion instincts, and managed to make her ache for him.

Cairo inhaled sharply. Solomon's playful, boyish streak reminded her of someone else.

She studied the lines of his face. Despite his long day, he seemed younger, less hard, and when he turned slowly to her, the dark warmth in his eyes shocked her. She rested her hand on the racing pulse in her throat and pushed back her chair. The knockout drops she had placed in Solomon's coffee would take exactly forty-five minutes to work. She had picked her special slow-acting flask, tucking it beneath the flounces on her wrist. "I believe I'll take my bath now, Quigly," she stated unevenly and stood. "Would you heat the water, please?"

Garnet looked at her sharply, leaped to her feet, and hugged Cairo's waist, burying her head on her stomach. "Don't, Ma. You'll hurt our baby. I once knew a woman who took a bath and lost her baby. They did that so's not to make a mess."

Cairo stiffened, stroking Garnet's neat black braids. She wanted to reassure the child, to ease her troubled past, but Solomon watched her in his quiet, assessing way. She blushed and trembled and swallowed repeatedly.

Then Quigly stood elegantly, cleared his throat, and said, "It's very late. But if you wish, I shall begin heating water."

"Ma?" Garnet pressed urgently, her expression worried as she smoothed Cairo's stomach.

"Ma has just had her bath, Garnet. Down at the stream," Solomon said slowly as he took Garnet's hand to draw her to his knee.

"Very well. If I am not needed, I shall say good night." Quigly nodded and closed the door behind him.

Solomon chuckled and caught Cairo's hand, drawing her down on his other knee. "Come here, you."

She sat very straight, aware of his large hand caressing her waist, of his hard thigh beneath the folds of her clean skirt and petticoats.

Quigly burst into the room, carrying her torn and stained clothing that she had worn earlier; she had hidden them from him. "I found these just outside the window—grass stains all over everything, straw and dirt and mud, and rips from one seam, a button is missing."

He threw the clothing into her padded rocker with claw feet. He looked at the rafters, as if asking for divine guidance, then shook his head. He muttered in a martyr's tone, "For this I worked night and day, pricked my fingers with pins," and stepped into the night.

"Ma had a bath—Do you think she's still got our baby?" Garnet asked brightly.

"Making a baby is pretty important work. If we get a baby, Cairo will keep him safe." Solomon gathered them both closer, and Cairo realized that she had never sat on a man's lap before or been cuddled.

"Important work," she repeated in a daze. Solomon's dark eyes met hers and she felt the fierce longing to have him locked in her deepest being. She blinked and swallowed, fighting the memory of Solomon's hard fullness erupting within her. She considered the thought while Garnet chatted about her day with Solomon. He bounced his knee occasionally and continued stroking Cairo's waist.

"Cairo is a strong, smart woman," he was telling Garnet. "Men and women don't always make babies. But if there is one, Cairo will know how to take care of it. Just like she takes good care of you."

Garnet stroked his beard sympathetically. "Pa, there's things that can help you if you can't do the job."

"I sincerely thank you for that advice, Garnet," Solomon returned in a serious tone, but Cairo disliked the humor leaping to his eyes and lips.

Garnet studied Cairo, who was trying desperately to suggest an alternative to the conversation. "There's things for you, too, Ma. Like teas. Course, most of the teas used on the Barbary were to get rid of babies and we want ours, don't we?"

"Weren't the apple dumplings lovely?" Cairo managed finally.

Garnet yawned. "I'm sleepy. Gotta go tell Quig his bedtime story. Told him about life on the Barbary last night. About how I helped shanghai drunks for ships. Tonight I'll tell him about the pimps, 'cause I like to see him shiver. It's like a whole mountain moving in little tiny jiggles," she said as she slid off Solomon's lap and kissed him. "Night, Pa. You look different tonight. Kinda—" She tipped her head, studying Solomon.

"Tired in a good way. Ma won't mind if you don't try to make a baby tonight," she said after a yawn.

Cairo bent to receive Garnet's kiss. When the door closed behind the girl, Solomon lifted Cairo into his arms, carried her to the bed, and tossed her onto it.

She leaped off the other side, her hand to her throat while Solomon quickly stripped away his clothing. "Not again," she said firmly as he walked toward her.

"You're shy, Cairo Wolfe," he murmured, touching her hair which she had left down. "Shy and sweet and soft. Just like a bride."

"I am mad, that's what I am," she began as he backed her against the wall and placed his hands on either side of her. "You can't maul me when you feel like it. And any honest man would sleep in a nightshirt."

He nuzzled the side of her throat, kissing her. "You taste sweet and new. Like a daisy smells at sunrise. Why did you save yourself?"

She angled her throat away from his lips and found his hands at the buttons on her back, loosening the fragile pearls that Garnet had fastened. "Don't you dare tear this dress. Quigly spent hours, weeks on it," she ordered huskily. She wondered how Solomon would look, standing in nothing but his boyish grin and fairy dust. "Ah . . . aren't you tired?"

"A little. I'm improving. Haven't undressed a woman before you," he murmured against her cheek as his fingers moved down her back.

While she mulled over that distracting thought, Solomon drew her arms from the sleeves, unknotted her petticoats, and eased her out of the dress. "Well . . . ah . . . you mean you . . . ah . . . just . . . do it with their clothes on?"

He chuckled and the rich sound curled around her. "That or they take off their clothes."

"How many times have you . . . ah . . ." she began, curious to know more about this man who fascinated her, who ran his trembling hands down her body and cupped her breasts. She hoped he would be awake long enough to answer her.

She gripped his shoulders with her fingertips when he began brushing kisses across her cheeks, tantalizing her lips, demanding and urging her to respond. He'd fall asleep at any minute, and then she would have the night to rest. Solomon yawned, the movement brushing his hard chest against her. "It was so long ago that until last night, I thought maybe I'd forgotten how."

Solomon looped his arms around her and began to ease backward to the bed. He lay down with her on top of him. With their fingers intertwined, palm to palm, he rested beneath her. A thrill shot through Cairo; she had him in her clutches again. Victory was close. She'd make him pay . . . drive him into the ground and make him admit that she could best him.

"I wonder how long it will be before you stop blushing," he said tenderly, nibbling at her lips. "You're warm all over, Mrs. Wolfe," he noted huskily.

His dark gaze flickered down her body and she shivered. "Are you going to terrorize me again? Run me down and have me?"

"What do you mean?" She was thinking how best to vanquish him.

"Why don't you show me?" he invited softly as her eyes grew heavy and she yawned.

She couldn't take advantage of a sleeping man.

She wanted a battle, one in which she would reign as the absolute champion.

She yawned again, then settled her head down beside Solomon's on the pillow. She held her prize; he wouldn't get away from her without admitting she had bested him. Before he fell into a deep sleep, she'd make him admit that she had gotten him well and good. "You'll be asleep at any minute. The knockout drops I gave you are very effective."

"I know," she heard him say as his hand found her breast. Then she snuggled her face to Solomon's warm neck and hovered near sleep.

"Thank you," she heard herself whisper. "Now that my maidenhead is no longer a problem, I can have lovers in New York and be elegantly gay . . . and . . . and . . . don't . . . curse, Mr. Wolfe. . . . Garnet . . . is . . . progressing nicely. . . ."

"Solomon Wolfe!" Cairo shouted angrily at midmorning. The double doors to the bedroom crashed open.

Quigly stopped polishing his huge, ornate black stove with warming ovens and massive hot water reservoir. "Thank you for journeying into town this morning to retrieve my beloved stove, sir. However, now I must tell you that you are in for an unpleasant experience," he murmured.

"Thanks," Solomon murmured.

Cairo stood in the opened doors, her black robe with dragons shining in the sunlight. She covered her eyes against the bright light, then slowly lifted her fingers to glare at Solomon. Her frown turned to the butler. "Quigleee!"

The tall butler swallowed, blinked, and his white glove trembled as he reached for an elegant coffeepot. He poured the freshly made brew into a warmed china pot and placed it on the table.

Then he looked at Solomon and raised his eyes to the rafters. "Thank goodness the child is outside playing and won't see this. They pass it on, you know. From woman to girl."

Solomon leaned back against the wall and Cairo's eyes cut to him. "You," she said darkly, in a tone that said she wanted to destroy him.

Instead she reached down to her thigh, ripped a small knife from its sheath, and threw it. The blade struck the wood next to Solomon's head. "You," she said, walking toward him, her robe sweeping behind her.

Quigly's seven-feet height and broad shoulders seemed to grow smaller as he whispered to Solomon. "I had hoped your recent marriage might have changed the schedule of her indisposition. I fear it has not. In another week to the day, the war will end and she'll have one miserable day at the onset."

Solomon nodded, watching her. "Thanks. From what I hear they can be contrary."

"Contrary isn't the word. Try fire-breathing, dragonlike. Toss in warlike and the need to torture."

"Exactly what are you whispering about, Quigly?" Cairo demanded as she advanced on the two men, glancing at the stove in passing. She noted the boxes of elegant cookware and foodstuffs. Quigly's precious herb starts seemed to quiver as she passed. "My, but haven't the two of you been busy this morning," she stated in a dark tone. "Moving stoves like little fairies, scurrying around to have everything tiptop."

Solomon crossed his arms and enjoyed the wild flush sweeping up Cairo's throat to her cheeks. "She's pretty as a daisy."

She pushed back a heavy swath of disheveled curls,

grabbed a kitchen knife from the side table, and hurled it at the other side of his head. "Stop that daisy-talk." Then she hurled another knife at him; the blade sank into the wood at his shoulder.

"Good shot," he said, enjoying the way the sunlight caught the shimmering softness beneath her robe.

She placed her hands on her hips, tightening the material over her breasts, and glared up at him. "Well? What do you have to say for yourself?" she demanded.

"You look good enough to take back to bed," he said honestly. "Primed."

She pivoted, throwing out her hands in a gesture of frustration. Quigly grabbed a copper pot from her reach. "Not that one. I've just polished it."

"A wife usually kisses her husband in the morning," Solomon offered. A fourth knife thrown by Cairo could hit some vital spot on his body. From the look of her, she was just getting warmed up.

"Ha!" she threw at him, gathering her sash around her.

Solomon leaned against the wall and studied his wife's elegant backside as she flounced back into the bedroom and slammed the doors.

"Living with women is not the easiest thing in the world," Quigly stated sagely. "I find it best to hide during this time."

The doors crashed open again and Cairo leveled her dueling pistol at Solomon. "I know how to shoot this," she began in a low tone. "Quigly, he gave me knockout drops and I have no idea what happened to my person. It was a low, dirty trick that only a no-good, low-down coward would use."

"You're scaring me," Solomon murmured, walking toward her.

"I'll blow your black heart out. Any fiend who would use knockout drops on a woman is lower than low, dirtier than dirt, and needs—" She glanced over his shoulder to Quigly, who was watching with interest. "Uh. Solomon, step into the bedroom please. Quigly?"

"Just leaving to check on the young mistress. She's been too quiet, and that always means one more adventure," he said in a hopeless tone. "Perhaps you should not have slipped him the knockout drops. He appears to have experience in dealing with that matter."

"Quigly. Out. Now," Cairo said too quietly.

"I'm off to plant my new herb garden," Quigly announced, sending Solomon a sympathetic look. "I'll make certain we have a good stock of chamomile."

Cairo pointed the pistol at Solomon's chest, then motioned him into the bedroom. She carefully placed the dueling pistol back into the velvet case, then closed the door. "Only a villain would use knockout drops to have his way with a lady."

"Was it fair for you to use knockout drops on me?" he asked cautiously.

"Of course. You're devious. You're stronger. And you seem . . . insatiable for the marriage act. I have decided to reclaim my person and to set the game rules."

"Where did you learn to throw knives like that?" Solomon asked, admiring the proud lift of her head.

"Every lady acquires certain defenses," Cairo returned.

"What made you think I had you last night?" he asked, intrigued by her started look and then her flush.

"Well . . . I . . . assumed."

"You assumed wrong. You had me in bed and you—"

Cairo's hand went to her throat. "You will not tell me that I . . . that I . . ."

"A man gets tired and used up if his bride keeps taking

him. But if that's what I have to do to keep you happy, then I will try to live up to the job. Seems like a hard way to start the day though. You still have the cow to milk," Solomon said, unstrapping his gun belt and placing it on a small, elegant table by the bed. Then he gripped the robe's sash in one hand and pulled her to him. "You talk too much."

"You're not getting away with this," she said as they tumbled into bed, rolled across it, and landed on the floor in a tangle of blankets.

"Off," she ordered, breathing hard beneath him.

"Make me," he invited, watching the sudden awareness leap in her eyes. It matched the fire surging through him, the need to press himself deep into that hot tight core of her, to take her softness and hear her cry out for him.

He'd never needed anyone. But with the bright morning light catching in the tangle of her hair, the sudden shyness of her half-closed lids, and the rise of her breasts, he needed—

Solomon brushed his lips against hers and inhaled her feminine scent; he swept his open mouth to throat, just over her rapidly beating pulse. He had to be inside her, to the heat, to the softness where she clasped him.

Cairo met his kiss fiercely, holding his face in her palms, driving her tongue into his mouth.

He tore at his trousers, freeing himself, spilling against her, already heavy. She cried out when he entered her, a high sigh that held him still as she lay very still. He breathed hard, aware of the softness beneath him, the long, soft thighs quivering along his. She pressed against him delicately and whispered, "Solomon?"

He watched her rosy nipple shimmer in the morning sun, the slight pulse causing her breast to quiver. Then nothing could have stopped him from bending to kiss it, to open his mouth and to tug the sweet taste into his mouth. He cupped her other breast, caressed and drew from it until the rosy tip stood upright and begged for more.

Cairo tightened around him instantly; her sigh trembled in the close air filled with her scent. "Deeper," she ordered huskily, wrapping her legs around him. "Deeper, Solomon."

He breathed heavily, watching her parted, swollen lips, the delicate flick of her tongue over them. Her heart raced against his and he feared that they were forging deeper bonds than this raging heat. Then Solomon let his body take her quickly.

Later Cairo stroked his back, tracing the scars through his shirt, and Solomon breathed heavily, his heart racing as if it would explode.

She moved restlessly beneath him, and Solomon wondered when a woman had needed him.

He had to keep her from getting inside him.

He had to bar her from his senses, from the drive to take her again. He wanted to feel no tenderness for this woman. He wanted no ties, no guilt when it was time for her to go.

Solomon inhaled her perfume, the scent lying along her throat, and noted the fine perspiration on her forehead. "Don't make more of this than it is," he said roughly.

She turned her head to look at him, her light-brown eyes still dark with the flame of their passion. "Of course not. Why would I?"

"To get to me," he stated roughly. "To bargain."

"Maybe I'll rip your heart from you and feed it to you

on a platter," she returned tightly after a heartbeat, and he knew he'd hurt her. "You drool when I take off my gloves."

She lay there beneath him, her body locked to his, and challenged him with queenly dignity. He remembered women with hard eyes and automatic movements; he thought of staged sounds in beds that had welcomed other men. He studied Cairo with her hair spread out around her, the sunlight catching sparks in it. Her soft, drowsy look that reminded him of Aphrodite sliding down on a moonbeam. Just for him. "You do not know how to win this game, Mrs. Wolfe," he whispered unevenly.

"I'm certain it's a skill that can be learned, Mr. Wolfe." Cairo's hands smoothed his shoulders as she bit his lip lightly. "I've always liked a good challenge."

twelve

Cairo reached into the basket Quigly held and pinched a bean seed between her gloved thumb and finger. She dropped the seed into the furrow, then pushed dirt over it with her foot. She adjusted her parasol against the midmorning sun and trampled the seed, just as Solomon had stomped on her New York dreams. She didn't want to feel tenderness toward him, to ache for the scars on his back. She didn't want to tighten deep inside when she thought of him lodged within her, nudging her into blazing hunger. She didn't want her heart to flip-flop when he called her "Daisy-girl."

The time she had spent memorizing "One Hundred Selected Toasts" and her research on how to interview a successful parlor pianist was wasted.

She dropped another seed into the ground and stomped on it. If only Solomon hadn't acted astonished when he tried on his new clothes. If only he hadn't seemed suddenly shy. She knew instantly then that he'd never had gifts and was uncertain how to say thank-you.

If only she hadn't put him out of his misery, when she should have tortured him. She should have let him simmer in his own juices, looking helplessly boyish and uncertain. "Good Lord. All I did was to choose him new clothes. I can't have him running around in rags," she muttered.

"I beg your pardon, madame?" Quigly asked in his cool tone.

"I want my replacement today. This instant," Cairo stated firmly, and ground her heel into the last seed she had planted.

Adele Cobb stepped from the steamer and surveyed the western town. At twenty-five, she was past her prime and eager to grab a husband. If a farmer's wife wanted a "replacement," Adele had no problems filling the position. She longed for a good sturdy life, for a home and a man to call her own. She pushed away her fear and adjusted her bonnet against the late-day sun. Now was no time to falter. Sitting Bull had surrendered today—July 19, 1881; she would not. She intended to grasp her opportunity in both fists.

She glanced uneasily at the two other women who had just left the steamer and were standing surveying Front Street. She was a practical woman who had spent her life tending her minister father. The rancher would be getting an educated, self-sufficient, hardworking, God-fearing Episcopal wife. She noted the town's Episcopal church; Mr. Wolfe would find himself seated in the front row every Sunday, and she would govern the church with a tight rein, just as she had her father's. The congregation would be led down a righteous path, just as Mr. Wolfe would be.

Two hours later, she sat sipping tea with the current

Mrs. Wolfe. She answered questions concisely and waited for her first sight of her potential new husband. Adele saw immediately that Cairo Wolfe was unsuitable for farm life, dressed in her silken day dress and doing little while her manservant served tea and prepared dinner. Cairo was not the name of a God-fearing, Episcopal rancher's wife; Adele promised herself that Mr. Wolfe would become Episcopal as soon as possible.

"Do you like children?" Cairo asked.

"Adore them," Adele lied, and smiled briefly at Garnet who had been banished from the interview and the house. Unwilling to leave the field, she sulked and scowled through the window. "A good switch on the bottom never hurt, or being sent to bed without dinner. Soap in the mouth for foul language."

Cairo's lips tightened, her fierce frown temporarily shocking Adele. "You can teach Garnet how to read and write then, and do her sums?"

"Of course, and spank her hands with a ruler when she is remiss. And I can mend and cook and garden and tend the stock very well. Mr. Wolfe's ranch will prosper under my care—" She glanced up as a sharp rap sounded on the door.

Quigly opened the door to find two ladies. They introduced themselves as wife applicants. He apologized for not collecting them and was assured that the matter was not bothersome.

Adele eyed the two other women, her competitors for the hand of Mr. Wolfe. She pressed her lips together as the women reintroduced themselves, Maureen from St. Louis and Della from Iowa. Adele thought they looked much too soft, probably church backsliders or, at the worst, Methodists.

Quigly seated the women and added tea servings.

Adele noted that Cairo seemed very pleased with the bridal selection. They were poor specimens. Adele refused to enter into their inane chatter. "A nervous, high-strung woman will not do as a good Episcopalian wife," she stated firmly.

"I am certain that I can make him happy," Della said. "A man's needs are not met by the church alone," she added with a meaningful lift of her eyebrows.

Maureen giggled. "Yes. I agree. There's a tidy, well-managed household and food on the table."

Della eyed her. "Really?" she asked in a taunt. "You don't think a man needs to come home to a warm bed?"

Adele breathed tightly. No doubt Della referred to the animal needs of men. "A man must be led in the right direction. He must be *told* what is good for him. I suppose along the way, they must be allowed a quick dollop of animal needs."

Cairo sipped her tea and smiled sweetly. "I believe Solomon would appreciate being told about such things. Oh, really, I do, Adele."

Adele preened slightly. The current Mrs. Wolfe did have a small amount of good sense.

Cairo smirked when her husband opened the door. "Hello, dear. We've been waiting for you. Quigly will have dinner ready in a moment. We've all been chatting about your needs."

Adele's heart quickened. The man was dirty, shaggy, and looked dangerous. He looked like he needed care and a good home. She sucked in her breath and pressed her hand to the stay that was knifing her breast. Mr. Wolfe was uncommonly appealing in a rugged fashion. She ached to rip off his clothing and touch those broad, Adonis-like shoulders. She closed her eyes briefly against the waves of heat smashing against her. Her fingertips toyed with her bodice, then stilled; once Mr. Wolfe was in her possession, she would draw his shaggy head down to her bare bosom and let him suckle her. Then she stealthily glanced at the other women who were wide-eyed, flushed, and licking their lips.

"Lawsy!" Della's tone dripped with hunger.

"Oh, my, yes. Yes! Yes! He'll do!" Maureen added when she could breathe.

The child attached to his leg glared at the women, and Solomon placed his hand on the girl's head, shaking her gently. His gaze found and latched onto his wife.

Adele perceived that something hot and tangible throbbed in the air between Mr. and the current Mrs. Wolfe. Adele decided that Mr. Wolfe was not happy about his ill-run home. Cairo shivered and flushed. "This is Solomon. Solomon, meet Adele Cobb. She came all the way from Kansas just to meet you. Then this is Maureen and Della. They are spending the night with us . . . in our bedroom. Oh, dear. You'll have to sleep in the barn, I'm afraid," she informed him lightly with a cat-and-cream smile.

"Charmed," he murmured, glancing at Cairo, who sat very straight.

Throughout supper, the women commented on favorite recipes and how mended clothes saved money and how children should be raised. Garnet clung to Solomon, clearly defending her territory. Adele noted with distaste that he coddled the child and kissed her cheek. After they were married, Adele would send the child to bed at sunset, so the hateful brat wouldn't interrupt dinner. She inhaled again sharply as she noted the muscles in Solomon's upper arm flexing; Adele wondered if she could nip him there as they frolicked in bed.

* * *

Cairo enjoyed Solomon's obvious discomfort, but Adele would not do as her replacement. The woman's attitude toward children was unloving. Maureen twittered and Della was slovenly. Cairo left Solomon in their care after supper and lay on the hay with her skirt pulled up behind her, her arms crossed behind her head. She refused to open her eyes as she caught Solomon's scent. He lay down in the hay beside her. When he didn't speak, she rolled on her side to look at him. "Well? Which one?" she demanded, noting Maureen's heavy perfume. "And where are Garnet and Quigly?"

"Garnet is doing her worst and so is Quigly. I left that lace battlefield when Adele tried to force me into the bedroom."

Cairo sat upright. "She didn't! She's leaving in the morning. None of them is suitable, Solomon."

Solomon must not have known her indignation, because he added thoughtfully, "Della seems—"

"Fat and slovenly. She'd let Garnet run wild."

Solomon turned his head to her and lifted his eyebrow. "They all talk too much. Sounds like clucking. They're soft and rounded like hens."

A tingle shot through Cairo; he'd left the women and come to her. Solomon stretched and closed his eyes. She edged closer and stroked back the strand of hair crossing his brow. He looked so tired. "They're not so bad. You need a bath," she whispered, fighting the protective tenderness blooming within her.

Half an hour later she sat on a blanket by the stream while Solomon bathed. When he stepped from the water and dried himself with his clothes, Cairo looked up at the full moon. "I'll try to see that the next applicant doesn't talk very much," she informed him.

She really disliked making Solomon uncomfortable after a hard day's work, especially since Garnet depended on him for reassurance. She glanced down at the shredded grass in her hands. Once she found a suitable wife for Solomon, she'd be free and waltzing in New York.

Then Solomon was easing her to her back, lying over her and finding her mouth with his.

She hated him for his tenderness, detested him for his quiet need of her, tangling her with emotions she didn't want to feel. "You are not what I want," she whispered shakily as he nuzzled her throat and his hand found her breast.

"You're hot and wet," he said simply when she was eager for him.

"Not here," she managed as he eased up her skirts.

Then Solomon was kissing her hungrily and she clung to him, complete only when he lay deep inside her. "Villain," she whispered, arching against him hungrily.

Her need for him shocked her. After her ultimate starbursting, fiery shattering, she savored his tenderness, the unsteady caress of his hands soothing her. She lay quietly beneath him, stroking his hair and listening to their hearts slow. She bit his ear playfully, then kissed it.

Still lodged inside her, Solomon tensed. "I didn't tear anything," he stated moodily.

"You can't just flop me on my back and have me when you want—"

But she'd wanted him and the thought frightened her. She turned her face to the moonlight sifting through the cottonwoods and closed her eyes against Solomon's rugged face over her. She couldn't bear to think of the women in the house having him like this—fevered, hungry, magnificent, and shaking with need.

The tear trailing down her cheek fell onto the blanket as Solomon's cheek rested on hers. "Don't worry," he murmured.

"I have to. I have all of us to take care of. I can't bear another lifetime of doing that."

"What do you mean?" he asked after a long time, and she refused to answer.

When he began to withdraw, Cairo clenched her legs on his. "Where do you think you're going? You can't just start a conversation like this and then leave."

"Then you'd better talk fast, because—" he said even as he was moving deeper within her and she was gathering him closer, pouring herself into each kiss, each flow of their bodies, and moving into the desperation she needed.

"You can't have them," she cried aloud—just after her cry echoed through the night and Solomon gathered her close. She held him fiercely. None of the women who wanted Solomon was getting him. Not tonight.

In the morning, Cairo evicted Adele, Maureen, and Della. They planned to share a room at the Choteau House hotel and look for other potential husbands.

So much for yesterday's Adele, Maureen, and Della. Nancy arrived that afternoon afternoon. She was pretty, young, and she knew how to slop pigs and hoe the garden and tell Garnet entertaining stories. Nancy could read and sum and she couldn't wait to play billiards.

Solomon noted Nancy the instant he returned home at dusk. He approved of her neatly folded laundry, the meal she had cooked, and seemed charmed by her conversation.

"You adore her," Cairo shot at him as they rode to check on the cattle by moonlight. She sat very stiff in front of him as they circled the cattle and then moved toward the sheep. "She's perfect for you and Garnet."

"Could be. She's eager, too," he noted, studying the new ram. "She knows how to weave wool."

"She's not for you. She's too sweet," Cairo stated. She looked down to Solomon's large hand, which was skillfully unbuttoning her bodice. Cairo closed her eyes, pained by the thought that Nancy's breast would soon be filling Solomon's hand. "You tore my camisole lace," she noted though her throat was closing with tears.

"You smell good," he whispered against her ear, finding her nipple with his thumb and brushing it gently. "You've got a smell that's like—"

"Don't accuse me of daisy-dom again. Nancy is very suitable." She pushed again, adjusting her legs across his lap, allowing for the slow intrusion of Solomon's hand on her thigh. She inhaled and tightened her thighs as his fingers stroked her delicately and she melted.

"Why don't we stop awhile and talk about moonbeams and such?" he invited huskily against her ear.

In the morning, Cairo told Nancy that she was not a suitable replacement. Marjorie, Pearl, a child called Daffodil, and Stella, who had already buried five husbands, were not suitable wife material either.

Two weeks of wife applicants passed. Every night Solomon came to Cairo for tending and she comforted him. She was exhausted and tense, faced with women drooling for her husband. Solomon, however, seemed quite happy with the events, despite grumbling for his bed.

When the last applicant of the week drove away with Quigly and Garnet, Cairo glared at him. His silence drew women like flies to honey. "You remind me of a bull sniffing at his cows."

He continued to hammer boards on the house's new

addition. "Maybe I should fix up the barn, so you can invite more wife replacements. We could rent out the stalls."

She hit him with her parasol. "They are too good for you."

Solomon leveled a dark look at her. "Is that why they've been ripping open their dresses and pushing their hands down my pants?"

When she could speak, Cairo managed, "Who? Which one would dare assault you while you're under my protection?"

Solomon ignored her and began pounding nails. A muscle on his jaw flexed and Cairo's eyes widened when he turned to her. "Let's go to our bed," he said; then before she could find her voice, Solomon bent and tossed her over his shoulder. She took great care not to damage her best silk parasol while he carried her into the house and tossed her onto the bed. "It's daylight," she whispered as Solomon stood over her.

"Sure is. Yes or no?" he asked softly. "I've been pinched, grabbed, and buried in hungry females for two weeks. It's more than any man can take," he grumbled. "Sheer hell and not a daisy in the lot."

He was so disgruntled that she wanted to remind him that she hadn't completely deserted him. "Solomon, I didn't toss you into their hands. I took very good care to see that you were protected. And I—" She hesitated. "You must admit, you weren't in torment, not the entire time. I—uh—did try to comfort you."

He began to undress. "What color drawers are you wearing? Ones to match this blue dress?"

Solomon stood beside the bed, all masculine angles and looking moody. Just looking at him, ready for her,

her body heated and tightened. "You'll have to find out," she whispered unevenly, because she wasn't making life easy for him. She fought the smile tugging at her lips.

"You're a daisy," he murmured with a slow, devilish grin.

"Beast . . . villain . . ." she protested breathlessly as his hand circled her ankle and began to work upward. Before he tore away her drawers, she discovered that she loved placing her bare soles against his hard, hair-roughened chest and wiggling her toes upon his glorious nipples and teasing his exciting little navel.

That night, nestled in the spoon of his hard body, she noted with satisfaction that he hadn't mentioned her feet.

Alone for the first time in two weeks, Cairo and Solomon looked at each other in the dawn. Sunlight hovered in the morning air, tiny gold flecks twisting, floating, and through them came the sound of Garnet's urgent call. "Ma! Pa! Come quick. There's someone coming."

When Garnet called again, Solomon, lodged deep inside Cairo and aching for more, eased slowly away.

Cairo drew a sheet across her chest and met his gaze as he fastened his clothing. Then she looked away to her billiard table. "Go," she whispered too quietly.

Solomon paused at the door and looked back at her.

He wanted to go to her, to hold her, to reassure her that someday another man would hold her and give her what she needed.

Solomon flung away that tenderness. He might not be able to stop the pent-up needs of his body, but deeper emotions would only bring pain to them both. He gripped the door and forced himself through it, answering Garnet's call.

* * *

Joseph led his horse toward the ranch. The travois—
two long poles crossed over the horse's back and dragging
on the ground behind it—left thin trails in the old dried
weeds and bent the new ones as it passed. Garnet walked
beside the travois, big-eyed and solemn, clutching her
kitten.

"Joseph," Solomon said, raising his hand in greeting.
He walked to the travois to see a young Indian woman,
badly beaten, and unconscious.

Joseph's expression softened as he looked at the young
woman. "She is my sister."

Solomon's first thought was that Garnet should not
see the pain of a beaten women. She already knew more
than she should. "Go tell Quigly that we have company,"
he said quietly after placing his hand on her head.

"Put her on the bed, Solomon," Cairo said quietly as
the two men entered, carrying the girl as gently as possible.

Joseph stared at Cairo, her hair piled high, and her
day dress of the finest material. "Boil water, Quigly, and
stay out of the way," she said, meeting Solomon's questioning look. "Quigly has an uneasy stomach where these
matters are involved."

Solomon spoke softly, pushed aside his quiet rage, and
placed her on the bed. "I'll get Mrs. Smith. She's the
closest woman. She'll know what to do."

"This girl doesn't have the time. Just help me, then
stay out of my way," she ordered, elbowing Solomon
aside.

Garnet hovered in the shadows, clutching her kitten
and looking very small. "My ma almost died when they
did that to her," she whispered unevenly.

Solomon inhaled, pain slamming into his heart.

Cairo flicked him an impatient look. "Get out of my way, Mr. Wolfe, and take Garnet," she said quickly. To the little round-eyed girl, Cairo said soothingly, "Shoo. Your kitten needs you and so does Quigly. Garnet, I need your help. I want you to take Quigly out to the barn and tell him stories. He's needing comforting just like this little kitten."

Garnet's eyes lit up, losing the solemn sadness. "Quig? He's scared?"

"Mortified. Hurry, before he faints. Solomon, please place my medicine chest on the bureau."

Then she bent, hugged Garnet and kissed her, and whispered, "There take that with you. And this, too—" She tossed imaginary fairy dust into the air and Garnet stood very still, letting it settle upon her. She threw it back and then she was gone.

Joseph lifted his head proudly. "What do you know about healing?" he questioned arrogantly.

"I've helped women like this before." Cairo glanced down at the girl, who was very pale.

"They will die, the men who did this," Joseph stated tightly, his head high as he walked out of the room.

"Get me hot water and my best lavender soap," Cairo murmured to Solomon. After Cairo made the battered girl comfortable, Joseph sat with her. The scent of burning sweet grass, the natives' healing medicine, filled the room.

"She's dying," Cairo said, leaving Joseph with the girl. "She could live, but she's been badly shamed. She wants to die."

She gripped the cherrywood table and crushed the Irish linen cloth. "It was Edward. I've seen his work before, and Duncan's, too."

Solomon continued sharpening his hunting knife.

Less than an hour ago, Cairo had been lying beneath him, tight, hot, and welcoming. Now she was furious and a girl lay dying in the next room.

Cairo reached for his knife and hurled it at the wall. Tears filled her eyes and she shivered, glaring down at him. "Don't you sit there looking like it didn't touch you, Mr. Wolfe. You went white when you looked at Garnet. She's only a little girl and she's seen too much." Cairo brushed away the tears dripping from her cheek.

Solomon rose slowly to his feet, uncertain how to handle an emotional woman or his own anguish. Cairo hurled herself into his arms. "Hold me, you black-hearted villain. Just hold me."

Solomon gathered her tighter, fighting visions of Fancy, lying beaten and cared for by a small child.

Then he gave up fighting and buried his face in Cairo's throat, holding her softness tightly against him.

Solomon looked at the woman riding sidesaddle beside him. Cairo held the parasol that matched her dress with one gloved hand and the reins to her horse with the other. She looked little like the woman who had held the dead girl, mourned for her. Now her ostrich feathers quivered and gleamed in the early-afternoon sun, and she sent him a dark, meaningful look.

He flung it back.

"You will not go to Blanche Knutson's house by yourself to avenge that poor girl. As your wife, I am going with you."

He hadn't gone to a fracas with a wife at his side before, much less one in a high, fine temper. "This is not a social call," he repeated. "You're in the way."

"I am accompanying you," Cairo returned evenly, sitting very straight. "You've got murder in your eyes and I will not have a husband of mine put in jail for revenge on a sixteen-year-old boy. It will surely make the newspapers and then I'll be ruined in New York."

They both knew that Edward would not pay for his crimes. Cairo was worried about Joseph and how revenge could turn to take his life. Solomon reluctantly admired her decision. The boy, Edward Knutson, son of an influential, powerful family, was in awe of her, and that edge could save his life. "What are you going to do if I land in jail? Throw more knives at me?"

"I may. Watch your back, Mr. Wolfe. It's big and wide and makes a good target." She glanced at Joseph, riding beside them. "I don't want him hurt. You know as well as I do that he doesn't have a chance alone."

"I'll take care of him. Go home," Solomon ordered. Cairo and Blanche were unsteady as a miner's blasting nitro in the same box. "A woman's place is at home. This is a man's job."

"Is it now?" she asked lightly, and twirled her parasol.

Solomon took a deep breath and she glanced at him. "Your nostrils flare when you get mad. They have been flaring since you saddled my horse—"

"Hell, yes, my nose probably does need more air with you around. Strapping a sidesaddle on a horse is just what a man wants to do when he's out to make someone pay," Solomon muttered darkly.

"Of course I'm riding sidesaddle. I'm wearing an expensive day dress," she returned logically. "You've got that dark, closed-in, angry look. I will not have Garnet's only relative and my husband running from the law because he's murdered a boy, despite the fact that Edward needs trouncing."

"I will kill him," Joseph stated quietly. "I will hand his scalp to our mother."

Cairo straightened and guided her horse close to Joseph's. "Taking a man's pride could be just as effective. Edward is smaller than you are. I ask you to consider other ways to shame Edward. Losing face is one of them. A jail term would do that."

Joseph scowled at her and she glanced at Solomon. "Calm yourself. Your nostrils are flaring."

"This is not a church box social," he returned tightly, and wondered why he had allowed her to come.

Cairo drew up her gloves in brisk, efficient movements. "I have determined that you need me—the both of you—to save your necks. The Knutsons have always had hired guns, and you're riding into this affair as if blazing guns would settle everything. Admit it or not, Solomon, my presence adds to the civilized legality of bringing Edward to justice."

Solomon forced his groan back down his throat. He tried to keep his nostrils from flaring.

They rode past the Knutsons' elegant windmill, the varnished paddles slowly rotating, the big wrought-iron K gleaming in the sun.

Joseph and Solomon swung down and Kipp helped Cairo from her saddle. She smoothed her skirts and smiled warmly at him. "Kipp. I'm so glad to see you. You'll come visit, won't you?"

He looked away, his face reddening. "Yeah. Well. Maybe."

Blanche sailed down from the porch, beaming at Solomon. "Solomon, you've come at last—" Then she glanced at Cairo, who had been shielded by the horses and the men. "Oh. You're here," she added hollowly.

Cairo moved to Solomon's side and he shifted away slightly when her body blocked his gun hand. He moved again and she followed, placing her hand through his arm in the picture of wifely elegance coming to call on a neighbor. "Is Edward home?" she asked, but Blanche was staring at the young warrior. "Edward?" Cairo prompted. "Is he home?"

Duncan limped toward them, Edward at his side. The boy's thin face was ashen, and he sulked near his mother. Duncan moved closer to Joseph, studying him closely.

"We've come after the boy," Solomon said quietly. "He's going to jail."

Blanche's pale hand rose to her throat. "Jail? Why?"

"He has killed my sister," Joseph stated harshly.

"Who are you?" Blanche asked shakily.

"I know," Duncan said slowly, thoughtfully. "I'd know those eyes anywhere. He's the right age, around seventeen to Kipp's eighteen and Edward's sixteen. He figures to be right in the middle."

"No!" Blanche cried out as if her heart had been torn from her.

"I knew his ma didn't have it in her to kill her whelp."

"Let's go, boy," Solomon said, trying to ease away from Cairo, who held his gun hand. He expected Duncan and the ranch hands to fire, and no matter how he tried to shield Cairo, she moved slightly in front of him.

Blanche's hands went to cover her mouth and tears filmed her eyes.

Duncan began to laugh, a deathly echo that lifted the hairs on the nape of Solomon's neck. "Now, isn't this nice? A real family reunion," Duncan murmured, and winked at Blanche.

"I will kill him," Joseph stated, and threw his knife into the earth between them.

"Nobody is killing anyone," Solomon said. "You're coming with us for trial, Edward. The girl named you before she died."

He shuddered and tears dripped from his eyes. "Ma, I

didn't do it. You've got to believe me—I didn't hurt any squaw."

"You won't make it off the ranch," Duncan said to Solomon, flicking his hand toward his men, who circled the group, rifles and guns ready.

"I'll bring him in," Kipp stated, facing Duncan.

"That would be lovely," Cairo said brightly. "It would be to Edward's advantage to arrive on his own—with a brother—wouldn't it, Solomon?"

"Do I have your word, Kipp?" Solomon asked, facing his son. Edward, a pampered coward, would run at the first opportunity.

"You do," Kipp returned, and shook the hand Solomon had extended to him. "But if you try to take him now, I'll have to draw down on you. He's my brother."

"I'm not going to jail," Edward screamed, drawing his gun.

Kipp hit his wrist and the gun fell to the earth; the back of Kipp's hand sent Edward reeling.

Duncan made a feral, protective noise and Edward launched himself into his mother's arms.

Blanche continued to look at the young Indian, her face very pale as she soothed Edward. "It's only a matter of letting a lawyer set bail, darling. You'll be home soon enough."

"Well. There. That's settled," Cairo said, linking her gloved hand with Solomon's gun hand. "We're going to the sheriff now . . . with Joseph, so he can make his statement. He is staying with us until the matter is settled."

"You'd keep a dirty—" Duncan began, and Cairo leveled a dark stare at him.

"Yes. He's welcome at our home for however long the process takes to judge Edward's guilt. The girl died horribly, Blanche. If Edward is guilty, he should pay the price. Come along, Solomon. Kipp always does what he says he will."

"Yes, come along, Solomon," Duncan mimed, and Solomon's hand hovered over his gun.

He fought the easiest solution—that of shooting Duncan on the spot. Then he slowly lowered his hand and said to Kipp, "Remember this. Sometimes it's harder to walk away than to draw down."

"Now he's giving Kipp lessons in a man's pride," Duncan said mockingly. "Are you a man, Solomon? Or are you hiding behind that skirt you married?"

"Shut up, Duncan," Blanche snapped.

"I'll ride out with you, pilgrim," Kipp said. "Then I'll come back for Edward."

Kipp stared at Edward. "I'll check on that stock on the north range. That should give you three hours to say good-bye to Mother. Better pack a change of clothes."

He looked at Solomon. "You have my word. It will be easier on Mother to have some time to get used to the idea."

thirteen

Blanche watched as Joseph rode toward her. She recognized him as her child the moment those brilliant blue eyes burned into hers. Joseph's eyes reminded her of her father's and her brothers'. Pride welled within her. She would fight to keep him safe now as she did when she first held him in her arms.

Kipp had started back to the ranch. He would find Edward gone. She had tucked her Edward safely away and then had ridden out to the knoll to wait.

"Mother," Joseph greeted her solemnly when they stood, facing each other, a lifetime swirling between them.

"How did you know?" she whispered, shaking.

"We have the same blue eyes. Your man saw that I am your child. The one called Edward is his son, and the one called Kipp is my friend Solomon's son. You are a good woman to bear all sons," he said with pride.

Tears blurred her eyes. He was so young and yet saw so much. This boy, her son, was proud of her. She, who had been rightfully hated and scorned, felt the unfamiliar bite of tears at her lids. "I . . . I am sorry about your sister, Joseph."

"You love your sons. Do not cry for me, Mother. I have been treated well."

She touched his arm lightly, sensing the strength and tension running through him, though he looked very calm. "Joseph . . . please . . . don't stay here. They will kill you. I cannot protect you—"

"Protect me a second time, Mother?" he asked with a touch of warmth around his mouth.

He looked so young and strong, filled with life, and her heart bled for the time lost between them. She dug in her saddlebag, tugging out a bag filled with coins. "Joseph, take these and go," she begged, already knowing that he would not take them as she held them out to him.

"Tell me about my father," he said quietly, the prairie grasses rippling around him like old dry secrets.

Buck. She hated him fiercely for this. Hated him for tearing her girlish body with his beastly one . . . hated him for goading her into what she had become . . . for taking lovers. . . .

"His name was William. He was a gentle man," she said honestly, remembering William fondly, remembering how she wanted Solomon's fierce, hot loving and had received William's tenderness and caring. "His death was because of me—"

"Because of me," Joseph corrected. "Was it not? Yet you kept me alive."

She fought the image of Buck's big hands reaching for the infant's fragile throat. How she had begged to kill the baby herself, though she knew then that she would fight to keep him alive. "Giving you away was the hardest thing in my life," she returned honestly. Just two hours after having Joseph, then being beaten by her husband, she had managed to cradle her baby in one arm and ride off the ranch. Weakened, terrified, and crying, she'd managed to find an Indian woman who wanted a strong son. Blanche inhaled the sweet evening air and closed her eyes. Despite the pain, she was pleased that she could be honest in this small matter. She pushed away the small tremor of pride. She was Blanche Knutson, and she had survived, just as she wanted her son to live. "Please, Joseph. Go."

His head lifted and the thrill of a mother's pride shot through her. Joseph looked like her father now in the evening light, fierce and honorable. She fought the tears in her eyes and found Joseph through the filmy veil. "Here. Take this," she whispered, slipping a large coin into his hand. It was pierced for a necklace, and it was all she had to remember William. "It was your father's. They killed him."

Then because he hadn't judged her, hadn't seen the evil in her, she took the gold necklace from her throat and pushed it into his hand. "I am your mother and I want you safe. Go to Canada and stay there."

"I cannot, until my sister is avenged," he returned simply. "I will not reveal your secret," he added, bringing his knife to her face.

Blanche closed her eyes; Joseph could do no worse than Buck had. . . . Perhaps she deserved this justice from a son she had given away. "There has always been a place in my heart for you, but I love Edward, too," she said simply, and started when Joseph's blade slid through her bound hair to cut away a black strand.

"I keep this for the children I will have, Mother," he said before leaping to his horse. He tucked the strand into a pouch and nodded good-bye to her.

Blanche watched him ride to rejoin Solomon, who would keep him safe.

Then she fell upon the dry prairie earth, grasped the weeds in her hands, and wept.

The tense tableau at the Knutson ranch had distracted Cairo throughout the visit to the sheriff and the visit to check on her parlor. She'd been wrapped in her thoughts of Kipp, looking dangerous as he faced Duncan.

Without his beard, Solomon would have the same fierce look. She'd thought about the shape of his jaw and chin and the angles of his forehead beneath his shaggily cut hair. In her passion, she'd gripped his face, soothed his hair away from his brow, and saw that his features had been stamped on Kipp's youthful face.

Now the fading sun caught Quigly's bloodred turban and his caftan as he ran across the golden prairie toward Solomon, Cairo, and Joseph.

The bull buffalo bellowed wildly and pawed the ground, staking his territory against the flying red cloth.

The old longhorn bull returned the bellow and shook his horns.

Quigly's terrified expression wiped away any humor. "Garnet is gone," he whispered hoarsely, and swallowed. "I've looked everywhere. I was just fixing dinner—capons in wine—"

"When?" Solomon asked tersely as an owl hooted and the night settled gently upon the prairie.

Fright scurried through Cairo like tiny mice.

"I've been calling and hunting for four hours. I found her footprints leading to a clump of sagebrush and there were horseshoe marks—one with a nick in it—and then her footprints were gone. I was searching for them when I saw you coming home." Then all seven-feet, three hundred pounds of Quigly's red-caftan-clad body fell to the earth. He began to retch. Before Cairo could reach him, he groaned and flopped to his back, unconscious.

"He's fainted," Cairo said, putting her hand to Quigly's forehead. "Help me get him back to the house."

Despite the news of the missing Garnet, Solomon and Joseph looked blankly at her.

"Quigly is overwrought," she informed them indignantly.

Half an hour later Solomon pushed food and warm clothing for Garnet into his saddlebags. "I am going with you," Cairo and Joseph stated in union, then looked at each other.

"You are a woman," Joseph noted arrogantly in tones that scraped her nerves.

"I am the current mother of the missing child," she announced firmly.

Solomon filled a coal-oil lamp. "Joseph, stay here. I need you to help Cairo. Left alone, she'll wander out into the night and get lost—"

"Why, you—" Cairo began, then she caught Solomon's deep fatigue, the worry in his eyes. "Yes. I'll stay and if Kipp comes here after delivering Edward to the sheriff, I'll ask him to help find Garnet."

He nodded and then was gone.

Cairo blinked, then followed. She caught him as he was mounting his horse. "Take me with you, you stubborn son of a—"

Solomon reached down and scooped her up against him with one arm. "Give me a good one," he ordered as she held him tightly, fearing for him and for Garnet.

"I'll give you nothing—" she began, relying on her instincts to save her from the fear wrapping around her.

Then Solomon gripped her tightly, so hard that he lifted her feet from the ground. "You keep my bed warm," he ordered unevenly before he found her mouth hungrily.

Cairo poured herself into the kiss, a talisman against harm. Solomon's horse could stumble in a gopher hole, he could be shot— She broke away for air.

Then she closed her eyes and gripped his shirt with her fists. "Just don't you get lost out there in the night. And don't do anything to embarrass me. Bring Garnet home safe and don't shoot anyone, or let them shoot you, and make certain you don't tear your new clothes," she returned before she latched her hands in his hair and took his mouth fiercely.

"I will take care of your woman," Joseph said as Solomon carefully lowered her to the ground.

Solomon watched her for a moment and in those heartbeats she felt her heart leaking from her. "Keep safe, Mr. Wolfe," she whispered, pressing her hands to her bosom to keep from reaching for him. "Or I will be very angry with you . . . and . . ." She wiped away the tears that wouldn't stop flowing. "And if this takes longer than tonight, don't forget that Garnet likes butter and jam on freshly baked bread, and—"

She swallowed and found his hand with hers, needing the security of his strong fingers lacing with hers. "You get Garnet and come back here. Tell her I care for her, will you? Tell her that I'm waiting."

"Good enough." Then he nodded and Hiyu Wind moved off into the night.

"Wait!" she called, running after him. She jerked up her skirts and pulled off her drawers, stuffing them into his hand. "For luck. Oh, Solomon, I'm so worried. It's a big country and Garnet is only a little girl. You'll need every bit of luck possible to find her. I don't have anything else to give you. If you give them to a bawdy woman, I'll kill you."

He nodded, then stuffed her underwear into his shirt. "Now, that's a daisy-sweetheart thing to do," he murmured, looking angular and fierce in the moonlight.

"Well," she snapped defensively, "I'm worried about Garnet, that's all. You look like one of the Knights of the Round Table, running off to rescue a princess. Find Garnet and don't call me your daisy, cowboy," she shot back, brushing away the hot tears at her lids. "I am not dipped in dew or sweeter than sunrise."

"No, you're purely not," Solomon murmured, then nodded and eased his horse off into the night.

Cairo glanced at Joseph, who looked uncomfortable with a weeping woman. "I'm worried about Garnet. Add that to how much I detest Solomon and a woman has a right to cry. He's ruined my life, you know. It will take me a good two years to make up for what he's cost me," she snapped, and tried not to sob. "Oh, I pray he finds her."

"He will find the girl. But your spirit needs his," Joseph said quietly.

"Oh, no. I need New York, not Solomon Wolfe. And I need to know that Garnet is safe," Cairo stated shakily, then hurried into the house to cry.

"You scum-sucking behind-of-a-barnacle. Untie me!" Garnet yelled as soon as she managed to get the gag from her mouth.

Edward Knutson rode ahead of her, pulling the rope of her horse. "Shut up, kid. Or I'll put you back in the sack."

Garnet glared at him. "You come close to me and you'll pay," she threatened. Edward had tricked her with candy and scooped the bag over her head. He'd paid well and good, he had, because she drew blood the first time she bit him. A painful grab at his manhood had helped her pride and taught him a lesson.

"Just what do you think you're doing with me? My ma and pa won't like this. You know my pa, don't you, Edward? He could slap you silly without turning a hair. Oh, he's gonna be real mad about this, he is. Real mad. I'm Ma's little darling, you know. She does lots of good things for women and kids that men have knocked around. People like her and if she asks them to tar and feather you, they will."

Edward turned slightly in his saddle. "Kid, you really think they want you around? I'm doing the both of them a favor, getting you out of the way."

Garnet studied his evil smile. She hadn't thought about being in the way. Maybe babies didn't come if other kids kept their folks too busy. "Edward, I don't like you none at all."

"Now, kid, that hurts. Cuts me like a knife."

She studied the open, rolling land. Edward wasn't much, but he was all she had for a resource at the moment. "Edward, do you think folks can make babies with other kids around?"

His snicker carried back to her.

So it was true, Garnet decided. She just needed to give Ma and Pa time alone. They'd come after her as soon as they found the locket she left hanging on a sagebrush. "Edward, I've decided to let you take me on a grand adventure. But you come close to me again and I'll take a chunk out of any piece of your hide closest to me."

Edward rubbed his already abused hands and arms. He shifted uncomfortably on the saddle and adjusted his mishandled and aching man-parts. He glanced back at the girl who was more evil than Duncan and voodoo witches put together. Paying back Solomon Wolfe by taking his brat had seemed like a good idea. It still was, if he could find a way to manage the kid. "Yeah, kid. They need time alone."

"You think so?" Her reply was childlike, innocent.

"Yeah. You should give them plenty of time alone. They haven't had a honeymoon." The lie came easy. He hadn't hurt the kid and he didn't want to kill her. He just wanted to worry Solomon Wolfe. He'd take the kid so deep into Canada that Wolfe would have a hard time finding her. Edward would trade her off and keep the trail hot and moving away from himself. And while Wolfe was hunting the girl—who was mouthy and mean enough to leave a big trail—Edward would circle back and destroy Wolfe's ranch. He reached for his gold toothpick and found it gone. He eyed the kid suspiciously. She had fast hands, especially when she grabbed his man-parts. Now that was indelicate of a female.

"Okay. This adventure is starting to look good. Untie me and give me some candy. If we don't stop pretty soon, I'm going to pee all over your packs. They feel like they got clothes in them. Pee smells real bad in hot weather."

"Ah, kid. Don't do that." Edward rode back and slid his knife through her bonds.

"Help me down," Garnet demanded. "Now!"

"You bite me and the deal is off. You'll have to go home," Edward stated warily.

"Nope. Not me. I'm off on a grand adventure. That ways Ma and Pa can make me a baby."

* * *

Kipp ignored July's hot afternoon sun and leaned his forearm on his saddlehorn. He watched Cairo, clad in her silk pajamas, haul buckets of water to the small garden.

Quigly sat in the shade of a parasol, his caftan and turban gleaming bloodred in the sun.

Kipp smiled grimly and tipped his hat back. He was not too tired from chasing Edward to enjoy the scene before him. Cairo and Joseph slaved under the hot sun, hauling water, while Quigly read the fashion news.

Edward had disappeared. Their mother was protecting him.

Kipp worried for his mother, for her long silences, for the hours she spent drinking privately. Blanche moved like a woman without a soul and never left her bedroom. In the two days since Edward had disappeared, Blanche had aged ten years, tiny lines appearing around her eyes and mouth. Her mind was fragile, unlike the willful mother he'd always known. Duncan ruthlessly pushed her toward an edge from which she might never return.

Duncan knew where Edward was; the two men always knew each other's whereabouts, like dogs of a pack. Garnet had been taken and Edward was missing. He was just ornery enough to take his revenge out on a child. In Kipp's experience, when Edward was missing, trouble was afoot.

Solomon had left Cairo under the protection of Quigly and Joseph. Reluctantly, Kipp admired the older man, the way he kept his head when shooting Duncan would have been easier.

Edward would not be far from Duncan's protection or advice.

His mother had always protected Edward. Kipp forgave her now, even when he knew Edward must pay. She seemed different from the moment she had seen Joseph.

Those blue eyes. . . . Joseph's blue eyes reminded Kipp of his mother's.

Kipp's horse started, rearing slightly as a jackrabbit escaped the sagebrush and zigzagged to a sarviceberry bush. The sun caught and glittered in the bush, and Kipp swung down from his horse.

Garnet's locket looked tiny and fragile in his hand. She'd always begged him to look inside, to see her grandparents. He opened the locket. The plain, dark-eyed woman had an inner beauty. The man was solemn, neck stiff in his starched collar and tie. Kipp eased the tintype out of the shadows.

He ran his free hand around his face. He sought the features reflected in the man who was Garnet's grandfather . . . who was Solomon's father. He had Kipp's squarish jaw, the dimple in his chin and slashing black eyes. Solomon's eyes . . . Kipp's eyes. . . .

Kipp swallowed tightly, the ground slanting precariously beneath his boots. He found the square contour of his jaw as he likened it to the man in the picture. "Solomon . . . Solomon is . . . is my father," Kipp whispered as a hawk keened through the clear blue sky.

After four exhausting days of following leads, Solomon could not find Garnet. He lay on the Canadian prairie, close to the smoking fire, despite the hot August night. The smoke shielded him from the stench of a wolfer's kill and the mosquitoes. Hiyu Wind was getting thin, despite the lush grass. The horse had been pushed hard. Solomon hadn't slept or rested; he knew he was running on bad coffee and nerves.

He had to find Garnet.

Mosquitoes buzzed furiously and Hiyu Wind nickered and danced in the lazy smoke, which protected him. Solomon scanned the stars overhead. Garnet was out there and he'd find her.

He wrapped that comfort around him and tried not to think about the lazy, vain, uppity, arguing woman who plagued his thoughts almost as much as the girl.

Cairo. She'd go to New York and he couldn't stop her. He drew her blue silk drawers to his face and inhaled her fragrance, wrapping her fierceness around him.

Solomon heard himself groan. He raised his gun hand and found it shaking.

He turned his hand, studying the swollen and bruised knuckles. He'd forgotten about protecting his gun hand; he'd laced into the man who had lied about Garnet.

Whoever had taken his niece knew how to make false trails and how to threaten and pay for lies. After Solomon's ungentle persuasion, two men had admitted to giving Solomon wrong information, and their description of Garnet's captor matched Edward. Later, a whiskey trader's woman noted a "brat with a foul mouth" in the company of Métis. A Blood warrior had seen the Métis bargain with trappers, and Solomon discovered the half-bloods had paid the trappers to take the "little poison-mouth."

Garnet had not made her captors happy. In the four days she had been missing, she'd stampeded buffalo, burned a tent, and ruined a whiskey vat. Spewing voodoo curses, she'd hexed a Métis and a trapper, who now feared her return. She'd been passed off several times in the four days. Her captors didn't want to keep her more than a few hours.

Solomon had heard about two Indian women who had

taken Garnet to a whiskey fort. Garnet was enough trouble that she'd been moved quickly from party to party.

He remembered Cairo's worried expression and her demand that he bring Garnet safely home.

He missed Cairo, despite his promise not to think about her. "Oh, hell," Solomon muttered. He had to do something to ease into sleep without longing for her.

He lay on the hard ground, the saddle beneath his head and the mosquitoes buzzing around his body, and tried to sleep. After a restless half hour, in which he fantasized about Cairo, he cursed again and sat up. He grabbed a pencil and paper from his saddlebags.

Solomon turned the paper to the moonlight, inhaled and wrote, "Without you, the lonesome hurts." He shook his head and wrote, "When sundown sparkles on the river and the wind sweeps across the prairie, I think of your sweet eyes."

While the words didn't sound like the grand plays he'd seen across the West, they were his, plain and simple.

Solomon shook his head. Every moment he thought of Garnet. But now with night around him, there wasn't a thing he could do but try a diversion to relax, then sleep. Garnet needed him to be sharp, and to do that, he needed sleep.

He wanted to write something about Cairo's lips, but when the words wouldn't come, he pushed on. "When you look at me with dark, hungry eyes, my heart goes wild as a rabbit running across the meadow. You're worried about Garnet. So am I. I'll find her, don't fret. Then I'll bring her home safe to you."

His body tensed with his next thoughts storming through him. "Those two strawberries on your bosom are the sweetest I've tasted. I've never tasted a woman in two places before. Never wanted to."

Then he wrote a promise he intended to keep. "Someday, my little daisy-girl, I'm going to make you take it nice and slow and this old bronc won't move so fast, but maybe he'll let you know what's in his heart."

Solomon inhaled and clamped his lips against the longing groan storming from the depths of his being. "I'm going to spread you out on the daisy field and cover you with them. I'll be tasting your strawberries— Oh, hell," Solomon cursed and knew that Cairo Brown Wolfe had finally driven him insane. He looked down at his sketch of her, a crude angular sampling with flowing hair and big, soft eyes, two round breasts with dark centers and a nest of curls between her legs. Solomon stared at the sketch and decided that it would have to serve as his sweetheart's photograph. He folded the crude sketch and tucked it in his pocket, only to draw it out again. He stroked the waving hair with a lingering fingertip. The Montana wind had caught her hair when she told him to bring back Garnet. He would, or die trying.

Solomon smiled briefly, surprised by the tenderness welling over him. He stroked the sketch's distinct large feet and thought about how he'd like to start kissing her there and work his way upward to where she was sweet and hot. "Oh, she'd be shocked with that," he whispered ruefully.

Solomon clenched his muscles against the taut need rising in him. After their loving, he wanted to start all over again and whisper something tender that sweetheart-daisies might like to hear.

But sugar and satin weren't in him. He'd been forged in cold steel and born to die alone with no one mourning him. He quickly wrote, "Lost the trail. Still looking. I'll find Garnet. Hope you are well. Your husband."

"Range-loco cowboy," he muttered, and tucked away

the sketch. He added more smoke wood to the fire, drizzling the last of his coffee over it. "Happy dreams are not for you. All you have to do now is to find Garnet and live long enough to raise her. Cowboy, you have purely seen the last of Mrs. Cairo Wolfe."

Then he placed his hand over the sketch in his breast pocket and forced his mind to empty.

fourteen

Cairo watched the crowd leave the tent. No one had heard of Garnet or Solomon. She felt empty, exhausted, and angry with Solomon. "Solomon should not have left me behind. That first night was horrible, worrying about them both. But once I'd made up my mind to enter the search, it was just a matter of raising the money. The ladies at Fort Benton understood and wanted to repay me for the help I'd given others. It was simple really, wasn't it, Quigly? We've transported the table so many times with Bernard that it was rather nostalgic getting back on the trail again."

"Yes, madame. Do you think Garnet is unharmed?"

"She'd better be. She's tough, Quigly. Don't forget that. She's had training in surviving since she was a baby." Cairo clung to that thought and prayed that Solomon already had her in his care. Fort Cyprien's fires rose high in the Canadian night. Cairo placed her cue in its case. It had just been eleven days since Solomon left her to find Garnet.

The third day after Solomon's departure found Quigly and Cairo pushing the horses' endurance and strength. She would put on the exhibitions and search for Garnet. Bernard had taught her well. *Not a gaudy medicine show, my dear. Rather elegance amidst the wilds.* Cairo knew how to pack her silks and satins and manage to look like a lady in the wilderness. She charged for her exhibitions, to finance the search, and asked questions.

At every stop—farms or communities—she asked about Garnet, prayed for word of her or Solomon. She asked the crowds in a sly way, so as not to alarm Garnet's captors. Garnet and Solomon seemed to have vanished. But she would find them.

The crowd continued to file out of her exhibition tent. She smiled and prayed Solomon or she would find Garnet. *Garnet! Where are you? Don't worry. We will find you.*

This Canadian outpost was the same as the last five. They had been pushing hard, the job of loading and unloading the disassembled table laborious. She pulled on her elegant French gloves and forced a smile when a man grabbed her hand and brought it to his lips. He was an American outlaw, hiding behind the Canadian borders.

Several North-West Mounted policeman had come from Fort Macleod to see her exhibition.

The men everyone despised, the wolfers, blended with aristocratic Métis who cherished a rebellious man called Louis Riel. American outlaws minded their tempers, glancing at the constable and the queen's men.

Cairo fleetingly admired the elegant beauty of a passing Métis couple, their clothing distinctive to their mixed blood and unique culture. They walked protectively on either side of a beautiful young girl disdaining the silent flirtation of the men.

A young Métis moved close to Cairo. Earlier she had

asked him about Garnet. He flicked the tiny pearls dangling from her ear. "So, if I find word of this small *poulette*—chicken—and take you to her, you will teach me, eh?"

She fluttered her fan; she wasn't falling under his charm. She was finding Garnet and Solomon and bringing them safely home. "Yes. I'll be happy to teach you at my billiard parlor," she answered.

He flicked her eardrop again and was gone.

Quigly polished the table quickly, preventing the night's dampness from ruining the wood, then covered it with a cloth. Cairo dully watched him check the overhead tarp's moorings, then return to lift her into the wagon—her traveling boudoir, when it wasn't supporting her beloved Italian slate. Gowns and plumes and petticoats hung from the slate's cradle now.

She pushed aside a drying silk camisole and sank onto a small cot; searching for Garnet had drained her.

These men would know where Garnet and Solomon were and they would tell her, or she would drag their tongues from their throats. She drew off her gloves and looked at her hands, which Quigly instantly began laving with herbal ointment. "We will find that little urchin, Cairo."

"She's only a little girl, Quigly."

"So were you, when Bernard took you."

"When my father sold me to him," she corrected wearily. "When he saw how much Bernard was willing to pay, he wanted me back. The old reselling-the-horse trick. I was supposed to run away from Bernard and come back to my family. I didn't. Selfish of me to want to survive, wasn't it?" She was tired, the years weighing on her.

"You cannot blame yourself for the circumstances.

Bernard offered your mother independence and a new life. She chose to stay with her husband," Quigly returned.

The wagon lurched and a large man stepped into the lamplight, stooping beneath the canvas. He was dirty, his clothing worn, and from the shaggy depths of his black hair and the shadows, his eyes accused her.

"I'll see to the horses," Quigly announced in his round tones, after clearing his throat. When he was outside, he tied the wagon's covering shut, enclosing Cairo with the man looming over her.

Cairo rose unsteadily to her feet. She placed her hand over her racing heart. Solomon looked worn, lines lying deep across his brow. Dark circles ran under his eyes, his clothing hung loosely on his body. "Solomon?"

"You're leaving here in the morning," he stated flatly, just as a woman's bawdy laughter shrieked over the camp, followed by men's shouts. Shots were fired, men yelled, and fiddlers played. "They're just getting warmed up."

"Have you heard anything of Garnet?"

"She's been moved fast. I'm on the trail now. She's with some traders who are known to follow this route. According to the farmers who saw her last, she was mouthy and demanding that the traders hop to do her bidding. She's safe, Cairo." His statement was so firm, his tone so determined that for a moment Cairo was relieved.

She fought the need to hold him, to wrap her arms around Solomon and— Pride bound her. She didn't want to care, didn't want to feel her heart warming and pouring joy through her. Solomon's black flashing eyes shot down her. "If you think that fancy silk get-up will stop any of those outlaws from having you—"

"You look ridiculous all stooped over in this wagon. You've ruined your new clothes," she said very carefully, fighting the urge to stroke away the wave crossing his forehead. Beneath his warrior's arrogance, he looked wary, barely standing on his feet, shaggy and uncertain. In the shadows of his eyes, she recognized the anguish she shared—Garnet must be found before winter choked their search. Cairo decided to deal with Solomon's dark mood and his impending dictum. "And I have every right to be here . . . just the same as you. I decided that the first night you left. It took me just one more day to water the garden and to make money for the trip. On the third morning we left. I am a woman of action, Solomon. And a determined one."

He whipped off his dusty hat and sailed it to her cot. Then he ran his fingers through his hair, the long strands arching out in deep waves, the lamplight catching his angular face. He'd lost weight, his bones thrusting at his skin. "I'm a man used to a hard trail. You should have stayed home where you were safe."

Cairo's hands locked to her waist. Tears threatened her. She'd hungered for the sight of him, wished for him, dreamed of him, and now he couldn't show her the slightest tenderness? "You can't enter my boudoir and order me to abandon my mission. I'm just as worried about Garnet as you are." She refused to say that no other man could take Solomon's place.

He hooked his thumbs in his gun belt and stood, immovable as the Canadian Rockies, long legs locked at the knee. "I thought you'd run. New York is waiting for you."

"I am going to rescue Garnet and then I'll find a wife-replacement and then I'll go. If you won't leave this minute, then I will," she said, brushing past him. She whipped open the canvas ties and began to step out.

Solomon's fist caught her bustle; her skirt tore away

from her bodice as he pulled her back inside the tarp. She glared at him, turned to look back at her abused dress, and stated too carefully, "You've ripped my bustle from its moorings. But then I could expect that, couldn't I, from a man who didn't have the decency to write?"

"You left right after me. A letter would have a hard time finding you, wouldn't it?"

"Now is no time to use logic." She had decided at the grip of that firm hand to attack at the first chance. She was worried about Garnet and here he stood, demanding that she leave. She wouldn't! Solomon deserved a good verbal mauling for leaving her, her heart breaking over him. . . .

"It's only been eleven days and I wrote plenty." He took her hand and studied the ring, then he fitted his hand to hers and studied the shape. She shivered under his thoughtful study, his hand moving slowly along hers, tracing each slender finger.

She watched his tanned fingers skim over her pale ones. She hated him for tearing her heart away from her safekeeping, just as he'd torn her bustle. She ripped away her hand, not willing to forgive him for her sleepless nights or her longing for him.

She took a deep breath and curled her fingers into a fist. Just one good punch at him, that was all she wanted. "You are infuriating. You know how worried I am about Garnet. The least you could do is comfort me, say something nice, and maybe, just maybe hold me. I don't suppose you even missed me."

He brought her fist to his heart, smoothed her fingers and her frustration. She fell before his tender, searching look. He lifted her hand to his mouth and kissed her palm. His eyes were soft upon her. "I thought about you."

Her pride threatened to pool at her feet and any minute, she'd grasp his dear face and press a million kisses over each hard plane, each worried line. "I actually fretted for your safety. Then you arrive, start tossing orders at me and act like I've invaded *your* private quest. Garnet is dear to me, Solomon. I want her back just as much as you do. I am horribly angry at you!"

She paused for breath. She couldn't have him locked sweet and gentle within her heart, with his shaggy, lonely looks and his soulful, needy eyes.

"Oh!" Cairo released the anger that she had nurtured. She hit his chest and paper rustled. "What's that?"

Solomon looked uneasy and guilty. The combination intrigued her. "I demand to know what is in your pocket, Mr. Wolfe."

"Can't say." He picked up his hat and nodded to her. "You just make sure you're headed back home at daylight. Make a quilt or something, if you don't take off for New York."

"Why, you—" Cairo launched herself at him, tripped on her torn skirt, and fell into his arms.

"You're a soft piece," Solomon stated huskily after a long moment in which neither of them stirred. He smelled the strand of her hair that had caught on his beard.

Solomon trembled, his passion clearly warring with his anger. "Didn't exactly have time to visit a tonsorial parlor. Get in that bed. I'll be back and I'll be wanting you," he said rawly. He nodded to the narrow cot in the wagon.

"I will not," she shot back, even as she knew she would be waiting for him.

Alone, Cairo began to unbutton her bodice. She'd pry his precious mystery from him. The secret of what lay within his pocket would be hers. She'd have her way with him, taking him in the wild, hot way she wanted, and then she'd fall upon him and tear out his secrets. She'd teach him he couldn't ride off like a knight on a mission without her. He couldn't incense his potential brides into a lustful frenzy, then leave her to fend them off.

She was stronger now. Just seeing Solomon had shot strength into her, lifted her from her tired, lonely depths. They'd find Garnet, and they'd do it together.

"Oh, yes. Solomon has lessons to learn," she murmured, delving into a chest and prowling through her best lingerie. No silk pajamas tonight because she intended to vanquish him, teach him more lessons than he ever thought possible, and then . . . She paused, her fists locked in lace and satin, and then she'd ruin him for any other woman, leave him so entranced that none of the wife-replacements could fill her place.

Solomon Wolfe was a marked man.

When he returned, Solomon had bathed, his hair and beard damp. She stopped brushing her hair and turned to him, her knees going weak at the sight of him. He flicked a wary glance at her and gripped his hat in his fist. "I made mistakes. One of them is ignoring how much you care for Garnet—that you want her safe. I've lived a hard life and haven't accounted to anyone but myself. I've always tried to hold my honor true. It was wrong of me to tell you that I wanted you. Haven't ever told a woman to get in bed that way before. I won't hold you to your wifely obligations."

"You think—you think that because we're married—that's why I let you have me?" How she'd wanted him—

"Women have minds that are hard to understand," he answered obliquely. "I don't have much to go on when it comes to women."

His apology sent her mission to devastate him skidding and wavering. He studied her long white lace negligee for so long that Cairo blushed and looked away. "You're a daisy," he whispered softly as he brought a strand of her hair to his lips. "Will you lie with me tonight? Will you let me comfort you about Garnet? Because we will find her. We have to."

A tiny skiff of pride shot through her, pushed aside by her need to hold him, to know that he was safe. She turned aside, shielding her tears from him. "You're not playing fair," she managed unevenly in a whisper that was torn from her very soul. "You know how worried I am about Garnet. I want to hold her in my arms and know that she is safe."

"You'll hold her again. Meanwhile, I don't know the rules to this one, but sweetheart, I purely want you," he admitted, easing his fingers through her hair, studying the lights. Solomon bent to kiss her eyelids, heat running from him like lightning setting off fires within her. "Don't want to tear anything," he murmured, standing back to look at her from head to toe. His dark gaze roamed down the thin straps on her shoulders, down to the white lace covering her breasts and the satin falling to her toes. "You've got nice feet," he noted before his gaze slowly rose. "Nice feet," he repeated unevenly.

But he looked at her nipples, which were nudging the lace, aching for his lips.

Her body went taut, needing his. Solomon looked so worn. His clothes needed washing. Quigly could help with that chore, while Cairo tended to Solomon's other comforts.

"Quigly!" Cairo called in an uneven whisper, unable to move, unable to look away from Solomon.

Solomon lifted a black questioning eyebrow and

brought her hand to his lips. He nibbled the soft center and placed her forefinger within his lips, suckling softly. "I'd like to call you my sweetheart."

"Sweetheart?" she asked in a husky thread of sound, remembering how he had tasted the word just moments before. She thought she heard the tinkling of her shattering defenses like wind chimes in the storm of her emotions.

"Haven't ever called a woman my sweetheart. Would you mind if I said that, just for tonight?"

Cairo's mouth dried as Solomon's heat swirled around her. He was hers; and she would wrap him softly in whatever she had to give, whatever she wanted to share with him . . . that she had given no one but him. "You're not going anywhere. You may call me sweetheart, if you'd like."

"Madame?" Quigly's deep voice rumbled outside the wagon.

"Mr. Wolfe's clothing needs washing. Please take care of it, will you?" she asked as she began to unbutton Solomon's shirt. She frowned slightly, listening to the odd noises circling the wagon. "Quigly?"

"Just oiling the wagon springs, madame. I've noted that they creak overmuch," he returned. "You might blow out the light. It appears that shadows can be seen quite easily behind the thin canvas."

After the wagon was dark and close and humming with desire and softer, silkier emotions, Solomon's lips drifted over hers. She sensed he feared, just as he desired. He touched her as if she were a fragile web trembling with dew, smooth as a rose petal. His fingertips drifted over her face, seeking, smoothing, learning. . . . Her hands stopped at his waist, fumbling with his gun belt. Solomon groaned, quickly unleashed his belt and tossed it aside. "We'll find Garnet. She's not hurt. I've been just a step behind her trail. But for tonight—"

"Yes, for tonight." Cairo's lifted her head proudly. In a wanton gesture that she'd saved all her life, she lifted her hair in both hands and let the strands slide slowly from her fingers. Cairo moistened her lips with the tip of her tongue, then leaned to taste his lips. She arched her head back, pride filling her because Solomon would not hold back this night. *Sweetheart*, he had called her, and his sweetheart she would be. There would be no lies, no layers of the past between them tonight, just the heat and the storms forging, burning them into one.

When he stood undressed before her, Cairo couldn't resist running her fingertips over him—his shoulders, the mound of a tense muscle, the rapid beat beneath his throat. She nuzzled the width of his chest, inhaling the scent of soap clinging to him, and was rewarded with his uneven groan. She skimmed his flat, hard stomach to where he was steel and silk. He inhaled sharply, his hands locking gently to her shoulders when she touched him, lightly and with awe, smoothing, seeking. She watched him surge, waiting for her. She gently enclosed him in her fingers and Solomon's eyes closed, color flooding his dark cheeks as he cradled her face in his hands.

He was trembling, layers of his heat hitting her like storm-tossed waves. "You think you're going to have me quick, don't you? Why?"

She lowered her lashes, fighting the need to nestle against him. She struggled with her crumbling pride and recognized her need for him, desperate and immediate. He raised her chin with his thumbs. "Look at me."

She refused to let him see her pain, her hunger, her need of him. "Still shy?" Solomon asked huskily, his lips roaming her cheekbones.

"Never. I haven't decided yet how to torture you . . . for leaving me like that and not a look back or a kiss blown in my direction." She lifted her head, allowing him access to her throat. Because she was frightened of herself, of her well-burnished defenses shattering, she pushed him away and quickly bent to retrieve his clothing, tossing it outside for Quigly.

"Sweetheart," Solomon murmured slowly, achingly.

Wrapped in the sweetness of his tenderness, she closed her eyes to draw the word deep inside her, treasuring it. He was right, she was shy of him because she had never opened herself to anyone as she would to him. She felt as if she were spinning out of control, like a billiard ball shot too hard and too fast and hovering in front of a pocket, poised to drop or to stay still. "I've never been anyone's sweetheart before."

"You're mine now. You're my bride, remember?" Solomon's finger slid under the tiny strap, snapping it gently before he kissed the curve of her shoulder. Then the other and the gown pooled at her feet.

"Sweetheart," Solomon murmured against her throat. Her weakened defenses shattered completely like crystal shards, leaving her vulnerable. She dug her fingertips into his shoulders, because she would break easily if he changed his mind.

She closed her eyes as Solomon took her in his arms. He fitted her carefully to him and sighed longingly against her hair. "Don't be afraid. There's a strong feeling running between us, just as much for me as for you."

His uneven admission tore at her. She struggled the old fight, to be free, independent of others, and lost, his tenderness snaring her more tightly than hemp.

Her fingers tightened on his shoulders, then skimmed them restlessly. He was hers again, hers to destroy and ravish and dine upon. Hers to resurrect, to comfort, to tend and cherish.

He stroked her back, finding the sensitive hollows and the curves. She placed her lips on his throat, exactly on the solid thud of his pulse. He was alive and in her arms, and that was enough for now. She closed her eyes, fighting the single teardrop lingering on her lashes, and nuzzled his clean, familiar scent.

"Hold me," he murmured suddenly, his heart thudding heavily beneath her palm.

Cairo slid her hands up his chest to his throat, then locked them around his neck. Solomon scooped her up, held her in his arms, and kissed her.

Cairo shivered beneath the tender assault, dazed by it, as Solomon sat on the cot and held her on his lap. He linked his fingers with hers and brought them to his chest. "We'll find Garnet, sweetheart."

"Yes," she answered simply, because they would. Because they were stronger together, forged by passion and the gentler joy humming through her.

She cradled his endearment to her, wondering, turning it in her heart as Solomon lowered her to the cot and spread himself over her.

"Solomon, I need you now." The words ripped out of her, shockingly.

He shuddered in her arms, touching her with shaking hands. He caressed her breasts, finding the sensitive tips with his fingers, circling them, then moving down her ribs, her stomach, spanning the softness of her belly and lower. She arched and gasped as his fingers stroked her, the intimate heat dewing gently. "Solomon . . ." she whispered desperately, her nails digging into his shoulders.

"I have to know you're real," he murmured against her frantic kisses, meeting them with his own.

She almost cried out when Solomon continued to stroke and caress and fit himself to her, lifting her hips in his palms and stroking her thighs. He smoothed the sensitive inner skin of her knees, lifting them, rocking his hard body gently against her.

Solomon placed his rugged, hot face against her throat and lay very still, his heart racing against hers. Her fingers trembled, hovered for a heartbeat, then slowly stroked his damp hair.

"Sweetheart. My daisy-girl . . . Touch me," he whispered urgently, then stilled as she timidly found him, drawing him into her so deep and tight that he could never get away.

She took him to her very heart, to the glittering crystal depths of what she was and would be. . . . To the woman of heat and passion and pride that she had closed to the world.

He met her there—a tall warrior, strong, proud, and arrogant, demanding his due and giving more. The colors burst around them, jet of night and scarlet of fire, and yet Solomon held her, protected her as she drifted from the sun.

She shattered, splintering into the sunburst, gathering Solomon, her own, tight against her.

She cried out, giving him more than was safe, a part of her sliding away, merging with him.

When he pulsated deep within her, taut in her arms and still gripped by their fever, she knew that he had given everything to her and between them, the bond had strengthened.

* * *

"Your nostrils are flaring," Cairo noted pleasantly late the next afternoon. Solomon was seated on the wagon seat beside her, handling the team of horses with ease while considering his unstable emotions. "You haven't spoken a word all day. Except that you believe Garnet was taken this way. And that the last people who saw her said she was safe and too mouthy for a child. And that you believe these people will follow this trail northward." Cairo twirled her parasol restlessly in her glove-clad hands. "So she's safe, we're on her trail, and you're angry. Why?"

He glanced at the passing band of Piegan Indians. He'd been shocked when he lifted the blanket this morning to look at her. Her pale body was marked by his passion. Men treated their wives with respect and care. While she was his, Solomon intended Cairo to have the respect of a wife. "You're going back after tonight."

She smoothed her gown and looked away. "Are you sorry about calling me sweetheart last night?" she asked too huskily, in a voice laden with tears.

"I hurt you," he muttered, uncomfortable with her and his guilt. He'd lost a bit of himself to her, felt it shifting away, melted by her heat, by his need to be so deep in her—but there was something else and he feared it.

Deep in his passion, he'd seen crystal flash in a myriad of colors, he'd felt as if he'd been so deep in her, so wrapped in her that he'd touched her heart. If she hadn't held him like that— "And wives don't take husbands like a prairie wildfire."

"You know so much about it, don't you?" Cairo asked hotly, glaring at him. "You're upset because I . . . I was forward and frightened you. I wanted you and I'm not afraid to admit it. I've seldom had an urge to run anyone into the ground, but when you act so arrogant, so high-and-mighty-lordly, breathing fire like a dragon, I react. Remember that, Solomon. I am no less of a competitor than you are."

He turned slowly to her, ignoring her comment, because she was right—she'd frightened him. "I meant it when I called you my sweetheart, damn it. A man sets the pace."

She sat very straight. "I challenge you to say it in the light of day."

He chewed on that, easing the wagon around a marshy hollow and skirting his emotions, which only Cairo seemed to nettle.

Her slight sniff gripped every nerve in his body and sent chills up his spine. His dependable instincts failed him as Cairo whispered, "I'm an athletic woman and I . . . I was glad to see you in one piece."

Solomon gripped the lines and knew he wanted to cuddle her. She acted shy and uncertain, nervous to be near him, despite her lofty statements. "Stop pushing," he warned unevenly. He turned to Cairo and shot "Sweetheart" at her like a bullet from his gun.

She twirled her parasol and lifted her chin. "You're just saying that because—"

He asked the question that had been tormenting him. "Why didn't Quigly harness the team this morning?"

She looked away at the burning golden fields spreading into the distant bluish mountains. "He held the rigging for me."

"You put on the tack, fitted the bits, and straightened the lines around the horses. Quigly kept a healthy distance apart."

"True," she agreed lightly.

"Don't tell me he's afraid of livestock," Solomon said, remembering how Quigly cooked and cleaned and laundered and helped load the billiard table.

"As a matter of fact, he is. On the rare occasions that he's had to travel alone, we pay for a stockman to help him. But don't you dare say anything. I'm perfectly capable of handling livestock."

He stared at her, trying to fit together the puzzle that was Cairo, and she returned a loftily ladylike look. "I dislike interrogation," she said finally. When he continued to study her, she said sharply, "Very well. Neither Bernard nor Quigly was worth anything around animals. Bernard was much worse, in fact. I've been tending livestock all my life. Quigly keeps the tack in good shape and does almost everything else."

She nudged Solomon with her knee. "Hurry up. Quigly should never be allowed to be in front. Unless it's a dire emergency. If the horses run, he'll panic."

Solomon eased the wagon in front of Quigly, who was decked out in his bloodred turban and his caftan and was cherishing a fine cigar.

"Hold this," Cairo ordered as she handed Solomon her parasol. She removed her gloves, opened her velvet and satin bag, and began laving ointment on her hands. Solomon caught her fingers and turned them to find what he had suspected—calluses. "You usually drive this rig, don't you?" he asked sharply.

"Goodness, yes. Did I forget to tell you that? Bernard never liked driving. I did. That parasol isn't your color," she noted critically, then patted his knee comfortingly. "You're tense because you're worried about Garnet, Solomon." Cairo drew on her gloves, reclaimed her parasol, and sat, like a tourist enjoying the passing scenery. "You've got to have confidence in my abilities as a detective. We will find Garnet, and soon. By the way, did I tell you that I'm not wearing knickers today? The freedom is wonderful."

Solomon tried to ignore the heavy pulsing of his hardened body and the thought that with very little effort, he could sink again into Cairo's smooth, hot, damp body. In seconds, she could take him from a logical moment into disaster. He wiped the perspiration from his upper lip. "How did you finance these wagons and teams?"

"The ladies of the county contributed to my immediate and dire problem. They understood my concern over Garnet and a missing husband—an arrogant selfish one, who had decided that only he should be endeavoring to find her. The ladies understood perfectly how helpless a woman can be when her husband controls the family money. The bank would not release funds to me or loan money to me without your consent," Cairo stated very distinctly. "Women-only billiards sessions at the Palace, an all-night affair the evening after you left, were more fun than a quilting bee. Quigly did all the ladies' hair and showed them how to make creams for their faces and hands. I demonstrated meditation and muscle control. You should have seen Lora McQuerty stand on her head. She can turn marvelous back flips, and she showed us how she can swing by her knees on a trapeze. There she was, swinging in her knickers above the tables. It was glorious, Solomon. The luxury baths sold for one hundred dollars apiece. Joseph carried the water. He's watching the ranch now and is eager to have Garnet returned. Then he'll go after Edward. I pray the law finds him before Joseph does."

She looked at Solomon, who was having difficulty with his breathing; every heartbeat told him to drag her back into the wagon and make love to her, until she was soft and limp, cuddly and obedient. "Women always wear knickers," he said instead, reverting to the previous logical arguement. "It's what they do."

She tossed her head. "I've decided not to. The heat chafes my thighs and makes me damp. Stop glaring at me and flaring your nostrils, Solomon sweetheart," she murmured. "Goodness, are we in the mood?" she asked as Solomon eased onto Hiyu Wind, who had been tethered to the wagon.

By the time they camped that night on the open prairie, Solomon had one thought—how quickly he could get Cairo to bed. Instead, after the horses were hobbled and Quigly was cooking their meal, he found Cairo on a moonlit knoll.

She dropped her silk robe and faced him. She stood naked, curved and soft in the silvery moonlight, her hair flowing around her. "We'll find Garnet, dear. Then we'll take her home," she whispered as he quickly undressed, tearing his clothing.

When they were sated, and Cairo's bottom nestled against him, his hand caressing her breast leisurely, Solomon covered them with a light sheet. Who was this sleeping woman in his arms? What secret past did she shield so well?

Where was Garnet? Was she safe?

Then Solomon gave himself to the sleep he'd lost and carefully lay his cheek upon her smooth one. "Sweetheart," he whispered, tasting the word, letting it fill him, sweeping away the lonely years.

She'd given herself to him passionately, demanded that he take her without waiting. . . . She'd stunned him, taken him before he could say the sweet words he'd wanted.

"Love," she'd whispered against his ear, stroking his scarred back and easing him back to earth.

Love. Solomon rummaged drowsily through the tenderness that filled him when he looked at Cairo, then drifted into sleep.

fifteen

"Mother stopped me from burning out that damned blue-eyed Indian," Edward muttered as Duncan poured whiskey into his glass. The torches lit the cave, flickering on the two men. "I had the torches and the men and was about to hightail it to the Wolfe spread and she caught me. I thought she was too far gone, drinking and crying in her room, then she comes running out of the house. When I told her my plan, she screamed and raised hell. The next thing I know, she had her horse saddled and was riding out toward the Wolfe place. She's protecting that red bastard . . . soft on him."

Duncan watched his son's flushed face and wondered how he could have spawned such a weakling. But Edward was his rein to Blanche and the Knutson spread, and Duncan needed that tether—until the papers legally named him as the rightful owner.

"He's watching the place for Wolfe, now that his woman and her man have taken off. You wait until Wolfe gets back and you've got hell to pay. They'll know by now that you took his kid. Now is the time to make your move, Eddie," Duncan prodded the boy, thinking him spineless.

"Don't call me that kid name. I measure up the same as the rest of you—and Kipp, too. No kid could have handled that Wolfe brat. She knows how to hurt a man so he can't walk or ride. That ain't natural for a girl-kid to know. I was lucky to get someone to take her off my hands. Cost a pretty penny, once she opened her mouth and started talking and biting." Edward rubbed his hand, scarred by several curved rows of small teeth.

Duncan leered at him; when Edward let the girl live, he'd proven his weakness. "Kipp's on your tail. He's been to Butte, I hear, hunting for you. He's given his word to find you and bring you to the law. He's always been Blanche's favorite. You two lock horns and you'll find out who's the better maverick."

Edward's expression darkened. "What do you mean, 'maverick'? We're the Knutson brothers, good and true."

Duncan laughed. "Sure. If that's what your mother says."

"I say. I say plenty, like I'm getting Kipp out of the way. He was always Mother's favorite."

"You deserve all of her attention. Maybe I can help you think of a way to get Kipp out of the picture. He's been running with a fast gang, and there's some talk about him thieving horses now. Seems like some Mounties had their own horses sold back to them and someone mentioned Kipp's name." Duncan omitted that he was the one to suggest that Kipp liked prime Mountie-owned horseflesh. "Now if he was to have the blame on him, your mother wouldn't be so high on him, would she? Or say, just maybe he gave that Indian girl your name before he worked her over. Then the law would come after you instead of him, wouldn't it? That would leave you in the clear. Have another drink, Edward," Duncan urged, knowing that Edward got his bravery from alcohol. Only then did he prove himself worthy of being Duncan's son.

That evening, Blanche was fully dressed and seated at the head of the dining table. She firmly placed aside her glass of wine and looked at Duncan. "Keep Edward in hiding. I don't want him found. Especially by Kipp. Kipp is incensed about Edward's dishonoring this family. Frankly—I am, too, but perhaps I'm responsible. I've known for a long time that you had your hooks into the boy and were guiding him."

Duncan threw his napkin onto his plate because he knew bad table manners angered her. "He's my boy, Blanche. A man wants to have a hand in his son's life."

"From what I know of your . . . adventures, you have other children. Leave mine alone," Blanche answered coolly. "Where is he?"

"Hiding out, like you ordered. He's safe." A man had to have his secrets, and his cave in the Highwood Mountains had served him well. He wished he'd finished Solomon Wolfe back then, when he was shackled to the walls of that cave. Duncan spat tobacco juice in a crystal glass and waited for her to rail at him. Once she was upset, she'd go running to her drink and her fancy "boudoir." Or she'd get hot—he bet on the latter—it had been too long for Blanche.

Blanche's nails tightened on her lace tablecloth and she remained cool, despite his taunt. "Duncan, Joseph has refused to leave his obligation, which is to take care of Solomon's ranch. I want the boy—Joseph—protected."

Her next words startled him, framing exactly what he

had planned to do. Blanche narrowed her eyes. "It would be only too easy for someone to place stolen stock on the Wolfe spread and make Joseph look guilty. I want him safe and away from here. You are to arrange for his safety, Duncan, for which I will pay you very well."

He leered and lifted a mocking eyebrow. Any minute she'd fly at him, and Duncan waited. He'd make her beg—pay for protecting Joseph and for playing Kipp as her favorite.

Expressionless, Blanche stared at him, and a swift, cold wind knifed through Duncan's confidence. She continued to study him, as if seeing him for the first time. "I am past disgust. Take care of Joseph if you want to retain your post here as my ranch manager. Otherwise, collect your pay. You may leave my table now, Duncan. And from now on, you'll be taking your meals at the cookhouse with the rest of the hired men."

Duncan stared at her, willing her to break. He fought the anger riding him; how he wanted to tell her that he'd done everything for her—even down to putting the pillow over old Buck's face. He would tell her someday. He rose from the table and said, "I'll take care of the breed for you, Blanche."

And how he would, he thought as he quietly closed the elegant door. Duncan spat tobacco on Blanche's prized rosebush. Blanche's bastard would hang from the cave's shackles the same as his father and Solomon.

Solomon and Cairo traveled together until noon. Then a Métis had mentioned Garnet, and Solomon rode out immediately. Garnet had passed through the area only two days ago, and Solomon followed the trail of the gang's horses until dark. The cloudy night sky prevented tracking them. Then he rode back to Cairo's camp.

Solomon eased Hiyu Wind down into Red Hole, a tiny farming settlement. Late at night, Cairo's exhibition tent was empty, the campfire burning outside her wagon. He needed more than his sketch of her; he needed to hold her before leaving at dawn.

He studied the bouquet of daisies and wildflowers tied carefully to his saddle horn, their stalks held in his dampened handkerchief to keep them fresh. Solomon supposed he'd get used to using Quigly's freshly starched and ironed handkerchiefs, but he wasn't certain about the packed lunch of watercress, chicken salad, and croissants. He couldn't refuse the dainty packed food at dawn, not when Cairo looked all drowsy and soft in her dragon robe, fussing about him.

There was more running between them than the heat and the storms.

In the light of the campfire, Solomon slid from his horse, inhaling the appetizing scent of whatever Quigly had concocted, and began unsaddling Hiyu Wind, though his thoughts locked on the woman who would be sleeping on that narrow cot.

Solomon studied the clear moonlit night. Tomorrow he would find Garnet, or come close to her. But tonight—he wanted what ran true between his sweetheart and himself. Solomon took the hot water kettle from the campfire and poured it into the basin. He shook his head when Quigly appeared, his expression worried. "Not yet. But we're close to Garnet. Maybe one or two days at the most."

"How I long to hear her little voice say 'Quig.' May I assist you, sir?" Quigly's booming voice asked quietly beside Solomon. He held out the expensive straight razor and a hot towel. "Allow me. My, that is a lovely bouquet."

Solomon nodded curtly, but was glad that the night covered his blush. "It's for her," he said unnecessarily because he was uncomfortable with the gentleness flowing through him. "Kind of a sweetheart-thing to do," he added uncomfortably. "She should have roses, maybe."

"Oh, dear, and I thought the flowers were for me," Quigly mourned, though he was grinning widely. "Yes, sir. It is a sweetheart-thing to do. There is plenty of water for a bath, if you prefer. I started filling it when I saw you in the moonlight."

When Quigly saw the game birds and the cheese rounds that the farmers had given Solomon, he acted as if they were Christmas presents. Quigly clapped his hands when presented with a sack of fresh herbs. "Rosemary! Thyme! Shallots? Oh, tell me I am in heaven," he exclaimed. "What's this? Fennel? Lovely fennel. . . ." He kissed the fragile green stalks.

Then he kissed Solomon, who stood very still and alert for seconds after. His hand rested on his gun butt, while he carefully wiped the kiss from his cheek.

Solomon locked his thoughts on Cairo and what was between them, and endured Quigly's pampering throughout his bath and meal.

Cairo awakened at the first lurch and squeak of the wagon beneath the cot. She held very still, easing her hand down to the garter on her thigh. The handle of her small knife fitted into her fingers as the wagon creaked again and she caught the scent of soap and a man's brisk aftershave.

Solomon's scents were woodsmoke, leather, and creek water, with a touch of arrogance that was all his own.

She lay very quietly as the scent of wildflowers swirled around her. The light touch on her shoulder brought her surging out of bed. Her knife flashed as her wrist was caught by a man's big hand.

"Now you wear your knickers," Solomon murmured, amused as he plucked the knife from her.

"You have frightened me, Mr. Wolfe," she shot at him, then stared at the bouquet of daisies he held out to her. She glanced at the caftan he was wearing, up at his cowboy hat, and back at the flowers. "You make a pretty picture. Did you find word of Garnet?"

"We're close. She's passed through the area two days ago. I lost the tracks at nightfall." Solomon flipped his gun belt over her hanging petticoat; he was clearly embarrassed. "For you. I'm only wearing this dress-caftan-thing because Quigly is washing my clothes. He's not getting my hat."

"You came back for me. You wanted me with you when we found her. Oh, Solomon, you are so thoughtful!" She slowly took the bouquet, and his endangered hat. She searched the shaven hollows of his face in the shadows. "Solomon?"

"I didn't exactly come back to—"

Nothing could have stopped her from leaping at him and bearing him down to her cot under a flurry of kisses. She wrestled him down, lay over him with the daisies crushed between them, and searched his rugged face with her fingertips. "You're safe. You're really safe, and you've come back for me. We'll find Garnet together. Oh, you've made me so happy!"

"You squashed the daisies," he protested in a rumbling, pleased tone as his hands found her silk-clad bottom and caressed it.

"I know . . . I know, and they're so beautiful," she admitted, studying at the jutting angles and planes of his face, his squarish chin and the dimple . . . oh, the dimple.

. . . She kissed it several times. "Oh, you're so pretty, Solomon," she exclaimed with delight. "And you have a dimple just like Kipp's! That's why you've been wearing a beard, isn't it? You look so much alike."

She raised to look down at him. "I know you're Kipp's father, Solomon," she stated slowly. "I probably knew from the first time I saw you together—equally tall, dark, and arrogant down to your boots. You share a certain cocky lone-wolf look and dragon-fiery eyes when you're angry. For a man with your reputation, you gave him too much rein. And your expression was so proud."

Solomon smoothed her cheek. "I never dared to think I could have a fine son like that, all straight and tall and proud. To think that he had my blood, that he came from my father's blood and his before him. That in him was my mother's family, straight and true and God-fearing."

Cairo placed her mouth upon his and kissed him slowly, thoroughly.

He went very still beneath her, his skin heated by her kisses along his cheekbones, his nose, the curve of his mouth. "This isn't natural," he mumbled finally, and she knew he was blushing, which delighted her.

"Ohhh!" She started to kiss him again and found her head caught in his large hands. "Don't be shy," she teased him, running her fingertip over the tiny indentation in his chin. "Look at you," she exclaimed, running her fingers through his newly cut short hair. It was crisp and clung to her fingertips, the gray trimmed away. Solomon looked younger and very sheepish and endearing. "What happened to you?"

"Quigly got me," he admitted reluctantly, clearly uncomfortable with how Quigly had expertly tended and shaved him. "I am not having any relaxing body massages from a man. My backside is plenty used to sitting on a saddle all day and doesn't need any massage," he noted darkly. "There are limits to how much torture a man can take."

Cairo paused in her exploration of him. "How soon do you think we'll find Garnet?"

"Tomorrow. Maybe," he added. "I want you to know how it is with me. How I feel about you. I want this settled between us before we collect Garnet."

sixteen

Cairo lay very still, watching Solomon.

He arose and moved slowly, methodically removing, folding, and placing the caftan over her cue stick case. He slowly rubbed his scarred wrists and she sensed him carefully aligning his thoughts.

When he sat, Cairo smoothed his back. She sat up behind him, gathering him close in her arms. She kissed the scars and he tensed, a withdrawal, but she held him tighter.

Then he was turning, bearing her down to the cot and lying beside her. "You have given me a good run, sweetheart," he said simply, holding her. "But there are things that need to be said."

She arched to kiss him, to hold him close, and he held her away, though his body had hardened at her touch. "Not this time," he said. "You won't have me fast, sweetheart. There is something running between us, more than the heat. This. We've got this," he whispered back, bending to kiss her gently, longingly. Then his hands caressed her too slowly, too carefully, removing her camisole and knickers until she felt like a willow humming in a sweet, hot summer breeze. Solomon touched her in ways he'd never done before, slowly, so slowly, running his lips across her ear, the heat of his breath filling her, melting her until she moved restlessly beneath him.

When she would have touched him, brought him to her very depths to fill the emptiness, Solomon caught her fingers, suckling them one by one. By the time he kissed her throat, Cairo was breathing unevenly, aching almost painfully for him.

By the time Solomon's open mouth suckled at her breast, she was trembling, her fingers digging into his shoulder. "Solomon, now . . . now. . . ."

His answer was to taste her other breast, to lick the hard nub of her nipple and gently bite it.

Cairo locked her fingers in his hair as he moved down her body, heating her skin, burning her with textures that caught her breath. His hands stroked her legs, drawing up her knees to kiss the sensitive inner skin. Images swirled around her enticingly.

Flames skimming across a summer lake.

Skin heated too hot, too tight.

Desire dancing along her pulse, igniting with each touch, each kiss. She heard herself call out, a desperate husky cry, urging him to take her.

He fought her taking him, kept her beneath him, her arms locking him closer, closer. Then Solomon rose above her, his fingers locked with hers, his hands pressing hers to the cot beside her head. He was her fierce dragon, eyes flashing, storms slashing, his shoulders taut and his arms trembling as his hips pressed hers down.

"Why?" she asked shakily, fighting her needs, her legs cradling his, hips moving up to take him.

"There's more than the quick heat between us. You missed me. Say it. Say you missed me," he demanded. Or was it a plea?

He caught the challenge in her eyes and the lift of her chin. "Not this time, sweetheart," he murmured in the hot, still, humming passion between them and entered her in one stroke.

She cried out when he withdrew. "I'll make you pay for this, Solomon Wolfe," she gritted between her teeth, realizing that she was trembling and their bodies were damp and slick.

Solomon's eyes were closed now, his expression withdrawn, and she knew he was centering on the lock of their bodies, riveting her into a trembling hot knot, buffeting her like a mountain lightning storm. "Say it. Say that it's more than a craving . . . a want . . . a necessity," he said between his teeth, his body arcing down on hers; he lay deep within her, pulsing and hard, and she cried out desperately.

She threw herself against him, locked him tight to her, and demanded fiercely, "I won't have this . . . you're going too far. You want too much."

She fought him then, wildly, drawing him deeper, keeping him and raising for his mouth on hers, on her body. "Yes . . ." she would remember saying later, the truth washing across her tender lips. "Yes, there is more."

When she could breathe, she lay half off the cot, limp as the mashed daisies between them, the waves of heat easing. Solomon gathered her closer, his heart racing against her breast, his hand smoothing her hip. She shot him a distrusting glance and found him looking at her. His hand smoothed her breast, the shimmering pulse beating there. "There's more," he repeated finally, drawing her into his arms. "When you go, I want you to remember this. How it was—here with me tonight. Because I'll remember and it will be a sweet memory to hold close when the years flow by. I'd like to think that this is how people love . . . how babies come to be, how a man gives a woman the best part of him."

Cairo shivered and kissed his chest with the tenderness running through her. She'd survived alone, willing herself to be strong.

The shattering had taken a part of her, had softened and melted and had slid it away from her keeping. She listened to the night and to Solomon's heart, and she feared the tethers of her heart. She let her teardrops fall, pool upon his chest, and gave herself to the gentling of his hands. She knew then why he had given her flowers and had allowed Quigly's tending. He'd prepared himself as a bridegroom for his bride.

"This is what I want for my son, when it is time for him to come to a woman—a woman who makes him feel new," Solomon whispered against her hair. "This sweetheart feeling when the night is soft and wrapped around us."

She closed her eyes against the wave of emotion slamming into her as he continued, "I'm thinking that if I hadn't forced you into this marriage, things could have been different between us. That maybe we might have a forever before us. Then I'd purely want to put a baby down in that hot, sweet, warm nest. When he came fighting into this world, I'd hold him tight against me and claim him and do my best to see that he'd get all the love he needs."

Solomon's eyes flickered warily and he looked away as she smoothed his lips with hers. "To hold his young . . . it is a need that comes on a man that is purely fearsome sometimes," he explained in a husky whisper. "Don't pay any attention to my wanderings. What is running between us would make any man proud . . . until you go."

Then he gathered her close and she held him.

Garnet drifted awake. The outlaws' cabin was dirty. Old Frank was a pretty good cook, though. She caught the scent of his molasses cookies and reached into her bag to retrieve one. She munched on it and listened to the men's snoring. Tomorrow she'd get them into a game of poker and make them clean up the cabin. Her next move was to get them to bathe and wear clean clothes.

She looked out at the moon and wished for her ma and pa. She fought tears. Things weren't so bad. Most of the time, she had things her way. If Ma and Pa didn't turn up soon, she'd have to pack up and leave her fun.

They would find her. Garnet allowed herself a sniffle. "Ma can be tough and Pa won't let nothing stop him. They love me."

Garnet sniffed again and spoke to comfort herself. "This sure was fun for a while. My big adventure. I sure hope Ma and Pa are working on my baby sister or brother, that's all. I'm sure giving them lots of time alone."

Garnet swallowed and stared at the big, lonely moon. "I sure need some of Ma's fairy dust now," she whispered. "But Pa can be real set in his ways when he wants something and I know he wants me. Back when I was a bad kid on the Barbary, he paid something fierce to bring me here. Ma, too. She talks sweet to me like my other ma." Garnet wiped her eyes. "They'll be coming. It's just a matter of time. Meanwhile the least they could do is make me a little sister."

"I don't want to hear any more about wife-replacements," Solomon muttered as he lifted Cairo from her sidesaddle to the earth. Most of the hard day of riding to the outlaw hideout where Garnet was reputed to be, Cairo had wanted to be close to him. She had ridden behind him, her arms locked around him as if she'd never let him go.

Solomon had focused on landmarks, seeking the cabin where Garnet would be and willing her to be safe.

When the pace was slowed to rest the horses, Cairo had snuggled to his back, riding behind him. Used to contemplating his plans alone, Solomon had been nettled at first.

He wasn't comfortable with Cairo's breath blowing in his ear—women shouldn't blow in men's ears. Men's ears weren't designed for warm breath and nibbling, and every time Cairo's tongue teased his ear his entire body reacted, jolted into a hard knot. As if the tip of her hot, moist tongue had shot right down through him and set him off. When she rode behind him, he sat very still while she toyed with his earlobes. The breath-blowing-teasing and the damp tip of her tongue put a strain on his control.

Cairo glowed in the dusk, her hair perfectly curled beneath her bonnet, and her lips looking luscious and soft and inviting. She adjusted the daisy in his buttonhole. Solomon scowled at her. "Stay out of this. This is dangerous work."

She lifted a challenging eyebrow, and he knew then that Cairo would be in the center of the fracas. Unless he stopped her. "See anything?" he asked of Cairo, who was hiding behind a sarviceberry bush, peering at the square log cabin.

"Shush. I'm looking for sign of Garnet," she returned in a distracted tone. She continued watching the cabin. "Oh, Solomon, I do hope she's safe. If they've harmed her in any way . . . What can I do?"

He handed her his rifle. "Watch the horses while I check for lookouts. Then I'll whistle like a mockingbird and you can meet me at the front door. Meanwhile, don't stick that sweet little busy tongue into another man's ears, if you know what's good for you. A torment like that could cause him to go blind or to embarrass himself like a half-grown boy."

"I intend to help you recover Garnet, Solomon."

"You stay put."

Solomon glanced at the cabin, noting the child's swing hanging from a tree. That was a good sign.

He moved swiftly toward the cabin, using the bushes for cover. He had no intention of whistling for Cairo until the outlaws were bound. He prayed that Garnet would be safe.

Rounding the cabin, Solomon glanced at Cairo and couldn't see her. He cursed silently. Damn, the woman wouldn't stay put. He crouched beneath the open window and listened carefully. "Boys, up the ante if you want to play," Garnet said firmly. "Old Frank, I'd sure like to add that last gold tooth to my poke. Now look at this fine gold toothpick I'm betting. Got it from a snot-nose named Edward."

Solomon smiled coolly. He stood upright, waited for the players to be locked on the new game, and then stepped into the window, his guns drawn. He prayed his speed and accuracy would keep Garnet safe if the men decided to go for their guns.

"Pa!" Garnet cried, leaping down from the chair, padded to raise her to the table. She ran to him as Old Frank and "the boys" eyed Solomon's dual revolvers.

He motioned her behind him. "Stay put."

* * *

The next afternoon, Garnet stuffed bread and jam into her mouth. Around it, she said, "Oh, Quig, you should have seen my pa."

For once the huge man did not protest her lack of table manners. The wagons were packed, the billiard table disassembled. Garnet beamed at Quigly. "Pa was grand. Just stepped into the open window, wearing a daisy in his shirt, and said, 'Boys, I've come for my little girl. I've had a bad day and I'm in no mood to powwow.' There I was, having taken Old Frank's last gold tooth in a blackjack game, and boy, was I glad to see my pa. He twirled his gun, sideways, forward, and then backward into his holster. The gang was scared, all six of them. Course, they scared me, too. But I didn't let on, and I got them buffaloed. They built a swing for me."

Garnet wiped the back of her sleeve across the milk left on her mouth. Her eyes widened and she chewed rapidly, anxious to get on with her story. "Then, Quig, here comes Ma. She knocked on the door like a lady does, you know. Then Pa looked like thunder and doomed for hell when he said, 'Open it, Garnet. That would be her.' Then Ma strolled in, pretty as you please, twirling her fancy parasol. She didn't spare the gang a look but went straight to Pa. Then she ripped out the daisy from his buttonhole, threw it at his boots, and pegged it with her knife. 'That was not a sweetheart thing to do, Mr. Wolfe. I never heard that mockingbird whistle,' she says with steam shooting from her eyes. She said something no-account about tongues and torments. 'Come along, Garnet,' she says after kissing me and making over me just like real mothers do, you know. 'It's time to go home, my dear,' she says with a little soft voice and a tear rolling down her cheek."

Garnet poured her poke onto the linen tablecloth. "I cried, too, 'cause I was happy. But Ma said it was okay and not to be ashamed of being glad to be with family. Look at my pickin's, Quig. Ain't they grand?"

She pointed to a collection of trade beads, gold buttons, and gold teeth. A glass eyeball rolled across the table and into Quigly's waiting glove. Then she yawned, stretched, and climbed up into Solomon's lap. She snuggled to him and yawned again. "Oh, it was a grand adventure all right. Lots a good folks along the way, except for that Edward at first. He's the one who got me from the ranch. Told me he had candy. Put me in a gunnysack to keep me from biting him. I was about to cut my way out when he passed me off on a gang and paid them to keep me. But after a while, they didn't want me. They tried to run off once and leave me. Most of them said I could go if I wanted. Sometimes they asked if I would leave them alone and not plague them anymore, but I said 'No, my ma and pa will be right along.'"

Garnet stroked Solomon's new short haircut. "You're pretty, Pa. Wasn't it grand when Ma handed out her best Nabob and Sultana cigars to the gang and thanked them for taking good care of me? Ain't that just like a lady? That's what I'm going to be when I grow up . . . a lady like Ma."

Cairo fought the deep fatigue of riding all night on the moonlit prairie. She refused to look at Solomon cuddling the drowsy girl on his lap, his expression tender as he listened to her explanation of her "pickin's."

They would start home before dawn, but now was a time for resting. Because the wagons were packed, Quigly had erected the camp tents.

Solomon looked at her over the sleeping girl's head and Cairo looked away, avoiding him. Her dark mood had swarmed like angry bees around her throughout the ride back to camp. She had trusted him, felt so alive after their lovemaking, and then he had tricked her.

When he'd entered the cabin, Cairo didn't want to feel the fear that almost caused her to empty her stomach. She didn't want to panic, to know that if anything happened to him, she'd never be the same because he'd taken away a part of her . . . or that she had given him something she never could reclaim. He had no right to offer himself up to danger, not while he was in her keeping.

The image of Solomon lying in a pool of blood had sent ice through her veins. She rose abruptly to her feet. She needed time to think, away from Solomon and the fire and growing tenderness between them. "It's the middle of August. It will take us at least until the end of the month to get home. We have to move quickly. I'm going to bed now. Please bring Garnet soon."

"I detest calluses and sweat and dawn," Cairo muttered sleepily after their first week of traveling. With Garnet in hand, they moved more slowly.

Solomon had learned that Cairo could sweet-talk a farmer's wife out of a meal and have her doing laundry at the same time. Exhausted and peeved by his absence from a regular stove, Quigly was glad for the help.

Solomon enjoyed every moment of her toilette, the smoothing and the oils and the luscious way she rolled down her garters. He'd never seen a woman do that so slowly, so elegantly.

He wondered if his skin smelled like hers, because they certainly were pressed together often enough, hungry for each other. That was when Garnet could be moved from their bed.

Cairo's long, mystical look over her shoulder winded him. One look, one touch set his pulse racing, and she met him fire for fire, until the embers eased and lay soft around them.

That was the time Solomon liked, the cuddling and nestling and the softness. He promised himself that once they were safe at the ranch, he'd do his best in the sweetheart business. He regretted forcing her to marry him, and now he planned to show her how much he cared.

While she slept, he lay in the soft tangle of her arms, breathing in her scent in the wagon filled with lace and ribbons and petticoats, and let it seep into him. When she looked at him, fire flashing in her eyes, he knew that nothing could keep them apart.

Now in the dawn, she snuggled on their pallet beneath the wagon while Solomon crouched beside her, fully dressed and ready to travel. "I want my bed and my bath and Quigly's wonderful massages," she added, turning away from the first light of day.

With his glove, Solomon smoothed the satin quilt down to her bottom and hit it once. Garnet's giggle sounded above them, in the wagon. "What do you think, Garnet? Shall I roll her out of here?" he asked.

Garnet giggled again. "She'll get you, Pa, if you do. You'd better be careful."

Cairo turned to glare at him, and the sight of her rumpled and warm and ready to sail at him caused him to smile. "You," she said grandly. "You will stop grinning and you will not invade my boudoir at this ungodly hour."

Solomon grabbed the canvas beneath her and slowly pulled her out from the wagon. Garnet peeped around the wagon's canvas cover and grinned.

Cairo lay glaring up at him, her bare shoulder gleaming in the pink dawn. He thought about the long, slender body beneath the elegant satin quilt and wanted to join her. "Do you think she needs a spanking, Garnet?"

"Nah. Kiss her. She always gets wilty when you do, Pa."

Cairo continued glaring at him. "I detest a playful man in the morning. Stop leering and stop—"

Solomon scooped her up and sat on the ground with her in his arms. She sniffed elegantly, then allowed him to hold her. "What's for breakfast?"

Quigly appeared with a platter of last night's biscuits. They had been warmed and were oozing with butter and jam. "Gad, how I long for a proper stove."

She greedily snatched a biscuit and curled prettily against Solomon. "Garnet, come eat."

Garnet, dressed in her long nightgown, a ruffled affair Quigly had made while worrying about her, slid onto Cairo's lap. Solomon sat, content with everything he wanted in his arms. "What about me? I don't suppose anyone thought about my breakfast," he grumbled, not unhappily.

Cairo shot him a sultry look that said he should be well satisfied from their last lovemaking. Garnet fed him a biscuit. Both females snuggled back against Solomon and Garnet mashed a berry-jam kiss to his lips. "My ma and pa and me. Ain't it grand, Quig?"

"Are we enjoying ourselves, sir?" Quigly asked with a broad grin.

Solomon returned the grin.

"Mmm," Cairo murmured, and arched to nibble his ear. She blinked when the first cold drop of rain hit her cheek. "Is that rain?"

That day, rain slashed across the prairie, lightning lashed the dark, rolling skies, and the wagon skidded in the mud on the slight slopes.

Walking beside the horses, Solomon glanced at Cairo on the wagon bench. Garnet was sleeping safely under the canvas-covered hoops.

His boots slid in the mud. He felt himself going down, too close to the nervous horses. As he fell, he saw Cairo, her face a pale blur in the storm. The horse's hoof caught his head and for a moment the pain did not come. Solomon knew in that instant, blood covering his vision, that the wound was probably fatal. He'd seen head wounds from kicking horses. The horse's hoof had caught him squarely, the iron shoe adding to the force.

Mud rose up to him and he prayed that Quigly and Garnet, traveling ahead of them, were safe and that Quigly could manage the teams. When the pain and the darkness came, he regretted dying and not seeing Garnet grown and happy, or Kipp settled in a good life. He regretted not holding his daisy once more—the only one he'd ever had—Cairo. *Cairo, take care of yourself. Cairo . . . Cairo. . . .*

He hoped that Garnet would grow up into a fine woman and have what she wanted from life. Live a good honest life, Kipp.

Cairo was talking to him urgently, demanding something he couldn't give. "Sweetheart," he heard himself say a distance away from the burning pain. "Sweetheart . . . I'm sorry . . . for leaving you now."

"You're not going anywhere, Solomon Wolfe," she stated unevenly. "But up in the wagon where I can tend you. Quigly, help me!" she called, her voice fading as Solomon sank into the hellish pain.

Cairo looked back to the man tossing restlessly in the wagon. Just an hour ago, she'd dragged him from the mud and tended him. Every second since the accident, she'd thought of nothing but keeping Solomon alive. She briefly released the reins with one hand and hugged the frightened girl on the seat beside her. "He'll be just fine. Quigly and I know how to take care of him."

"Pa is so white," Garnet whispered unsteadily, wrapping both arms around Cairo. "Like Ma . . . my real ma when she died."

"Garnet, Solomon won't die. He's sleeping, that's all. His body needs rest to mend."

"It's 'cause of me. 'Cause I was having a high time on my adventure and he had to come after me. Now he's hurt. When you weren't there, that Miss Adele said I should be quiet and leave grown-ups alone. Edward said you and Pa needed some time without me—"

"Hush. Edward is full of beans and Miss Adele is full of horsefeathers," Cairo muttered, damning the woman. "We came because we love you and maybe we had an adventure or two along the way, too."

Quigly drew his wagon to a stop and trudged back to them. "I could use company in my wagon," he said, eyeing Garnet. "It's bad enough that I'm forced to labor like this. I don't suppose you'd come keep me company. You could"—Quigly winced painfully—"tell me more stories of the Barbary."

"I'm staying with my pa," Garnet returned, though her eyes lit with the prospect of telling Quigly more Barbary Coast stories.

Cairo kissed Garnet. "Go with him. He needs you and your pa will be just fine." Cairo prayed that she wasn't lying.

Alone with Solomon, Cairo's fears enveloped her. They were miles from help; Quigly had looked at Solomon's bloody head and had taken sick. Cairo had cleansed the deep wound on Solomon's forehead with her best sour mash whiskey and padded it with yarrow. "He's wearing my best black silk thread in that arrogant, no-account, low-down skin of his. . . ." She wiped the tears from her eyes and Solomon's leather glove began to slide off her hand as she gathered the reins closer.

He had looked so vulnerable, so wounded lying in the pounding rain, blood gushing from his head and running into the mud.

Her Italian slate, her fine Belgian table cover . . . nothing mattered except dragging Solomon to safety as the lightning cracked overhead, startling the horses. She'd grabbed yarrow blossoms and pushed them to the gaping wound to slow the blood.

So much blood. Solomon's face was ghostly pale, lit by lightning.

She slashed her sleeve across her face, drying the trail of tears that wouldn't stop. Dosed with laudanum now, Solomon's feverish ramblings about his life told an ugly picture. He'd seen more than he'd told her . . . as a boy, he'd seen his parents tortured, his mother raped. He'd wanted to hold his son in his arms. He cried out for Fancy, cursing himself for not finding her. Then there was the darkness that was Duncan, dark, stormy memories as Solomon struggled against the cave's shackles. He'd called Duncan out, thought he'd killed him.

"*I'll take care of her, Fancy. She'll grow up in wildflowers and good fresh air, just like you want,*" he cried out deliriously, and pain slammed into Cairo. "*Oh, God, Fancy . . . I'm sorry I didn't find you. . . .*" His anguish shot into Cairo and she straightened, forcing herself to control the team, nervous with the man's feverish cries.

Their first camp was miserable. Quigly was visibly shaken by the accident, the storm, and Garnet's stories.

Cairo had cooked the trail supper of rabbit and barley broth. Quigly had carried off a sleeping Garnet soon after they ate.

The rain slashed at the canvas as Cairo tried again to feed Solomon. He called Cairo a "hot-tongued ear defiler" and accused her of violating his privacy with her breath and by nibbling on his earlobe where no righteous woman should prowl. "Oh, you'll pay for that, sweetheart," he threatened, fighting her broth of rabbit and barley, denying her access until he felt the nudge of her breast.

He'd nuzzled her softness, kissing her weakly, and she knew that he wanted her breast. She'd have given her soul to make him live. . . .

There he lay, all two hundred pounds, lanky tough six feet four inches of him, weak as a baby and needing her breast. What could she do but open her silk bodice ruined by the rain and mud and give him what he wanted? She'd held his bandaged head to her and rocked him, letting him doze upon her.

"Daisy . . ." he'd whispered feverishly.

"I'll plant no daisies over your grave, Mr. Wolfe," she'd told him unevenly. "Because you are not leaving me this way."

Then in a hoarse voice cracked with fever, he'd asked her to do something shocking, to place his fingers within her, so that he could feel her heat, to touch the sweet place where he'd wanted his baby to nest.

So, with tears streaming down her face, she'd eased his hand to what he sought. "To hold my baby with you, sweetheart . . . would have been . . . grand," he whispered, his black eyes bright with fever and hopelessness.

He began to slip away from her then, and in her desperation, she took his jaw to her breast and moved her nipple upon his lips. She willed him to taste her, to hold to life . . . and she'd clamped her thighs to hold his weak touch to life and the dream of the baby he'd wanted, and regretted never holding.

The slow curl of his tongue to touch her nipple stopped the frightened stroke of her heart.

She kissed him then . . . short, soft, tempting kisses, allowing him to rest before giving him another.

His face lay hot against her breasts as the thunder and the lightning rocked the dark world outside the wagon. She dozed, forcing herself to rest.

In the morning, the cold prairie wind whipped the wagon's canvas. This was the day after his accident; each day would add to Solomon's chances.

She pulled on the wagon brake with both hands as the team eased down a slight slope. They had to keep moving.

At the bottom of the incline, she looked back to see Quigly stop the horses. Beside him, Garnet scowled up at him and he shook his head fearfully. Sighing, Cairo slid down from her wagon and trudged back to his. She climbed up on the seat and guided the wagon down the slope. Then she hopped off and reseated herself in her wagon.

The tears rolled from her cheeks, dropping onto the saddlebags beside her.

Cairo threaded the reins through her hands, though the fingers of Solomon's worn gloves, and glanced at his saddlebags. The damning evidence inside them had torn her heart from its protective moorings.

To tend him better, she'd dressed him in Quigly's new caftan, a rakish fire-red affair.

Then because she needed him close to her and keeping her calm, she wore his clothing, burying her nose in the collar to catch his scent.

The accident was only yesterday and she smelled of horses and sweat now, working and sleeping in his shirt.

Cairo bit her lip. If only she hadn't looked inside his saddlebags to find his razor—a small area of his scalp had to be shaved to make her stitches hold—and then she found the sketch, crudely drawn, and the sweet, sweet, tender letters to his sweetheart, his daisy.

The loneliness of a cowboy at the night's campfire, the wolves howling in the distance, the need of a man for his woman, echoed in every word.

Cairo slashed at the tears blinding her.

He'd written so beautifully that he'd torn through the protection of her heart, sank the shaft so deep and so true that she couldn't forgive him. . . .

He'd touched her in places that were hers alone, kissed and nuzzled her in his shocking request, and his fingertips had gone to the very center of her, where he mourned a baby she would never have . . . and had never wanted . . . until that sharp pang of longing lurched within her, drawn from the gentle seeking movement of his hand—

She wept harshly, her heart tearing. Solomon Wolfe had no right to bind her with tethers of dreams and whimsy and longing. . . .

He had no right to draw from her very womb the awesome need to hold his child, to feel his baby suckle at her breast.

Cairo hunched beneath Solomon's coat, shivered with the surge of needs and dreams swarming around her, and knew that she couldn't allow any of it.

seventeen

"I t's only a kid." Outside the wagon, the wind carried a man's rough, quiet voice to Solomon.

He lay trying to push away the thundering pain in his head. He was too weak, straining to grip his gun belt and to stand. He shoved away the herb bundles dangling from the wagon's hoop and damp silk knickers hit him in the face. He ripped them away, struggling not to lose consciousness. He pushed aside the hanging smoked carcass of a duck; he had to protect Cairo, Garnet, and Quigly.

Solomon worked his way to the back of the wagon; the moonlit night outlined two men outside the campfire and a youth crouched by fire, tending it and cooking. A wave of nausea crawled over Solomon, making him sweat, but he forced himself to ease from the back of the wagon.

His bare foot caught on cloth and he realized belatedly that he was nude beneath Quigly's nightmarish creation, a caftan.

The men separated, moving like wolves around the

campfire, then came into the light, leering at the youth. He stood very slowly and beneath Solomon's hat, Cairo's pale face appeared. "Hello, boys. Care to eat?" she asked in a welcoming tone as Solomon edged closer, gripping the wagon spokes for support. He recognized the breed of these men—the look of predators, the lawless breed that preyed upon travelers.

"They're moving along, aren't you, boys?" Solomon said with strength he did not feel.

"Solomon!" Cairo's exclamation held joy and relief. She began to move toward him, her path blocked by the men.

The one with Mexican rowel spurs and a scar across his face, probably caused by a spur, leered at Solomon. "Now, ain't she pretty?" he said, noting Solomon's caftan.

"Pretty enough," Solomon said, leveling his gun and ignoring the cold wind sweeping up his backside.

"He means business," the other man whispered harshly. "Look at those eyes . . . they got that flat killer-look."

"Ah . . . we'll just be going, mister," the first man said quickly, then they rode off into the night.

Cairo hurried to Solomon just as his knees weakened. She eased him to the ground, then sat behind him, braced by the wagon wheel. He let her hold him and threaten him and kiss him until the woozy, weak feeling eased. He rested his aching head back against her shoulder. "Where's Garnet and Quigly?"

"Oh, Solomon, you're awake! You're alive! Oh, Garnet and Quigly? They're fine, asleep in the wagon. Oh, Solomon, I'm so glad you're feeling better." She hugged him and placed kisses all over his face, taking care not to bump his bandaged forehead. Solomon wallowed hazily, happily in a golden haze.

"You stink," he said finally, comforted by her arms around him, her hands smoothing his hair back from his hot cheeks.

"Hush. I'm your sweetheart. Your daisy, remember? Oh, Lord, I'm glad you're awake!"

He found a weak silly grin on his face and kept it there while she kissed his cheek and gathered him closer. He opened his eyes to see his white legs gleaming in the firelight. "This abomination is a fearsome trial to place on a righteous man."

Then he forced his head back, narrowing his eyes against the pain shooting through him. He studied her long, bare neck. "If you've cut your hair, there will be hell to pay. Here I am, weak as spit, in a dress, and—"

She swept off his hat and her hair spilled down around him. He welcomed the silken fall—like a drunken fool, he wallowed in the fragrance as a strand slid across his cheek. He nestled his back against the softness of her breasts and snuggled down with her arms around him; he could feel himself smirking, despite the pain. He was ashamed of his weakness, barely able to reach out and catch a fistful of her hair, bringing it to his face. "I didn't dream this. You holding me."

A sweet memory slid by him as she blushed. "Yes," she whispered simply.

He caressed her hair with his thumb as Cairo carefully fed him slivers of roasted rabbit, bits of freshly baked biscuits, and forced him to drink meat broth with barley. In the pungent tea she forced him to take, he recognized the taste of rose hips, yarrow, sage, and other herbs, sweetened with molasses. To his shame, Cairo helped him back into the wagon, fretting that the cold, damp night would make him more ill.

He roused when she came to him, clean and sweet from her bath and wearing nothing but warm silky skin. She cuddled him close and covered him tenderly, and eased his head upon her breasts.

"My ma sure knows horses," Garnet stated proudly on the seat beside Solomon. Cairo, dressed in his shirt, pants, and a woolen poncho, looked down at her boots, studying them as she talked with the horse trader. It was September now, summer pushed away by a cold prairie wind. After seven days, Solomon was aggravated by his weakness and this bold new woman who was the camp cook and one of the best teamsters he'd ever seen.

She could cuss like the devil during the day and love like a lady at night. Because Solomon's head throbbed with any noise, she'd tie the team and go running across the prairie with her rifle to return with game.

Solomon inhaled sharply and a pain ripped through his healing stitches. Here he was, weak as a child and having his woman feed, bathe, and love the living daylights out of him at night. To a man who always took care of others, this dilemma had to do with the rightful place of a man and a woman.

He glared at her. Something was making her happy. All the hard work had done nothing but place a bloom upon her face. And now here she was, his ladylike wife, enjoying haggling with horse traders.

They'd lost three horses to accidents and wolves. Cairo began inspecting the trader's herd, moving around each horse, looking at teeth, ears, hooves, and pushing at their sides. She finally selected three horses and paid the man.

Solomon gripped the satin blanket around him with one fist; he clamped his other hand to the side of the wagon, fear lurching through him. Cairo was preparing to ride a big outlaw horse, and Solomon didn't have the strength to stop her. Cairo swung up into the saddle and the horse began bucking. She clung to his back and Solomon made promises about what he'd do to her for scaring him. Then the horse ran into the wind and Cairo lowered her head, riding him across the prairie.

Garnet grinned up at him. "Pa, you just said a nasty word. You told me it was bad to say that."

"Well, don't you say it," he returned, following Cairo.

Solomon realized his mouth and throat were dried by fear, that his fingers ached from holding the wagon bench, and he realized, too, that if the animal was ornery, the woman was a fair match.

The gold sun silhouetted the race across the horizon, the woman bent low over the flying mane, the horse's tail streaming out in the wind. The horse reared against the big bright round sun and Solomon's heart stopped.

Cairo swept off his hat, her hair flying around her like a stormy halo. She whipped the horse's flanks, racing him around the wagon.

"Ain't she something, Pa?" Garnet breathed in adoration.

"She's something all right," he muttered darkly.

She was winding the horse, pitting her will against the animal's and finally guiding him back to the harnessed horses. Solomon met her triumphant grin with a scowl and wished he had his hands on her backside.

Like an experienced driver, Cairo lashed the horse to the harnessed horses, so that he would have to keep pace and learn how to pull.

"How was it, Ma?" Garnet called excitedly. "How

about me? Can I ride him? Will you teach me how to ride like that and trade horses? Huh? Will you?"

Seated on the other wagon, Quigly closed his eyes and shuddered. "Oh, please, dear Lord. Not two of them."

"Maybe. If your pa says so." Cairo grabbed the grease bucket from the side of the wagon and began swabbing the wheel hubs. She glanced at Solomon. "That frown must hurt."

Solomon struggled for words, and in the end, just glowered at her.

She swung up into the wagon seat. "His name is The Cuss," she stated before lifting her hand to test Solomon's forehead. "Did I forget to tell you that I know horses, from mangy nags to Thoroughbreds? That one just stood and eyeballed me—looked at me as if he didn't like me. I don't like him, either, so we're even. He's big and tough and reminds me of you. You're both contrary and surly and—"

He caught her wrist. "That was some show," he stated darkly, not trusting himself and hating himself for his weakness. "I don't suppose you've got a kiss saved up down in that evil heart of yours, just to let me know you're safe."

When she pressed a kiss to him, soft and quick, he caught her jaw and deepened it, trying to make her know that he cared, fearing for her. She did not respond and he whispered darkly against her lips, "Now I know you for what you are, ornery and contrary. There's not a bit of a daisy in you, just pure sheer pigheaded meanness."

Garnet moved behind them, standing with an arm wrapped around each of their necks. She watched them intently, curiously. "Is this a Ma-Pa fight?"

"We're sorting things out. Why don't you go ride with Quigly?" Solomon asked as gently as he could.

Garnet muttered and scrambled down to board Quigly's wagon. Cairo's expression revealed little as she said thoughtfully, "Imagine a girl Garnet's age, stuck on a horse like that, running it into the ground and terrified that she'd fall off. And knowing that everyone depended on her to live. That was what I was doing the day that Bernard bought me from Pa."

He knew then the terror she had come from and she shocked him by adding "My own father wanted me. I was just a little girl—"

The impact of that sent him reeling as he smoothed away her tears. Just as he had his scars, she had hers. She had told him that in the beginning, that not all scars could be seen, and now he knew the truth of it. "That was a long time ago, daisy-girl. You've done fine."

She glared at him. "Then you come along, just when everything was so right."

"Right? This dress isn't my usual gear. I want my clothes back," he muttered, embarrassed that she was tending him and he wanted to take care of her and cuddle her and ease her memories of a hard life. A cowboy in a caftan just wasn't right for taking care of sweethearts.

Her jaw set in a stubborn angle, giving him little sympathy. "You'll have your clothes soon enough. The ones I've been wearing are drying at the back of the wagon. That brown nag is the best of the lot and she's been doctored so much she's barely standing. The black one is a heaver, his wind is broken. I hate horse doctors and every nasty trick they do to these poor animals."

The bitterness in her voice caused Solomon to take her hand and she jerked it away, slashing at the tears in her eyes. "Yes, I know about horse doctoring. About a father who drinks away money that his family needs. About how he looked with his skin torn from him with hot tar and feathers. I know about no beans or bread and babies crying for food. I know what it feels like to have your stomach pushed to your backbone and how helpless it feels to have others depending on you and you just can't fill their needs. I know what it is to tend a mother who's been badly beaten—used roughly after just having a baby—and still won't leave her husband," she said tightly, lifting the reins as tears streamed freely down her cheeks. "Gee-ah! Giddup, you sons of—"

Then she turned to him, pain lodged deep in her eyes, tears welling up over her lids and spilling down her cheeks. He wondered why he hadn't seen this deep pain before. "This is what I am, a crooked horse trader's daughter. I've got a bit of Pa's wickedness in me, and the daring to pull it off. Bernard taught me the other, the smooth lady and polish. I've worked for everything, paid for it since before I could remember. You're a dreamer, Solomon Wolfe, with your sweetheart pictures and your sweet letters— Oh, yes, I saw your picture of me and my big feet. But the world isn't for sweethearts and daisies. It's for those who make their fortunes and don't get trapped."

She crumpled before him, vulnerable when a moment ago, pitting herself against the horse, she had been fierce and strong. He could do little but place his arm around her and she clung to him. "Oh, Solomon. I left them all—Ma and the kids—because I wanted to live and because I didn't want Pa to have me. He probably took one of my sisters instead. I can't stop thinking about where they are or if they are safe. Marsha Jane always wanted to call herself by a fancy French name, Désirée. I left all of them," she repeated in a sob.

He understood then how deep Cairo's emotions ran against the tethers of a family.

She cried in his arms that night, sobbing painfully.

Because, after a time, he needed the kiss as much as she, he lifted her chin with his fingertip; he tried to tell her with his lips that he understood how it hurt to lose a family.

"No," she whispered so quietly that the soft September wind swept away her words onto the prairie. "No. . . ."

The night before they expected to reach the ranch, Cairo moved over him twice, the second time more fiercely, more demanding, more urgently as she lifted her breasts to his lips. She cried out when he bit her gently. When they were done, she slept, holding him closely with arms and legs and stirring only to kiss him, here on his shoulder, there on his throat.

In her sleep, she guided his hand to her intimately and breathed unevenly. "Tell me about this baby you want," she whispered against his temple as his head rested on her breasts.

Because he thought she was sleeping, talking restlessly in her dreams, he shared that which lurked deep and sweet within him.

In the morning, The Cuss moved easily into his morning harness and Cairo fondled his ears as he preferred.

The Cuss's liquidy brown eyes swung warily to Solomon, who had come up behind Cairo. This morning Solomon was quiet, pale, and shaved. She regretted that she had not kept him better, that she had not had the energy to do more than keep the wagon rolling, keep the horses tethered for the night, keep the food over the campfire, and see that Solomon didn't slip back into his fever.

Cairo reveled in the wonder and the joy of him surging up into her, filling her heavy and hot and silky. She reveled in the knowledge that it meant something wonderful to him, not just a passing necessity as her father had shown for her mother.

Their coupling in the night was too sweet and lingering to be real. She flushed beneath the shadowy shield of her bonnet and stepped firmly away from him.

Solomon urged the team down the knoll near the ranch. They'd been gone over a month. Tumbleweeds spread across the front porch and the corrals and pens were empty. He sensed that something was wrong.

He was obligated by honor to free Cairo from her promise. He wanted her to know that if new trouble waited at the ranch, he would handle it alone. She'd done more than her share bringing them home safely. "You saved my life. It was wrong of me to force you into marriage when you were so set against it. When you've got dreams to follow. I won't hold you to your wager. You can go," Solomon said, his fingers tightening on the reins. "Just don't tell anyone about my sweetheart letters or my drawing. I'll deny it if you do and say you were so fascinated with me that you saw mirages."

Only a man driven mad by a woman who had defiled his ears would sit and write letters like that, Solomon brooded. He truly missed that agile little tongue.

Garnet raced across the dry weeds, and whitetail deer, grazing a distance away, peered at the wagons for a moment before lifting their tails and fleeing. Solomon did not look at Cairo, but her body straightened in the seat beside him.

"I think," she said very quietly, "that my word is my honor, just as yours is to you. We had a year's bargain, Mr. Wolfe, and I intend to keep it."

"Bargain," he repeated too quickly, the label scraping against his raw nerves.

"The bargain stands— Something is wrong." She leaned forward, scanning the ranch. "Joseph isn't here. He promised to take care of your stock, didn't he?"

"Ma! Pa!" The moment the wagon eased to a stop, Garnet scrambled up and onto Cairo's lap. She hugged and kissed her way to Solomon and then back again. She held up her locket. "Guess what? This was hanging from the door!"

Garnet sat very still on Solomon's lap, studying his face and smoothing his cheeks with her small hands. She opened the locket and studied it. "Pa?" she asked, timidly for once. "Did you know you and Kipp look just alike?"

She placed her finger on his dimple and smoothed his cheeks again. "Just alike," she whispered. "Just like me, with black eyes and black hair, and a dimple and—Pa? Why does Kipp look like us?"

Solomon placed his cheek next to hers and hoped she'd understand. "Kipp is my son."

Garnet's eyes lit up. "Really? Ain't that grand? That makes him my brother, doesn't it? Did you hear that, Quig?" she yelled. "Now I got me a ma and a pa and a brother! And my kitty and you!" she added.

Quigly helped Cairo step to the ground. She took the note pinned high on the door. "Vigilantes are hunting Kipp and say he's a horse thief. They want to have a necktie party. Duncan is inciting the crowd."

She took a second note and skimmed it. "Joseph's note says he won't be back."

Solomon listened to the faraway rifle shot. Duncan had been busy. "Joseph couldn't write," Solomon stated quietly.

A volley of shots sounded, rifles answered with a single pistol. "That's at the old trapper's cabin," he said, and began to saddle Hiyu Wind.

"Don't you dare leave here without me," Cairo said behind him. For an answer, he sealed her lips with his, then swung up into his saddle.

"Quigly, Mr. Wolfe will need my support," Cairo said as she began unharnessing The Cuss. "Garnet, stay with Quigly. I'm going with Pa. Solomon, don't you give me that fire-breathing-dragon look. Kipp is my friend and I want to help."

Garnet hitched up her pants. "I'd sure like to come. I just took my bath," she said hopefully.

"You stay," Quigly, Cairo, and Solomon ordered in unison.

"Please put me on The Cuss's back, Quigly. Give the horses water and I'm certain we'll be back soon," Cairo said.

"Do I have to touch them?" the large man asked fearfully.

Hiyu Wind left The Cuss behind, just as Solomon had planned. The coulee was treacherous and Cairo would need time to cross it with the heavier-built horse. Hiyu Wind nimbly went down the wall of the ravine, while Solomon leaned as far backward as he could.

Fifteen minutes later, he moved quietly through the dried prairie grass, until he saw the men circling the adobe trapper's hut. From a broken window, Kipp's gun gleamed in the sunlight. Solomon recognized several of the men, including Duncan, who was talking excitedly to five of the men, motioning them to surround the cabin and shaking a hanging rope.

A wounded man lay behind a stand of sagebrush, tended by Sam Wade, a riverman. Lying bellydown, Josiah Barnes, a saddler, pushed his buffalo gun onto a rock and fired at the cabin's wood door, splintering it.

Fear for Kipp caused Solomon to react instantly, and he trusted his instincts—he pumped his Winchester's slugs into the bright blue sky as he walked toward the cabin. Startled and realizing that they didn't want to challenge Solomon, the men held their fire. When Solomon was near, he ran to the cabin and shoved his way through the damaged door.

Kipp was in the shadows, pressed against the crumbling adobe bricks, close to the window. "Get out. This is my fight. I don't need you—*Pa.* . . ." The hatred lashing from his eyes cut into Solomon. This was the son he had to protect.

"We'll get out of this together," he said.

"Are you my pa?" Kipp demanded in a tone wrapped in agony; his pain sounded as if it had been wrenched from his soul.

"Yes," Solomon admitted, leaning against the other side of the window as a dirty rag, caught by the wind, flapped between them. He ripped it away, just as he wanted to erase the years when Kipp was growing up.

Tears ran down Kipp's dirty cheeks, his brocade vest torn and dirty. "You used Mother, then you left her. Just like you will with Cairo. It all makes sense now . . . why Mother is so hot for you, why Duncan hates you."

Solomon wished desperately that he knew how to give tenderness, how to form the words that would heal Kipp's discovery. He shoved Duncan out of his mind; revenge was a distraction he couldn't afford.

"Wolfe! This isn't your fight!" Henry St. Pierre yelled.

"Kipp's been stealing Mountie horses and selling them back to them and hereabouts. There's witnesses who say they gave Kipp sale money for Mountie horses."

Kipp's dark, tortured eyes sought Solomon's face, tracing their resemblance and looking away. He began loading his Colt. "What does any of it matter? I may as well shoot my way out of here and ride."

"You're not going anywhere," Solomon said, expertly taking the revolver from Kipp. He stuck it in his belt. "Did you do it?"

Kipp launched himself at Solomon, who pushed him away. "Stay put. You're my son, and you're not ending it like this. You're Cairo's friend and she wants you safe. Garnet wants her brother. I've already spent my life on the gun trail and at any minute someone might take me out. You've got to be there for them. I'll believe whatever you say."

Solomon awkwardly placed his hand on Kipp's angular shoulder and shook him gently. Kipp looked so fragile and worn. "If I could take back the years, I would, son. But this is where we are now, and your mother doesn't need more pain."

Kipp wilted back against the adobe, looking older than his eighteen years. "Strange to have someone believe me on just my word. I didn't do anything outside the law. We were just shooting off our mouths, telling big stories and having fun. I made some money with trick shots and poker and digging out loopholes in the law. There's sport and romance in the law that I like."

"I believe you, son." Because Kipp looked as if he needed a friend and a kind word, Solomon rummaged through his thoughts and settled for placing his hand on Kipp's hunched shoulder. "We stand together."

While he held Kipp's agonized stare, Solomon called, "I'm coming out."

eighteen

"Kipp didn't do it." Solomon's quiet voice stated as Cairo lifted her skirts away from a sagebrush. When she could get Solomon in her clutches, she'd throttle him for leaving her far behind.

She'd had to explore the crossing of a coulee, but he already knew the easiest way. That was a prime example of how he liked to stack the game in his favor. When she got his throat within squeezing distance, she'd . . .

The sight of Solomon standing outside the cabin door and facing twelve men with drawn guns and rifles tore into her. Duncan was in the lot, his face ugly. "What's the kid to you, Wolfe? Just why are you so interested in what happens to him?" Duncan leered knowingly at the men.

She loved Solomon Wolfe, and if he was hurt—

She loved him. The knowledge hit home like a massé stick plunging into her heart.

Nothing mattered if he was ripped away from her.

She'd kill him . . . for standing there, looking cool and

hard and immovable, his legs locked in a gunfighter's stance, his jacket tugged back, out of the way of his gun hand. . . . He was just asking for trouble, challenging every man in the pack.

There would be no man making his reputation by killing her husband, the man she had just discovered she loved from the moment she saw his shaggy head, not while he was hers.

He would write more heartfelt sweetheart letters and draw more ugly pictures and cuddle Garnet and teach Kipp that a man didn't have to use a gun to prove he was a man.

She couldn't waltz at her New York soirees with his death on her conscience. *New York. Was it her dream . . . or was it Bernard's?*

She pushed aside the cold wash of fear to curse Solomon, to curse herself, and then smoothed her bodice. She had no time to debate the past; she was claiming her husband. "Nothing is going to happen to that man," she muttered.

She tugged her gloves up purposefully and called, "Mort Jackson. Would you mind escorting me down there? I'd like to talk with my husband—if he's not too busy."

Solomon didn't move, but his expression shifted, darkened thunderously. His eyes locked with Cairo's unflinching ones and she lifted her chin.

"Well, look at that," Duncan crowed. "Here comes Mrs. Wolfe."

Mort Jackson looked sheepish when he came to her, but ignoring her impulse to throw him into the nearest sagebrush, Cairo smiled. She slipped her hand through his arm. "Lovely day, isn't it?"

Mort mumbled and the gang eased back from the

door. Except Duncan, who watched her like a badger, seeking a weak moment to rip into his victims. "First the son, and then the old man, huh?"

Cairo ignored him and slipped her glove through Solomon's right arm. She locked her fingers to the tense muscles beneath his jacket. "Is there a problem?"

The men looked at each other, realizing that she was Kipp's friend. "Kipp is inside. He's a horse thief bound to decorate a cottonwood tree," a settler answered.

"Wolfe won't let us have him."

"Get out of here, Cairo," Solomon ordered darkly, speaking quietly to her, his expression unchanged.

"When I'm ready, dear," she returned with a blithe smile. She was not leaving this prairie without her husband and her friend safely in tow.

"This is no game. There are no winners in this." Solomon's eyes narrowed to slits, swords flashing, thrusting at her, willing her to leave.

Cairo lifted her chin and tightened the satin bow of her bonnet. Solomon's raised hackles weren't driving her away from this battlefield. "I don't like the odds. I've never backed off from a challenge yet."

She expected his disbelieving snort. "What proof do you have that Kipp took horses?" she asked the men, smiling despite the wild beating of her heart.

Ned Parker spat on the ground. "It's a known fact. He's been running with a wild bunch—been mixed up with stealing Mounties' horses and selling them back, or to other folks."

"Ira McCullough said that Kipp sold him those stolen beeves from that Texas bunch," Duncan added.

Cairo knew that Ira owed Duncan more money than he was worth. By naming Kipp as a criminal, he could erase that debt.

"Stay out of this," Solomon said, easing away from her.

She locked her hand to his gun arm. "Most of you owe me," she stated in the round elegant way Bernard had taught her. "I've been busy lately, but I have a few IOUs in my keeping—yours, Mort—and yours, Ned. Ira and the rest of you have lost to me. I needed money recently and I could have sold those IOUs easily. But I didn't."

Ned shuffled his boots. "We . . . thought you'd given up the gambling business, Mrs. Wolfe. I mean—"

Pork Woods's beefy face turned red. "Wolfe don't want his wife supporting him. No righteous man wants his wife playing billiards. He wants her cooking his supper."

Cairo sensed Solomon's mood shifting, the thunderous heat settling, cooling, becoming icy and deadly. He reminded her of his namesake, a wolf going very quiet, his hackles raised and his teeth bared. "I'm a businesswoman. Solomon knew that when he married me. I intend to call in my debts this moment—"

"You are not doing this," he said tightly. "I'll handle it."

"If you shoot someone and they hang you, who will protect Kipp or Garnet?" she asked in a hushed tone. "Kipp could lose his life right here, right now." The muscle running along Solomon's jaw contracted and released and the scar on his head darkened.

Cairo pushed her point. "I still own the Palace and the debts stand. Gentleman, I am prepared to erase your debts to date and I will sell my jewelry to add an amount on top of that to everyone here." She met Duncan's furious stare with her cool one. "Except you. That amount to be divided equally. All of you be at the Palace tomorrow at one o'clock. Solomon will see to it and I'll have the papers drawn up for you to sign a statement that you understand the basics of the transaction. If Kipp is hurt or threatened in any way, I will order my attorney to publish my memoirs—"

"Memoirs?" Tom Livingston asked, scratching his head.

"The events in my life and those of the people I know. For instance, Tom . . . remember when you ran out of a certain house one night? You'd been surprised and left your pants and came to the Palace's back door? Wouldn't that make interesting reading in our local paper?"

"You're bluffing," a man muttered.

"Try me," she returned in a heartbeat.

The men moved restlessly, until one said, "I say take the money and let Kipp go free."

A man who never spoke unless he had basic truth to deliver cleared his throat. Towering over the men at almost seven feet tall, Big Jim Hawkes said slowly, "I've thought for a time that Duncan has more gurgle than guts. He does a good job of wakin' snakes and starting hurrahs. But you'd have to be blind as a post hole not to see that Cairo sets store by Wolfe. Look at her. She'll go down with him if she has to, and she likes the boy. I always liked her and the kid. Seems like a fair deal, and I sure don't need to pay back what I owe her. If she collects, that could mean my quarter of land."

"All or none, except Duncan, and never another word is said about Kipp," Cairo stated, smiling to veil her fear. She smoothed her gloves, studying her trembling fingers.

"Hiding behind her skirt again, Wolfe? And you've taught your bastard the same, eh?" Duncan shot back, furious that his plans were being thwarted. "Does she talk for you?"

"Take it easy," Solomon said finally, too coolly, and

Cairo held her breath because if ever she saw death ride a man's expression, Solomon was that man.

"You're all cowards!" Duncan yelled.

In that heartbeat, Cairo mentally saw the women Duncan had defiled, had taught Edward to torment. "Please excuse me, Solomon," she murmured as she withdrew her arm from his. "I fear that I must act, or I will explode."

Before Duncan could react, Cairo stepped against him, grabbed his wrist, kicked her leg behind his, and threw him to the ground. He scrambled to his feet, wiping mud from his face and swearing while the men began to snicker.

When Solomon stepped toward her, she leveled a look at him. "Stay where you are. My honor has been besmirched and I intend to reclaim it."

Solomon reached over her head to deflect Duncan's open hand from her face. Sarah Jones, a half-blood girl, had felt the blow from that hand. Cairo remembered Sarah telling her how Duncan had hit her. The girl had been left with a broken nose.

"Thank you, my dear," Cairo murmured to Solomon. She hit Duncan in his stomach with the full force of her body behind the punch. Her other hand clipped his jaw. Bernard had always taught her to hold her temper. But when she was forced to release it, to release it well with a thorough, good old-fashioned one-two punch.

Duncan crumbled to his knees and the men began to guffaw. Cairo was just bringing her knee quickly up to Duncan's chin, when Solomon's arm wrapped around her waist and hauled her back to where Kipp stood grinning.

His grin matched Solomon's. Aghast that the men had seen her display of unladylike gutter fighting, Cairo decided instantly to take the easy way out of her embarrassment.

She fluttered her lashes and allowed herself to swoon, draping herself successfully upon Kipp. The men weren't harming him.

"Or you," she muttered, grabbing a fistful of Solomon's jacket and dragging him to her.

When the men were gone, Cairo walked to the waiting horses. Solomon knew that she was giving him time to talk with Kipp.

His son watched her and said slowly, "I'll be moving on."

Solomon glanced at Cairo. If the dangerous play had gone wrong, he could have lost the only woman who made him think about daisies and moonbeams and made him mad at the same time. Right now he had to deal with Kipp. "I'd like to talk with you first, son. If you've got time to spare."

"Reckon I owe you that."

Solomon, a man who had never used words, realized that now what he said could change the course of Kipp's young life. He wanted his son to know that he cared. "What you owe yourself is important. I'm sorry I wasn't here for you when you were growing up. But what you do now shows just what you're made of. I'd like to think that my father's blood—you come from French, English, and Scots people—is going to go on in you. My ma was part German and said that there's usually more boys than girls in the families, so you could have a son. Garnet will have her babies, and if I'm lucky maybe I'll get to rock a few. But I'd like to hold my grandchildren from you, too. You're my only son, Kipp, and just watching you makes me proud."

Kipp kicked the prairie sod with his boot, studying the crushed weeds.

"I'd like to see you meet this thing, son," Solomon said. "Stay right here and face down your troubles. It's hard to come back once you go."

"You came back." Kipp slashed away at something in his eye and swallowed. "You've got Cairo. You've got what you wanted."

Solomon inhaled slowly, focusing his thoughts. "Maybe. I've made mistakes with her and I'll try my best to make it up to her. Right now, it's you and me."

He rested his hand on Kipp's shoulder and ached for the times he'd never held his son. "You're the best part of me, Kipp. The part that will go on through time. I'd like to get to know you and to have you know a little about the people you come from. That's all I can remember, just a little. They're buried on the ranch."

Kipp moved his hands restlessly on his hat. "I'm a maverick then. My mother married to a man other than my father."

"Your mother was young, too young to make the choices before her. There are more ways than one to have a hard life. She survived."

"She's still in love with you," Kipp stated shakily.

Solomon looked at Cairo, who was leaning against the Cuss. She might be thinking of the family she left to survive. He hoped that one day she would find them. If he could, he'd help her. "Blanche is a good woman. I've always thought that too much was stacked against her and, eventually, she'd figure out the right of it. But life changes and here we are and here you are. What's important now is how this is all going to work out."

"Work out," Kipp repeated hollowly, glancing at Cairo.

Solomon prayed silently that Kipp would understand. "I'd be honored if you'd stay with us for a while. There's Garnet, who's pretty happy about her new brother, and then Cairo, who needs to know that you're safe, because you're her friend. And me, because I know that running is no good and because . . ." He was floundering, unable to dig his feelings from his heart and spread them before his son.

How could he tell Kipp that he loved him?

The boy had grown up in a household of hate. What would he understand? While Solomon was floundering, he glanced at Cairo. As if sensing his uncertainty, she waved to the men and called, "Kipp, you're coming home to supper, aren't you?"

Solomon thanked her silently. He wanted whatever time possible with Kipp, to keep him from running. He tried a light tone. "You won't have to eat Cairo's cooking."

Kipp's head went up, his eyes amused. "She cooks?"

"Camp grub. Burned beans and rabbit. Bad coffee," Solomon informed him, not shielding his pride in Cairo. "She does what has to be done. She's twice as mean and ornery as that outlaw horse she's tamed to her hand. I wouldn't want to get on her wrong side. How about it?"

He reached out his hand and his heart missed a stroke as Kipp slid his hand into the firm handshake. It held, their hands locked. "How do you feel about her? Deep down?" Kipp asked.

"Soft. Real soft and gentle. She's my daisy and she always will be," Solomon answered truthfully.

"That's good. I'll stay awhile, but I'm pretty shamed that Cairo had to bail me out."

"You're her friend. Talk with her about how you feel and all the dust will settle down."

Kipp stood back and straightened his shoulders. "You two talk about things, don't you? Meaningful things."

"I'm learning that game. I've made some mistakes," Solomon admitted.

"She's worth the try." Kipp looked at his father. "Maybe you are, too."

Solomon fought the quick jerk of emotions that dried his throat and brought the threat of tears to his eyes. He swallowed and looked off into the prairie. Then he said what was in his heart. "Come home, son."

Blanche smoothed the fresh dirt over the new grave in the Knutson cemetery. She stood slowly, painfully, feeling like a woman twice her age and carrying too great a burden. In the last month, a streak of gray had entered her ebony hair. Now the September wind swirled her hair around her.

She turned to an old grave, ignoring the cold prairie wind sweeping through her cloak. The grave dominated the small cemetery framed by a black wrought-iron fence. "Well, Buck. Here we are. You wanted sons and I gave them to you. Edward is lying here beside you, trampled by the very cattle he was rustling. He wasn't a pretty sight, Buck, and I saw no reason to linger over burying him. Duncan has been gone for the past three days and something is wrong. The men are keeping to themselves and saying little. Of course no one in town will come out here to tell me what is happening. And I take the blame for that. I've made some wrong turns in my life."

She inhaled the cold air, no colder than the pain in her heart. "My life is gone, Buck. You took it from me. You made me what I am—selfish, bitter, as ugly in heart and deed as Duncan, Edward's real father. Not a pretty story, is it?"

She lifted her face to the clean, cold wind, letting it wash over her and take her hair flying wildly around her. "You know what I want, Buck? After all these years? Not money. Not this big ranch. I want Joseph to be safe and Kipp to have a good life. I hope Kipp will bring his children to me, because life is too lonely without family. Then there's Joseph. How you hated his father."

Blanche gathered her cloak around her and studied the clouds sweeping across the blue sky. The wind whipped the streak of gray along her cheek. "You did all this, Buck. Your legacy, the dynasty you wanted." She turned back to the grave. "Well, you're not here and I am and I'm living my life the way I see fit, old man—you bastard. I'm not spending it in a bottle or with Duncan trying to kill me slowly, taking what's left of me."

Blanche placed a rope around the old stone marking Buck's grave, left the cemetery, and got up on her saddle. The horse strained to dislodge the stone and it toppled, facedown. "That's how it's going to be with me, Buck," she said. "If Joseph can bring his young ones here, his family, he's welcome. Because he's *my* blood, *my* baby-child, the same as Kipp. But this is my land, Buck Knutson—and this is my life. And you can't do a damn thing about it."

She threw down the rope from her saddlehorn and sat looking out at the ranch that she would one day leave to Joseph and to Kipp, her sons. The windmill turned slowly and Blanche studied the big K in wrought iron. "That will come down, too."

Duncan raced toward her, slashing his reins against the flanks of his lathered horse. "That's no way to treat a good animal," Blanche said. "You missed your son's funeral. He managed to stay alive long enough to tell me that you wanted him to plant that herd on the Wolfe ranch."

"My boy is dead?" Duncan's once-handsome face crumpled.

Blanche recognized his false expression of grief. She admired his acting ability, for Duncan mourned for no one but himself. "He's lying over there by Buck. I want you off my property, Duncan. Now."

Duncan stared at the fresh grave, his expression hard. "You've become a hard woman, Blanche. Think about Edward and what he would want after he was gone. He'd want me to take care of you, with a husband's right. I think we should get married right away so that you won't let your grief and the struggle of running this spread ruin you."

"Marry you?" She began to laugh wildly, the absurd idea too crazy to consider.

Duncan's eyes were ice-cold. "Then you'll have your own accident. After you sign the ranch over to me, the rightful owner. Reckon you could have that accident now and some woman could sign your name later."

She should have known—she saw him draw the revolver and felt the slug tear, burning through her shoulder. "You always were a bad shot," she said as she bent her head low and kicked the fast horse beneath her.

nineteen

"You were right to come here, Blanche," Solomon said as everyone sat at the table. Cairo had tended Blanche's wound and drank tea beside her. Sound asleep, Garnet lay in her bed against the wall.

Cairo eased her hand to Solomon's, her face pale. He laced his fingers with hers, bringing their hands to rest on his thigh.

Blanche looked pleadingly at Kipp. "I'm so sorry. You couldn't hate me any worse than I hate myself."

Kipp turned away, pain riding his young, rawboned face.

"Listen to what she has to say, son," Solomon said quietly.

Tears ran down Blanche's face and Quigly slid a hand-kerchief into her hand. "Edward is dead. Duncan had pushed him into stealing the herd. It was supposed to be found on your land as evidence. The cattle stampeded and Edward is lying in the cemetery with Buck."

She shook her head, bracing herself to open her raw,

gaping past. "Buck wanted a dynasty of sons. I gave them to him—because I was young and weak and knew well enough what would happen to me if I didn't. There was you and Edward and one other—" She swallowed, tears flowing down her cheeks. "Joseph."

Kipp stared at her disbelievingly, then pushed his hands through black hair, making him look even more like Solomon. For a moment, time spun backward in Solomon's mind and he heard his father say, "You'll be having a fine son one day and you'll feel about him just like I feel about you.

Solomon ached for Kipp, who struggled with the knowledge that Joseph was his half-brother. "Where is Joseph?" Kipp asked finally.

"Duncan was to keep him safe. Oh, how I pray he hasn't hurt Joseph. You don't know what he is capable of—"

"Yes. I do know, Mother," Kipp returned in an empty tone.

Blanche stared at him as if realizing what probably had happened to him. "How you must have suffered." She cried out as if in mortal pain. "Without Buck, I gloried in my freedom, forgetting that you needed me in gentler ways."

Kipp took her hand. "Mother, stop that. We survived. Duncan spent most of his time tormenting Edward."

Solomon nodded. "Blanche, you've raised two fine sons. I thank you for Kipp and how you kept the land for me. Only a strong woman could have managed the Knutson spread and raised two sons. You've given Fancy's daughter a home. Garnet is where her mother wanted her to be, with wild roses and sunshine. Remember that."

Cairo stroked Blanche's tangled hair, comforting her.

Whatever Blanche had done in the past, she was paying dearly.

Solomon showed her the note that Joseph was to have written and Blanche frowned. "That is Duncan's handwriting."

Solomon prayed that Joseph was alive. He had to know that the cave did not hold another youth, shackled to the walls. "Kipp, it's a nice moonlit night. How about taking a long ride with me?"

Father and son shared a meaningful look and Cairo reacted immediately. She leaped to her feet and latched both fists onto Solomon's shirt. He covered her hands with his. In her fear for him, she dismissed his tender expression. "Oh, no. You're not going anywhere. I've just got the both of you under the same roof, and Garnet and Quigly, too. Nobody is going anywhere. Blanche needs to know that you're both safe. She's just lost a son and heaven only knows where Joseph is—"

She studied Solomon, her expression stark with fear. "Don't go without me, Solomon."

Solomon knew there would never be another woman for him. Cairo was lodged too deeply in his heart. If anything happened to her . . . But he shook his head, then kissed her palm, bringing it to rest against his cheek. "Not this time. You stay put. Blanche and Garnet and Quigly need you."

He looked at Kipp, still reeling with the news of a new brother. "Coming, son? Joseph may need two friends."

Kipp rose to his feet. "Count on it."

After a long silence, Cairo cleared her throat. Blanche sat, gripping the table, her eyes terrified. Cairo glanced down at her and murmured, "Blanche, Solomon has that look. Satan couldn't stop him from finding Joseph. He'll find him and he'll bring him safely back to you. Quigly, I believe I would like more chamomile tea, please."

"No, madame. It would not be good for the baby."

"Baby?" Solomon managed as the blush rose up Cairo's cheeks and the silence hovered and stretched between them. He studied her face and the impatient lash of her eyes at Quigly. Solomon forced himself to breathe and carefully placed his hand over her stomach. "How long have you known?"

Cairo's hands covered his and she blinked up at him innocently. "Oh, dear. Did I forget to tell you? Well, really there hasn't been time, and I only suspect because there hasn't been time to know for sure. I think it's only two weeks or less. I . . . I think maybe we . . . you know . . . when you were recovering so nicely and I was so happy you were alive. . . . Well, anyway. There I was upside down the other day, meditating and chanting. I heard myself humming lullabies and tuning myself to a certain warm, snugly feeling and the changes in my body. . . . And then the loveliest feeling wrapped around me and I thought, I'm having a baby. Solomon gave me his baby."

Her blush deepened. "Just like that. Wonderful how meditation clears the mind."

"Wonderful," Solomon repeated hollowly. Cairo had known—suspected a baby and hadn't told him. He looked deep into her glowing, whiskey-brown eyes; he wondered when and if she had planned to tell him. He'd already lost a lifetime with one son whom he hadn't known existed.

"Solomon, you look like your heart is bleeding right out of you," Cairo said softly, placing her palm along his jaw.

Solomon realized how deeply the wound ran through him. He instinctively sought to protect himself by leaving. "Kipp, if you're riding with me, say good-bye to your mother and give her a kiss. Women need comforting," he said impatiently before he kicked the door shut behind him.

Cairo caught him before he got on Hiyu Wind's saddle. She grabbed his shirt and locked her arms around him. "You are a blackguard, Mr. Wolfe. I meant to tell you, but I had to take the idea inside myself and wrap it around me first. I make decisions like I play billiards, I have to study the shots. It's only been a few days since I've missed my time, three to be exact, and everything has been moving so fast. I could be wrong. But I've certainly been exposed."

" 'Study the shots.' Like putting spin on the ball?" Solomon said, shielding his pain and fear behind an impassive expression. What if she didn't want that tiny part of him? What if she decided to tear it away now? What if—Solomon stood very still as the thought slammed into him that women died in childbirth. "You be here when I get back."

"You just make sure you don't get hurt, or I'll come after you and make you pay," she tossed back, her eyes brimming with tears. He'd hurt her, shamed that his bitterness had rolled out to consume her. He inhaled the cold air and waited for her to tell him that it was all over. That she was walking away from him, despite the wager. He didn't want to tether her when she wanted to be free; that game between them was ended long ago. "I won't hold you to that wager," he said finally. "But I'd appreciate holding my child, if there is one."

He had no pride where she was concerned. Was his

heart bleeding into the hard Montana ground? Or was he sensing what his future would be without her? The decision was hers and he could only wait.

Cairo folded her arms, bit her trembling bottom lip, and glared at him. "I am not going anywhere without you, Mr. Wolfe. You are mine and a hard game at that. I love you, Mr. Wolfe. It came to me several times and not during your damnable sweet lovemaking or your mind-drugging kisses. It came to me when I realized I might lose you, that you might die from your accident, or when you faced that gang. I realized as you faced that gang that New York society was Bernard's dream and not mine. Because I've got my dream. I've come a long way down the daisy trail to get you and you're not getting away from me now. Got it?"

But she was asking, not telling, her eyes pleading with him to understand as her hair flew away from her pale, moonlit face.

He caught a wild, silky strand in his leather glove. He wanted to believe her. Wanted to drag her into his arms and hold her tight. Instead he looked at her, bound by his old ways and trying to shield his joy and his pain.

"Don't you want this baby?" Cairo demanded, the tears streaming down her cheeks. Shivering in the wind, she looked as fragile, vulnerable, and aching as he felt. "Or don't you want me?"

"Haven't got a thing to offer you but hard times," he said truthfully, wanting to place his face in the soft curve of her throat and tell her of the sunshine filling his heart. Instead, he pulled her against him, tucked her under his coat, and wrapped his arms around her to keep her warm and safe.

"Ha!" she returned hotly, but warmth spread from her eyes to the curve of her lips. She wrapped her arms around him and snuggled close. "You'll be drawing no awful pictures of other women and wearing them in your shirt pocket. You won't be talking to any other woman about her looking like Aphrodite sliding down on moonbeams. And if you call another woman 'daisy-girl,' I'll show you the painful uses of a cue stick. Because I'm canceling my ad. There'll be no wife-replacements bulldogging my husband."

"See that you do that," he said, allowing her warmth to race through him. She glowed just like his Aphrodite when her eyes met his, filled with promises. She was uncertain and proud and afraid and her love for him shone like moonbeams. It wrapped around him and he started to go dizzy with the thought of his child lodged so deep and nestling inside her.

But he had a job to do, maybe save a young boy's life, and he always did the job. Solomon considered the thought and began to grin. "I always do the job," he said cockily.

Cairo's smile lit her face. "Why, Solomon, you're glowing," she exclaimed in delight.

"Pretty near walking on air. In another minute, I'll be leaping over the moon," he said goofily, because that was how he felt.

"Kiss me," she demanded, making him take the first step between them, challenging him. But her eyes were warm and gentle upon him. "Do it now, Mr. Wolfe."

He locked his mouth on hers and told her with his lips how he felt. That there was love deep inside him and he'd do his best for her for all their years. Cairo returned the favor and shivered when he put her away and swung up on his horse. Kipp was mounted and clearly enjoying the moment. "Kids" was all he said, grinning at Cairo and then at Solomon.

"I'll be expecting the both of you to come home with Joseph," Cairo called as they rode out into the moonlit prairie.

The next evening, Blanche rode to meet the spring-board wagon bearing Joseph. Feverish and near death, Joseph had wanted to be away from the cave and Kipp had compared the youth's brutal wounds to Solomon's scars. Duncan had become skilled in keeping his victims alive; it had been nearly a month since the boy had seen daylight. After one look at Joseph, Solomon told Kipp to find a wagon and warm blankets for traveling home.

It was time for the raw, gaping wound of the past to be aired, then forgotten. Riding back on the wagon, Solomon had told his son everything. "Why didn't you kill Duncan when you came back?" Kipp had asked.

"Because revenge isn't a trail I want to ride," Solomon returned honestly. "Revenge grows and jumps outside of what was intended, like a prairie fire. I had Garnet to keep safe and I had you and Cairo. I didn't want you to see me kill him. Killing leaves a sour feeling that doesn't heal. I didn't want you to be a part of that, to remember me with guns blazing and another man dying. It isn't right for a son to see his father filled with hatred. And there is a look in Duncan's eyes that asks for death. I wouldn't give him the pleasure."

"So you walked away?"

"I tried. I wanted a new life and one for Garnet."

Kipp had studied his father. "I know Duncan. He won't leave it at that."

"Duncan is going before a judge. That's a job I will see to," Solomon had promised.

Now Kipp helped Blanche board the wagon.

"Mother," Joseph murmured as Blanche cradled his head to her lap.

"You'll be fine," she returned, softness and strength blending in her expression. She tucked the buffalo robe and blankets closer around him, frowning when he whispered to her. "You are not dying. You will not be buried in a ravine or tied to a scaffold," she stated, bending to kiss his forehead.

From the driver's bench, Solomon turned to look over his shoulder and met Blanche's anxious gaze. "Duncan has Cairo. He wants you to come after her. He said 'a life for a life.'"

Cairo studied her bound hands and the flickering campfire, tormented by the prairie wind. Her cheek throbbed from Duncan's blow, but her fear for Solomon dimmed the pain.

Duncan didn't like the many uses of a cue stick, nor her accurate aim with billiard balls. There were other men, threats to Garnet, Quigly, and Blanche, and so she had let them take her.

Moonlight glinted across a rifle barrel; Duncan and one of his men lay in the coulee. Another hid behind a sagebrush, his revolver gleaming. Five men lay in hiding and Duncan had promised that Solomon would be dead before the night was over.

Anxious to kill Solomon, and aware of his danger to them, Duncan and his men—who hid beyond the firelight—had not yet bothered her. If Solomon— She shoved that deathly thought away, but knew that Duncan's men would fall upon her like beasts when they thought they were safe. She still had her knife and her knockout drops. They would not hurt the baby within her.

Wind swept the vast high plains, dried weeds crackling. "Don't come, Solomon," she whispered, even as she knew he would.

A cloud crossed the moon, darkening the night, and Solomon loomed in the firelight. His gaze flicked over her, shifting as it touched her swollen cheek. An elemental emotion moved within him then, something dark and fierce and frightening, like a dragon rising to strike its enemies; after that heartbeat, Solomon's expression was flat, revealing nothing. "I'm here, Duncan. Let her go."

Duncan climbed awkwardly from the coulee and stood. "Drop your gun."

"Not until you let her go," Solomon returned, appearing lethal in the moonlight. "Are you hurt?" he asked Cairo, his hand hovering over his revolver.

He was an easy target. "No. But he has five men," she replied.

"Figures," he said quietly, the tone causing her to shiver. There would be no mercy for Duncan this night.

Duncan started laughing, peppering bullets into the ground around the campfire. "You've come at last, dead man," he crowed.

"Let her go. You have me."

"She'll draw a ransom. Meanwhile we can have the use of her. But I'm going to kill you for the pleasure of it." Then his damaged hand shot out, the back of it hitting Solomon's face. "Drop that iron."

"I gave my word to bring you to the law," Solomon stated coolly, his eyes narrowed and gleaming in the night. "It's time."

"Not tonight, sweetheart," Duncan returned in a venom-dipped tone. "Drop it."

Solomon began to slide his revolver from the holster.

Then he flipped it over, gripped the barrel, and neatly tapped Duncan on the head with the butt.

Duncan crumpled just as Solomon threw his body over Cairo's, flattening her to the ground. "This is what I do, sweetheart, and I'm good at it. I've collected kidnapped children and ransomed wives. Got myself a name for it. I'd rather grow tulip bouquets for you from now on though. Just this once, don't fight me," he whispered.

"Who, me?" she asked innocently.

Shots flew across the night and suddenly Solomon was picking her up in one arm and firing with his other hand. While he ran with her to the coulee, another rifle blazed.

There was a man's agonized scream, and another. The Cuss reared in the moonlight, tossing a man's body to the ground and trampling it.

"That would be Duncan. He picked the wrong horse," Solomon stated quietly, his body trembling over hers.

He looked down at Cairo, frowning when he saw her swollen jaw and kissing it lightly. He ripped away his coat and tucked her into it. "Have I told you I love you?" he asked tenderly as if gunfire were not blazing over their heads, as if he had to tell her.

She sensed that, in a heartbeat, Solomon would leap into the fray and that he was giving her something to tell the baby they might have created. She wanted to lock on to him and keep him safe. Her need for him was selfish, because now he was a part of her life and her heart.

He kissed her lips and pressed his hand to her stomach. "Take care of my son, daisy-girl. Be right back." Solomon scrambled over the rim of the coulee.

"Tulip bouquet," she muttered, then prayed and wept and dug through her petticoats as guns blazed. In the next moment, Solomon was lifting her in his arms. She looped her bound wrists over his head and clung to him, shaking.

"You're ornery and mean and no righteous husband would leave his wife tied at a moment like this."

"Are you all mouth, or can I have a kiss?" he asked gently, and she realized he was shaking as much as she. She held him tightly, because he was never escaping from her again.

"I poured Duncan's body into that coulee and covered it. The rest are gone. Is she hurt?" Kipp asked, and Cairo turned to see him reloading his revolver.

"Not that I can see," Solomon managed between Cairo's kisses.

She stopped to glare at him. "You didn't tell me you had help. I thought you were all alone."

"I guess I forgot that part," he said between more kisses.

"Did you tell her you love her?" Kipp asked with interest as he kicked earth over the fire. "Did you tell her that your life wasn't worth beans if something happened to her? Like you told me?"

Solomon grinned, clearly loving Cairo's tiny healing kisses on his swollen lip. "I thought I'd do that with no other ears around and then I'd ask her to marry me again and tie her up right."

"I studied how to do it right. You have to set the mood, candles, wine, a good dinner. You have to soften her with romantic poems, and then you have to go down on one knee and ask her," Kipp stated wisely as Cairo reached to rumple his hair.

"Not tonight, Kipp. I've got plans to talk about tulip bouquets," she said with a grin.

After Kipp had taken Blanche home and Garnet and Quigly were quiet in their new bedrooms, Cairo latched the bedroom door behind Solomon. She stepped on a chest to bolt the upper latch and stepped down to face Solomon. "There. Now you have no one to protect you. At dinner you said we needed to sort things out and meanwhile I might move back into town. I don't believe that excuse about me being more comfortable. What exactly did you mean?" she demanded.

Solomon finished the bath he'd taken after Cairo's and tugged on his caftan. He faced Cairo, taking in her long legs and the drape of his flannel shirt over the rest of her, to the top of her light-brown hair. He studied the rich color, lightened by sun; if she discovered he knew her lemon-sun-lightening trick . . . he decided that information wouldn't be pried from him. "This nightshirt isn't too bad," he said, delaying the moment when Cairo would dig and pry and run him to the ground.

He inhaled; tonight he was making his stand.

Cairo ripped out her leg knife and threw it into the wood near his head. "Ooo. You're not making this easy, Solomon Wolfe. Explain yourself."

He needed more time. "Let's play a game, sweetheart."

She placed her hands on her hips. "The only game I'm interested in is you. You're acting skittish and wary, Solomon. Did you not tell me only a few hours ago out there on the prairie that you loved me?" she demanded. "Why are we not in that bed?"

He picked up a cue stick and burst the triangle, the red balls zinging into pockets. He wondered when his instincts would save him from Cairo's dark frown. "We need to think this thing out, Cairo. Sometimes people regret decisions made in haste. I don't want to tie you down when New York is waiting. I don't want you lingering after what never was and blaming me because of it." He sighted down on the deuce ball and Cairo caught it before it sank into the pocket.

She swept the remaining balls into the pocket. "Game is over. You win. You don't think I know my own mind?"

Solomon's gaze locked with hers. "First we'll find out about the baby, and since women are delicate at first and sometimes later on, I think you should move back to your apartment. It's warm and comfortable. I'm told that women with babies coming sometimes get too emotional, and right now you might not be in control of your logic. Then . . ." He floundered, uncomfortable because Quigly had told him women were sometimes late due to stress and emotions. "It could be the other reason, too."

She glared at him. "What other reason?"

He studied his gun belt and hoped he'd say things right. Cairo was making her way around the billiard table to him. She grabbed his caftan with both fists and pushed him until he leaned backward over the table. "You're mine, Solomon Wolfe."

He went dizzy with the scent of her freshly bathed body, with the thought that she could be carrying his child. "Would you want a baby with me?" he asked rawly, fear gripping his stomach.

"The thought has crossed my mind. You have to agree about multiple exposure to the possibility," she returned impatiently. "Maybe that was why I wanted to take one from you. I knew that I wanted a part of the man I loved to go on and I wanted to hold his child. Selfish, aren't I?"

He considered that thought and the long, slow night of her loving him, while he returned the favor. He caught her hand as it eased under his caftan. "There's more to be said, daisy-girl. Like you can't just carry me off like a Sabine woman when you want me."

She began to smile; she plucked a whorl of hair on

his chest and stood away from him. "You're too big for me to put you over my shoulder, Solomon," she stated, grinning up at him. He admired the sway of her hips as she walked back to their bed and placed her arm around a post.

"You can't just have me where you catch me, daisy," he muttered. The shirt covering her slid open and his mouth dried at the sight of her breast shimmering in the lamplight.

"Who's going to stop me?" she asked, unbuttoning the shirt. "Come here, you big, tall, tough sweetheart, and tell me about how you're going to grow wheat and raise cattle. Tell me about how you'll cry when Garnet is grown and how you'll linger with me on the porch in our twilight years. Tell me how you'll grow tulip bouquets and how you love me," she invited softly. "Tell me about moonbeams, sunshine, and daisies in the meadow and I'll tell you that I love you and I might just nibble on your ears."

Solomon cleared his throat, every muscle in his body taut, needing her and what was between them. Cairo had painted a picture that he'd carried in his heart; he read her love in her expression and didn't try to shield the sunshine in his heart. Cairo would be the match of his life, the best and only game. The rough times would come, but together they would meet the future. Because Cairo loved challenges, he gave her one. "You know what that ear business does to me. You could be delicate now."

"Sweetheart. Come here and we'll talk about it." Cairo shed the shirt and eased into bed. The wind howled outside and his heart missed a beat as she looked at him. "Solomon, I know now that Bernard's dream isn't mine. I love you. Do you think we could change the rules of this game and make it a lifetime?"

"Call it," he said simply, walking toward her and the future.

Epilogue

Three and a half years later, Solomon stood in the shadows of an elegant New York billiard parlor.

After Cairo had qualified to play world-class billiards in St. Louis, a special challenge match had been arranged with the current New York champion.

The champion, a short, fat man, had been contemptuous of playing a woman, believing the match to be beneath him. A New York banker, the father of a child Solomon had rescued from kidnappers, had applied pressure to the arrogant champion. Now, dressed in a bright blue evening gown—Quigly's masterpiece—Cairo stood in the lighted room and began drawing off her long evening gloves.

Cairo was elegant and graceful, listening to the referee's rules with her small, practiced smile. Solomon knew she was watching the arrogant champion and his disdainful gestures. Right now, while the cocky little man boasted to his friends, Cairo was taking him apart systematically. She'd already studied his technique, and his arrogance only made her more determined to take the title from him.

Dressed in silk and ruffles, Cairo looked little like the seasoned Montana ranchwife she was and little like the mother of two-year old Diamond.

Diamond. A beautiful baby; Cairo's gift to him. He'd never forget the months before Diamond's birth, the changes of Cairo's body and her moods. Amazingly, after months of worry and the easy birth, he had quietly shattered and Cairo had comforted him. She was never more beautiful than when she nursed the baby.

Or when she looked over his first bouquet of home-grown tulips to tell him she loved him.

Solomon had plans for later in the evening. This time it would be rose petals crushed beneath them.

He wondered briefly how the newly married Jacob Maxwell was managing at the Wolfe ranch.

"Lordy, who is that beautiful man?" Blanche had breathed huskily when Jacob arrived at the Wolfes' wedding.

For the next three years, Blanche fought a losing game. On his wedding day, Jacob grinned and murmured to Solomon, *"Veni, vidi, vici."* Its Latin translation—I came, I saw, I conquered—was too true, when applied to how Jacob had enticed Blanche into the idea of another marriage. His courtship of her had started after Solomon and Cairo's wedding; Jacob simply served punch to Blanche, chatted intimately with her, then lifted her over his shoulder and carried her out onto his horse. Five days later, he deposited a very happy Blanche at her ranch and rode off. Fort Benton watched the progress of the strange courtship with interest, because clearly Blanche had found her match in Jacob Maxwell.

During Solomon and Cairo's trips to St. Louis for billiard tournaments, Blanche and Jacob watched the children. Now with Kipp at law school, and their parents in New York, Garnet and Diamond would torment Joseph, who clearly adored them. The girls delighted Quigly and frequently visited his millinery and beauty center in the old parlor. The town's ladies enjoyed billiard lessons from Cairo and luxuriated in Quigly's mud baths and facials later. Quigly's beauty oil and herbal business thrived.

Solomon inhaled slowly, calming his nerves. He was proud of his wife; he wanted Cairo to have what she wanted, what she had worked for and deserved, a world-class title.

He shifted restlessly and leaned back against the wall. He had his dreams . . . more than he ever thought possible . . . and he wanted Cairo to have hers.

Before the game began, Cairo turned slowly to Solomon, finding him in the shadows of the elegant parlor and in the midst of a crowd. Their eyes locked and Cairo silently formed the words "I love you."

Unable to move, praying for her, Solomon nodded. He'd be there for her always.

If her win tonight took her away from him, he'd understand and wait. Because nothing would change between them; he'd still love her and she was the sunshine of his heart.

"Mrs. Wolfe has something to say," the referee announced to the well-dressed crowd.

Cairo lifted her chin and looked every inch a queen of the billiard parlor. "I dedicate this game to the memory of Bernard Marchand, who taught me to play," she stated clearly in the eloquent way the Englishman had taught her. "And to my beloved husband, Solomon Wolfe, who has always unselfishly supported my wishes to hold this great title."

Solomon held his breath and knew that pride shone in his eyes.

Cairo made short work of the overconfident champion, who played sloppily. The referee proclaimed that the title went to Mrs. Cairo Wolfe. After the congratulations and when Cairo held the huge trophy cup, the announcer held up his hand. "Mrs. Wolfe wishes to speak."

Across the crowded room, Cairo met Solomon's eyes. "I have not said enough about my husband. He has encouraged me when I would have withdrawn. He has sacrificed to see me here and for every woman who loves the sport and the romance of this great game, billiards, I encourage you all to aspire to men like Solomon—men who recognize that women are competitors and equals."

The former champion muttered ungraciously and stalked out of the room, unnoticed by the elegantly dressed men and women. Cairo nodded to the announcer and continued, "Because I have reached my goal and have taken the title, I want to thank you all. I give back the title. I am going home to my family and to our wheat harvest. If you visit Fort Benton, Montana, I invite you to stop at my billiard parlor. I always love a good game."

The crowd went wild, cheering for Cairo as she handed the trophy back to the announcer and moved toward Solomon. He met her halfway in the crush of the crowd, and when she would have thrown herself into his arms, Solomon took her gloved hand and placed it through his bent arm. "Give them a show to remember, Daisy," he said, proud of her and the love running between them. "Do it right. Walk out of here smiling and head up. Because this is one night they'll never forget."

"I love you, dear," she murmured as she walked beside him, looking very ladylike and elegant.

"I love you, Daisy," he returned, pressing her gloved hand on his arm closer to him.

"Take me to our room," she ordered, while smiling at the cheering crowd. "I'm ready for another game, one without a crowd."

"Can't."

She allowed a nobleman to capture her gloved hand and bring the back of it to his lips. "Why?"

"Did I forget to tell you that I waltz?" Solomon asked as he moved expertly around the crowded, ornate ballroom with Cairo.

"You did forget that tidbit, dear. You waltz beautifully." She frowned at a society matron who was openly ogling Solomon in his black evening clothes. He was gorgeous, and every day she loved him more, for his honor, his kindness and patience.

She loved him when he was a scoundrel and a pirate and a demanding lover.

She loved him when he drew her upon his lap and sat quietly, holding her without words.

She loved him when he talked with Kipp, helping ease the painful past. Solomon wanted the best for his son and for Joseph, whom Blanche adored.

And she loved Solomon because he had planted a bed of wildflowers for his sister, Fancy, keeping her close to Garnet.

Cairo allowed the waltz to flow into her and smoothed Solomon's powerful shoulder, the one she intended to nibble upon later.

She'd never forget his awe and pleasure, the tears on his lashes when he held Diamond for the first time. "Thank you, Daisy," he'd said simply in a deep uneven tone that she knew came from his heart.

She drew his hand to her lips and, loving him, nestled her cheek against his palm. The music swirled around them as Solomon gathered her closer. "Happy?"

"Yes. Tell me you love me again."

He grinned wickedly. "Can't."

Then she knew she had to run him down and have him. Because Solomon was the best challenge, the best game of her life. "Call it," she said, loving him.

"Love," he returned, his eyes soft upon her.